About the Author

Force Majeure is Graziella Montalbán's debut novel. She lives happily in Albacete, Spain, with her tequila-loving grandmother and her two cocker spaniels – named Mia and Sebastian, of course – always ensuring she's in good company. She is also a frequent guest at the city's three functional movie theatres, to keep her out of touch with reality as often as possible. Graziella remains unwilling to halt her efforts of shunning spectators whenever they do not conform to her highly-set movie etiquette standards. It is expected this will lead her to the hospital or prison or both in the foreseeable future. She does not mind in the slightest.

Graziella splits her time between writing far too weird screenplays that will probably never get produced, and a thankless (yet ultimately reliable) job as a data analyst, although she is gearing up the engines to make her big jump to the world of cinema anytime soon…

She consciously stays away from any form of social media except for Tinder, which she is an avid user of.

Just like Carla, Graziella carries on with her fight one day at a time, and hopes to continue this way for many years to come.

Force Majeure

Graziella Montalbán

Force Majeure

Olympia Publishers
London

www.olympiapublishers.com
OLYMPIA PAPERBACK EDITION

Copyright © Graziella Montalbán 2023

The right of Graziella Montalbán to be identified as author of this work has been asserted in accordance with sections 77 and 78 of the Copyright, Designs and Patents Act 1988.

All Rights Reserved

No reproduction, copy or transmission of this publication may be made without written permission.
No paragraph of this publication may be reproduced, copied or transmitted save with the written permission of the publisher, or in accordance with the provisions of the Copyright Act 1956 (as amended).

Any person who commits any unauthorised act in relation to this publication may be liable to criminal prosecution and civil claims for damage.

A CIP catalogue record for this title is available from the British Library.

ISBN: 978-1-80439-102-0

This is a work of fiction.
Names, characters, places and incidents originate from the writer's imagination. Any resemblance to actual persons, living or dead, is purely coincidental.

First Published in 2023

Olympia Publishers
Tallis House
2 Tallis Street
London
EC4Y 0AB

Printed in Great Britain

A WORD FROM THE AUTHOR

This book is a testament to the dangers arising from keeping within the compounds of ourselves the unbearable shouted whisper that self-destructive behaviour can be, and to the inherent healing power that lies in letting our loved ones finally in. This effort was carried out in the hopes that every single person who has ever felt the same way Carla does – be that a moment, an hour, a day, a year or a lifetime – knows that they are not alone, that their lives have meaning, that their feelings (as troubled as they may be), are not permanent, and that they still have plenty to experience before ultimately reaching their final destination.

Although written with nothing but good intentions in my attempt to address this epidemic by bringing mutual support, understanding and empathy into the hearts of readers, it is important to inform readers that **this book contains details and elements that may trigger especially sensitive people to this subject, as it includes descriptions of suicide, suicidal ideation and suicide attempts.**

If you or someone you know is experiencing thoughts of suicide, for more information please go to https://www.opencounseling.com/suicide-hotlines on International Suicide & Emergency Hotlines.

(Mostly) based on a true story.

PROLOGUE

THE MOST HORRIBLE ACT

A few days ago, whilst I scouted the endless corridors of my town's public library as part of my Friday night routine, I was fortunate enough to come across *The Longest Suicide in Hollywood*, John William Law's skilful account of the last years in the life of one of the most troubled souls to ever walk the Earth: acting legend Montgomery Clift. Although the outstanding thespian eventually passed away not by his own hand, but by what could be interpreted as a much-desired occlusive coronary artery disease heavily fuelled by his years-long substance abuse, the book got me thinking: can suicide be elongated through the years? Can someone be dying purposefully, consciously, madly, irreparably, for years and years on end?

The thing is, tragedies are not just wars and climate crises and pandemics and murders. They too can be the irreparable fracture of a family because of two siblings refusing to talk to one another, the unexpected rise of self-destructive behaviour resulting from troubled relationships, or, in my case, all of the above. In a similar fashion to the boxing match analogy described by the great Richard Burton when explaining his alcohol addiction, suicide postponement entails daily suffering in the shape of hopping into the ring and defeating the other fighter: your inner impulse to do something permanent and irreversible. Some days you win the battle by a long stretch; others, you come close to never boxing ever again. But no matter what, you take no pride in winning, because the victory comes in the shape of staying alive. And that is no prize at all.

When one witnesses life through the prism of such a deeply corrosive mindset, it is only inevitable to come to the realization most of us pretend not to see, few actually notice and even fewer are brave enough to deal with: there are only a select number of things that are truly enjoyable about the life we are given—and most of them are gone before we are even mildly capable of learning how to truly appreciate them in the manner they deserve. Once you arrive at that demoralising yet eye-opening destination, you begin to wonder…what is the purpose, then, of coming out of your bed every morning? Finding someone to share your life with? Having kids, perhaps? Buying a house? Becoming the manager of your branch? And then what, huh? You're just another name in the graveyard where teens go to get drunk, and goths knock on Satan's door through heavily misguided seances caused by childhood neglect and Barbra Streisand aversion. But in reality, ask that random father walking down the street—you who I am talking about: the guy with few hairs garnishing his scalp, eternally dressed in a crappy eighty-dollar-suit and driving a hideous, egg-shaped blue Chrysler van to take his five children (three of whom are likely unwanted) to Sunday school, always walking in a perennial state of looking on the verge of declaring bankruptcy after getting divorced from the woman half his age for which he will soon abandon his family at the first sight of a middle-age crisis. Ask him, then, if he likes his job. Ask him if he loves his partner. Ask him if he loves his children. Ask him and, in the process, ask yourself, if he loves all of that, or if he *must* love all of that. There is nothing to love about the things we foolishly dedicate our lives to pursuing, nor about the constant mending of relationships we blindly try at all costs to preserve in the face of failing to notice they have long been broken. Marriage? An arrangement with a statistically proven expiration date. Children? A burdensome, bottomless well of disappointment. A job? Good luck finding a fulfilling one; and if so, good luck paying the bills; and if able to do so, good luck balancing out that position with your personal life before you reach the age of retirement; and if so, good luck with avoiding a severe cardiac arrest; and if so, then, by all means, share with the rest of us your secret, for you'd be the first person on Earth to successfully navigate such treacherous vital waters.

That is why, once we sever ties with the fantasy meticulously crafted and effectively enforced upon us all that our life path should fit the desires of a despotic society with no place for those who have the audacity of not fitting in into one of the carefully manufactured categories designed for us, it is important to find an anchor that endows our lives with alternative pathways towards survival, mild fulfilment and, ultimately, something moderately resembling a purpose. Because otherwise, the outlook seems dire—unavoidably so. In my case, I was lucky enough to have a father with plenty of good taste and human decency to introduce me to the world of cinema, one masterpiece at a time, which effective immediately fuelled my need to keep feeding myself with the enigmatically magical mysticism with which each of the twenty-four frames per second that conformed a shot, each shot conforming a scene, each scene confirming a sequence, and each sequence conforming a movie, had all been inherently endowed with.

Art, in whatever shape we are lucky enough to witness it, has the ultimate purpose of easing our transition out of the world of the living, as the master Andrei Tarkovsky wrote in his book

Sculpting in Time, for within it lies the ability to elicit inside every one of us the very best we have to offer, something which, if true, would ironically make me readier than ever to face my final sunrise. If I didn't know me any better, I would say that my disenchantment with living—undoubtedly stemming from an inability to truly appreciate life in the midst of a problem I had no role in creating, yet thoroughly accentuated by relegating myself to constant complaints and self-torture instead of actively searching for a way to try and put an end to it—would have made me succumb to my impulses at a much earlier stage, had it not been for my early passion for the art of moviemaking—the microcosm on which the macrocosm is reflected— which proved to be surprisingly useful in keeping me alive…for a while. Because the inherent flaws lurking underneath our ability to find a remedy which prevents us from an early grave of our own making arise whenever that method of bringing comfort ultimately fails for whatever reason, be that because of *inherent vice* on those times when we've unapologetically brought it upon ourselves, or due to standing in the presence of a case of *force majeure*, when our safety net is bluntly unravelled by the forces of nature, and there is nothing standing between us and the tangible nothingness or the hypothetical beyond, anymore.

Don't get me wrong, while I see my final outcome as nothing short of inescapable, I still remained the first one who wanted to find happiness, and feel understood, appreciated and loved. But I hadn't, or at least I *felt* I hadn't, which is often worse. It had become clear to me that the way I was going through life was simply no way to live, and the resulting pain was far too much to bear. Due to that virulent mental state, my brain found itself constantly being hijacked by an impending, all-encompassing, deafening sound; an irrational order cunningly camouflaged and subsequently misidentified as inoffensive by my emotionally feeble and excessively vulnerable mind, until grasping all-too-late the vast space such a poisonous, dark thought had permanently rented inside of me; one that kept softly whispering in my ear at every chance it saw fit, at every moment of strength and of weakness, every turn and every tumble, every step in vain and every decision confidently made, every sleepless night and every second spent daydreaming. A command that turned me into a fiercely devoted believer of the Church that predicated I had no choice in life but to carry out the most horrible act one can commit against oneself.

Bubbling within every single one of us lies a desire—already awakened in some, whilst dormant in many others—to play our part in making the world a better place by putting an end, somehow, to the many troubles plaguing our collective existence on a daily basis. As noble an aspiration as this may be, saving the world does not necessarily entail saving every single one of its inhabitants, for saving just one person should be as rewarding an achievement as saving a thousand, especially if the person you are saving is your own self. Well, the only way to save myself, I reckoned, was to carry out that which the circumstances surrounding my life had successfully convinced me I had no other choice but doing. Because I was losing the battle on the ring, just like Mr Burton did back in his day. And with each fight, I progressively developed an inability to feel love or joy, instead beginning to truly believe that every event surrounding my life had become the pre-show, the opening act, which implied a harsher reality: that the real show would never arrive. Having long accepted the relentless Diabolus ex machina that reigned over my days, it nevertheless took me thousands of white nights to finally understand that there was no point in hoping for a future where I would somehow find a way to fit in this world of ours, because, quite simply, by now it had become self-evident that this world had no room for me. What was the point of going on? What was awaiting me after all the painful daily suffering I had gotten used to calling "life" was all finally over? And more importantly, did I want it? Did I even deserve it? When the answer was as clear as it was for me, there was only one way to go, and that way was down. Six feet under, to be precise.

I

THE ACCIDENTAL(LLY SUICIDAL) TOURIST

My arrival in Switzerland on that cold, early spring morning was nothing short of traumatic, as if I needed more reasons to put a bullet through my skull. With a suitcase filled with clothes that didn't fit me anymore and sporting a pair of boots I would never wear during my stay, I walked confidently into the wrong door on my way out of Geneva's airport. The result? I ended up seven miles out of town, being fined three hundred Swiss francs by a ticket inspector who struck me as the kind of person who needed to be hugged a little tighter by his parents as an infant.

"Well, if this is not where I'm supposed to be, then would you be so kind as to tell me how to get to *insert name of the street where my future flat was located* by bus?" I asked. The sexually dissatisfied inspector shrugged his shoulders and handed me the fine, nonetheless. Using every ounce of my scarce intelligence in the face of a phone with no reception, courtesy of Swiss-European internet space agreements, I (believed to have) managed to arrive to the location indicated by my landlord on a text message with as many spelling mistakes as female characters in Michael Bay movies who failed the Bechdel Test. In spite of the orthographical butchery, the instructions were patently unmistakable: all I had to do was find bus no.5 and get off at the last stop, near the *Lancy-Pont Rouge* train station, and walk for a hundred metres to my left until I saw a pharmacy with bright, neon lights; the flat was (apparently) right next to it. Simple. Easy-peasy, lemon squeezy. Well, as it later turned out, I severely underestimated my natural ability to attract and effortlessly generate chaotic energy everywhere I went, as things made an unexpected turn for the very worst, shattering all preconceptions held up until then of what reaching "rock bottom" actually meant.

With the confidence of someone who licks the floors of the New York subway car at eight a.m. on a busy Monday, I conjured up (what I thought to be) an impressive level of French to approach the moustachioed driver after bus no.5 came to the end of its tour, in the hopes of confirming I was indeed not lost yet again in another Swiss village where (I assumed) the most popular pastime was eating a pot full of cheese and casually implementing policies of ethnic cleansing. I, with my perfectly idiotic face and my much-to-be-desired French, remained convinced I had asked the driver something in a more than appropriate and, frankly, quite eloquent way. The lady remained quiet for an entire minute, after which a sudden grin—half disgust, half confusion—started to form on her face. Only a handful of things in this world can be considered as total absolutes, completely immovable and unchangeable facts. One such truth, one which I am confident is corroborated by significant medical and empirical evidence, is that Swiss citizens (while being fully capable of speaking the English language) would inexplicably sell their respective grandma's titanium knee prosthesis to the Devil herself before speaking a single word of English.

So, imagine what state of absolute emotional breakdown one such person must experience to tell *me*, a person who looks like you could casually spit in my mouth and I would probably be the one doing the apologising part to you, the words, "Could you…could you please do yourself a favour and speak in English?" in a way that gave me yet another reason to love the Swiss: their limitless ways of telling foreigners to go fuck themselves. Such a massive medical breakthrough did not dawn on me until months later, once I had lived amongst the flora and fauna of the region.

"Is that the way to the *Lancy-Pont Rouge* station?" said the sweaty tour of meat I had become by that point. After a dramatic pause (God knows why she needed that), she nodded. It must be clarified that there was no room for error. Nothing was lost in translation. A nod is a nod. Perhaps there are some areas in the world where a nod means "no" and a finger up the ass means "it appears today's a bit windy, don't you think, Harold?" But in this context, her nod clearly translated to an affirmative answer to my question.

I hopped off the bus—which, unbeknownst to me, had crossed the France-Switzerland border *and* entered into French territory—and headed over to what would turn out to be the Customs Office, a massive enterprise which screamed "mass shooter energy" through the thousand different shades of grey paint covering its walls. Located right in the middle of the road, the only way to access the area separating the border was to kamikaze your way across the road, dodging the buses drifting by at an illegal and immoral speed.

"A lot of freakin' buses over here today. There must be an important event going on around the area," I wondered, you know, like a fucking idiot.

When I arrived at the Customs Office, the first thing that I noticed was the lack of people, which, as a general rule in my life, tends to be what I look for in any given place and situation, but not when it comes to a Customs Office—or any place where you're about to make a life changing decision, for that matter. In those cases, you want to be surrounded by as many irredeemable imbeciles as possible, to learn from their mistakes by eavesdropping your way across the long queues. The road lanes surrounding the security posts were filled with massive trucks and buses, but no people on foot, though.

"How weird," was all my sleep-deprived mind could come up with. Ignoring even the most blatantly obvious signals, I decided to join the queue of vehicles, suitcase in hand, and ended up between two immense omnibuses, those green ones that cross the continent exclusively carrying bi-curious exchange students, snoring Belarusian ladies who smell like pickled herring, and shady-looking men with an endemic need to overcompensate their insecurities by dedicating over half their working schedules to various forms of catcalling and mentally undressing strangers just to feel like an even lesser person than they already are. The disposition was as follows: large vehicle, large vehicle, enormous vehicle, fragile human being carrying luggage in the middle of the road, large vehicle, large vehicle.

Interpreting the looks daggered at me by the astonished crowd inside their respective cars and buses as part of the country's customary welcoming to strangers, particularly if they have a skin colour as dark as mine, I decided to turn a blind eye. In my mind, I assigned their celery-looking faces some thought bubbles to pass the time, so I imagined they seemed to be thinking, "God, what went wrong in this girls' life?" Oh, if only they knew… But their looks did not bother me, or at least I could not allow myself to let their looks bother me, because it's not as if I would have done something about it, either. I am so emotionally feeble that if you stop me for directions in the middle of the street, the anxiety brought by casual social interaction that requires me to be a functional human being would be too overwhelming for me not to be invaded by a sudden urge to kill myself dead. It is just as important to fix the problem than it is to know how to best cure it, and it takes a high degree of introspection to know oneself to the point of identifying exactly what it is about you that needs a remedy. A totally different discussion is, however, what you can and should do about it. But enough about my Freud-fuelled introspection slips. My turn finally arrived, and a young muscular officer looked above his manila file (for the first time that week, I'm sure), and stared at me, top to bottom, before saying something that I deduced was French but in fact sounded like the Swedish Chef from The Muppets choking on a dry piece of chicken breast at the Thanksgiving dinner with his third underage spouse.

"*You are not truck,*" the officer solemnly declared.

And I replied, always so eloquently, "Well, that depends on how you look at it." Soon after, I found myself being escorted to the Geneva police station by the Customs agents. That is the way Switzerland and I met for the first time: on a highway, with my luggage on one hand and with handcuffs around my wrists. It was as if the wrong person was at the wrong time in the wrong place in the wrong country on the wrong border.

The Swiss may have a proper-functioning democracy and the right to have an abortion, sure, but one thing they lack (and as much as I hate to hammer down on the clichés) is a sense of humour. Because the truth is that I had no intention of illegally re-entering Switzerland, as the agents claimed I did. All I was trying to do was to appreciate the Swiss landscapes from a bit up close. Sprinting? Well, in the heat of the moment people have been known to lose control of their limbs. And it is true that I was not carrying the contract that proved I had somewhere to stay in Geneva, nor did I have a working permit that verifiably showed the reasons why I wanted to enter the country, because it hadn't been issued yet by my employers. So technically, it may have *looked* like I was trying to sneak into the country. And yelling "You motherfucking pigs! Who do you think you are? All you have is cheese and bad breath!" to them, as they handcuffed me in front of the speechless crowd quietly staring at me from the comfort of their cars outside the Customs Office, may not have helped—let me be the first one to admit that. But all I did was to try to finally arrive at the flat and get some rest. I am an emotional person, what can I say? If that's illegal, then I'm guilty as charged.

With the help of Google Translator, and the physical re-enactment of every word we said during our conversation held in front of all other detainees—courtesy of the English-speaking arrested mime patiently awaiting (ultimately in vain) at the police station for his charges of public indecency to be dropped— the misunderstanding was quickly solved, and they let me go without pressing charges. One of them, a lady whose named tag read "Grtl", as if her mother had not only cursed her with being Swiss but *also* with having a white noise-sounding name with no vowels, even had the Christian decency of showing me the way to the street where my future apartment was located. When I (surreptitiously) logged onto their Wi-Fi, I received a message from my landlord, claiming—sure enough—that he'd mistakenly sent me the wrong directions to get to the flat.

Ten hours after I had landed in Geneva, and eighteen since I left Albacete, I successfully took the right bus to the newly indicated location and almost instantly broke down in tears of confusion and regret as soon as I saw the famous pharmacy and the building next to it. Across the pavement, the thousands of small pieces of glass spread across the sidewalk informed me of the cosy environment I was about to step into. To my left, a couple of drunken middle-aged men with their hairy bellies sticking out, wrestled one another over what I can only imagine was the trophy for "Most likely to commit rape in the next fifteen hours." To my right, an elderly woman defecated on the street, making eye contact with me all the way until completion. After quite an eventful day filled with memories I would yearn and struggle to forget, I finally arrived at what was to become my residence and took out a Kleenex out of my pocket to press the doorbell and avoid catching syphilis.

As I headed to the elevator after the landlord buzzed me in, a flock of rats decided to greet me with their characteristically delightful screeching, further confirming my hypothesis that there is a select, extremely idiosyncratic number of small pleasures scattered around Earth (or found all along within ourselves in the best scenarios), which make life a little more pleasant and our troubles a little more forgettable. A screening of a movie crafted by the one and only Ernst Lubitsch where the moviegoers act respectfully, for once. A cold beer after a day of doing absolutely nothing. Unexpectedly petting a playful dog while walking down the street. A tight hug from the ones you love most after months of being apart. But even those are ephemeral. Perhaps that is why they are so valuable. The perception of having acquired a state of happiness is something only consciously registered in our brain as soon as we find ourselves no longer in its possession. Because we've been looking at it the wrong way: happiness is not a destination; it's an occasional pitstop along our path of inexplicably trying (albeit always unsuccessfully) to indefinitely postpone the imminent. Now, even though I am wholeheartedly and irrevocably incapable of successfully managing my emotion(al breakdown)s, I am a woman fully capable of living in the most inhospitable places—the benches of Thessaloniki where I slept for three weeks during an eventually prosperous job search around the country bear witness to that. But there is a difference between adaptability and survivability. And not even being perfectly aware of my privilege as the first woman in my family to ever get out of Albacete under the pretence of pursuing a better life elsewhere, and having lived in more than a few places, including a room next to a (regrettably) bloodline-related psychopathic crusher of one's will to live, could prepare me for what I was to encounter at that God-forsaken apartment—even spoken from a true agnostic like myself.

The elevator doors opened, lights flickering, and as soon as my right index finger came into contact with the button for the third floor, a deafening sound—just the kind you don't want to ever hear at an elevator—drilled my eardrums and made me fear for losing a life I did not even want in the first place. I would have been shocked, had it not been for the fact the elevator decided to violently plunge into the void instead of going up, where the third floor is usually located. Funny how one comes to appreciate life much more when being constantly exposed to the lack of it, or to repeated environmental attempts against it.

Once I finally managed to arrive at the third stage after taking a detour through the stairs, the *mise en scène* all around tried to warn me of what was to come, in its defence, as my shoes progressively got stuck in the filthy tiles that covered the floor of the ominous corridor, a surface that might as well have been the "before" picture of a Cillit Bang commercial. Only the (masochistic) thought of walking around barefoot made my stomach start doing nineteenth-century Russian folk-dance moves, causing an instant indigestion of the quickly improvised breakfast I had had nearly a day ago at that point. Sharing the interior design with that of a second-rate penitentiary, I started to gather the oozing impression that the residents living amongst those ochre-coloured walls seemed to have momentarily exited one of Luis García Berlanga's films, as colourful individuals kept endlessly opening the doors, shouting at one another from across the hall only to immediately close them, exiting their houses mid-conversation and entering that of a neighbour, and shouting a symphony of orgasms and borderline-divorce arguments to one another. The door of "my" (far from mine alone, partly where the problem lay) "flat" (*latrine* was more suitable) opened and a fetid odour hijacked my nostrils, curling every inch of my body and effectively making me lose a year of good health. Standing there was my landlord: a bald man wearing a red Adidas tracksuit and a pair of white sandals which left his filth-covered toenails out in the open for only the luckiest to see and smell. His round and frankly unpleasant face was presided by an unnerving gaze that seemed to be busy making an estimation of how much he could get for selling my kidneys in the black market. His knuckles were visibly red, which made me wonder whether the noses of the other tenants, my flatmates, were at the other end of such injuries. He smiled as I approached, revealing a deranged look with his only four functioning teeth, making him closely resemble what the live-action, long-lost brother of John Silver in Disney's *Treasure Planet* (2002) would have probably looked like. Once I got close enough and was subjected (against my will, I might add) to three greeting kisses on my cheeks, I realised the smell was coming not only from him, but also from the flat itself.

"Something to look forward to during these months," I

guessed.

With an overly boyish excitement, which only served to accentuate his *rapey* vibes, he showed me the place in a few, quick strokes. The bathroom, to all intents and purposes designed *for* and *by* a toddler, was composed of a minuscule sink where my left ass cheek could barely fit, and what I assumed was a minimalist toilet, as there was none, and all that remained in its stead was a squared porcelain structure with the silhouette of two footprints and a hole in its centre. Above it, my gaze was set on a string attached to a red bucket—you do the math. The kitchen was no better than the bathroom, both in terms of space and general proportion of diseases per square meter. Being more than aware of the apartment's limitations, he wisely decided to omit opening the fridge or any of the cupboards out of fear for what might pop out of them. But the *pièce de resistance* was my Sark Prison-dimensioned room. That must have been what Harry Potter felt like, I reckoned, when he was relegated to living in the room under the stairs of the sexually arousing icon who totally monopolised my attention in *Killing Eve* (2018-2022), when my landlord opened the door and showed me that I was about to pay him seven hundred euros a month for living in a glorified closet. A table had been miraculously inserted in between a modest wardrobe and a bed out of which I suspected my feet would be sticking out—the perks of being nearly six feet tall—which he at least had the (in)decency of previously covering with a blanket so filthy it almost impregnated me by just glancing at it.

I somehow managed to fit inside the room, and just when I was about to slide right into a comfy nervous collapse, he said in a thick Eastern European accent, "No curtains: you wake up with morning light," to which I replied with an articulate, "Oh…"

"Also," he proceeded, "the tram line passes by the street

right below us. *No worry*, you get used to it: there is no better place in the world than here," he continued. There are comments which are not worthy of an answer, but of a sucker punch right in the responsible person's Beef Stroganoff, and this was one of them.

My question of "How often does the train pass by our street?" was interrupted by a vigorous tremor that shook the foundations of the entire building and prompted a pile of dust and clay to fall from the ceiling, confirming I had certifiably been *catfished*.

"Every ten minutes. Good luck," he said, and just before he closed the door, he crowned his unforgettable first impression with, "If you *have problem*, don't call me unless it is something police can't do." And after a wink that made my libido decrease to worrying levels, he disappeared from my sight.

Once I had had the customary daily mental breakdown, I crept out of the room, determined to find bed linens that would not immediately give me HPV. On my way out, I realised the tour was not over, as I had yet to meet the other patients of the twisted experiment which living in this place seemed to be. All glimmers of hope stemming from my delusional fantasies of meeting interesting people I could potentially become friends with while staying there were instantly shattered as soon as I headed towards the kitchen and saw a dark shadow lurking across the room. Standing there was a man who turned out to be named Ronnie, a twenty-year-old-ish young man with a face that I deduced had seldom seen the light of day, perpetually hunched over and sporting big, squared glasses around his slanted eyes. His skull was ninety percent covered with a massive headset and surely filled with thoughts about how much of a disappointment he was to his parents: wouldn't you know it, I was about to be living with a gamer. I observed him from a distance—him completely unaware of my presence—and witnessed how he put all of his freshly used cooking utensils inside a kitchen drawer and then proceeded to put a lock on it. We unexpectedly made eye contact, and he acknowledged my presence with a small nod, after which he disappeared into his room. And that was the last time I saw him. Not because he died, but because Ronnie would effectively avoid human contact by scheduling his day so as not to make any social interaction with anyone else in the flat, something I would come to practice after merely enduring five days in a flat that looked and felt like Kevin Spacey's sex dungeon. Because even though I never saw him again, he would make us very much aware of his presence, as he incessantly played his video games out loud, laughably shouting instructions to his virgin peers as if in the midst of childbirth, starting at six p.m. and ending at eight a.m. One of those Jeffrey Dahmers in the making, I reckoned.

Leaving behind the anxiety-inducing atmosphere from the building did not mean that things would go much better for me out there, as my shopping duties were deemed unsuccessful, given the Machiavellian opening and closing schedules that run the country in times of COVID and mandatory lockdowns. With everything closed by six p.m., how did Swiss people who worked nine-to-five manage to buy toilet paper or supplies for their alcohol addiction or cucumbers for lonely nights? On the bright side, it did give me the time, however, to get to know the neighbourhood a little better, away from all the commotion of daily life. The only two places to quench one's vices—the nearby Protestant church and the clandestine bars—were the only locations which remained open at that time. Being welcomed in none of them, I continued my tour and walked around the industrial-park-like beauty of the streets around my new shared apartment, until I found the only vestiges of mild beauty in the area embodied in a humble park where one could see the *Mount Salève* in all its splendour and, if one squinted tightly enough, the tower of Saint Peter's cathedral presiding over Geneva city far into the distance. Entranced by the inherent beauty in the eyes of a child who was being pushed on a swing by her father, her laughter, her total ignorance of the world that awaited her as soon as she hopped off the swing, I failed to notice the abundant syringes which carelessly laid on the ground, unbothered. Soon after, a pair of skinny dudes in dark sport clothes, who looked like a self-produced rapper with thirty-four followers on Instagram and a Ditropan addiction which your mother would never approve of, zigzagged their way to where I was standing, me fearing their likely approach to sell me drugs or ask for my number could easily turn—as many interactions had in the past—into the kind of situation you read in the papers on the next morning. That was one of the things I learnt from an early age after my family and I crossed the Atlantic and arrived in Spain in search of a better life: my pigmented inheritance carries with it an overwhelming, undue and unwanted burden on those of us who had no choice in its selection, although if I were to be given the chance, I wouldn't change a single shade of it. Anticipating the misguided comments that were going to ensue as a result of their fragile self-importance having been undealt with for that long, I decided to head back before they made first contact, not out of cowardice but sheer accumulated collective tiredness of dealing with a problem that did not belong to me yet constantly felt the consequences of.

    Since there were no police officers in sight, and bearing very much in mind that I could always play the "lost foreigner card", I decided to venture outside the streets of *Carouge*, where my flat was located, and properly explore the city, given that all the *excitement* of my arrival had prevented me from taking a single, honest look at the city of Geneva beyond its police stations and Customs Offices. In all seriousness, the quick search I had carried out prior to buying the plane tickets revealed that Geneva may have been a city endowed with geopolitical and economic relevance, but the place in and of itself was far from a visually remarkable destination. In fact, the most thorough of Google searches is only bound to result in the overwhelming monopolization of pictures of the *Jet D'Eau* from a thousand different angles: a massive waterjet that occasionally changed colour and, apparently, the most recognisable symbol of the city. It was like having only one picture on your Tinder profile—all alarms immediately go off. Thus, my mind was more than prepared to encounter a sea of grey-coloured buildings, where buying a sandwich was as expensive as a heart transplant and where the national sport was knitting the rope with which they hang themselves after they're done with building clocks and miniature trains to fill the empty void left by an unfulfilled life.

But, as luck would have it (and despite the fact that my ignorant disposition got mixed with a clear unwillingness to learn more about the city prior to my arrival, something which back in Spain we call *"Se ha juntado el hambre con las ganas de comer"*), things turned out for the best, as I was more than pleasantly surprised when Geneva pulled an unexpected power play by revealing the many wonders it had to offer along a single, three-hour-long walk across the city. Because what Google had left out was something that could never be captured in a mere picture, like a smell or an uncontrollable impulse; it was what made Geneva a city with a different molecular structure than anything that came before it: the atmosphere around it. Very much like a Bloody Mary or mayonnaise, if you eat its raw ingredients on their own, you may end up viciously vomiting on the street. But mix it all together in the right order and with enough precision or lack thereof—the *Rhône* and the *Arve* rivers with their secret shorelines and Parisian-looking bridges majestically leading the way into the *Léman* Lake; the vintage trams frantically driven by coked-up drivers; pedestrians constantly walking on the path designed for bikes and being threatened to death by incoming bikers; the eternal protesters fruitlessly holding demonstrations in front of the *Palais des Nations* in support of a resolution that will never see the light of day; ladies giving their breasts a tan at the female-only *Bains des Pâquis* section; the possibility of always falling prey to a burglary in front of *Gare Cornavin*; the smell of joints and cheese on the *Marché des Grottes*—and you have an unforgettable end result.

Even though I was not in the best company, the city instantly captivated me with its seemingly boundless possibilities, its public bookshelves which stored knowledge anybody could freely acquire, and its quiet parks hidden across narrow streets, only accessible for lost souls in search of a way to drown out the thundering noises of the occasionally maddening city. And as I walked across the empty streets of the Old Town, it suddenly hit me: I finally understood that what had so far kept the seemingly unremarkable city of Geneva from being great in my mind was not its ordinary nature, but my lack of sight in being able to look a little further, underneath the apparent trivial beauties of the world, and appreciate its hidden greatness. Even on the streets near the flat, there was a bubbling underground culture of secretly opened bars and illegal neighbourhood gatherings raising a firm middle finger to COVID curfews, which flowed through the veins of the city and made the hideousness stemming from each building peppering the virtually identical streets of even the least visually appealing district, become instantly trumped by the unique atmosphere created by its inhabitants. There was something innately authentic about its people, who crowded the patios of the residential buildings, and seemed to embody the popular saying that "it takes a village to raise a kid", as it gave the impression they were all related, if not by blood, then by postcode, which can often be more meaningful.

On my way back, I noticed that waiting for me, a couple of feet away from the entrance to my building, was the same lady I had earlier seen defecating on the street. She once again made a conscious effort to lock eyes with me whilst she manoeuvred her way out of the *clay statue* she was squeezing onto the sidewalk. You have to watch out for these things, before they become a ritual. I guess it's like your first day in prison; you have to establish your dominance, so I made a vow right then and there to one day pull off a "UNO Reverse Card" and poop as she poops and make sure our eyes met while I performed my excretive duties.

"Who knows, maybe that way I'd find something new about myself," I wondered. When I arrived back at the flat, I was (un)pleasantly greeted by the other flatmates: Carmen and Marisa, two unemployed Ethiopian ladies in their late 50s who were flamenco dancer wannabes and felt the need to rehearse every day to avoid "losing their magical touch." Unless that magical touch was the one that resulted after the doctor accidentally dropped them on the floor as infants, I remained thoroughly unaware of what that could be. Forever covered in high leather boots with fishnet stockings and thin sweaters that overemphasised their respective hysterectomies' scars, these two avid chain-smokers with no apparent penchant for personal hygiene, as evidenced by their constant flickering of boogers, made me feel like I had been transported to Paris' red-light district in the 1960s.

Partly the exhaustion, and partly the trauma dawning in from coming to the realisation that I was supposed to live amongst such specimens for six months, my judgement was clouded to the point I decided to venture into humankind's most perverted invention to date: our apartment's shower—*enter suspenseful sound effect*. With the drain inexplicably built on the highest part of the porcelain shower structure, the water instantly flooded the shower plate and overflowed the bathroom floor, creating the perfect breeding ground amongst the wooden floors for mould and a delightful smell of putrefaction to become the newest members of our flat. The small dimensions of such a devilish creation placed the person inside of it at quite a close distance with the shower curtain, to the point it was almost inevitable that it got stuck to your body. Oh, yes, the thought of those tobacco-infused ladies and the hacker guy scrubbing themselves onto the plastic curtain, and then my body sharing the same fate, made me cheer with delight in the face of such a beautiful connection. The alternative was to stick yourself onto the tiles of the wall, a place I suspected had been the frequent target of bodily fluids. What a time to be alive.

I got undressed and stared at my naked reflection in the mirror: looking back at me from the other side were the stretch marks softly ploughing my pronounced curves after years of dietary ups and downs, the countless freckles and few pimples around my discreetly flat nose, the scars resulting from deep cuts along the upper part of my inner thighs and forearms, the life in my ocean-blue eyes which had progressively escaped pill after pill, the hirsute armpits and eyebrows I had gladly inherited from

Grandma Lupe…

Little did I know, this new phase of my life was the beginning of a heck of a ride. More specifically, the beginning and the end of my happiness, and the first step towards my eventual death.

II

GET ANXIOUS LIVING OR GET BUSY DYING

How ironic is it, that when you need to sleep the most, you end up barely resting at all and looking like Christian Bale's double in *The Machinist* (2004)—pointlessly wandering around the house, unable to reach a decent level of productiveness, with your confused mind wondering why you refuse to relax and give her some rest when she knows that's all that you need and ever dream of.

As one might have deduced after the previous day's interactions with the other roommates, my eventful night included an eight-hour-long *concerto* filled with stellar interventions, ranging from Ronnie's masterful rendition of "The Thousand Years' Drought of Female Genitalia" as he shouted at his fellow incel companions during their nightly Call of Duty virtual gathering, to an era-defining performance from Carmen and Marisa and their inability to snore like human beings. Every time one of their mistreated lungs emulated what can only be described as the momentary escape of a centuries-old Irish ghost's trapped soul, the wall's foundations trembled like they were in the middle of a Macarena dance exhibition, a state of snoring so remarkably outrageous I previously thought only my father was capable of. Of course, it could not have been a party without the special appearance of the Genevan public transport, which I quickly corroborated indeed ran every ten minutes, each time nearly inducing me into a premature heart attack with its dramatic entrances into scene.

It took me a little longer to fully wake up that morning; not only was I supposed to face a new day, but also, potentially, a new life. Purpose was something that kept evading me, escaping through my fingers, even when it seemed like I was finally on the right track of life. But it was too early in the morning to start thinking about that kind of thing, so I decided to consciously get lost in my delusional thoughts and aspirations for a better life as I stared out the window and down into the busy streets of *Carouge*. My momentary entrancement was interrupted by a notification from my phone—an unsubtle call to get back to reality, which just as soon as it was registered, was instantly erased from my brain. Those streets out there…there was something about them that kept urgently demanding my attention. After the second notification loudly resounded over the room, I grabbed the phone and in its black mirror saw my reflection staring back at me.

And so, I began my daily cycle of misery by opening up the respective bottle of antidepressants. At this point, the routine had become quite clear: one blue pill before going to sleep, to numb the pain and manage to get some hours of rest, and one red pill in the mornings, to numb the pain and be a somewhat functional Homo sapiens by momentarily parking the most troubling thoughts in a dark corner—because forcibly repressing one's most violent impulses has always worked wonders, right?

It has always amazed me the frighteningly quick speed with which doctors decide to rock the pillars of your life by diagnosing you with depression, as if they obtained a commission each time one of their patients walked into a pharmacy with a Zoloft prescription. Despite having nothing that resembles a medical degree diploma hanging on my wall, I carefully manage to keep my balance when walking along the tightrope between stupidity and common sense, at least enough to know that what a clinically depressed person needs most are not profit-driven pills, but to be *heard*. Makes one feel like a complete idiot after finally taking the courageous step forward to ask for help. Like the school nurse relegating the treatment of your broken ankle to covering it with a bag of ice, when in fact what you needed was to immediately go to the ER to receive medical care by a qualified professional, treating depression, anxiety and suicidal thoughts with a bottle of pills is, as Selina Meyer stated, like using a piece of bakery as a sex toy: not only does it fail to fulfil its intended purpose, but it also makes matters considerably worse by creating additional problems that are even harder to scrub out of your system. Grandma always says a fool's money always comes twice to the store, and the irresponsibility some doctors exhibit by carelessly prescribing pills to everyone who happens to walk through the door, like they're Gaspar Noé adding more psychedelic strobe lightbulbs to the shopping chart ahead of shooting one of his movies, only serves to expand the problem and devalue the real solution: the combination of opening up to your closed ones and proper psychological counselling. But that would require taking some time and actually sitting down with each person to get to the bottom of their problems, and time is something we apparently don't have anymore. That's what happens when you live in the Empire of TikTok, where a two-hour-long movie is considered to be never-ending, and reading a book is discarded as a tedious, time-consuming task. Why read when you can watch? Why watch when you can listen? Why listen when you don't have the time?

Yes, I feel that my health is a commodity, that is, the lack of it, as I get sucked into a perpetual torture chamber where I get punched until I become senseless at night, only to be yet again knocked out of my nightly coma by the incoming trains of the morning pills. Before arriving here, Dr Nguyen used to call me every Monday evening, without fail. But in a house with paper-thin walls, where one could neatly follow each other's digestive processes, my answers to the doctor were limited to monosyllables, and she seemed to be content with such replies.

"Less work for me," she probably thought. And so, the world keeps turning, drawing a thick veil over the fact that close to a million people take their lives every year, far more than the ones losing their lives in traffic accidents, and with countless more suffering from deteriorating mental health conditions in plain sight. Lost souls of a world that it seems stopped caring about them long ago. Problem solved, I guess.

It should come to no surprise that I was not feeling particularly great on that morning. Could have been that there were still three days before I started my internship and had no inclination to start thinking about the fact that I was vastly unqualified for the position. Could have been the horrible Tinder conversations I'd been having and the constant apprehension that plundered my thoughts every time I fathomed the dreading moment where I'd meet one of those girls in person and they would realise the pictures on my profile were, at the very least, five years old. Or perhaps it was the fact that I still hadn't made any progress making friends in that inhospitable territory, a state of affairs undoubtedly of my own making. Maybe the pound and a half of Emmental cheese I had eaten the night prior for dinner had also played a part in failing to improve my characteristically depressive state of mind by adding physical discomfort to the list of things I was forced to withstand on that day. Who's to tell? My diet had been relegated to baguettes and the smelliest selection of local cheeses, which I simply inserted into a loaf of bread in an effort to avoid touching with my bare hands the shamelessly repulsive filth covering the flat's cutlery, pots and pans. Although, it must be said that by then I had grown so accustomed to the place's characteristic repugnant state that I didn't even scream anymore whenever I saw a four-feet, emerald-coloured, slightly overweight snake crawling across the kitchen floor. She was lovely, actually. We decided to call her Myriam—at least I did. Apparently, she was one of the many pet snakes from our upstairs fakir neighbour that escaped everyday out his window. Certainly instigated by the fact we could never have a pet growing up, for obvious safety reasons, but also fuelled by my desire to give out some of the love and affection that I had carried with me for so long but which nobody seemed to want or value, Myriam and I quickly built a strong affinity for one another during the many visits she used to pay us, as if she could feel I was clinging onto anything that could get me out of the hole I found myself in. A few weeks before I arrived in Geneva, one of my closest friends innocently replied to my stated wish to someday adopt a puppy with a sharp-edged yet totally on-point reply of, "You're too nuts to have a pet."

    What many people around me fail to grasp is that depression is neither prolonged sadness nor something that can be cured by simply "cheering up". The lonely women and men that walk down that road are essentially de-facto ticking time bombs, accumulating energy as days go by; energy that they have nobody but themselves to share with, and which, over time, is only bound to get out, one way or another. So, they spend their days just waiting for the moment when themselves and the joke of a life they have pretended to build for all these years finally crumble by their own weight, shattering into a thousand little pieces the farcical porcelain mask placed over their faces in an attempt to fit into the norm and continue senseless and purposelessly navigating through life, eventually landing in the comfortable coffin they've yearned for so long. People who have nothing to lose are walking, talking catastrophe precursors, because anything can happen when you are beyond the point of caring, beyond fearing the unknown reality that awaits us after death, when the tiniest, smallest kind of disruption can make you go off and you would not only be at peace with that, but crave for it to happen. That's why you have to be careful when you are around somebody like me, someone who suffers from (or who you think suffers from) depression, because an innocent statement, such as the one my friend made, can trigger unexpected consequences and make an already flammable individual permanently go off. But was it true what my friend said, anyway? Or was the insanity located at the other side of the accusatory finger pointed in my direction? By painstakingly analysing his self-perceived harmless statement, it became apparent to me that—even if it was at a deeply internalised, subconscious level to the point of complete lack of self-awareness—it had become common knowledge amongst my friends that there was something not right about me, whatever that meant, and that at this point in time, they had no prospect in their minds that such a condition was ever going to change.

Loneliness can be the deadliest of companions, not because of the synthetically designed and unrealistic need to be constantly surrounded by others which is perpetually taught by common practice, but because it's the one carefully loading the bullets of our guns behind our backs, and in the worst cases, with our permission. And before you know it, the trigger has been pulled and now you are part of an annual statistic of a problem nobody takes the time to pay any real attention to yet takes all the time in the world to gossip about. All this confusion arising from my sleeplessness got me thinking that I may have gotten myself into a bigger mess than I expected, as the reason why I left the inhospitable terrain that I used to call my home back in Spain was in the search for the prospect of a better life, away from Him and, without being overly greedy, for a chance to finally reach something that resembled peace and quiet. But so far, the one thing I genuinely felt was that the only place I was gonna be able to get some true rest was whenever I found myself pushing up daisies.

Perhaps my frustration arose from the fact that I had managed to personalize all my mental troubles, comfortably tracing the root cause of my decaying physical and mental state back to someone else's behaviour. But I had every reason to do so, as the amount of pain suffered by his own hand cannot even be quantified. How, I wonder, by sleepless nights? By suicide attempts? By number of sore or broken knuckles? By stitches from the self-inflicted cuts on my body? By the amount of destroyed relationships? I guess, like everyone else, I try to make the most out of the hand I am dealt, and in my case, it has taken the shape of simplifying my trauma and attaching to it a name other than my own. Because the truth is that ever since I can remember, he has been the author of my insomnia, the proud sculptor of my mother's tears and the sole architect of the rupture of our home. He has broken her down and, by sheer force and unconditional motherly love, she has picked herself back up so many times after each and every one of his twisted words and violent outbursts, that she now finds herself unable to feel a single thing. Emotionally lobotomised and perennially stuck to a bottle of wine, that poor woman, guilty only of giving him all the love one can possibly give, now faces the reality of living with him each day, with nothing but her own resilience to keep her company.

Easy problems require easy solutions, so I tricked myself into believing that the Devil cannot be escaped from, but could be temporarily fooled, since theoretically he couldn't possibly hurt me anymore if he couldn't see me anymore. This turned out to be untrue, as nothing brought him more pleasure than the sport which he has become the master of, always making his way out of finding convoluted ways to get a poisoned dart right to its target, as far away as it may be. Even though being voluntarily evicted from my own house—since a better life would surely be found anywhere but there—was certainly a step in the right direction towards the path of self-improvement (or at least so I thought), the repercussions of my rushed decision were now momentarily exposing themselves. If life had not worked for me back at home and was not working now in Geneva—at a different town, a different city, and even a different country where he couldn't find me anymore—then Aristotelian logic points to the one variable in common: me, myself and I. So, what if, like my friend's comment casually implied, there is no remedy available for me? What if my brother was not really a villain, but a demented perversion engineered by my irredeemable impulse to blame all my problems onto someone else? What if the premature grave I now find myself in is of my own making?

To understand where I am coming from, and the state I permanently found myself in, picture yourself having a pair of overweight Cossacks performing a traditional folk dance on your chest all day long, puncturing your lungs with each step they take, undermining the task of breathing to the point of near impossibility. At every turn you make and every place you visit. When you're on the toilet. When you're out buying groceries. When you're at the movies. At the park. In your bed. Outside of your home. While driving in your car or when taking the public transport. With friends and on your own. When you're wide awake and when you are deep into your dreams. In class and at work. Now imagine if that was not a momentary instant, but prolonged for long enough for you to grow used to it. That's what is called anxiety. In a world where we devalue the meaning of words by constantly and erroneously overusing them—a sin of which I am the guiltiest one, because if acting is about reacting and writing is about rewriting, I manage to suck at both, even though I react quite a lot, and overwrite in excess—there seems to be little understanding and proper treatment for this affliction that silently affects many more people than we care to bother. The tragedy lying underneath this pervasive disease is that, in the face of its protracted presence, I have confused familiarity with normality, falling prey to the worst remedy available for it: getting used to that feeling, and developing my own ways of adapting to it. In my case, looking down, purposely not wearing my round, metal glasses and avoiding eye contact always helped, especially when waiting in line (which always made me uncomfortable) and in crowded places, since I'm hardly ever not by myself, accompanied only by my fiercely loyal companion of social awkwardness. Because if you can't see anything, then you've got less reasons to be anxious and have one of those panic attacks that occasionally frequented my long weeks.

The problem is, however, that the effect that prolonged social inanition can have on a human body can very likely turn out to be irreparable. In the absence of meaningful connections with others and with the real world (in that order) given the overwhelming presence of loneliness, your body drastically changes, your mental constitution acclimatizes to that state, and as such, you will remain forever changed, even if you somehow manage to put an end to this endlessly destructive condition.

Having been on my own for as long as I have has made me become more aware of my surroundings, where everybody always seems to be in groups, and especially in pairs. And an odd number always stands out, and not for the right reasons. One could argue I may be biased about this, but I wholeheartedly feel there is an inherent prejudice towards people just casually hanging out on their own in the face of limited social abilities and a roster of toxic friendships filling their days; people who we instinctively tend to label as introverts, as lonely individuals, as someone to take pity on, to ostracise or to assume *is* ostracised, taking for granted that such persons *must* be at the very least weird enough to have nobody to go to a concert or a movie theatre with. Leaving prison, personal losses and illnesses aside, feeling completely alone is one of the most hurtful states of mind a person can experience: unable to make a connection with anybody else, like being forced to stand still whilst watching everyone else move forward. It seems today that everywhere you look there are people carelessly living their best lives, and they stand at a numeric majority. Loners by choice at least have somewhat of a chance at being happy. But loners by default, by total inability due to their inner or outer surroundings, are amongst the most tortured souls walking this earth. Worst of all, they tend to have a low life expectancy.

Yesterday, for instance, after almost being run over by a pair of kamikaze bikers (whom I would soon learn have more rights than the President of the Swiss Confederation), I realised that regardless of where you are, even if you are in the most Microsoft-Windows-wallpaper-worthy of all places, it is futile to try and believe you are experiencing the best that a particular place has to offer. Drinking a coffee at a bar on your own is not the same as going at prime-time golden hour to the busiest and fanciest cafe in town with a friend, or a date. Same thing with going to the movies, or with visiting any given city on your own. It's not that I am reliant on others in order to enjoy life—then again, how can one be reliant on something one does not have?—it's just that the same way that I think movies like *Lawrence of Arabia* (1963) or *There Will Be Blood* (2007) are best enjoyed on the biggest movie screen you can get your hands on, the discovery of new places, new cities and new countries is a dish served and enjoyed best whilst in company. And now, the prospect of walking on my own across Geneva makes me feel as if I went shopping while my bank account was in red numbers, even unable to afford tap water: I see love, beauty and happiness all around me, and I feel those are things I used to enjoy, things that I *had*, when I was not on my own and that are now positively lost and completely out of reach. That said, when wasn't I on my own? I can no longer remember.

This pain stemming from an inability to connect with others is where I believe the root of unhappiness and the recipe for death lies, as it endows individuals with a lack of purpose and, above all, solidifies the idea in their minds that there is no room for them in this world. Because it doesn't get any better than fitting in and feeling you belong somewhere, and it doesn't get any worse than being utterly unable to achieve so. My mind is filled with regrets of a life I wish I could live, of an ideally devised existence where I could go through my days not caring about what others thought about me, but as soon as I step out the door my behaviour is tailored to trying to be as pleasant to others as possible, an attitude where my wellbeing clearly lies at the bottom of the scale of priorities. That is why I envy people who can go places on their own, meeting people they *matched* with on Tinder, and making friends around the world during improvised gap-year trips. But I am not that kind of person. My friends are those that were formed almost out of sheer coincidence and certainly a lot of patience on their side. Quite a lot of patience from me as well, I might add, as I have quietly become their confidant and main support, always ready to listen to their problems yet unable to open up enough to them to reveal my own—partly due to a (somewhat founded) fear that they will be unable to help and cope with such existential, life-defying dilemmas that are best suited for someone with a degree in psychiatry, or a priest, and if heard by them would result in a one-way ticket to a white room with foam walls.

Life would be so easy then, I guess, if human interaction was something I did not avoid but actively seek. Unable to do so, when my friend Lucas sent me the number of a friend of his that lived in Geneva, a girl apparently named Lara, I thanked him for the opportunity whilst simultaneously becoming perfectly aware of the fact I would never talk to nor have any interaction with his friend. What a shame; I bet she's great and a lot of fun to hang out with, but that's something for someone else to discover. From the bottom of my broken heart, I wish I could say that I hoped I had friends in Geneva, but the apparent truth is that even when given the chance to do so, my instinctive loneliness, heavily ingrained after many painful years of experiences that solidified such state, told me otherwise. It was too late for me; I was too far deep. There was no turning back. Self-imposed preventive solitude was the destination that awaited me, so there was only one place where I could go and be by myself without the looming weight of the social judgement being constantly passed upon me everywhere I walked on my own, and where I could finally enjoy the company of silence and quietness: the mountains. Luckily for me, the country was filled with them.

The 7.45 a.m. train passed by, and I swallowed the morning pills like a good girl. As the chemicals went down my throat and into my stomach, I wondered, "What came before, though, the anti-depressive or the anxiolytic?" Of little importance was the answer to that question, because, if you can't tell, then what's the difference? The pills started to kick off immediately, and with it, the morning ritual officially began.

III

TROYAN HORSE

Despite being fully aware of the highly flammable cocktail that could potentially result from the combination of my emotional shortcomings being paired with my deeply unqualified disposition for the internship I would end up being selected for, my desperation to get out of that house made me dive head on into hastily applying for such position in perhaps one of the worst states that you can apply for any job: being COVID-19 positive. Like virtually all decisions that I had made up until that point, I had no idea where I was getting myself into. All I knew was that I had to get out of Albacete as soon as possible, and this seemed to be the perfect way out. But having pneumonia on my left lung and a fierce desire to collapse with every breath I took—partly the effects of the virus, partly the result of my depressed, and physical activity-deprived default mode—made me quite an undesirable candidate. But still, as part of my desperate efforts to emancipate, I applied to a number of human-rights-related positions, the only field of work my *expertise* had been relegated to, in the hopes that there would be someone out there foolish and desperate enough to hire me. After all, there were far more useless people in much more demanding positions out there into the world—I should know, I (reluctantly) lived with one for nearly a quarter of a century. And quite surprisingly, or perhaps not, given my penchant to colour up my professional abilities—

AKA blatantly making things up, a tendency of which my CV had not gone unscathed—I was contacted by three different NGOs interested in "scheduling an interview with me". And me being who I am, saw myself at a loss for words when I was notified this world's chaotic energy had somehow managed to schedule my three interviews on the same day, one right after the other: ten a.m. – ten thirty a.m. – eleven a.m..

"We've come to play," I thought. And play I did, indeed.

The doctors who had prescribed an immoral amount of drugs to numb the effects of COVID on my body had the last laugh when I woke up on the scheduled Monday at five minutes to ten a.m., severely lacking any sense of temporal or spatial perception as if I had just woken up from a naughty four-hour-long nap, which was then followed by an absolute state of panic, with my face looking like an extra out of one of Fritz Lang's earlier movies, and no ironed items of clothing in sight. Still, I pulled through in the face of adversity and managed to tune in to the virtual interview via Zoom just in time.

For what appeared to be an eternity after the preliminary greetings, I monologued when asked the question "Why do you want to work for our organization?" Somehow, I managed to nail every single rehearsed beat, courtesy of lengthy periods of thoroughly researching that NGO in particular, which prior to my inquiries I had never heard of—and, as it turned out, never would again. Because, after a solid four minutes passed by telling the poker-faced interviewers how since I was a little girl, I had dreamed of working for "Peace and Prosperity International", I was corrected by a nonplussed interviewer, who merely resigned to say, "I am sorry, Madam, but I think you have us confused with another organization. We are 'Peace and Development International Coalition.'" Yes, I had logged onto the wrong link and entered the eleven a.m. interview, instead—why these people were already on the call is beyond me, though. Trying to get out of that pickle as best as I could, I blamed the name slip on the fact that most NGOs have similar names, which did not go well with the interviewers, who turned out to be the founders of the organization themselves. After wiping away the copious sweat from my forehead, and with a combo of fifty percent adrenaline, fifty percent painkillers flowing through my veins, I logged onto the first scheduled call of the day, for which I was now late, and went on to have the shortest interview in the history of humankind, as I arrived two minutes before the end of the agreed upon time. It also did not help that my father made an appearance in the background, vacuuming the floor whilst singing in a Scottish kilt to his collection of National Hymns, completely oblivious to the fact I was in the middle of a job interview. As if the world was conspiring against me, my brother casually and innocently—as he typically did—decided to restart the wireless internet router to be able to play on an Xbox FIFA tournament, and I ended up abruptly disconnecting from the interview before being able to say goodbye, which in all honesty was probably for the best—the less time for me to embarrass myself any further, the better.

Having lost all faith in humanity at this point, I logged onto the last virtual interview in the hopes of getting it over and done with as quickly as possible and return back to my bed to continue my self-designed Thomas Vinterberg movie marathon. But it turned out the young, lively women in charge of the interview were incredibly friendly, to my amazement, and in between a surprisingly refreshing set of questions we instantly formed some unexpected complicity; a space where I could liberate myself from most tensions and no longer felt the need to give the prepared and phony answers which I had carefully written down on a notebook next to my computer. Saving distances, I could say with a straight face that it was the first time that I had been myself in a job interview...even though I claimed to know how to use Excel and social media, and to have experience in web design, and in the heat of the moment described myself as a fluent French speaker—the latter of which they tested me on, those bitches, and I ended up looking like what I am: a fool, because I had not spoken a single word of French since I was in primary school and now all the residual knowledge which remained in my brain was *"Bonjour, bonjour! Bienvenue dans ma maison, il y a quatre fenêtres et un grand port!!"*

Against all odds, I got a call a week later stating that I had nevertheless been chosen for the position, which inaugurated a varied roster of moral dilemmas and spearheaded an avalanche of emotional turmoil, the effects of which I have not yet recovered from. Over the subsequent three weeks, what followed were a series of mental breakdowns that filled my days from dusk till dawn, internally battling whether to leave my mother all alone, defenceless to the long claws of emotional torture that had left such deep, invisible scars which she wore in silence, or instead opt for a brief period of desperately-needed internal and external healing after having reached rock bottom long enough for it to become my permanent state of mind. Even after I bought the plane tickets, I kept torturing myself for having chosen the latter, and it took me more than a few sleepless nights to understand how profoundly broken I was to prefer to abandon the place where I was needed most in the pursuit of something I no longer thought I deserved. But like the best decisions, the counteroffer must involve a certain risk of loss in such a way that, when looking back, one sees how much one has sacrificed in order to give up not being happy. So, the rationale that kept me away from insomnia was the thought that having two inconsiderate children is better than having one of them permanently underground. I just hoped she would eventually see it that way, too. Opting to think short term in favour of having a long term to speak of, a month later I was flying away from my domestic problems and on route to the city of Geneva.

Ahead of my first day at work, and having grown (kind of) accustomed to Switzerland's wilderness, I decided to kick things off in this new life of mine by adopting a somewhat healthier lifestyle. So, I decided to go on the Swiss equivalent of Craigslist and get my hands on a bike to go to work every day, and perhaps go on some adventures of my own (as if I had ever done that back in Spain for a single day; you can say whatever you want about me, but I surely have a wide imagination for devising scenarios whose occurrence is questionable, to say the least). The bike seemed like a good option at the time, because Lord knows I didn't have the money to pay five Swiss francs a day for hopping onto a foul-smelling tram where a knife at the heart and a racially-motivated random police search were two likely outcomes I had to face on a daily basis, and my thighs were acquiring such massive dimensions people could hear me coming from a mile away just from the mere sound of my groins thrusting against one another. Who knows, perhaps it could even put an end to the random chest pains which persistently made their presence very much felt at the most inconvenient of times, comforting me by falsely predicting the end was nigh.

One of the shadier ads on the website offered a perfectly serviceable-looking, yellowish bike for around ninety Swiss francs, so I sent the buyer a message and around two hours later I was meeting with a gypsy woman who smelled like the most fetid odours from one of Geronimo Stilton's books in an abandoned parking lot on the outskirts of the city, each minute becoming increasingly afraid I was going to be kidnapped and my organs sold on the Deep Web, like one of those kids in *Slumdog Millionaire* (2008). The bike in and of itself was designed for a much smaller person with ass cheeks made of concrete, because the chair was so hard and so loose that each time I went over a bump on the road, the chair would violently get lowered to its smallest height, effectively making me lose my virginity all over again. But very much like Swiss people's emotional depth, it was cheap and functional, and even though the posterior brakes did not work (something which would turn out to be important, apparently), I decided to purchase it, nonetheless.

Everything was now ready for my first day at work, so I hopped on the bike and headed North with an adolescent smile painted on my face, thinking about the many possibilities that day and the months ahead, could possibly offer. What did not come to mind, however, was the need to wear proper clothing for riding said bike, particularly in the early hours of the morning, nor adequate cycling equipment, like a helmet, nor to bring a change of clothes—you know, like normal people do. The result? After battling with that devilish creation called Google Maps, which kept redirecting me back to my flat and suddenly switching from Spanish to German and from German to Afrikaans, and then opted for vaguely stoic instructions like "turn right whenever you have to turn right" or "go South", I counted at least a few dozen occasions where I came close to forming part of the Swiss road map, thanks to the Formula 1 aspirations of Geneva's tram conductors. The instructions from the navigation system, paired with the frenzy morning wave of mechanically morose drivers arriving late at their twenty-year-old unsought desk jobs that routinely prompted them to gag from repulsion, made for quite a ride. Written on the side screen of one of the buses, I read the name of the street where the NGO was located as its next destination, so I grabbed onto its posterior lights with my left hand and prayed for the sake of my teeth that the brakes from my new bike would not suddenly stop working. For some reason I still am unable to grasp, I miraculously arrived—completely covered in sweat, I might add—to the front door of the NGO, right across the *Palais des Nations*, unscathed and with every bone in its proper place. But life, as it often does when it comes to me, was just getting started with this maniacal game. As I hopped off the bike, I could tell something was wrong, the day seemed…particularly windy. Since I was already forty minutes late, I made nothing of it and walked up the stairs, all six floors of them.

The sweaty mess that I was at that point in time—gasping for air, my grey suit visibly wet around the chest, back and armpit area—was greeted by Konstantinos, the organization's Director, a chubby Greek man with a penchant for colourful shirts who did not miss a beat when he immediately called me by the name of the previous intern. Next to him were the two ladies that I had seen at the interview a month prior: Cassandra, a ginger British expat with a round face and an overall lack of style, and Lucille, a French lady with a bright and sunny disposition painted all over her freckled-filled face, who uttered the expression "Oh my God" for every other four words that came out of her mouth. And then there was Vero, dear Vero, a Spanish compatriot in her early thirties yet somehow looking younger than me, who ran the Communications Department with far more efficiency than the NGO had any right to demand of her. With just one look at her, you could tell she emanated a kind of rare beauty that'd make everyone turn around at a party whenever she walked into a room—a perfectly imperfect idiosyncratic beauty of long, frizzy hair eternally wrapped in a tight bun.

After the awkward introductions, and perhaps motivated by the inescapable collective realization that I was pouring sweat like Orson Welles' Captain Quinlan in *Touch of Evil* (1958) every time he took one breath too many, we moved the conversation to the Conference Room, where we had our very first staff meeting. Somehow, I could still feel the breeze even though we were indoors and the radiators were on full blast, something which I attributed to my agitated state and inner panic attack upon realising the indelible and certainly unforgettable first impression I was leaving on each of their minds. Presiding over the room was a massive banner with the organization's logo, looming over our heads like the sixth staff member, silently judging the drops of sweat flowing down my spine. We all sat on opposing sides, and so the meeting began, without any lube, anaesthesia or preliminaries whatsoever. What ensued was a collection of incomprehensible verbal exchanges that would make the dialogues in *His Girl Friday* (1940) seem like a pair of senile war veterans with hearing loss trying to talk about the weather at a nursing home through two plastic cups connected by a string. Names, projects, bills, lawsuits, United Nations' mechanisms, meetings, events, phone numbers, statistics, street names, schedules, all kinds of information flying around at a speed that made it hard to comprehend, let alone take note of.

"Did you get any of that?" Konstantinos asked.

To which I nodded affirmatively and replied, "It's all here," pointing at the notebook where I had just coloured a few round hearts around a poorly executed drawing of Adèle Exarchopoulos and carefully perfected my signature for the past ninety minutes. What became apparent after the meeting was over, was that I had no right whatsoever to be there, and that I certainly lacked the ability to perform the tasks that were expected of me, whatever those turned out to be.

But well, *"Por peores plazas hemos toreado,"* I thought.

It was only when we all stood up that I finally understood what was behind the meteorological condition that *I* was experiencing and apparently nobody else was: along the way of the noble efforts I made to try and lead a healthier life by riding a Mephistopheles-hand-crafted bike across a city through which biking was a feat as appealing to me as a colonoscopy, it became apparent that such endeavour had resulted in the tearing of a massive hole in my pants...right on the area underneath my crotch. My survival instinct prompted me to drop the folder Cassandra had just carefully handed me, and to cover the area with both my hands in a move as elegant and unnoticeable as Cardi B walking into a silent retreat temple. Indeed, this turned out to be quite an unfortunate manoeuvre, since as soon as I executed this move, the entire team turned around, now joined by the complete staff of the neighbour NGO with whom we shared the office and who now were coming out of their own Conference Room themselves, and stared at me grabbing what appeared to be—to all intents and purposes—my genitals in the middle of the Conference Room on an otherwise ordinary Wednesday morning. The look only lasted for a few seconds, but the effect was expected to have long-lasting consequences—that was for certain. This regrettable instant was then followed by an unsuccessful attempt at disguising the move by pretending to kick some crumbs off my now wrinkled and sweated suit, and dust off my pants whilst progressively lowering my knees to get a hold of the dropped documents. I then opted to ignore the entire ordeal by covering the clothing fiasco with the large folder during the entire day. Never in my life have I carried so many things around.

Mere minutes after this episode, Cassandra, who would turn out to be my supervisor for the remainder of the internship, gave me a briefing of the entire organization and the projects I was going to assist her on, none of which interested me in the least and all of which seemed like they would require me to be. It was too late to change course, however, as they wanted me to start ASAP developing Excel spreadsheets, scheduling appointments, handling social media accounts and updating the website of the organization, whatever that meant. Although Cassandra was initially unaware of my shortcomings, certainly clouded by my quite ironic ability for self-promotion in the face of my inner animosity towards myself, the truth would not take too long to emerge, like a turd in the A/C ventilation system, as every single task she assigned to me, as rudimentary and uncomplicated as it may have been, was followed by a mental crisis and an extensive Google and YouTube search.

The cherry on top of the proverbial shit cake came later that day, when Konstantinos gathered us all at the conference meeting to report some serious news: somebody had entered a pornographic illegal website with a laptop from the organisation, resulting in the appearance of a virus in the online system which endangered all the documents uploaded online.

"We do not know from which one of your computers it came from, but we know it was from here in Geneva, and it took place around twenty minutes from now." Konstantinos, being the Director and the one who brought up this issue to the staff members of a child rights NGO, was excluded from being the culprit. Lucille and Cassandra, with just taking a look at them one could deduce they were not responsible for anything other than looking like they had never masturbated in their lives. Vero was the Communications Officer, so one could infer if she were to search for porn, that she'd be careful enough to avoid being caught. All eyes were now on me. And rightfully so. Because yes, it was me. But hang on, it's not what you think, but it's also not *not* what you think.

"It might have been me, but it's not what you think," I started off, balancing out what was to come so perfectly. "I was on an illegal movie website because there's this new movie they just released online and I wanted to take a quick look, only a quick one, I promise—I've been known to do that when I feel a bit stressed out—and I accidentally clicked on one of the pop-up ads, but there was nothing related to porn, I swear. It's just that today was a bit stressful, so I needed to blow off some steam," I said to the people in charge of an organization dedicated to defending the human rights of children on a daily basis. There was not a single person who was not utterly confused and also genuinely worried about the person they had just hired.

An awkward silence filled the room, only interrupted by my tachycardic heartbeat, until Konstantinos finally revealed the real depth of the problem when he said, "Well, that's perhaps the dumbest thing that has been said in this room since I started working here, and bear in mind that Boris Johnson once sat on the chair right next to yours. I have no idea why you would do that during working hours, and worst of all, get caught doing it. But because of your *movie site*, the virus has permanently deleted the files from the past five years."

Repressing every muscle of my body to avoid breaking down right then and there, I somehow managed to say, "Are there no security copies?" trying to be helpful, not recriminatory, although it came out as the latter and was rightfully interpreted as such.

Konstantinos calmly stared right into my soul, and then said, "You better pray there are, because I don't know what I'm gonna do if there aren't." He gawked at me for an additional moment, trying to break down a soul that was already broken before I walked through that door on that morning, and then left the room.

There was no point in repressing the feelings at this point, so I could not help but start sobbing as soon as Cassandra and Lucille left in order to discuss what I assumed would be a lifetime of gossip supply. Vero calmly approached me and put her hand on my shoulder. She took out a handkerchief from her purse and wiped away my tears. Even though I could not put my finger on it, I could tell there was something unconventional about her that made her distinguishable amongst the sea of homogeneous, flavourless people who populated the office, the city, the country, the planet. There was goodness in her; genuine, disinterested, selfless goodness which came out to the surface that day when she consoled me after I needed it most, and when she healed a potentially traumatic wound by laughing the whole thing off.

"Come on, the Conference Room is no place to cry. I'll buy you a beer after work," she concluded. After she singlehandedly managed to get rid of the virus in the system and upload the security copy of all endangered files, the rest of the day went by surprisingly quickly, and before I could realise it, I was walking out the door with Vero on our way to a nearby bar which faced the *Gare Cornavin*, a place where, against all odds, I would end up becoming a frequent customer at: *Les Brasseurs*. Joining us was a friend of hers, also a Spaniard who worked at a local chocolate shop.

What can I say, it was fun to hang out for the first time with people, instead of succumbing to my newly tailored routine of walking the streets on my own, for a change. We had a few laughs, and got to know one another a little bit, occasionally letting each other take a peek through the cracks of the deeply flawed people that we were, just like everyone else. Then, just when I was slowly beginning to creep out of the comfort shell I had carefully built around me, I remembered the following day I had an appointment at the bank, so I had to leave a bit early in the morning to be able to arrive in time for work. As much as I wanted to stay, it was better to leave things before I found a way to screw them up, and that moment was as good a time as any.

"Bye, Vero, see you tomorrow! Oh, it was a pleasure to know you, _Cecilia_. We should meet up another time!" I said whilst standing up to leave.

"Yes, for sure. Let's do this again next week!" Cecilia replied. I then hopped on my bike, and proceeded to spend the entire trip to my horrid flat aggressively cringing at the realization I had called her by the wrong name the entire night, as Vero's friend was named, in fact, Camila.

IV

WRONG PIN

The day I told Grandma Lupe that her granddaughter was opening a Swiss bank account, she laughed her ass off for two straight minutes before replying, "It figures; after all, you've always wanted to be a politician." She was not wrong in her rationale, I guess, even if my dreams of becoming involved in politics were long gone. Given the impetuous need I then felt deep down to recount in painstaking detail the series of misfortunes that ensued as soon as I made the decision to open a Swiss bank account in Geneva, what will follow is a retelling of true events seamlessly mixed with the delusional fantasies developed whilst waiting in the eternal queues of the customer support desk at a bank which shall remain nameless, presented to you in a movie screenplay fashion. See if you can spot the difference.

INT/EXT. BANK - MORNING

We open on **CARLA**, a slightly overweight, dark-haired young lady who's waiting in line outside of (judging from the twelve stores that conform the building) what appears to be a reputed bank. Her face showcasing the exasperation of the tedious, slow-paced bureaucracy, something present even in a country that runs (and, to a larger degree than any other place, is) like a Swiss clock, she nervously stares at the time on the vintage Casio watch on her wrist, uncontrollably tapping her foot on the ground.

Surrounding her are a sea of **ELEGANTLY DRESSED MEN AND WOMEN** from all ages, who, in addition to their stylish clothes have the habit of shouting in various languages whilst on the phone as a common trait. One of them, a **MIDDLE-AGED LADY** holding a baby who has a face of being very much aware of the neglect he will experience in the years to come, ignores her kid's excruciating screams, and carries on with her conversation about financial downturns of the Dutch sausage-making market, and takes a long drag out of the cigarette she's holding. She offers some to her baby.

Another **REFINED-LOOKING WOMAN** waiting in line, whose ass cheeks are large enough to hide Anne Frank's entire family, calmly yet effectively lets out some gas from her prominent posterior, a substance whose use was explicitly outlawed after WWI under the 1925 Geneva Convention for being considered a "method of bacteriological warfare". CARLA's tightly wrapped French braid is then instantly moved from a careless position of resting on her shoulders to her back, courtesy of the recently propelled gas, which effectively makes her lose roughly forty percent of her pulmonary capacity.

We set our eyes on the clock inside the building: it's 08.05.

MATCH CUT TO:

The same clock now reads 08.45, exactly fifteen minutes before CARLA's shift at work begins.

Just then, the **BANK TELLER**, a chubby man well into his forties who looks like he has skipped potty-training for the past couple of decades, sticks his head out the window and calmly signals CARLA to approach the customer help desk. By the time she arrives, one can easily tell every ounce of patience in her body is about to expire as soon as she takes one good look at the BANK TELLER, who's comfortably sitting behind the desk.

      BANK TELLER
      (*in French*)
  How may I help you today, Madam?

        CARLA
      (*you go, girl*)
  Oh, *je ne parle pas* French...English?

      BANK TELLER
Sure, I can speak in English. But just so you know, you should at least try to make an effort to earn the language from the country you're in, okay?

        CARLA
      (*not okay*)
     ...excuse me?

BANK TELLER
I don't suppose you go to Germany, for example, and expect people to talk to you in whatever language they speak in the country you come from, no?

CARLA
(*Listen, you piece of human waste, I am working ten hours a day at place that I am not entirely sure I want to work in, only to go back to a snake-filled flat that I don't want to live in. I know you Swiss people have a more than decent education level that allows you to learn as many languages as you please, but you also have quite a high suicide rate and for centuries have had the indecency of outlawing gay marriage until only a few months ago, so stop pretending like you don't sleep in your mother's attic and like your shit doesn't stink, and maybe just shut your mouth and let me open a bank account in peace, because otherwise your greedy money-laundering-enabling government will take thirty percent of every single Swiss franc I make in this country*)
Thank you, I will take it into account.

BANK TELLER
(*Karen-like smile*)
So, how can I help you today?

CARLA
I want to open a bank account.

BANK TELLER
(*startled, as if his job was other than opening bank accounts for new customers*)
A bank account? Here? Why is that?

CARLA
I need it for work.

BANK TELLER
Oh, and where do *you* work?

CARLA
(*none of your fucking business*)
Here in Geneva.

BANK TELLER
Perhaps your English is not so good, after all. I said *where* as in which company, I did not mean here in a geographical sense.

CARLA
(*Where in a geographical sense is your Adam's apple, sir?*)
Oh, of course, I work at an NGO.

BANK TELLER
And for how long do you expect to have this account?

CARLA
For six months.

                    BANK TELLER
                         Only?
              (*looking at her, head to toe*)
         They already told you they would not be renewing
                    your contract, huh?

                        CARLA
           No, that's how long the internship is for.

                    BANK TELLER
        Yep, that's exactly what we say to underachievers
                        around here.
He stares at her for some time. Then...

                 BANK TELLER (cont'd)
        Take the third door to your left—that means the
        door number three—and ask for Erika. She will answer
          any of the many questions you will surely have.

She nods and paints a fake smile on her face, but not before discreetly staring for a little too long at the grease stain on his shirt, in an effort to prompt the disgusting Monsters Inc.-looking creature to direct his attention towards his lack of decorum, perhaps in the hopes he realised his body and overall obnoxious behaviour was a temple whose worshippers were all atheists.

As CARLA walks through the corridor, we linger on the BANK TELLER facing his stained shirt...slowly leaning forward...a little more...closer now. He seems to stare at the stain from up close, his encrypted thoughts a gift only available to him. He carefully examines the stain, deeply entranced by his inner world as he smells it...and eventually proceeds to(perhaps too enthusiastically) lick it.

       MANAGER
      (from far away)
       FREDERICK!

The BANK TELLER stops mid-lick.

      MANAGER (CONT'D)
      (in French)
   Oh, Frederick. <u>Not again</u>!

          CUT TO:

INT/EXT. ERIKA'S OFFICE - CONTINUED

We pop in mid-conversation with **ERIKA**, an elegant blonde woman that is, to all intents and purposes, the living and breathing Swiss-VHS-B-movie-version of Hannah Waddingham.

        ERIKA
   (incessantly typing on her computer)
  --don't worry about the working permit. The Swiss authorities barely give them out to foreigners, anyway. Besides--

>   (*she looks both ways, even though there is
>   nobody else in the room*)
>   Most of our customers also have some form of,
>   uh, documentary irregularities...
>   (*wink*)
>   ...if you know what I mean.

CARLA
I, uh, I would pay for the permit, it's just that my boss has told me they never have done so for an intern--

ERIKA
Oh, honey, nobody does. Interns are at the bottom of the food chain in this city, right underneath bikes and Jews.
> (*awkward pause to let the antisemitic air
>   suddenly fill the room*)
> Well, I think everything is clear then, right?

CARLA
Yes, thank you.

ERIKA
Remember, all the payments must be done online with *both* the card *and* 10-digit pin you'll receive next week, and also with the pin machine you'll get in two weeks' time.
> (*handing over a series of papers*)
> Sign there, there, and right there.

CARLA does as instructed.

                         ERIKA
              (*taking over the documents*)
           Fantastic. Your soul now belongs to us,
                      congratulations.

                         CARLA
                  (*immediately after*)
                         What?!
                       ERIKA
                         What?

After a somewhat uncomfortable pause…

                    ERIKA (cont'd)
                 (*excessive hand gestures*)
                     I'm kidding!
                      (*not really*)
        Now, my dear, if you have any questions that a
        bottle of tequila or a tantric foot massage can't
                          cure--
                  (*handing over her card*)
                 --don't hesitate to call.

As if held at gunpoint, a smiling CARLA forcibly
takes the card and exits.

                       ERIKA
            (*now on her own, in French*)
                  Now, where were we?

Out of her drawer, ERIKA takes out a large Iberian

ham leg and presses 'play' on her music system. Just as Chenoa's "Cuando tú vas" starts resounding all over her office, ERIKA inexplicably pulls a massive katana sword out of a violin case and proceeds to subsequently sharpen its blade to the rhythm of the music.

FADE TO:

INT. CARLA'S BEDROOM - SUNDOWN

Sitting down at her paper-filled desk, CARLA opens her laptop and starts typing on a brand new Celtx document the setting for her newest screenplay…

INT. CARLA'S BEDROOM - SUNDOWN - ENTER SCREENPLAY WITHIN A SCREENPLAY

Our protagonist, a slightly overweight, severely misguided in her fashion choices, deeply broken Latina in her early 20s, CARLA, stares at the empty page she has just opened on her Celtx account.

                    CARLA (V.O.)
    I still can't process what has just happened to
me. When that Brownshirt down at the bank explained
it a couple of weeks ago, it all seemed so easy. She
failed to mention, however, that in order to be able
   to make a single money transfer (a process whose
step number sixteen out of twenty-four actually read
      "at this point, it is advisable to burst into

tears"), lied a quasi-Catch-22 scenario: if you dared to introduce one number out of place in any of the seven required 20-digit PIN security checks, your account will be instantly blocked, and you'll have to order another ID card and start the entire process all over again...which, by now you can imagine is something that effectively happened to me.
(*beat*)
Two months. I have to wait two fucking months to access my bank account because I forgot to press the Caps Lock button.

INT. CARLA'S BEDROOM - THAT MOMENT

CARLA stares at the pin machine in her hands. The computer in front of her reads "WRONG PIN: ACCOUNT BLOCKED". Her hands are visibly shaking, her mouth wide-open...she looks on the brink of having a heart attack...

                    CARLA (cont'd) (V.O.)
As soon as it happened, I experienced what many often call "acute myocardial infarction", thinking my account would be frozen and the Swiss army would kick me out of my horrible flat, straight right into my parents' home back again. My body was in fifth gear, racing for impact, ready for a physical fight with 'Ms. Goebbels' down at the bank in case she dared to dismiss the case by suggesting I started the procedure all over again. One of the most secure financial institutions in the world, and instead of

running on ones and zeros, they run on paper envelopes and the postal service. Makes one wonder about the location of all the progress constantly in the mouths of others.

INT. ERIKA'S OFFICE- LATER THAT EVENING

CARLA, on the brink of losing control, nervously paces the room, looking down as a katana-wielding ERIKA tries to explain to her how to handle the situation.

                        CARLA (cont'd) (V.O.)
Being a writer at heart, I started anticipating what the conversation between us both would look like. It would all start as most things in his life do: with a fight.

CARLA plunges into ERIKA.

                        CARLA (cont'd) (V.O.)
Unsurprisingly, I would lose my temper and try to wrestle with that corpse-looking albino bitch, and two security guards would have no option but to escort me out of the premises and report me to the police--

EXT. BANK - MOMENTS LATER

TWO SECURITY GUARDS enter and break up the fight. Soon after, half a dozen **POLICE OFFICERS** enter the premises and escort a handcuffed CARLA into their car.

                    CARLA (cont'd) (V.O.)
...where the authorities would discover that not
only was that my third offence in the country—
running into France plus the fine at the public
transport—it was actually my fourth, as they would
also come to learn about my non-existent working
permit, thus effectively making me an illegal
                immigrant in the country.

INT. NGO - THAT EVENING

Sporting a look as if he had just been through my browser history, a befuddled KONSTANTINOS, now wearing his most outrageously colourful shirt which screamed "in desperate need of attention and fashion validation from my emotionally detached partner", does his best to keep his composure whilst answering the questions of the POLICE OFFICERS.

                    CARLA (cont'd) (V.O.)
    When the authorities would head own to the NGO
   to ask Konstantinos about my working status, and
    enquire about the working permit, I am more than
    certain that he would reveal the porn incident that
    tainted my first day impression, prompting him to
    sever all ties with me after becoming aware of my
                  troubles with the law.

INT. PRISON - THAT NIGHT

Two **PRISON GUARDS** close the bars behind CARLA's prison

cell. She's now wearing an orange vest, and takes a
scared look at her **CELL COMPANION,** a morbidly obese
woman who pulls a fully live trout from her throat
and starts menacingly slamming it against the palm of
her hand.

                    CARLA (cont'd) (V.O.)
All these elements, when put together, would lead me
  into a jail cell in a remote Swiss location, where I
      would spend the next two years imprisoned--

INT. PRISON SHOWERS

Completely naked, CARLA takes a carved toothbrush and
mortally plunges it into the heart of a SKINNY INMATE
taking shower whilst smoking a cigar.

                    CARLA (cont'd) (V.O.)
...and an additional eight more for taking the life
  of one of the inmates after she dares to question
  the delicate shot composition of Tarkovsky's *The*
Sacrifice (1986) and argues the movie is nihilistic
and pedantic in nature, failing to live up to any of
            the author's previous work.
                        (*beat*)
  Naturally, I would be forced to take her life.

**MONTAGE. PRISON LIBRARY/PRISON COMPUTER ROOM -
VARIOUS**

Over the course of days, weeks, years, we see CARLA,

now a fully-grown woman with numerous tattoos visibly covering her once delicate skin, with her head deep inside a wide roster of thick books.

              CARLA (cont'd) (V.O.)
During the ten years that I would spend behind bars, I would nurture myself with all kinds of knowledge, particularly regarding technology and informatics, which would eventually lead me to get more than comfortable around computers—

On Thursdays, **CARLA** attentively listens at the **INSTRUCTOR** during their weekly informatics workshop, easily standing out amongst the rest of the inmates there present.

The eternally longed day finally arrives, when an **OFFICER** lets CARLA know, she has mail: a manila envelope has arrived for her. With her heart about to exit from her chest, she tears it open and takes out a diploma...

              CARLA (cont'd) (V.O.)
...but also, to a long-distance degree in computer engineering from the University of Geneva.

MONTAGE. VARIOUS EUROPEAN TOWNS (SOMEWHAT REMOTE LOCATIONS)

Dead set on crawling out of the hole her life had become at that point, CARLA travels across a colourful roster of somewhat remote locations scattered across

Europe: from small towns to more prominent cities.

We see her making her way through small-scale computer firms up until massive conglomerates that host thousands of jobs or technicians.

              CARLA (cont'd) (V.O.)
Those troubled years would be followed by numerous months of travelling across Europe, making my way as a computer technician and cybersecurity expert, always in places with an assured failure to inquire about my past run-ins with the law.

INT. JARDIN ANGLAIS/MONT BLANC BRIDGE - MORNING

Bag over her shoulder, CARLA walks the Genevan streets with optimism for the first time in years.

              CARLA (cont'd) (V.O.)
Having gained the discipline and the knowledge required, I would then return to Geneva, my 'beloved' city—

MONTAGE. ENGINEERING COMPANY

An **ELDERLY MAN** extends his hand to CARLA and welcomes her into the STAFF of his company, all wearing dark blue jumpsuits and wearing a dark beret—the company's uniform.

Across various months, we see CARLA quickly acquiring

a masterful dominion of her craft, advancing the ranks of the company with speed and precision.

                      CARLA (cont'd) (V.O.)
...and progressively start to make my dent on the market in the hopes that my extensive experience covered up the desire to dig into my past for more than it may be strictly necessary.

INT. ERIKA'S OFFICE - MORNING

With a few timid rays of light making their way past the curtains of her office, we see ERIKA —now looking significantly older, which is what happens when you look like a block of Gouda cheese, you age just like one—ending to some **CUSTOMERS**.

                      CARLA (CONT'D) (V.O.)
Then, on a sunny morning down at the bank, Erika would be busy in her full-time job of being a totally useless human being when—

A tall, dark moustachioed man in a blue jumpsuit and sporting a dark beret, the ELECTRICIAN, walks past her office, carrying a toolbox, and shakes the hand of the BANK MANAGER.

                      CARLA (cont'd) (V.O.)
...barely managing to catch The Electrician out of the corner of her eye, now leaving the bank after successfully carrying out his duties.

ERIKA makes nothing of it—how could she, that poor thing? —and carries on her conversation with her **CUSTOMERS** until...a notice pops up on her computer, in bright yellow letters and a noticeably large font, blocking the entire screen and urgently demanding her attention.

The message reads "<u>SECURITY ALERT: IDENTIFICATION REQUIRED</u>".

                    CARLA (cont'd) (V.O.)
      Given that it would appear on a highly secured
      network, and carrying the logo of the bank, Erika
      would have no hesitation when promptly introducing
        her name and PIN number to authorize the demanded
                         dentification.

ERIKA presses 'Enter' and waits for what amounts to an eternity, after which the screen turns completely white, and among the abysmally empty screen, the only space is suddenly filled by two simple words...

                    <u>WRONG PIN</u>.

Immediately after, ERIKA, along with virtually EVERYONE on the payroll of that bank, impotently stare at their computers, witnessing how their bank accounts and accumulated assets are being emptied directly into their customers' accounts, effectively inverting the pyramid of power.

As chaos effectively takes hold over that Genevan office, with the rest of the branches promptly following suit(papers flying around, **EMPLOYEES** shouting over the telephone, losing all decorum with greed and desperation clawing out of their shells and revealing their real selves—a phenomenon only seen when you mess around with unearned money and possessions), we slowly leave the Bank, while a befuddled ERIKA anxiously looks for a culprit.

ERIKA

(*in French*)

<u>THE ELECTRICIAN</u>! WHERE IS HE?

Outside, we continue zooming out, now crossing the sidewalk, where **PEDESTRIANS ON THE STREET** stare at the notifications received on their phones, looking around, confused and suspicious on equal measures, witnessing the recent deposits in their bank accounts.

We continue moving away from the chaos and arrive at the sidewalk on the opposite side of the road, facing the bank, where a discrete cafe lies.

Calmly sitting down, we see the blue jumpsuit of THE ELECTRICIAN, as well as a fake moustachioed nose and a dark beret, sitting on an empty hair at the cafe. **A SKINNY WAITER** brings out a tray carrying a hot cup of coffee and serves it to a **YOUNG LADY** sitting down at the table...CARLA. Her phone, too, dings and reveals her account at the bank has been credited. She peacefully takes a sip of her coffee, unbothered by the surrounding pandemonium, and we see a bright devilish smile forming on her face.

FADE OUT.
BLACK.
END...?

INT. CARLA'S BEDROOM – MIDNIGHT - EXIT SCREENPLAY WITHIN A SCREENPLAY

CARLA closes her laptop and rubs her tired eyes. Next to her lies a bottle of melatonin. She takes three pills and uses a glass of water to make them go down.

In the background, we can hear the incessant clacking of flamenco shoes from **CARMEN** and **MARISSA** practising their dance moves, **RONNIE** shouting at his online friends, and the Genevan Public transport, always on time for its appointment every ten minutes.

We stare out the window at the full moon, and then swiftly lower our gaze back inside and into the bed, at eye level...where we see the collapsed body of CARLA, completely beaten up after her medicinal vomiting of frustrated dreams, fantasies and life projects out of her system and into the page.

HARD CUT TO BLACK.

V

GRANDMA GOES TO THE MOVIES

A drop of blood completely wrapped itself around the bell from my bike. And just as it arrived, the raindrops washed it away, like the pain never existed in the first place. Unaware of the thorns heavily inserted onto my flesh, I kept cycling down the road that crossed the untamed forest, putting the exhaustion of a long day at work well behind me. After all, it was Wim Wenders' *Paris, Texas* (1984) that was awaiting. Near the cinema entrance, a moustachioed man holding a little girl's hand put out a cigarette butt and entered. That instant transported me back to my earliest memories, when back in Mexico, Dad used to take me every Saturday to *La Casa del Cine*, an independent arthouse movie theatre near *Plaza de la Constitución* where I discovered Harold Lloyd and Buster Keaton, the great Edward G. Robinson and the poker-faced Greta Garbo. I should call him; it's been too long.

Looking like *The Babadook*'s (2014) physically revolting home-schooled cousin, I stepped onto the movie theatre in an attempt to avoid facing the fact that the overwhelming loneliness and general lack of purpose that invaded me was the true reason why I had been a regular at cinemas for the past fifteen years. That could perhaps explain why I kept myself busy at every chance that I got by immersing myself into some movie that I was either completely incapable of properly appreciating or ashamedly enjoying way more than I had any right to—I'm looking at you, *Hitman's Wife's Bodyguard* (2021)—Jesus, what does that say about me? Imagine my surprise, however, when after the treacherous road I had to cross to get to that obscure indie movie theatre hidden in a questionable alley on a shady neighbourhood placed at the very outskirts of Geneva, that they had cancelled the screening due to a COVID-19 outbreak originating from an *anti-vaxxer* who refused to wear a mask in a session on the week prior. With my stomach fiercely roaring for attention to be fed a bunch of junk in subliminal hopes of eventually adding diabetes to my already advanced drug dependency, I headed to the only store open on a Sunday, a place which would turn out to offer one sole item with a morally unreasonable expiration date.

As the cashier packed the fifth tin of canned pinto beans, she succinctly looked at me, almost with pity in her eyes, after picturing the poor state my bike seat was about to be left in after those beans had been consumed. And what can I say...her feelings were well-placed. I packed all my groceries in a bag and carried it on the right handlebar of my bike. The substantial weight of the canned pinto beans, combined with my sub-standard biking abilities and an almost conveniently placed Swiss wind, made me oscillate from side to side of the narrow road as the bag containing the groceries kept sliding back and forth, which is why I discarded using the road and opted for the sidewalk instead. One of my many encounters on my way home was with another fellow biker, who saw me riding right down the middle of the sidewalk, making no attempt at moving either right or left to let him through. He was thus forced by my nefarious driving skills to change course and continue riding his bike on the road, unaware of the fact that had he continued down the sidewalk, our fates, bikes and bodies would have eloped like a rapist uncle approaching you at your cousin's first communion. As he passed me by—the cyclist, not my rapist uncle—yelled, "*Merci, canard.*" My French abilities allowed me to understand "*canard*" meant "duck" in French, so I laughed and blew him a kiss, because my mother always taught me to be polite above anything else. It would take me a couple of months to learn, however, that the man had said "*connard*" not "*canard*". Didn't matter, though. He was Swiss, after all, and that must have been insulting enough for him, I reckoned.

The only other available alternative to my frustrated moviegoing evening was to head to the *Grütli* cinemas, where that day they were playing that God-awful sugary suppository of kindness handled with the subtlety with which Christopher Nolan integrated Hans Zimmer's score into the dialogue of *Interstellar* (2014): the monstrosity that was, is, and forever will be *E.T. The Extra-Terrestrial* (1982). Since repeatedly puking in my mouth for the duration of the entire film was not in my plans for that day, I opted for a domestic cinema session, instead. Back in the flat, and after the fifth attempt to watch *Sátántangó* (1994) in a relatively quiet space was proven unsuccessful by the weekly power cut resulting from strong weather and lack of payment of the building's electricity bills by the vast majority of its tenants, for no particular reason I began reminiscing about that time Martin Scorsese's took over all kinds of sensationalistic headlines that made all newspaper owners sinisterly rub their hands at the chaos that was about to be ignited at the very heart of Tinseltown. Little did the renowned author of *After Hours* (1985) know when he charged forward against current superhero movies, going as far as drawing a comparison between them and amusement parks (later detailing the anxiety and profound sadness he felt due to the current route cinema had taken as a result of the severe alterations brought upon by streaming platforms), that not only was he correct in his predictions and assumptions: he fell abundantly short.

In this fast-food culture of immediacy of ours, how could you expect any given person to sit down in a dark movie theatre and not check their phone at least twice during the remainder of the film? How could you expect, like I foolishly did, that people would not dare to play a YouTube video—spam ads included—during a screening of Florian Zeller's *The Father* (2020)? Or that teenagers becoming increasingly impatient at having to remain quiet and steady for a couple of hours would not start kicking the seats in front of them at a session of *North by Northwest* (1959)? Or that someone would not cough and sneeze loud enough one could have easily guessed that young woman to be an eighty-year-old Portuguese sailor in the 1780s about to die of gout and depression during a screening of *Les Diaboliques* (1955)? What about that time a man farted out a cackling laughter during the iconic closing scene of *The Godfather* (1972) after Michael Corleone delivered his history-defining negation of a self-evident reality to a wife who would never forgive him? Different countries, different movies, statistically divergent movie audiences all lead to the same result: a commonly shared disdain for the cinematic experience. And every time people decide to act like they are the only ones in the cinema they not only take themselves out of the experience; they take all others present in the room with them, thus instantly placing us all back into reality, which defeats the entire purpose of going to the movies in the first place and instantly shatters the illusion planted by the inner nature of the Seventh Art. What can I say, I love cinema, but I'm beginning to hate cinemagoers.

Going to the movies used to be something precious, a

collective adventure into the unknown, easily yet inferiorly replicated at home, properly unachievable anywhere else other than a movie theatre, where a group of strangers experience the same reality each in their own idiosyncratic way, succumbing to an illusion that takes us far away from our reality. This spell can be easily broken, as it often is, by the generalised inability to momentarily sever ties with the world we left at the entrance, effectively taking out of the rabbit hole those there present in the theatre with you. Now, in the age where you can stare at content anywhere and everywhere and be "entertained" or momentarily anaesthetised until boredom kicks in a couples of minutes or seconds after, from the comfort of your house or while commuting to work, and are endowed with the ability to pause it, rewind it, lose interest in it and change to something else, the essence, the appreciation for an event now forgotten has been lost in between the pixels of our TV screens and the cushions of our sofas. With our collective attention span having been drastically lowered in the presence of an endemic inability to stand in a room for more than twenty minutes before checking for non-existent notifications on our cell phones, how can we expect people to temporarily forget about their troubles and completely surrender all inhibitions to a film and the people who have put their time, effort and money into making it come to life? Until we are able to collectively respect one another and become mindful of the repercussions our actions can have on the communal experience of going to the movies, and realise what the purpose of cinema is and should be, moviegoing will continue to be downgraded, its value forever lost in time. Packed movie theatres are no longer something desired but dreaded; in cinemas, spectators have begrudgingly hijacked movies themselves by suddenly being the ones doing the talking in the room; while, in my view, most things can wait, restoring respect for the inherently rich and currently endangered cinematic experience of moviegoing simply cannot.

This problem is clearly exemplified (yet not relegated to) the entertainment industry, although it serves to shed a light onto the bigger picture, onto the fact that our current way of life is making us dumber, fatter and more useless than we have ever been. Most of the efforts to increase our efficiency are oriented towards achieving a lower efficiency: TV remotes, Amazon's Alexa, self-driving cars, pre-peeled fruit, or even parking spots and buffets at the top of mountain ranges. All of the technological prowess has resulted in the predominance of the "culture of immediacy", something perfectly embodied by Netflix and its wannabes: easily digestible, easily forgettable. Just like the laxative effect of a morning cigarette after a large cup of coffee, what has come in immediately comes out. And with our addiction to emotional masochism acquiring exorbitant toxicity levels by being promptly satisfied through the rise of social media, things are just getting started. We are half a second away from entering the realm of infinite content, where countless algorithms battle to get hold of our attention, to organise our lives, surreptitiously profile our tastes, all in the hopes of eventually turning us into emotional cripples who have developed a long-term emotional reliance on technology just to be able to feel complete again. Have you been to a supermarket as of lately? The frozen sections, the pre-prepared dishes, the energy bars, the already-assembled salads, the restaurants inside of supermarkets: everything is pre-cooked, pre-prepared, pre-effort. All designed so we don't add the one thing that distinguishes us from others: a little thought and a little effort into what we do. That is not *just* the way we consume food, or *just* the way we consume content, or *just* the way we watch movies at the cinema or *just* the way we relate to each other. That is our new way of life. All of which made me come to the realization on that very morning that I was coming close to (perhaps irreparably) losing all faith in humanity. Just like that.

VI

WHEN GOING UPHILL GOES DOWNHILL

Two large cheese sandwiches conceived from the mother-of-all-baguettes, a rusty water bottle filled with poisonous tap water, three heavily bruised bananas and a warm Kronenbourg beer. That's all I carried and all I needed for my trip up *Mount Salève*. The rough conditions, both geographical and existential, meant that I had to download the map on my phone, as I had no Internet connection the very instant I stepped out the door. To say that I extensively prepared for this trip would be to severely misrepresent what really transpired, but in my defence, I did browse through Google Maps the path that was (technically) scheduled to take me up there, at nearly fourteen hundred metres of altitude. In total, the nineteen-kilometre-trip should not have taken me more than two hours to complete, but reality, as you might have guessed by now, had other plans for me. With my thighs forcibly vacuumed into my dark leggings against their will, worryingly assaulting the integrity of my circulatory system, I played the entire Chayanne and David Bisbal-filled Spotify playlist that I had prepared specifically for that day. Do not ask me why, but the music from those two men filled my soul with more energy than ruining a civil servant's day.

Frantically pumping each pedal stroke given, I went across the French border and arrived at the crossroads outside of France fifteen minutes before scheduled. Easy—all I had to do was take the roundabout's third exit, and then turn to my right after I had passed the little bakery near the Town Hall. That's what Trip Advisor said. That's what Google Maps said. That was not, however, what life said. As I took the third exit, I realised the bakery was nowhere to be found, nor was the name of the street where it was supposedly located. At that moment, I was not able to grasp what was about to transpire, but it turned out that the reason the bakery was not where it was supposed to be was not due to the fact that such a small business had disappeared in the maelstrom of a colossally devastating capitalist world order, but, in fact, it was because I was not on the right village—not even remotely: I was twelve kilometres off the intended location, as I would find out later on.

After touring the main streets a few times too many, and being further away to the top of *Mount Salève* than I had ever been, I took the (flagrantly misguided) approach that most fathers take after being offered at Ikea the possibility to pay an extra supplement for getting their newly-acquired furniture assembled: rejecting common sense and opting to do something which I was unashamedly unfit or even mildly capable of doing. The spirit of Bear Grylls took hold of my body, I reckoned, because I decided to "guide myself by cardinal directions"—you know, pretending that I did not get lost in shopping malls until I was well into my teen years. The result of such an adventurous turn was that the map on my phone went full Charlie Sheen and started making a few suggestions which, at first, I found somewhat questionable.

"Are you sure?" I kept inquiring the map out loud, like the lunatic I had become. The reason why I was openly talking to an inanimate object was that, at that moment, I found myself riding my bike on the train tracks—not close to, next to, or on the side of—*on the train tracks*.

"It's not that bad, at least the tracks are aband—" I couldn't even finish my thought because the trail began to vibrate with such inclemency that I inevitably looked like an elderly man dancing at a wedding. With the impending thrusting of the Swiss train coming towards me at full speed, I immediately lunged myself onto the nearby grass, making a front flip and landing on my backpack, just in time before a <u>TRANSCONTINENTAL TRAIN</u> passed by at a devilish speed, its driver quite rightly honking the train's horn at me. Before I could begin to process the entire event, the momentary unmovable truth that the surface where I had landed was far away from soft, comforting grass was not apparent at first, and took a minute to crumble and reveal I had instead placed my fully exposed back and ass crack on a delightful field of nettles.

Among the other magnificent locations which the downloaded map on my phone fooled me into visiting, my favourites of the bunch, and the ones that stole my heart with their inclement beauty, were the Genevan highways—wonderful to visit them that time of the year—a breathtaking touristic destination where every driver felt the need to honk at me to let me know that I was not supposed to be there, as if I was not very much aware of the fact that I was driving a used-up bike with no reflective vest, no lights, no bell and with purposeless posterior brakes in the middle of a highway I had no right to be on in the first place, surrounded by cars going at one hundred miles per hour, and following the directions of a map that seemed to have been designed by Lars Von Trier himself

After what amounted to a couple of hours but felt like the runtime of anything directed by Kevin Costner, I took the very first exit and turned off the phone, for real this time, making the decision right then and there to follow the signs along the way which read *"Mount Salève"* and ask the locals in case I got lost at any point throughout the rest of the trip. Seemed reasonable enough. The signs along the way, however, turned out to be exclusively for cars and similar vehicles, and pointed at the direction of the way to the mountain top, which was only accessible by car, something which I became aware of only after reluctantly embarking on a dozen additional kilometres of highway. It was as if someone was intent on me exploring the Swiss road system. By now, four hours had come and gone, and fifty-five kilometres in, I was nowhere near the top of the mountain.

With the sun now at its zenith and no clouds in sight, an unheard-of phenomenon in the country, desperation began to steadily crawl into my body to the point I let all inhibitions and social anxiety aside and decided to ask a shepherd (which apparently continue to exist outside of Scandinavian, straight-to-DVD fiction) for directions. Unimpressed by my level of spoken French and slightly bewildered by my abundantly amicable breasts remarkably enclosed within the confines of a Nike sports bra, it seemed to me the man had no intention of really giving me any valuable information. It also did not help that my ADHD-curtailed attention span was monopolised by the drops of slime creeping out of his mouth and into the ground. So, all I was able to gather from his drunken gesticulations was that I had to cross the wheat fields until I arrived somewhere he called *"cimetière"*, which I guessed was a small town where I could finally get some proper directions. What ensued was approximately four kilometres of racing past golden fields next to which vast green pastures were located, as I forcibly discovered when I was involuntarily compelled to dodge bovine and ovine livestock which, every time they noticed my presence, felt the need to start charging forth, making me wish I was not a vegetarian anymore. There is no doubt in mind that those entitled pieces of shit certainly ensured the entire trip to the nearby town went by at a much quicker pace, in their defence. But between you and I, a little more time surrounded by those creatures, and I would have been lighter thanks to my contributions to the fields' fertility with the fabrication of my own compost.

Had I known the real meaning of the word "*cimetière*", I would not have cheerfully celebrated my arrival at the location in the eccentric manner that I did, nor would I have entered the outdoor compound where this place was located by loudly singing and dancing to the tune of David Bisbal's "Ave María". Being a permanent resident of my absorbent inner world, I failed to realise the dozens of people grimly walking around carrying flowers, or the crowds of people gathered around a priest, or the hundreds of crosses and marble tombstones.

Because I was too busy singing to a catchy Latin pop song, my traumatised body, which that same day had experienced the anger of GPS systems and trains and cars alike, now was about to witness the rage of God in the shape of a priest who sprinted over to where I was and shouted at me in a French accent thicker and more outrageous (if possible) than Sacha Baron Coen's in *Talladega Nights* (2006) to rhetorically inquire to me "DON'T YOU HAVE ANY SHAME?", to which I was about to reply "No, and also, about what exactly?" when he continued with "This is a place of God, we're in the middle of a funeral!".

After I had recovered my breath from peddling my way out of there as fast as I could, I managed to regain my composure and ask for directions to get somewhere other than the previously unfortunate locations I had visited on that day. The top of the mountain was still three and a half hours away from that town, over a roughly four-kilometres treacherous road that was so steep the elderly lady I asked for directions had to raise her arm to an almost completely vertical position, in what could either be interpreted as her taking any chance life gave her to polish the Nazi salute she was unable to use during the war, or as the indications for a destination that was located at the end of a road which was completely uphill. I like to imagine it was the former; makes me sleep better at night.

The fascist lady turned out to be right, as even the professional cyclists I encountered along the road struggled on their way up. Just the bare sight of their calves about to burst like a Taco Bell victim's anal cavity in the bathroom after devouring five chili-cheese burritos, made the rational side of my brain take the helm for once as it urged me to get off my bike and start pushing it up the road. This small manoeuvre added around one extra hour to the journey, and while gravity was starting to take its toll on my nearly exhausted and positively dehydrated body, my sheer stubbornness fuelled up my veins in the hopes of reaching the top at any price, since I wasn't going to give it all up now that I was that close. To reward me for not collapsing thus far, and to make the rest of the way up a vastly more interesting experience, I decided to open up the now-warm beer inside my backpack, to make sure that if I was going to die from exhaustion, I might as well do it whilst being moderately inebriated.

There were still three kilometres more to go, and the familiar pain manifesting itself all over my chest began to spread to comfortable lengths, letting me know organ failure was on the horizon. Just as my body began flirting with coming shockingly close to a state of non-responsiveness, the path reached a small farm in a rough terrain just as steep as the previous one, yet the road had now been replaced with massive pebbles instead of smooth concrete. With my forearms screaming in agony, I had no idea how much further I could take the bike uphill. Everyone I encountered, all on their way down, as it was already well past midday, looked at me as if they had seen a (mildly overweight) ghost, murmuring to one another and exchanging looks which predicted the incoming topic of conversation that was about to fill their trip back home. Every hundred metres I had to stop and get some air because I was running progressively empty on my energy supply, and my body had been engineered for a different kind of sport, like professional whining, sumo wrestling or ASMR YouTube content creation. The large blocks of stone that covered the ground did not present any good news for Future Me, as I could already picture the speed with which my chin was going to hit the ground after I pulled the brakes and only the frontal one would be operational, something which, paired with my hefty corporal mass and the high speeds at which I would certainly be going downhill on such a steep road, was only bound to happen sooner or later.

After the path came a small meadow, then I finally entered into fully mountainous terrain. The narrow rocky paths and alpine cliffs were no place for a bike, lest of all for *my bike*, lest of all one that was ridden *by me*, so I chained it to a tree and continued my way up. From here on, the path was considerably smoother, and much to my physical exhaustion, I managed to reach the top in just over an hour. Up there, at *Col de la Croisette*, one could sit and observe in awe as far as the eyes could see into the distance, the entire city, even that goddamn waterjet. There was nobody around, no noise, no cars, no children screaming, nobody taking pictures to immediately post on Instagram or share with friends who could not be bothered to download the images you send them. Just Carla and the cows calmly grazing a few hundred meters away from me. Barely keeping it together, and more grateful for having survived the trip than for being at the top of the mountain, I sat down on the rocks near the stone tower that remained from a medieval castle, and presided over the city of Geneva, admiring the paragliders and the decadent air pollution. Eight hours. It had taken me eight goddamn motherfucking hours to do the first part of a two-hour trip. But that was of little consequence, as all that mattered was that I was there then.

"If I were to take my own life right here, right now, by throwing myself off the cliff, how could anybody ever find me?" I wondered. The ground below was inaccessible, and the only witnesses were the distant cows which each time I turned around seemed to be coming closer, or perhaps it was just the accumulated exhaustion. Food for thought, I guess.

As soon as I opened my backpack, I realised much too late that the cows had speedily arrived at the tower, and now had me completely surrounded. The only way out was over the cliffs or over the cows, none of which seemed viable enough. But there was something about these animals that made them somehow approachable, somehow friendly. My guess is that they looked at me and clearly saw, just like anybody with a pair of decent eyes would, that I posed no threat to them: they need not protect from me as I was, in fact, the one in need of protection. They seemed warm and tender-hearted—which I now realise are not great adjectives to describe cows— like big puppies that I wanted to give a meaningful hug to. I observed them for a while, how relaxed they seemed. If only I could be a cow: waking up, eating grass, taking a shit, eating some grass, taking a nap, eating some more grass, and back to sleep. If I managed to squeeze in watching a few movies into that tight schedule, I can think of few other lives worth living. With both my hands up, in a sign of submission my mind believed to have seen in a Werner Herzog documentary at some point in my life, I calmly walked towards the cows until I finally locked eyes with one of them, the one I would later observe was considered to be the leader, a massive specimen with toffee-coloured fur and eyes that seemed to sparkle with sympathy, and I gently laid my hand on her head. Out of all the things I thought I would be doing, and despite the insane events that had transpired over the course of that day, I would have never said I would be petting a cow in the middle of a mountain top. She looked at me, and I don't know if I imagined it in a self-delusional effort of wishful thinking, but she stared at me with her glistening eyes, as if we were both tied up in the same cord through which we held a shared moment of happiness. She playfully licked my hand (always start with the preliminaries, kids), which initially frightened the living daylights out of me because she could have just as well devoured my entire arm, but I persevered and continued to pet her, putting my unconditional trust on such a heavenly creature. At that moment, there was nothing else in the world—no troubles, no dark thoughts, no honking cars nor furious priests. Just two living beings enjoying a small moment of ephemeral joy. In what (I later discovered) amounted to a twisted move, my absent-minded nature felt the need to share my meal with her, so, I took out the Brie sandwiches, now as flat as my aunt Luli's chest due to the whole murderous-train-front-flipping fiasco, and ate one while I gave the other to my newly found friend. She would never know that she was eating some other cow's pasteurised milk, so we opted to turn a blind eye over the matter, and nobody was the wiser.

How lucky was I not to have encountered anybody else up

there, partly explained by the government-imposed curfew that I had no intention of obeying. Since I was a kid, I had always loved to get lost in nature and go on top of mountains, because it allows you to see everything from a different point of view, from the alternate perspective we often lack to incorporate into our lives and stare at our troubles with. From up there, all your crises suddenly become irrelevant or at least take a supporting role in the story of your life, and the actual scale of our national, global and cosmic triviality begins to dawn on you, becoming fleetingly ingrained on the deepest part of your skull. How right Mr. Chaplin was when he complained about our alarmingly chronic overthinking and "under-feeling" in the closing moments of his visionary WWII-inspired masterpiece. Momentarily gone were those troubling thoughts I had recently had after my botched attempt at going to the movies because, going up here, admiring the beauty put on this earth, thinking about my bovine friend, made me think, if only for just one moment, that life may just be worth fighting for.

VII

THE THEATRE OF WAR

Could this be true? Could life be cutting me some slack? Was I on pace towards having a reasonably comfortable, decently ventilated room for me to live in? It certainly looked like it. It had been a week since, after I quickly declined Carmen and Marisa's proposal to have lunch together, I had potentially found a new apartment to stay in, this time located closer to the northern side of the city and roughly fifteen minutes by bike to work. Beatrice, the landlady, and I exchanged a couple of messages online after I expressed interest in the room, and we set a rendezvous for the following day. In the scale from psychopath (the standard set by the previous person fulfilling those duties in my previous flat) to normal human being, she ranked as a solid 7, which was good enough for me at that point in my life. The place in question was considerably bigger, with a bed large enough for my sovereign ass, sound-insulated walls that would soon seductively incite me into binge-watching entire filmographies, breathtaking views to the *Jura* Mountains from my bedroom window and floors clean enough for me to walk around without fearing the amputation of my feet after catching Tuberculosis, or worse, as my racist Uncle Tomás used to say: homosexuality. Too late for that, I am afraid.

We shook hands right then and there, and scheduled my arrival for the following week, giving me some wiggle room to sort it all out with my Harvey Weinstein-y landlord. Since the man was as dumb as a bag of nails, I wasn't expecting him to realise the contract specified no permanence clause, so my plan was to leave my old place with the luggage I never bothered to unpack (perhaps in a play of wishful thinking from the by now marginalised self-loving part of my brain), and text him about the recent shift of events; mainly, that I had grown a conscience, and that he should, too. On my way out the door of the new flat, I met Agnes, a tall, thin girl with delicate factions and blonde hair, who was to become my new flatmate. Even though she looked just like every single German person you've ever imagined and spoke with a comically thick accent—think Ines from *Toni Erdmann* (2016), but with a worrisome obsession for rye bread and melatonin— she would end up defying all predetermined notions in my head that I was going to end up alone throughout my stay in this country, as she and I would end up forming a moderately agreeable, somewhat forced, never truly emotionally satisfying, friendship. But let's not get ahead of things.

    A week before these events, I was yet again woken up from a self-induced Eszopiclone sleeping coma by the severely misguided flamingo spectacle put on by Marisa and Carmen, something which, at first, I thought I would get used to, yet caught myself progressively hating even more as days went by. Little did I know, however, that the reality that awaited me that evening was far more unpleasant. My mother, God bless her, had told everyone in the family how proud she was that I was travelling abroad to work at a human rights NGO, in Switzerland of all places. If only she knew why I left... Part of me wants to think she does, because deep down, nobody knows her children better than a mother does. Perhaps they are unaware of the specifics, but they *know*; they know when we're down and when we're bubbling with excitement, when we are not comfortable with ourselves and when we make others feel that way. And a good mother, the kind I was lucky enough to have, knows how to tell which of her children is doing the former, and which is doing the latter. My guess is that what motivated my Aunt Rocío to offer her help as soon as she learned about my destination to Geneva was sheer kindness, a random act of selflessness motivated (I am certain) by her religious upbringing, but which was nonetheless reluctantly accepted on my part, as her offer translated into the scheduling of an appointment for lunch between some friend of hers who lived in Geneva, and myself. Despite using every trick in the book to get out of that pickle, I was eventually unsuccessful in passive-aggressively implying to my dear aunt that a retired sixty-eight-year-old nurse and her dementia-inflicted husband would be of little help to get me adjusted in this foreign city. But it would make my aunt happy, and her friends were excited to meet me, and what the Hell, it never hurts to have a nurse on your contact list when abroad—or anywhere else, for that matter. Thus, I took a few more anxiolytics than medically advisable and braced for impact, mentally preparing to park aside my inherent awkwardness and severely curtailed social abilities. But before lunch I had to buy a small detail for them, a bucket of flowers or a box of chocolates, perhaps. If history has taught us something, it is that it's never advisable to enter foreign territory with empty hands. So, I put my headphones on, called my grandma (the "good" one) to kill time on my way to the market, and rode off on my bike.

If, by any chance, I was bestowed by some cosmic superior entity the ability to choose who lives and who dies on this Earth, I would certainly pick my grandmother Lupe to outlive us all. She never had any political aspirations, but there is no doubt in my mind that she would make Albacete a world power in a matter of weeks, were she to be given the chance. With the inner strength to raise nine children whilst simultaneously working two jobs and pushing her body to the limit by becoming the town doctor after years of studying overnight, that lady redefined all previously held conceptions of what it meant to be a hero. Perpetually respected and occasionally feared (don't you dare mess with her *Alioli* sauce), my grandmother stood as the last uncorrupted bastion of human decency, the result of a life filled with hard work and an honesty-first approach to everything she did. Always unreasonably talkative, a level of which not even the combined efforts of the great Aaron Sorkin and David Mamet could ever possibly capture, whenever I called, I knew what was about to take place was not going to be a conversation, but a monologue.

From a very early age, she taught me on one of the occasions where she picked me up from the principal's office after talking back to one of the teachers for their misogynistic remarks, "If you have nothing intelligent or insightful to add to a conversation, then just shut the fuck up." So shut the fuck up I did whenever I called her, because out of the two people on that call, she was the one which definitely had more interesting things to say.

It was precisely in the middle of one of her Shakespearean soliloquies, my mind focused not on my poor bike-riding abilities but on her soothing voice, that a woman pushing a stroller somehow found it a good idea to lunge herself onto a crosswalk mere metres away from me, without even checking whether incoming vehicles were coming her way, whilst having what appeared to be a quite intense conversation on her phone. Had I been riding the bike at a reasonable speed, I would have noticed in time both the lady *and* the two small, friendly faces sticking their curious heads out of their blankets inside the baby cart. Right at that instant, I had a *record scratch* moment when all time was momentarily frozen, and I became a passive spectator in my own life and in the events that were about to transpire. Even though I was not fully aware of having made that move, my hand had instinctively pulled the brakes of the bike all the way, prompting the only operational brake system to violently halt the path of the front tire. Like swerving the steering wheel of a car that's going at a hundred and fifty miles per hour, anything that abruptly interferes with the significant speed of any moving object is bound to end in disaster, especially if the one doing the driving took five attempts (and a little sprinkle of bribery) to finally pass her driver's test. The first thing to exit through the forum were my headphones, which flew across the road with the sound of Grandma's voice still hearable in the distance. The laws of physics propelled the bike—and her rider—upwards then forward, doing the heavy lifting in terms of completing a front flip, one of those that by now had become my signature move. Mid-air, body and vehicle parted ways, and in the midst of my acrobatics, I was able to watch from the very first row of the theatre where this macabre play was being staged how the bike headed at a potentially mortal speed towards the peeking babies and the reasonably frightened yet careless mother. Some divine intervention diverted the trajectory of the flying bicycle, which ended up passing right between the woman and her offspring, the tire coming close to nearly imprinting life-defining skid marks on those babies' foreheads.

This time I landed on grass, certainly more hospitable terrain than in previous incursions, and in a matter of seconds the entire street was filled with honking cars screaming all sorts of obscenities at me in French, failing to realise that the kamikaze was the lady, not myself, and that I was merely suicidal, not homicidal. Trying my best to repress an anxiety attack making its way up my stomach and crawling through my throat, I walked up to the woman and her babies in order to make sure everyone was okay. The lady ran away with her kids, and continued with her important call, whilst everyone else aggressively stared at me. The entire neighbourhood was now present: those constantly fighting next to the fish shop were now menacingly looking in my direction, the old lady taking a shit was—sure enough— taking a shit, but had her eyes deeply fixed on me, and even the corrupt members of the Genevan police force (with their zippers down, very much in character for them) exited the local brothel and pretended to do their job for once. In the midst of such flora and fauna, I picked up my bike and the headphones from the ground—with my grandmother still rambling about the different approaches taken by Michael Haneke and Lynne Ramsay in the depiction of violence in cinema, completely unaware of all that had just transpired—and rushed back to the flat, checking all the way over my shoulder that nobody was following me, before getting ready for one of the weirdest evenings of my life.

When you expect something to go awfully wrong, and then it actually does, do you think your mind plays an active role in ensuring that is indeed exactly what eventually ends up taking place? As if unintentionally hijacking any kind of event just to give oneself the reassuring feeling of being right all along. Well, the encounter with my aunt's friends turned out to be just as I imagined: all the dull conversations about COVID and political radicalization of the youth happened; every single imaginable moment I feared would keep filling my stay at that house with awkward silences effectively did so. But something unexpected, however, did take place, which made me appreciate a life I had recently discovered could potentially be spared from an abrupt conclusion, when I found myself recreating (against my will) one of the most disturbing scenes of David Fincher's *Zodiac* (2007). Without going into unnecessary details, because Lord knows this book is not at all filled with that kind, at one point in such movie Jake Gyllenhaal's character is in the house of a man helping him in his investigation to track the Zodiac Killer. The other man speaks in a calm, collected yet unnerving manner, letting us know that he knows more than we know he knows. Well, the chills down my spine created by the impeccable dominion of director David Fincher over the atmosphere of that scene (hell, of the entire movie) was what came to mind after the husband of my aunt's friend, Lorenzo I believe his name was, asked me whether I liked trains. To be polite, and in an attempt to avoid yet another uncomfortable moment of quietness in that house, I replied affirmatively in what, thinking back, was perhaps a bit too enthusiastic a manner. Like a heroin-addicted junkie after stealing fifty dollars from his mother's purse, a wide smile was painted on the man's face, and his speech pattern radically shifted into a boyish, almost giggling nature.

"Would you…would you like to see my train collection?" he asked. I guess I could have just refused, but after all, I had nothing better to do on that afternoon, so I nodded and rolled along with that poor old man's way of coping with his emasculated nature.

As we walked down the stairs into his basement, and making a conscious effort not to think about the *Don't Breathe* (2016) turkey baster scene, I started wondering what on Earth had brought me to the Genevan suburbs on a Sunday evening to stare at the train models of a retired, well-off man with a large bald patch and an advanced case of erectile dysfunction that probably led to his wife's evident emotional dissatisfaction and subsequent development of her suicide-inducing favourite topic of conversation—the various types of handmade wool tapestry of the sixteenth century.

Inside, it became apparent that Lorenzo had failed to mention that 1) his train collection was located on the government-decreed house's mandatory bunker and 2) that he had built an entire city through computerised systems that filled a complex web of hand-made trains, entire Genevan streets and blocks of buildings completely identical to their real-life counterparts, and even a proper functioning waterfall. After my jaw was about to sprain from fake smiling too much at his moderately impressive yet ultimately worthless endeavour, I took the fake call I had scheduled—courtesy of my phone's alarm—and announced I was expected elsewhere. And by elsewhere, I obviously meant my sad apartment, and the Leo McCarey movie I had been dreaming of watching since I stepped foot in that house.

A couple of weeks went by, and after I was all settled down at the new flat and finally managed to get some decent rest, my blood pressure started to benefit from entering into routine territory. No more gang fights, no more demented ladies searching for eye contact in the worst possible scenarios, no more flamenco dancing. This soon-to-be twenty-four-year-old was finally able to enjoy her eighty-year-old life filled with peace and quiet. Or was she? Because that would mean that more silence would ensue, opening the door for a deeper inner self-inspection, which in my case was never a good thing, as my wild imagination could quite easily take the reins and change course towards a darker destination. You see, I occasionally get this impulse which takes the deceitful shape of a seductive voice, a villain of my own creation that usurps my mirror and occupies my throne and whispers to me credible alternative scenarios, life trajectories, futures where the choices that I made had led me to a life better enjoyed yet never achieved. But so far up until that moment, life was treating me well enough for me to pay little attention to those impulses.

At the flat, it took some time to get adjusted to the radically different dynamics. Agnes and I quickly got along, both of us being in an initially-hidden-later-on-openly-disclosed state of depression—in her case, prompted by the death of her father, who died in her arms when she was only seven; in my case, prompted by the death my brother made me long for—and as the two emotionally crippled individuals that we were, we bonded over sleeping pills and our shared obsession with battling noisy environments. She knew nothing about movies, and I knew nothing about music, but somehow, we made it work, with our mutually shared dark sense of humour—Nazi jokes were a frequent guest at our conversations—keeping us both constantly laughing and, eventually, sufficiently comfortable being around one another. At one point, I even gathered enough courage to reveal to her how annoying I found her constant noises of banging pots and pans over at the kitchen (instinctively praying for her not to be messing around with the oven; you never know, old habits die hard).

It seems silly now, but looking back, what initially felt like a friendship born out of necessity between Agnes and I in the face of nobody else to hang out with, eventually bloomed into a strong bond between us both. All the trips I had made on my own, to the mountains, to Bern and Lausanne and Basel and Zürich—trips that, like going to the theatre to endure a Vin Diesel movie, had come in and out yet had left no indelible impression other than a diminishing bank account—had now been replaced with proper journeys with Agnes to places that were permanently inscribed into my retina, skyrocketing my serotonin levels, and making my weekends no longer be relegated to a relentless succession of watching depressing Armenian movies. The sunny walk across *Montreux* surrounded by the kaleidoscopic pigments of a hundred different flowers; the eye-opening experience atop *Mont Blanc*, where I forgot to bring proper pants to the highest geographical location in all Europe; the nearly religious experience I had whilst tasting a proper beer in *Mürren* with the *Jungfrau* as the prime exhibit of that immeasurable nature exposition... Each week, provided that Agnes (out of the two of us, the one who owned a car), had slept well—fifty percent chance—we would go on one of those trips, just us two or occasionally with her work colleagues.

Things at the organization were not particularly remarkable, however. Although the catch-up process was over, as I had finally managed to get used to most of the tasks that I was required to learn prior to starting the job in the first place, contact with everyone at the office was (probably for the best) somewhat limited, motivated by online working and the fact I never managed to overcome the powerfully unforgettable self-portrait which I skilfully painted on the first day for everyone else to see. Vero still stood as the island in the middle of that insipid ocean that was our working space, and perhaps because of our cultural proximity, we started growing closer to one another with a soothing easiness, now organising small coven meetings in between coffee breaks to whisper one another the newest gossip around the office. As if I had opened a door she was desperately waiting to cross, I think about how lonely she must have felt during her long years working at the organization, having been completely shut down from the team's out-of-work social events for a reason neither she nor I would ever learn. Now that the Pandora's box had been opened, and she could rely on the safe space we had built to talk amongst us two without being judged, gossip without fearing others hearing, and share existential crises without receiving stoic and impractical pieces of advice, we easily formed a strong bond with the speed and intensity of a film by the Safdie Brothers.

What initially began as an occasional beer after work, paired with a visible reluctance on her behalf to chaperone me around the city during my first weeks (a perfectly understandable position given my energy-engulfing depressed propensity), eventually blossomed into something more profound and meaningful and, Hell, life-saving even. Virtually every day that we worked remotely, I went over to her place, and we would have a beer both during *and* after work, even though her busy social life prevented us from seeing one another during the weekends. I cannot pin down what it was about her, but she made me feel comfortable and safe and at ease with myself and with her. Like, don't ask me why, but I would be more than happy to let her babysit my hypothetical children. Her boyfriend Leo was the definition of a Swiss-army knife. Genetically engineered by ¼ Egyptian, ¼ Swiss, ¼ Colombian and ¼ Sri Lankan genes, the man spoke eight languages and at age thirty was poised to become the CEO of the engineering company he worked for in a matter of months. This relentlessly resourceful and eternally quick-witted handyman genuinely gave the impression there was nothing he could not do, which is why he seemed the perfect match for Vero, if there ever was one. A couple of nights a week, the three of us had dinner at their place, and watched a film from Emir Kusturica—her favourite movie director—a plan which, in all honesty, made me feel on top of the world: that's all I needed—good movies, good company and a feeling of belonging. One could even say I was about to find my spot in this city. Who knows, perhaps on this planet, too. The lens through which I looked at life was becoming much clearer now, no longer darkened yet not quite fully transparent, either. But clear enough to start to appreciate the view.

On that rainy Saturday which inaugurated the month of June and the Euro Cup soccer tournament, with Agnes gone for a family visit back in Germany and Richard (our other flatmate, a Canadian man in his late thirties whom we barely saw, and whose passion for CrossFit tutorials was just about the entire span of information we knew about him) on a trip overseas, I was bracing myself for a weekend of binge watching Andrei Tarkovsky, Max Ophüls and Yasujirō Ozu films (in that order). Imagine my surprise, however, when I opened the door to see my landlady Beatrice, a passive aggressive 50-year-old, Tilda Swinton-looking, lower back butterfly tattoo wearer, slightly cross-eyed Swiss lady, eating yogurt in the middle of our kitchen while only wearing her panties and bra. She was listening to *Push it to the Limit* by Paul Engemann, staring into the distance with a demented look on her face. Out on the terrace, I could see our clothesline was now filled with thongs—one of which had the McDonald's logo underneath a caption which read "Happy Meal"—and various lace clothing items of a much older woman than Agnes and myself. To my right, I noticed the bathtub was not empty, as most ordinary bathtubs tend to be, but was instead occupied by 5 massive leopard-striped suitcases. For a moment, I quietly debated whether to call the police or an exorcist altogether to save us some time, but I opted for the option that would require less effort when I knocked on the door, which startled Beatrice and made her instinctively jump out whilst letting out a shrieking howl of non-human origin, and instantly prompted her left saggy breast to leave the bra that had previously contained it and start dangling all over the kitchen. On some nights I swear I can still hear it hitting the ground. For some reason only she was aware of, Beatrice violently thrusted the yogurt into what I assumed she thought was the garbage can but was, in fact, the kitchen drawer. Jesus Christ, all I wanted was to detest life through Tarkovsky's films, not to fear death because of my landlady's psychological precariousness and lack of spatial calculation.

"Well, I guess I have no choice but to go to watch that stupid soccer match," I concluded. It was certainly a better plan than having to pull out a knife from my chest after my landlady went into one of her tantrums, and that day I was simply not in the mood of getting viciously murdered.

***

A broken glass on the floor from which a Guinness beer now sadly poured onto the sidewalk was stepped on by a clueless pedestrian. It was game night: Germany and France battling, blood and tears, for international validation…and the Euro Cup trophy. The environment around Geneva was truly kinetic, contagious even. So, hoping that the beers I was about to chug down would give me the confidence to venture myself into speaking some moderately functional French, I joined Vero and a couple of her friends over at Mr Pickwick's pub to watch the soccer game.

At this point it must be stated that I have no interest—nor have I ever had any interest—in sports. It was only during international events such as this one that I could understand the furore and passion with which people lived these competitions: saving distances, it was easy to root for (basically your country, unless you are from Latvia, then I guess you root for anyone else), it was easy to understand and everyone was invested and found enjoyment in it, with even the busiest streets being completely emptied during match time. Attempting to get rid of the subconsciously assumed belief as a non-sports enthusiast that soccer was always the same, with the sole novelty being the change of players and playing fields, I equated it to the thing that I love most. Because it turns out that one could argue that soccer is kind of like movies—the trainer is the director, the players are the actors, the staff is the crew, the referees the critics, the World Cup is the Oscars and the audience, well, they're the audience. And even though we like to think that each movie is its own independent thing, they are very much not, because the master Mike Nichols once pulled the rug from beneath our feet and shattered this myth when he revealed that each movie scene is, at the end of the day, either an argument between two impetuous forces clashing against one another, a negotiation to defend one's position and achievements whilst simultaneously pushing personal aspirations over the opponent's under the pretence of reaching a mutually-beneficial common ground or, whenever this fails, a seduction. Indeed, soccer is all about attack, defence, and somewhere in between. Once you start to appreciate the art, the path of getting to a destination and leaving along the way all fixations on just the final result, soccer can be quite a fulfilling experience, especially if enjoyed among the right audience.

As the game went on, I put my overthinking abilities to good use and started to analyse what had made me become so entranced by that soccer match, to the point I managed to identify what I thought was a common trope in soccer matches: whenever a player vigorously charged against another player, or injured him in any conceivable way, as soon as the other was—quote unquote—hurt, and almost always before they even reached the ground, they started screaming for their life. With the convincingness of a veteran stage actor, players wisely simulated being deeply hurt, as if they had become desperately in need of immediate, life-saving surgery, regardless of whether it was because of a kick in the shin or a slight push on their shoulders. But why go all the way, thick and thin, rain or shine, severe or unimportant, giving their all in each curtain call? Because they know they have greater chances of being paid more attention if they cry from the get-go, instead of waiting and seeing whether the injury is indeed worthy of wasting everyone's time. That is what I like to call "the theatre of war". And I guess that's what prompted the creation of this book: an open-ended cry for help its author has not even had the decency of mildly covering up. In the hopes of finally coming to terms with who I truly am, I use writing to cope with the painful anxiety inflicted by life upon me, by me upon me, and by those around me—whether close or anonymous—upon me. There is something deeply empowering about putting into words exactly what it is that one feels, which can only arise after arriving at a point of sincere awareness about your own self by being both brave enough to develop a willingness to know the person that you actually are, and patient enough to take the time for inner reflection—to know what you like and what you hate, who to keep in your life and who to forget. Because every single day, couples split up, families are broken, resentment is slowly built among friends, and all for failing to understand oneself, and for failing to either internally or externally communicate what infuriates us about ourselves and about others; what makes us feel like our heart no longer belongs to us and is instead in someone else's hands, or what makes our blood boil and makes us at a certain point want to strangle the life out someone we hold dear to our heart. So many "I love you's" and "I hate you's" that have never been uttered and never will, but which could have saved relationships or protected us from those we should have stayed away from, had they been screamed out of our systems just as we felt their very first foul impact on our bodies, like soccer players, before even reaching the ground; before it became far too late.

VIII

WHAT WOULD IT TAKE?

"Ariadna is coming," Agnes said. "You're gonna like her." What might have seemed as just another passing comment with the relevance of a Mormon church recruitment ad, instantly lit a lightbulb in my mind and prompted a painstaking process of overthinking that the pretentious mobs hiding their inability to function as proper human beings behind lengthy Letterboxd reviews can only dream of. And once this process had begun, there was no turning back. As soon as Agnes uttered those words, common words, simple words, innocent words, the nuts and bolts began working full time inside my mind, obsessively crafting the many unlikely scenarios that could potentially unfold during our trip to *Gruyères* on that sunny summer day. The fact that all of this had come out of a "you're gonna like her" exemplifies the place where I found myself in, mentally and emotionally, desperately refusing to see this reality that was smacking me right in the face. Even when our evening included many of the events I fantasised about—inside jokes, flirting here and there, a casually developed mutual attraction between Ariadna and myself, and even a heart-stealing reference to François Truffaut by her own hand—I could not escape the thought that my judgement was being clouded: did I really like Ariadna, or was I so desperate to love and be loved in return that I just couldn't help but fall head over heels for the first person that showed me the slightest amount of decency, kindness or affection? The answer to that question was quickly answered in the shape of a dagger to my heart that permanently altered the nature of Agnes and I's relationship, as the (at least perceived) mutual attraction between Ariadna and I went straight out the window when Agnes took me aside and revealed to me Ariadna had, as a matter of fact, a boyfriend back in Bolivia whom she dearly loved, and Agnes had merely told me I was going to "like her" as a way to make sure I would come on the trip, because they were not really that close to warrant an evening plan just the two of them. What a bitch. And what a naive imbecile I was to fall for it.

Felix, Agnes' boyfriend, had joined us when he came to visit a few weeks prior, and I think this also partly contributed to the erosion of our relationship, because I am a friendly gal by nature and I do not have the ability nor the confidence to flirt, but apparently in this world every single gesture a woman makes to a man—from a blink out of rhythm, to accidentally bumping into someone whilst dancing at the club, to leaving your house without wearing a bra just because you feel like it—can be interpreted as a sign of flirting or of being in the mood of wanting unwanted attention. It is so utterly dumb and pervasive that even us women have it ingrained both in our subconscious and very conscious part of our brains. We have become part of the problem, because we've been told for so long that we are to blame for the impulsive and animalistic behaviour of those who have "no other option" because they "can't control themselves", as if we were the only ones who had a choice of behaving like conscious human beings, as if we were the only ones to be held responsible for both our and *their* actions... The problem has taken roots so deep we have begun implementing a self-destructive witch hunt amongst ourselves; a preventive process to root out any possibility of behaving in a manner which we have been told to be "inappropriate" by those who have done nothing but behave in that way. So, we routinely bring each other down as a way to protect ourselves, to protect their behaviour, to protect this system that makes no effort to hide its omnipresence, and which so far has remained unchallenged ever since it established a long time ago who is to hunt and who is to be hunted. But how gut-wrenching it is when the latter are helping the former carry out their duties, as acceptance of this devastating reality's existence should never fall into complacency, as much as they try to make us believe so by installing the foundations of such system as early as we step out of the womb.

No, Agnes, I had no wish to have sex with your boyfriend. Not because he is a man (Heaven knows I have had more than a few pleasant surprises along the way), but because *he is your boyfriend*, and I respect you and I respect that, even if you don't, with your imposed insecurity about the rest of the women that are out there doing their best to survive the constant unwanted advances resulting from misread signs they had no role in creating. Because, at the end of the day, you're not afraid that I want to sleep with your boyfriend—what you're scared of is that in case I do, you are not entirely sure your boyfriend will be able to "control himself", not because of my physical attractiveness or lack thereof, but because he has never been expected to do so. So don't lay the blame on those at the other end, whether we have good or bad intentions, because in fact all those other women are more than likely doing their best to navigate a sea of enforced gender roles and undeserved expected behaviours, which come with far too many homework exclusively designed for us, as well as precautions from actions we should never be ever exposed to in the first place in the absence of any restrictions imposed upon the often abusive, unfair practices of a large part of the opposite sex.

Oh, apologies for the meandering detour, but it feels amazing to finally get this out of my system... Now, I can say all this to *you*, but how could I say that out loud to *her*? Immediately in Agnes' mind I would be sown a scarlet letter on my chest and labelled as criminally insane. The Freudian side of my brain made me think that maybe that was the reason why she tricked me into believing Ariadna was interested in me: to make me atone for the crime of wanting to be with Felix, a man whom in reality I had no interest to be with in the first place. Even though it would take a couple of additional weeks for Agnes and me to get to that point of mutually eroded comfort of being surrounded by one another for her to reveal this to me, this rage she felt quickly began to brew inside of her, one misinterpreted gesture at a time.

At the time of the reveal, I was in the midst of a sea of people, with the town of *Gruyères* being filled with young people taking part in a vibrant LGBTQ+-themed parade, shedding powerfully positive energy and catchy tunes onto the streets...and yet, my entire body ached from feeling completely powerless, alone, unable to make a connection. This planet of ours can be quite a lonely place. And when you have a bottomless roster of traumatic memories to choose from, you start questioning if it could perhaps be a situation of your own making. When your brain goes into full *conspiracy mode*, all alarms are rung and there is simply no way back. It's like that scene in *Ratatouille* (2007) when all the rats rapidly exit the pantry and flee in a thousand different directions as the first signs of human presence in the kitchen become self-evident, but in reverse. Once formulated, the pervasively corrosive ideas flow into my brain and set roots forever. The feeling of not belonging—accentuated by my clearly inappropriate winter clothes that hid my scars, my inability to dance a single step on beat and Agnes telling me to "have fun" and "relax" and "wow, I assumed all Latinas knew how to dance and have a good time, but I guess I was wrong"—was then extrapolated from a simple event into my entire life. What if I did not belong anywhere? I am almost twenty-four years old; statistically speaking, I should be able to fit in perfectly in events such as that one. And yet, on that day I never felt more like leaving and going home to watch a David Lynch movie.

The last nail in the coffin of the fleeting feeling of opportunity and hopefulness I had about my chances with Ariadna—something which very much embodied my tendency to daydream and over-rely on foolish fantasies about ideal lives that I will never get to live—was finally drowned out for good when I saw a bunch of notifications on my phone: two missed calls and a worryingly long text, all from Dad.

"Don't be scared, *little one*. But your mother is in the hospital. Her stomach is acting up again, you know, one of those infections she gets every once in a while, ever since her surgery. But everything is under control. Me and your aunts will spend the night here with her and hopefully she can return back home tomorrow. She's asleep now, so if you want to talk to her, it's best to wait until tomorrow. Take care, little one."

Underneath those simple lines lay a darker secret, yearning to come out of the walls of the home where for so long it had been confined to. Because it turns out this was not her first trip to the ER for almost identical reasons, with the other stomach infections having manifested in the presence of large daily intakes of alcohol in her system. While I can only speculate about the reasons for her to end up at that dark place, as she would always try her best to shield us from any pain that may come our way, even when that pain stemmed from our own actions, one can trace an abundantly clear line between the time my brother's behaviour around the house became far too aggressive, uncontrollably so, and the amount of secret trips my mother would take in the middle of the night to go to the gas station, only to return home tiptoeing her way into her studio, with the sound of clinking bottles announcing her arrival. That night, there was no need to receive confirmation from my father of the presence of yet another violent argument between her and my brother; the truth was more than apparent, as it had been all along. The real culprit of her state, ironically enough, did not even care to show his face and spend the night with her at the hospital, perhaps out of disgust with the circumstances he had just created. It was precisely the generalised aura of mysticism with which his explosions of rage directed towards us three were covered, both outside and within our family, paired my mother's toxically unconditional love for this person who never for a second was worthy of it, and the irreparable harm it would enforce upon her in particular, far more damaging than the more recent wounds she was currently recovering from, that prevented any of us from actually seeking real help.

    The art of navigating across the sea of depression means perennially swimming in treacherous waters that drown out the cries of those standing on nearby boats, tending their hands, offering their help. Once again, the dark glass of melancholy resulting from an irreparable state of mind, was placed over my eyes with the sole purpose of severely clouding my judgement, depriving me of the little happiness that came my way as soon as the thought of him entered my mind. Hate can be a powerful source of motivation to create, but also to destroy. It acts in the manner of a corrosive substance, making its way onto your emotional stability, tainting your memories and toying with your perception of reality altogether.

Thus, with the force and effectiveness of a meteorological catastrophe, just contemplating the scenario of going back to that house, of once again being forced to schedule my life according to another person's preferences in the hopes of reducing the chances of crossing paths and bumping into undesired and undeserved conflict, the constant weeping from my mother which even in her silence invariably echoed through the walls, our occasionally bruised bodies and permanently shattered souls, instantly annihilated the little progress made since I arrived in Switzerland, blatantly exposing the fragility of the emotional equilibrium I had just reached up until then and opening up the door wide open for all the dark thoughts to come live in my head rent free. The man had risen from our collective nightmares and made it his life mission to make us all yearn to be stripped away of our most valuable gift. My life was now lived in death, and my days were now filled with an asphyxiating feeling that reverberated across my spine every time I had to get in touch with the world he inhabited and which I desperately craved to leave behind. And every phone call with my parents, every picture from the weddings they attended, every piece of news that came from Albacete was a constant reminder that opened the scar and rubbed salt into the wound, putting back on the table an option my mind struggled to ever let go off.

With no real solid ground to keep my feet from hovering suspended above the floor with a rope around my neck, the scenario of carrying out an irreversible decision had never been banished, but I had certainly managed to anaesthetize it for some time, in the midst of other problems monopolising my attention.

Somebody had to pay for the crimes committed, somebody had to die, and if it could not be him, well then, I would have no other choice but to follow the path he had carefully built for myself, and let him win the twisted game he was making us all play. And all of this from a hypothetical thought I think Agnes had had and from Dad's text which contained no mention of my brother whatsoever. It was, in fact, the act of thinking about the advanced preparedness with which my mind was ready to embrace such a grim vital outlook what made me suddenly wonder if I was beyond redemption, if my days were truly numbered and I was on borrowed time just looking for the tiniest excuse, or my brother's next attack against human decency, to put an end to it all. Or whether the pervasively poisonous and psychologically torturing relationship with him was indeed a problem that did not take place in my mind alone, but was palpable enough to make a person want to take her own life, and to ultimately consider that outcome as nothing short of unavoidable. The blackened lens through which I looked at life, and whose creation he heavily contributed to, made me feel like Paula Alquist, twisting my reality and making me doubt my own shadow. That unbearable pain created deep scars that were invisible to the eye, but which weighed heavily on one's soul, enough for one to carry them forever regardless of whether the one doing the harm is sleeping in the room next to yours or thousands of miles away. The answer then, to what it would take for me to create a hecatomb in those around me by going somewhere with no return, was frighteningly very little.

IX

…AND ALONG CAME THE LADIES

The Euro Cup was at its zenith, its deeply enveloping collective obsession having trapped me under its claws and turned me into a true devotee of the competition. Certainly instigated by the fact each match became an excuse to get out of the house and grab a beer with Vero and her friends, I became so invested in the cause I surprised myself watching the soccer matches of countries other than my beloved Spain, countries which nobody but the people who lived in them ever believed they truly existed—I mean, what is the *real* difference between Slovenia and Slovakia? Who knows? Who cares? With Vero having already finished up her master's thesis and with our homeland team about to enter into the quarter-finals against Switzerland, of all teams and out of all places, the stars aligned to mend the up-until-then incompatible schedules, endowing us with the perfect opportunity to finally gather enough courage to venture into inviting the Spanish colleagues working at the NGO right in front of ours, Anna and Montserrat, during our otherwise gossip-designated coffee break, to come join us after work to watch the soccer match. The team we had gathered on that day needed an adequately Spanish-friendly location to rise to the occasion: a Spanish bar in the middle of Geneva, run by Maribel, an overweight lady from Galicia whose voice pitch sounded exactly like a dog whistle, whom before you could even start to think about your order had, very much in Spanish fashion, already opened up a bottle of *Estrella Galicia* beer and had anticipated the food cravings you were unaware you even had by laying down a plate with *tortilla de patata* and another with *croquetas de jamón*. What can I say, that made me feel as if I was back home. So, the four of us—later joined by their Venezuelan co-worker, Michaela, and by Agnes, who soon regretted not having taken seriously her Spanish lessons back in high school—entered the crowded bar and took a discrete table near the area where it looked like we had less chances of being knifed to death in the likely scenario that Switzerland were to be ultimately defeated. With two TV screens on each side of the bar effectively dividing the crowd by nationality, tensions progressively grew almost as fast as the temporary sense of camaraderie and community that flooded the two teams of strangers that had gathered that day on a rainy afternoon.

Very much aided by the exorbitant amounts of alcohol which, courtesy of our beloved Maribel, by now had well-entered our bodies, we began to lose all inhibitions and get to know one another outside of the dreaded and all-encompassing workspace which we occasionally frequented and in which we had seldom gotten the time to go beyond a casual "hello" or a furtive "goodbye" on our way out the door. It was curious, however, that such an intimate connection was being formed in an exceptionally hostile environment, a ticking time bomb of a setting waiting for a lawsuit to happen. Sure enough, by the time we had reached the penalty round, two fights had already broken out, countering what common belief might have otherwise led us to assume, as they were not in the least instigated by Spanish people but in fact by two Swiss gentlemen who were simply in the mood of losing their molars that evening.

In the meantime, I managed to squeeze some quality time with the girls each time a quiet moment took place throughout the match. Out of the entire group, Michaela seemed to be the most mysteriously inaccessible one, always an intriguing presence and the first one to crack open the can of worms of dark humour jokes. Her seductive brown eyes seemed to hide a secret nobody but her had access to, and which, despite the many walks we would go on to take on our own on nights of heavy drinking and excessive ingests of falafel, I was unable to unlock the safe containing the answers to who she truly was. A lost soul that had found her place on Earth, and with a permanent slick look that made us all know she always knew exactly what she was doing, Michaela would make me fall back in love with the Nouvelle Vague after it became clear we were the only people in Geneva under the age of seventy-five that got excited about movie theatre cycles of French New Wave movies. That is what remained with me, the little she felt comfortable with revealing, the *cinephiliac* passions and the laughter that filled our walks back home; the unpretentious and the authentic, nothing more and nothing less. Montserrat, on the other hand, was an entirely different case. Inexplicably hilarious at all times, not in the least instigated by her severely heightened sombre disposition—she once managed to impressively steer in a matter of seconds Michaela's Tinder date story about a guy who begged her to take a dump on her chest into the sanitary health crisis experienced in some East Asian countries— but by her obsession with K-pop bands, whose songs she kept singing in Korean and dancing to poorly executed TikTok dances, whilst simultaneously managing to have absolutely no regard whatsoever for the concept of rhythm. And then there was Anna, the quieter one of the group, selflessly refusing to step into the spotlight despite the genuine light she inherently emanated. She inexplicably struck me from the very beginning as someone who made kindness her way of life. Perhaps the way she attentively listened when you spoke about even the most trivial of things, or the way her eyes tenderly closed when she laughed, or her inability to brag about her impressive resume and academic accomplishments, or the way she kindly and softly spoke to waiters, or the way she would sweetly pet the two dogs at the bar which immediately found their way to her. There was something powerfully authentic about her, a carefree, generous energy that constantly flowed from her into the room and into everyone else around her.

To my left, Agnes found herself to be completely out of the conversation, given the materialization of one of the biggest and truest clichés about Spanish people that tend to circumnavigate the cosmos—our tendency to speak in our language amongst ourselves whenever possible. In the face of her level of Spanish being not that far away from that of a construction brick, she was understanding as much as Terrence Howard did in Math class. Upon realization, my attempts to hush the rest with a loud whisper of, "In English, in English", was met by Agnes with a condescending "You don't have to pity me and speak in English, you do what you want with your friends", which indeed hid a much deeper meaning, a threatening one even, and effectively took away every single motivation I had had up until that moment of making an effort to include her as part of the conversation, something which she had failed to do on more than a few trips which we made with her German-speaking colleagues. Her attitude did not matter, then, because I was in good company, and all can be forgiven and forgotten when in good company. That dinner on that match day, as it later turned out, was going to be a turning point, not just in terms of my stay in Geneva, but in my life as a whole. Because sitting at that table, which would eventually become metaphorically larger to accommodate for others, were the people who made me want to give myself a second chance, even when I thought I no longer deserved it, and even when that turned out to be true.

Imagine the extent of the ecstatic feeling that took over my entire body, that I found myself unable to contain the impulse to kiss Maribel right on her virtually non-existent lips after Spain won the nail-biting, ultimately futile penalty round. God bless her and God bless Galicia. As if Genevan streets were suddenly turned into Nazi-occupied Paris with our spoken language—saving distances—becoming the equivalent of a Star of David sewed onto our clothes, us Spanish people found ourselves unable to celebrate the victory as soon as we stepped out of the sacrosanct safe haven provided by Maribel's bar and into a city filled with disappointed citizens who were looking for someone to blame, for an escape to their frustrations and Euro Cup national aspirations, and we just seemed like the perfect target. Being well aware of the power of male frustration—two World Wars can testify to that—and having developed some expertise in the field of dealing with analogous incidents (swap a soccer fan for a frat boy at a nightclub), we drunkenly walked back to our respective homes speaking in as discreet a tone of voice as humanly possible. On our way to the tram stop, Vero invited us all to join her at the party she was going to host the following weekend on the outskirts of Geneva, at the house of her de facto father-in-law. Her boyfriend Leo and his friends were going to make *sangría* and *paella* for all, and I offered to make a Spanish *tortilla* myself—not that I had ever made one back in Spain, but what can I say, you probably can tell by now that I am a messy, incomprehensible, impulsive person who was recently told by my dear friend Mónica that she took a look at my LinkedIn profile, and she laughed out loud for five solid minutes, claiming that I was a walking and talking contradiction…but, aren't we all?

The day of the party arrived and, after realising I had no clue of the ingredients nor the way of properly cooking a *tortilla de patatas*, but very much remembering that scene from *Madres Paralelas* (2021), I ventured into the kitchen and made the first attempt at preparing the dish, which all things considered could not be entirely labelled as a success, given that it almost featured the intervention of the fire brigade and what could have perfectly resulted in my second visit in just shy of two months to a *cimitière*. The second time around, I managed not to spill (again) the mix all over the kitchen floor and ended up with a more than decent-looking *tortilla de patatas* (with onions, of course) that I nonetheless had the unavoidable certainty of having undercooked. When everybody at the party seemed to enjoy it, some even asking for the recipe (completely unaware that the dish had been the result of one part sheer luck, two parts impulsive irrational behaviour and two-thirds divine intervention), all I could think of were my agnostic prayers to prevent salmonella from entering the party and confining us all to the compounds of our respective bathrooms on the following morning.

Except for Agnes, who had agreed to come yet was eventually prevented from doing so due to a fake headache that she engineered on the last minute, the entire group from Maribel's bar was there. Sitting at the table next to Anna was a gorgeous blonde girl, with heavenly, deep eyes endowed with a thousand hues of blue and a small touch of grey emanating in gently mercurial arcs, and the kind of smile that beautifully captured her compassionate soul—Lara, Anna's roommate whom I had heard so much about. The two last working brain cells operating on the rough terrain that had become my neurological tissue immediately made a connection—I knew someone by that name, someone familiar. I had seen her face before, but where?

Given that Montserrat and I had chosen the same remote destination of Odessa for our student exchange experiences (five years apart from one another), and Anna and I had studied the same pompously flashy yet ultimately useless degree in International Politics at the same university (merely one year apart), and Michaela was the one that got the job for which I was (briefly) considered, yet managed to say the wrong NGO name at the disastrous interview I had, there was a running joke among us that I inevitably had mystical connections with everybody in the group, which only served to emphasize in my mind that in a way—a corny one—we were all destined to meet one another.

It was only when Anna said, "You're not going to believe it: we have found your connection with Lara," that reality hit me: the phone number my friend Lucas had sent me over three months prior, the number of his best friend who was living in Geneva and who I regretted not having the kind of life that would possibly conjure up a reason for the two of us to cross paths...a friend whose name was Lara. That same Lara that would go on to tell me she had just arrived from a trip to the oddly remote Greek destination of *Khalkidhiki*, where a year prior, in an attempt to survive the first COVID-19 lockdown within my home's inhospitable territory, I had worked as a bartender during the summer. The same Lara that devoutly listened every Friday evening to the *Estirando el Chicle* podcast which had filled my otherwise miserable evenings with uncontrollable laughter.

Indeed, the very same Lara who revealed she was reading Cristina Morales' *Lectura Fácil*, incidentally, the book I was viciously devouring night after night, as part of an almost religious experience of self-acceptance and enlightenment about one's position in the world. The Lara that loved *L'Événement* (2021) and *The Worst Person in the World* (2021) and Céline Sciamma and Virginie Despentes. The same Lara who told me about the concert of Mumford and Sons she had recently been to (and of which I had been prevented from going due to a much-to-be-desired financial situation), where the band had played arguably the best song in living memory—*"There Will Be Time"*. After having the kind of conversation that entrances you to the point of forgetting about your surroundings altogether, I felt like we were embodying Rick Blaine and Captain Renault, for as time would later on prove, that day an invaluable, life-saving friendship was born. From that moment on, rock bottom was left long behind.

Almost without even realising it, these people who just a month earlier had no idea one another existed, quickly formed a close group in the best way for a relationship to get started: quickly, intensely and developing a deep-rooted and genuine affection for one another. Although things had not been ideal after "Ariadnagate" and "Felixgate", I must admit it was not easy when Agnes finally ended her internship and returned to Germany, her presence being sorely missed back at the flat after what amounted to an eternity of days eating breakfast on my own without having to smell her reeking herbal infusions. Even walking by the parking lot and seeing the spot where she used to park her light-blue, dusty old Honda Civic—by then having been occupied by a rapist-white van—instantly filled my days with nostalgia, as I longed for the time prior to her duplicitous gimmicks, and wished that things had turned out better than they did, had she seen not only how much I valued our otherwise gratifying friendship and the memories we had shared together and how we had managed to make a hospitable home out of that inhospitable flat, but also how my friendliness towards her beloved boyfriend did not prevent nor had ever prevented my lack of romantic or otherwise intentions from remaining unaltered in his presence. But I decided to adopt a pragmatic disposition on the matter, given that she had willingly made her own choices, having opted to silence all rational behaviour, even if the charges brought about stood in direct contradiction with the Carla she had come to truly know during those intense months, all in lieu of a crime that had not been committed and for which there were no grounds to indicate otherwise. Hopefully, time would make them both get back in touch with reality and out of touch with fantasy through finally becoming able to discern the relationship they have from the relationship they think they have. Because whenever you find yourself doubting your significant other's intentions, instead of being quick to assign blame to whomever either hypothetically or verifiably finds him or herself at the other end of such advances, take the necessary time to question what kind of partner you have chosen to spend your days with, because that is often where the real blame ultimately lies, even if it is almost never properly assigned to its real culprit.

The blow of her absence was nonetheless softened by the presence of whom I would end up referring to as "my Genevan ladies", those guilty of being behind the momentary hushing of dark thoughts in the mornings where I used to feel my life had absolutely no purpose whatsoever—a dangerous side effect of awakening from the dream state we're all put into throughout the course of our lives, after realising you don't want to live anymore, and you can die at any minute and responsibilities instantly fly out the window (Oh, how much damaging enlightenment has Mr Camus brought upon this world...). Though those thoughts were not gone entirely, they had been surely relegated to the far corner of my brain, no longer having uninhibited access to rational thoughts nor largely determining my behaviour, anymore.

Like being offered a cold glass of water after wandering for days in the desert, it almost made me feel ashamed to say it, because my friends back in Spain were incredible people whom I loved dearly, but I had never been more comfortable with a group of friends in a very long time. And Spain seemed far away now, and they all had their own problems to worry about, and for once, I no longer worried that much about my own. In any case, all of them, particularly Sara, had shown an interest in me and my mental health since I came here, and I had been in regular contact with all of them, so my conscience was clear. With my birthday coming up the following month, and given the girls were leaving on that week back to their homes to go vacation with their respective entourages, I planned to momentarily return to Spain for a quick visit, which would give me the chance to test the waters both with my friends and back at home; especially back at home, where I could see if any progress had been made while I was away. It was not a big birthday, twenty-four, but I felt like spending it with the few people who still (intermittently) stood the sight of my face and the sound of my voice and noticed my absence and appreciated my presence...even if some had a lot to be desired when it came to the "giving" part yet were first in line for the "needing" one, a sharp contrast with what I discovered here in Geneva, and an eventual wake-up call regarding the people I had in my life, the people I wished I had and the people

I deserved to have around.

The month that followed can only be described as pure bliss. The movie tickets I bought for indie films at ungodly hours in remote cinemas were no longer for one, the pain in my muscles after hiking routes around the mountains were no longer (just in) my legs but also on my stomach from uncontrollably chucking all the way as a result of being in the right company. Step by step, I began to loosen all inhibitions around them, peeling away the most burdensome layers and taking away the mask I always wore when trying to please others, and replaced it for a mask that I had not worn in a long time, something I feared had been lost over the years in an attempt to please others first and never myself: my own face. It is so hard yet so important to find people that bring out the best of you and make you believe in yourself even when that seems like an inconceivable thought you have no right to have. Especially then. But you never know for sure how people are really going to be once you pass the point of acquaintance and become friends. So genuinely opening up, becoming vulnerable for others in the presence of mutually perceived trust, can be quite a daunting task, especially if you have been hurt before. That's a leap of faith I thought I could never take, but I could not be more thankful that I eventually did.

It still makes me laugh whenever I think about how I met Arantxa and Claudia, Lara's friends from university whose alcoholism and predisposition for twerking and gossip inevitably made our paths cross and turned them into the last constituents of our tightly-knit group, the aptly titled "*Abordaje*". They reminded me of Bert and Bertie: Claudia, a short Chilean girl who looked nineteen yet neared thirty, with puppy-like energy, confidence in every step she took—she was poised to become one of the country's leading dental health researchers—and the most contagious laugh I have ever heard, to the point of being medicinal, more efficient in calming me down and letting my mind get rid of bad thoughts than melatonin ever could; and Arantxa, a six-feet-tall Basque beauty in her early twenties, who had the physical resilience of a professional athlete and a heart large enough it surprised me it fit her chest, who gave some of the tightest and most sincere hugs anyone has ever given me. On one of our drunken nights, as we did every Thursday (or any day of the week other than Mondays and Tuesdays, to be honest), we gathered at Anna and Lara's place to play board games, nonchalantly drink cheap wine as if it was tap water and talk about our misfortunes in life, which was well worth the (rocky and legally questionable) forty-kilometre trip it took to get there by bike and get back home.

Don't ask me how, or why, but Claudia, a wild spirit who everything she lacked in height she compensated with fiery Latin character, told us about a failed attempt of hers to see the fireworks on Switzerland's national holiday from Lake Geneva, which entailed getting a boat, and more importantly, finding someone who was *in possession of* a boat. Tinder, as it turned out, proved to be a surprisingly effective place not necessarily for going on dates, but to acquire things, like used furniture, hallucinogenic drugs or, if you're lucky, chlamydia. So, in the hopes of fulfilling her plan, Claudia hijacked Arantxa's Tinder profile and texted all the people she had *matched* with without any preliminaries or Vaseline with the line "Do you have a boat?" They all laughed whenever she told that story and how unsuccessful her technique had been—of course, it would take a few more months for Netflix's *The Tinder Swindler* (2022) to come out and make us all realise the absolute mess they could have gotten into—but not me, because a thought invaded my mind, and took me back to when, on a regretfully vodka-filled night, courtesy of receiving the family pictures taken of my parents with my brother at my younger niece's first communion (to all intents and purposes, and judging by their faces, pictures that looked like they had been taken at gunpoint), I re-opened my Tinder account, I guess because I was in the mood of making deplorable decisions. And I soon got a text from a Spanish girl I had matched with, even though none of us took the first step to talk to the other...until, two weeks later, she suddenly texted those exact words to me: "Do / You / Have / A / Boat". And funnily enough, I did not have a boat but when we opened both our profiles back at Anna and Laura's place, I did have something else, as it turned out Arantxa and I had technically met each other before, when I became one of the victims of Claudia's capitalist impulses. It was a glorious moment, one that solidified our (by-then collectively shared) thought that this group somehow belonged together. We had found our final connexion.

Individually, both at work and when surrounded by sane people in public, we were calm and docile, like little endearing lambs merrily trotting along Swiss grazing fields. But together we were like putting Kanye West and Frances McDormand in the same room, forming chaotic energy bound to degenerate in the kind of memories one always chases and never wants to forget. Like that time we drove the DJ at *Village du Soir* out of his mind by taking turns to ask every person in the room to head over to his booth and incessantly ask him to play Farruko's *Pepas*—"*Arrete toi!*" he desperately cried at one point—until he reluctantly agreed...for the fifth time in a row to play such a melodic masterpiece. Or that evening when we found ourselves at a movie-themed indoor mini-golf and Anna broke a bottle of tequila and the entire glass counter during her first attempt at hitting the ball on the Fifty Shades of Grey-themed green, eventually seducing the bartender into not only getting away without paying for the damages caused, but somehow managing to make him prepare us *piña coladas* we did not even come close to paying, all night long. Or that time we went paragliding in *Annecy* and Lara puked all over the instructor mid-air, prompting him to forcibly swirl the sail and stumble upon a flock of sparrows that got inside his seat and tickled him into deviating his path right into a near-crash collision against an elderly lady trying to enjoy her paragliding birthday present, and effectively causing her a cardiopulmonary arrest that we assume—though have yet to confirm—eventually led her to a tardy grave. Or that sunny evening when we inexplicably made the decision to go paddle surfing all of us on the same massive board, and all it took was five minutes out of shore for us to reach a small yacht inhabited by two sixty-year-old men in the midst of their fifth divorce and awaiting arrest for a soon-to-be-discovered pyramid scheme, smoking cigars, making laughable efforts at covering their bald patches and drinking aged wine that smelled like the unpaid labour of the interns that had probably financed it. We quickly pretended to become friends with them by simulating our interest in real estate and offshore tax evasion, until they let us inside to get very drunk on their expensive wine. Hell, we even got one of them, an alcoholic who up until that day had spent nearly ten years sober, irresponsibly drunk to the point Michaela—for whom that day marked the first time in years since she had even come close to a boat—ended up being the one sailing the yacht back to the harbour herself…to inconclusive results.

And then one day, when we were having cold drinks at *Bains des Pâquis* and it looked like Lake Geneva had been emptied out just for us, admiring the sunset and the golden light reflected on our faces, I became fully aware of what I had, right then and there. The kind of thing you always search for and never realise until it's gone. Happiness, that's what it was. On my fingertips. With names and surnames. After I came back from my momentary trip to my private (and as of lately somewhat abandoned) inner world, I saw those ladies in their element, cracking jokes whilst eternally holding onto their cigarettes on one hand and gin and tonics on the other, and I realised how mathematically improbable it was to cross paths with someone— let alone an entire group of people—in a remote environment with whom you share tastes, vital perspectives and a common interest in each other's well-being. Indeed, I have seen many movies, and had (as well as observed other's) many friendships, at least enough to accurately spot the kind of people that make your life worth living from the moment you first meet them. It did not take a lot of thinking on my side to know that they easily fitted into that category.

A foreign feeling began to creep into my body, a blunt emotion that covered every inch of my being, an instinct that I had no right of having yet made me feel that somehow, things were starting to change—for the better, this time. It is funny, when you are in the right mood, in the right mindset, the perception of your reality radically changes, even if the entire world around you has remained the same, because while everything has remained static, you have not. Feeling as the earthly embodiment of the character about to be executed who, when faced with the impending prospect of a tangible death, felt how the limited moments ahead of him seemingly stretched in time (eventually becoming utterly unbearable, in his case), as the case described by Prince Myshkin in Dostoyevsky's *The Idiot*;

"an enormous wealth of time" of all the possibilities life could potentially have in store for me were unveiled before my eyes, one which had always been there before, only now it was being looked at from the right perspective. Like a colour-blinded woman who was suddenly presented with the chance to look at this multicoloured life of ours in all its splendour, I began to wonder about all the experiences had, all the movies seen and the songs listened to, the places visited and the parties avoided, that I had missed by my own hand, by my own willingness to be unhappy. When the remedy to the pain ailing you is at the tip of your fingers, one can either try to endow life with meaning by pursuing similar moments like that one for the rest of your existence, or dismiss this discovery as a one-off, as the product of a desperate mind who is dying for someone to save her and feels unworthy when someone finally does. But I would not be making the same mistake twice, after life had painfully taught me the importance of keeping close to us those people who make us feel like the persons we truly want to be, even if (and precisely when) we think we eventually never will. Most cases of depression and suicidal thoughts are rooted in the belief that this world has no place for us, no seat at the proverbial table. So now that I think about it, and leaving hyperbole out the door, those ladies saved my life, because I finally felt, somehow, that I belonged somewhere.

X

CONQUERORS AND CONQUERED

Regardless of how hard I tried to forget, it always found its way back: all the unbearable misery dragged across never-ending years that I endured in that house, the pain whose full extent only the walls had borne witness to and now anxiously awaited to welcome my arrival, the ever-ready nauseating anxiety which never for a day dared to fail attendance while I stayed under that roof for what amounted to a lifetime suffered in silence and excruciating agony. It was my birthday, after all, and coinciding with the fact everyone in Geneva was taking a few days off to visit their respective families for the summer, I decided to come back to spend this day—for a long time assumed to be my last, given the lengths my thoughts had been reaching—with my loved ones. It is important to bear in mind that, back then, I was in a state where my unreliable perception of reality made me foolishly use the term "loved ones" quite cautiously, as I stupidly believed out of all the people I was to encounter upon returning to Spain, there were only a few that I really loved, and fewer even that I truly liked. Out of my closer friends, most of whom had taken a backseat in my life as I had in theirs while I was away, Mónica worked long hours so nobody ever saw her anymore, Antonio and Miriam had started aggressively dating and only had eyes for one another, Luna was abroad on a student exchange program, and Sara had simultaneously enrolled in two master's degrees, effectively depriving her of a social life already scarce in the midst of everyone else's priorities having been recently rearranged. So, during those months we were like the Baldwin brothers: still tied together by an unbreakable bond, yet each of us following a *very* different path in our respective lives.

We did text every couple of days, to mutually let us know about recent developments—them, confiding in me their intimate inner troubles in the hopes of getting some guidance from this old dog who has seen far too many films to know what should be done yet remained utterly incapable of applying those same pieces of advice to herself (why is it that the people who give the best advice are the ones who need it the most for themselves?); me, being perfectly aware that my suicidal tendencies would instantly make their blood run cold and radically change the dynamic of our entire relationship, given that the massive scope of the problem understandably fell well out of their purview, thus relegating myself to only letting them know about the most trivial parts of my life, the punchlines, the funny stories into which I constantly managed to turn all the misfortunes that happened to me (as well as the ones of my own making), perhaps in an effort to let them sleep well at night thinking nothing at all was rotten in the state of Denmark.

We also called one another at least once a week so that the sound of our voices would not turn into a distant memory. But it certainly was a drastic change to radically switch from seeing one another virtually every day to exchanging a few text messages over the course of the week. But quantity can never be more fulfilling than quality, and relegating our contact to fewer instances made them feel more special and substantial, even in the absence of my verbalisation of the reality whose existence I kept hiding from everyone but myself.

Only somewhat healthy friendships with strong foundations, carefully and unexpectedly built over countless years filled with non-replicable experiences, could stand the test of time, the concealment of the devastatingly inflammatory affliction that internally corroded me, and the thousands of kilometres that for nearly four months and a half had separated us, without significant alterations to the pillars of the building which our friendship symbolised. Or at least that was what I thought until I arrived, and a dose of reality came out of the oven and smacked me right in the face when nobody came to pick me up at the airport upon my arrival. My parents were enjoying an express one-day trip to a SPA in the mountains, courtesy of my anniversary gift to them, the monetary effects of which I am still recovering from, while all my friends mysteriously alleged to have been busy with convoluted excuses and implausible last-minute commitments. The truth behind their absence at the airport was that they had all gathered at Sara's place to prepare my surprise dinner party on that evening, but since I was unaware of it at that moment, and would take months to get rid of that toxic feeling and come to that seemingly-obvious conclusion, I couldn't help but feel that I would have liked to be someone else's priority for once, taking into account it was my birthday and that I had not seen them all for quite a long time. Not only because I knew I would have done it for them, but mainly because I had in the past.

Thus, after the plane landed, I took the train from Madrid's airport straight back home, then pushed my far-too-overweight luggage for approximately a mile until I reached our humble neighbourhood. Located right across the city's largest mall, and barely a ten-minute walk away from the *Castilla-La Mancha University*, my home stood right at the epicentre of all places worth going to and of all gossip worth learning about in the city, certainly instigated by having virtually all student homes surrounding our nearby streets. As I walked along the avenues of my beloved Albacete, the foundation of the layers upon layers of self-delusion that I had carefully built around the elephant not-in-the-room-yet-about-to-finally-be, began to tremble as I reached into my pocket in search of my house keys…and came to the gut-wrenching realisation that I had left them back in Geneva. With no other option but to ring the doorbell and let Him open the door for me, given that by my own estimation my parents were still anywhere from four to seven hours away, I found myself gasping for air, fearing the encounter that was about to take place, and hoping to get out of there as quickly and unharmed as possible. As if the Bard himself had written this tragedy, I swallowed my pride and my grandmother's genes came afloat in the shape of the deliriously optimistic thought that He would just open the door without any further conflict. That would be all. No need to panic, we were all grown-ups.

"And who knows," I thought, "perhaps he's changed whilst I have been away." No doubt he had changed. For the worse.

You see, preparing for the worst possible outcome in pretty much any situation is something that I tend to prioritise over wishful thinking and empty prayers for a best-case-scenario, if nothing else for my mental health, as it saves me the trouble of crushing disappointment. But even though I am not a praying kind of person, when faced with your worst fears, with the author of your pain, a person you are forever cursed to share a surname with, and in the presence of even the slightest chance to get out of there having endured as little damage as possible, even the most atheist person on Earth would turn into a believer. When I rang the doorbell, after noticing that the light in the kitchen was on and saw somebody had moved the curtains inside to take a peek at the person standing on the street, I knew that I should have done a little less praying and a lot more preparing for the worst-case-scenario, as it turned out my brother's endemic inability to put a halt to the corrosive hatred he inexplicable felt for my very existence not only remained unchallenged, but had in fact been invigorated over the course of my absence. I guess it's on me, for underestimating the power of sheer hatred—after all, it is what makes the world go round. Displaying a desperately urgent need for personal growth and in a move very much in-character, he refused to come down the stairs to open the door. And so, I kept ringing again and again, for what felt like an entire hour, and in fact became longer than that; and so, he kept ignoring my presence at the door of what once I had thought to be my home. From the comfort of their houses, I could see curious neighbours peeking through their windows, their initial discrete looks transforming into reprimanding ones after forcing them to incessantly listen to the annoying tune of my doorbell.

Just as I was about to give up my seemingly futile efforts, I heard some footsteps inside the house, and immediately the lock on the door began to be slowly unlocked. As the door began to seemingly open in slow motion, I had to remind myself to breathe and stand strong, no matter what. Nothing had prepared me for this encounter which I hoped with every bone in my body I was somehow spared of. When he finally opened the door, it was as if two strangers, in every sense of the word, locked eyes in the middle of a busy morning on the public transport. After spending years avoiding contact with him, making an effort not to direct my gaze in his direction during car trips and family dinners, mentally blurring his face in pictures and blocking him on social media, I realised I had forgotten what his face looked like, and it took me a few instances to recognize the person that had been responsible for my self-enforced eviction of my own home. There he was, looking like a recently escaped inmate of the Guantanamo Bay prison, the glorified cum sock that I was forced to call my brother Diego.

Always an unassertive, skinny little boy with a prominent skull-complexion and almost see-through skin that made the veins on his face look like prison tattoos, the bullying he suffered at school at the hands of those who made fun of his squalid physique progressively determined the code of conduct which he would end up applying in his later life, building a resentment towards himself he became so sick of he had no other choice but to vomit out of his system and into the nearest target, which I was lucky enough to be. This Napoleonic bitterness only worsened over time, as he realised he had been cursed with the face his actions deserved: a crooked, aquiline nose that covered half of his mole-filled face; round, corpse-like eyes, deeply embedded into his skull, of a tone of grey so clear it became hard to distinguish when he was rolling his eyes as if possessed by the devil he enjoyed incarnating from when he was just staring at you with his spiteful gaze; a small head accentuated by two large, slightly bent forward ears he seldom cleansed, at each end; his virtually non-existent lips unable to contain the long rows of yellowish teeth which popped out of his mouth; all topped with a hideous odour resulting from a combination of poor dental health, distaste for deodorant, and constant use of muscle-developing remedies, a potent mephitic *bouquet* which followed him around everywhere he went, announcing his presence long before he entered a room, and letting everybody know of his appearance long after he had left.

Diego found refuge, once he turned sixteen, in the world of

gymnastics and steroids, and it did not take him long to fall down the rabbit hole of a delusional reality where he could potentially have a chance at finally being happy with himself, in the shape of dumbbells and protein shakes. If he had a good-looking body then perhaps others would accept him, and after they did, perhaps he could himself, too. Being only a few years younger than him, I confided in my friends that this decision secretly made me happy, as it potentially meant his toxic aggressiveness would be drowned out, and the environment at home would be noticeably less testosterone-charged, which for the first months made me sleep a little better at night, knowing that at the very least he would be getting the peace he needed and no longer felt the necessity to disrupt my own. But, having conquered the summit of carefully traceless abuse, the gym only made the ongoing fire burn brighter than ever, as his initially verbal attacks progressively acquired a physical dimension, and I no longer felt even remotely safe in the comfort of my home in the presence of an abuser with the strength to overpower me and the will to consistently do so. Diego found in the gym the ability to take control of his body, sharpening his thug mentality of paying the pain forward in the hopes of letting go of the agony of being himself, which only emboldened his actions, no longer camouflaged in the midst of nobody to stand up to him.

And so, we quickly entered into a dynamic not dissimilar to the one most recently portrayed in *The Power of the Dog* (2021), where, by someone else's hand, I had become permanently uncomfortable in my own house in the face of someone who took pleasure in torturing others into lowering to his level of misery, thus ending up relegated to the confines of my room, aching with every step he took, trying to find solace in any form of evasion from reality available at my disposal. The person he had been all along was revealed for everyone to see, in plain sight, yet not a soul dared contradict the vision of reality he kept trying to shove down our throats. Even though the invisible abuse had become evidently perceptible, its non-resolvability led my parents to implement a policy of blindness and complacency that drowned out the few complaints I attempted to raise on the matter, and ended up turning such a stark reality into the norm for the many years to come: my mother, never prepared to have that conversation and pursuing an empathetic approach that justified her disposition to act like there was no conversation that needed to be had in the first place, despite her occasional attempts to expand her horizons; my father, opting to choose comfort in his silence for many years, an indecipherable mystery until the cathartic moment upon my return home during the summer, which came much too late and long after far too much damage had already taken its (potentially deadly) toll.

And now, there we were: two people who used to be blood before they were darkness, now unrecognizable to one another in the presence of decades-long pain that instantly labelled us as combatants with fundamentally different visions of reality, and placed us both on opposing sides, immutably so, rendering impossible any attempt to put a peaceful end to our fraternal conundrum, especially conditioned by his inability to even consider such a possibility. Without even as much as a gesture acknowledging my presence, and before my blood started to boil over the accumulated pain I had endured as a result of childhood trauma we both never managed to get past, I put my hand on the door with the intention of coming inside my home. Before I could do that, he violently shut the door and swiftly locked it without any hint of remorse, as if he had spent the entire day rehearsing this moment, salivating with anticipation. With a smirk on his face, he put his headphones on and vehemently bumped into me with his shoulder with so much impetus and unrestrained rage it almost threw me down the stairs, and began walking down the street, cheerfully saying "hello" to the neighbours without a worry on his twisted mind. In all honesty, I was not expecting anything from him, not even the delivery of an insincere "happy birthday" at gunpoint in case the two of us would be in the same room with the rest of the family, as it had happened once before, a gesture that, as you can imagine, meant everything to my mother and absolutely nothing to me. But even if this was to be expected, it did not make it any less hurtful. This thought was carried away by the incoming rain, which left all my clothes and luggage completely soaking wet before I could even reach the bus stop across the street to protect myself from the storm. Cold, alone, and desperate, making an effort to forget the fact that it was my birthday on that filthy corner where I used to wait each morning for the bus to take me to school, I finally broke down in tears, completely helpless, after the realization that this problem was never going to go away became clearer than it ever had before.

Pain, like love or justice, is an impossibly abstract concept that resists definition despite the many attributed to it. What is painful for some may not necessarily be unbearable for others, and the amount of resistance to it—as well as the conditions under which one suffers it—vary significantly from person to person. The pain I experienced was visible at first; the scars and bruises that often covered my body were so frequent at one point I felt like they were never going to heal, and I would always have them tattooed onto my skin, something which, much to my attempts to clarify their origin to anybody who would listen, he successfully trumped by attributing to my absent-minded nature and never to his perverted traumas and inferiority complex. The worst part was they all believed him. Denying that growing up in a conservative family, where the older sibling tended to be right, did not play an important role in the collective imaginary of the events witnessed by my family, would be to blindly reject a very tangible reality that meddled with the creation of my personality's building blocks. After having established himself as someone who in the eyes of all spoke the truth, and with the certainty that every word that came out of my mouth was instantly labelled to be of dubious veracity given his thorough efforts to clearly delimit the role that I was to play in everyone else's minds, the cogs inside his perverted brain started to turn. His kind of evil is so pernicious, so self-assured, so tragically effective, that it does not feel the need to hide its face, in view of having been overwhelmingly accepted as part of the circle of life, allowing it to break out of its confinement and no longer feel the need to act quietly and in abandoned places, as it can now operate in plain daylight with no repercussions whatsoever.

When he reached that point, he promptly entered into the second phase of his long-gestated plan: when you establish a lie at a sufficiently frequent pace, and for a repeated number of times, there is no other choice for people but to assume that such fiction must be reality, thus establishing a pattern of conduct and linking any kind of similar behaviour to the person you have been pushed into believing is responsible in the first place. Because after bruises came bone fractures, and after came being blamed for the money he took from my mother's purse and the alcohol he drank from my father's cabinet, and the windows that were broken after he played soccer inside the house, and the TV he smashed in a state of rage after being dumped by his girlfriend at the time, and the cigarettes and porn magazines he hid under my bed. The image everyone had of me in my family was, to say the least, soul-crushing, particularly because there was nothing I could do to swim against such a powerfully crafted stream of believable lies, which by now had become common knowledge shared by all members of the family and close friends. It would take me years of hard work at school and countless hours of depriving myself from playtimes, parties and other social gatherings in order to excel in my exams, a territory where he no longer had as much agency as he did in other fields—although he missed no chance to make the most out of us sharing contiguous rooms by routinely playing his music at deafening volumes whenever it became known to him that our parents were no longer at home—to wipe away this image he had carefully built of myself for me against my will. Not unlike the disturbing reality portrayed in *The Hunt* (2012), once you open the door to the mere possibility (not necessarily the certain occurrence) of a reality too distressing to bear, the inherent irresistibility endows such perception others have of you with an everlasting longevity, with the image of yourself in the mind of others becoming more powerful than ever for the easiness with which it is to picture it and the near impossibility of ever forgetting. Thus, despite my laborious efforts to show my unequivocal innocence and prove the incompatibility between myself and the version of myself in their mind, the legacies of such a long and pervasively persuasive image of myself which my brother took good care in propagating are still felt today, when I continue to be subjected to comments in the vein of "You used to be a little devil when you were a kid," and "Oh, how you've changed since you would pickpocket our wallets at family dinners." It seemed like neither my parents nor the rest of our family were able to see past this illusion, and so the image of whom he presented himself as being, and the one he presented myself with being, remained unblemished, year after year.

The invisible pain one wears inside, the one that cannot be traced, the one you carry for all of your life and tears wounds so deep it makes you curse the day you were put on this earth—that was his favourite kind. He understood far too quickly that my wounds from his outbursts eventually healed, and the stoicness he forced me to develop meant he had to turn to a different target, my mother, to take on the mantle of the victim. That way, we all suffered, one from the blows and one from being forced to witness them. But as hard as I tried to develop a certain numbness that acquired not only a physical but also an emotional dimension, I always found the little things to be the hardest to withstand, far more than anything else. Because they could happen anywhere, in any form, at any time, and their profitability for their creator never ceased to grow. The hurtful comments launched quietly enough to be registered by my targeted ears only, the packages I ordered home and found almost smashed in the trash with marks indicating someone had clearly stepped on them and wanted me to notice, the top-to-bottom looks at me whenever I was about to go out and the giggling that proceeded after, the disappearance of my favourite clothes from my closet, the erasure of countless of pictures from my childhood from family albums... The never-ending hate which had become the fifth component of our family.

One case which encapsulates the kind of person he truly was, was the way in which he would violently kick my door every single morning to wake me up hours before I was supposed to go to work, being fully aware that I, a light sleeper, was unable to go back to sleep once awakened. He continued this twisted impulse, randomly waking me up each day at a different time, thus rendering me completely incapable of anticipating his actions. Worst of all, this began to affect me before going to bed, constantly worrying about not falling asleep in time before he would come waking me up at unpredictable hours of the early morning. On those occasions when I tried to confront him, fully aware such an impulse would bring me nowhere, he would claim to be on his way to the bathroom, like that time he woke me up at two a.m. in the middle of my finals week, prompting me to finally go off and lose all control, shouting at him in the middle of the night and waking my parents up in the process. Given my mother had an exceptional ability to justify it all, whilst my father had a remarkable gift to ignore it all, my complaints were easily dismissed as, from their side, it looked exactly like what he wanted it to look like.

"Go to bed, both of you. And you, young lady, we will talk tomorrow about going to that therapist. You should know better than throwing these tantrums in the middle of the night, you're too old for this kind of behaviour," my somnolent mother managed to say, confirming that I had become the embodiment of the character Thomasin in *The VVitch* (2015), the person in the family nobody believed anymore and whom everybody blamed for their own shortcomings—emotional or otherwise.

Certainly nothing to be proud of, my brother Diego had an exceptional ability to learn with distressing exactitude that which you loved most, and subsequently come up with a way to prevent you from enjoying it any longer. In my case, he always hated that I loved movies as much as I did, because my father and I had formed a tight bond around the Seventh Art, with Dad having introduced me to the world of the Marx Brothers, Harold Lloyd and Buster Keaton from an early age. And it corroded his insides to know that every time I sat in my room to watch a movie in the hopes of evading myself and being transported into a different universe, I suddenly became out of his reach. There was nothing that I loved more as a kid than, after having finished homework every day, sitting down with my father to watch one of the classic movies from his treasured, massive film collection that covered the entire walls from the office he had built for himself in our home's basement. Shelf after shelf was filled with the amateur films he made while he was a kid, and with the precious copies of movies hard to find anywhere else in the world—the result of off the grid auctions and friends in important places—and the kind of movies for which putting a price tag would be a futile task. But when he had to start working extra hours to pay for my brother's private school tuition for the seventh year in a row, he started arriving home at night-time, so with his permission I started to watch them on my own. It was a territory that only my father and I inhabited, a taste Diego had not acquired and had developed no interest in, as it seldom revolved around boobs, soccer or both.

But as everything mildly fulfilling that came into my life, all's unwell that ends unwell, as my movie sessions down in my father's basement did not go unnoticed by my brother, who suddenly felt the need to inexplicably start moving furniture each time he saw me heading downstairs. All efforts to try and rise above the toxicity oozing through every corner of our home were deemed unsuccessful, as the relentless dedication he poured into preventing me from harmlessly enjoying my movie sessions after long days of studying never ceased to pay off, constantly and effective immediately taking me out of the experience. Thus, regardless of the quality portrayed on those films, I became unable to enjoy the beauty of the images projected, all efforts thwarted even in the presence of the kind of noise-cancelling headphones used by construction workers. His presence and his absence were notably felt and equally feared, the former due to his pseudo-torturing activities and the latter due to the possibility of his presence. Peace and quiet became scarce commodities, but it was when the occasional occurrence of mild entertainment was thrown out the window for good, never again to be considered attainable, that my long-term existence ceased to be a certainty, and what and who I was and why and where I stood no longer were apparent, anymore.

By far, my favourite of Dad's movies was a short film beautifully titled "*The Tomato Affair*"—his first short film, shot with the Super 8 camera he received as a present for his thirteenth birthday, a story which revolved around a resurrected mummy (played by my late grandfather) obsessed with eating breadcrumbs with his *gazpacho*. Despite the little artistic value of this amateur ghost story he recorded with his friends when he was the age that I was when the described events transpired, I loved to watch it again and again, not only because it was one of the few recordings we had of my grandfather, but especially because I could see in those frames the person that my father would grow out to be and the person whose daughter I was proud to be. A couple of days went by when I was unable to watch any movies due to a heavy exam period, which used to leave me too exhausted to even hear my door being kicked in the mornings. But on a December night that to this day I painfully remember with the exactitude only traumatic memories can evoke, I was woken up from a deep sleep by my father yelling my full name, as he only did whenever I found myself in deep trouble. While I slowly walked down the stairs, still in the midst of exiting a dreamlike state, I saw my dad holding in his hands a white cloth with a few uneven pieces of what appeared to be a broken CD.

"*The Tomato Affair*" had now been completely destroyed. After swearing in between tears and copious sobbing that I had nothing to do with such an outcome, that it would make no sense for me to damage in any way the film that I so dearly loved, he phoned Grandma Gabriela, her mother, who had "taken care of us" that evening (and by that, what I mean is she locked herself up in the attic with a bottle of Gordon's, a bag of ice and her old portable radio), and she promptly confirmed she had seen me going into my father's studio that evening, having witnessed me doing so many other times before and fearing my father's repercussions in his state of anger would lead him to dig in a little deeper into her whereabouts on that evening. The accusations I laid against my brother were immediately dismissed by Grandma Gabriela, who went as far as to swear on my grandfather's grave that not only was my brother Diego innocent, but he had actually been in his room studying during the entire day, setting an example for his little sister. Like a game of the insensitively named *Chinese Whispers*, the truth was distorted and diluted along the way, particularly when there was no truth to begin with. Because in this world it does not matter who you are or what you do, only what others think you are and are convinced you have done. My father did not speak to me for three entire months, rendering my efforts at school meaningless by sending me to a reformatory up in Zaragoza until the following September, to "finally make me come to my senses", senses to which I had come to long ago, unlike everyone else around me, apparently.

And I'm sure you're right now thinking, dear Reader, "what a bunch of fools your family members were, how could they not know?" But the truth is that we never truly know what happens on someone else's household. And when you have an eloquent teenager describing the horrible things that a little girl did—

always at the hospital for getting into trouble, a liar, a thief who was consistently behind every single thing that went wrong at our family, and who even tortured her dear brother by incessantly playing her music as loud as she could to intently disrupt his sleep cycles—was very much consistent with the kind of person he had convinced others I actually was. And that kind of reality where the defenceless one is predetermined not to be believed regardless of what she says, is a much too seductive spell to fall under, rather than taking some time to actually understand the force depravedly operating behind it all. With reality being distorted, and the pain on my body camouflaged and accepted, my brother carefully staged his psychological manipulations at the right time so that I would finally go off right whenever he wanted me to: in front of an audience. And thus, they only saw the trick, not the magician operating behind it. So, I was sent to all kinds of psychiatrists who wanted to help me deal with my "emotional instability" and my "inability to control impulses". And I must admit that I was indeed in need of help, but I just felt it was funny how you put on trial the person whose throat has been strangled (physically and metaphorically) instead of the one doing the strangling.

Back then, the predominant stigma which dictated that going to a psychiatrist was something that only crazy people did was very much present—and is still being currently enforced, albeit to a lesser degree. Every session in which that creepy woman with her lipstick all over her teeth and her fake Pedro del Hierro suits asked me why I thought I needed to be receiving such treatment, I felt like standing up and saying, "Well, doctor, I need to come visit a psychiatrist's office three times a week because the people that really should be coming here instead of me, actually won't". But I knew that level of insight for a precocious child forced by her circumstances to relinquish her childhood and graceful innocence, would ring all the wrong bells and land me right straight into a mental institution. So I went along with her hypnotherapy sessions and learnt absolutely nothing except my parents were struggling financially and forking out one-hundred euros a session for a middle-aged, white-privileged lady with two divorces and a questionable involvement in hedge funds to waste nearly fifty minutes of my time (and hers) by playing "relaxing" music of Gregorian chants in the background whilst explaining in far too much detail how to breathe deeply when having an anxiety attack, instead of being useful and helping me deal with (and hopefully eventually overcome) my abundant traumas— you know, the kind of thing one comes to expect from a therapist. What followed was a couple more sessions I made at the behest of trying to invest in my parent's mental health, where I pretended to make progress to calm their nerves and let them sleep better at night, while also making a remarkable effort to get out of there as soon as possible, because I was depressed enough to know that I was in need of emotional assistance, but also smart enough to realise that that lady's office was not the place where I would be getting any of the useful help I desperately needed.

And so, with no bearable or useful solution within reach for this scared little girl, the cancer he had been meticulously planting kept growing, log after log, year after year, day after day, a fire in my brain which would progressively lead the self-destructive thoughts I had been having from as early a time as when I was nine years of age, into its natural lethal destination: a tombstone I craved for and soon began to think I deserved. But even though the proverbial match was lit on numerous occasions, a result of loving myself too little or hating him far too much, it never reached the gasoline-impregnated pile that would lead to a harrowing explosion, with the rational hemisphere of my brain eventually emerging victorious. This struggle was kept away from my parents, as revealing this would entail that my brother was right all along, that the reality which I had worked so hard to avoid from materialising had actually come to pass, because letting them know of my inner troubles would mean that I had become exactly the monster that my brother Diego had deluded us all into thinking I was. Thus, with the lies having acquired the status of truth, the prophecy would be fulfilled after he had trapped the last survivor of common sense under his puppeteer strings: myself. Rarely have I ever felt so identified onscreen as when I saw George Cukor's masterful *Gaslight* (1944) and saw in myself the vulnerable Paula being constantly fed distorted fragments of reality in an environment relatively malleable for the person in control. Just imagine what that kind of suffering can cause on a child's body and mind. The constant feeling of neglect, of incomprehension, of lack of belief in oneself, of conceiving the person that you are as inferior to anybody else, as unworthy of love and affection and understanding. If anybody should be refusing to open up doors to anyone, it should be no other than me; I believe I have more than earned that right.

In retrospect, I guess what bothered me most was his lack of remorse, his ability to absent-mindedly walk around the house like he was paying the bills, pretending we all remained unaware he had not worked a day in his life, like that scene in *Atonement* (2007) when the rapist played by Benedict Cumberbatch comfortably takes a nap on the sofa while the police set out to question (and blame) an innocent (albeit somewhat excessively horny) gentleman played by James McAvoy. His capacity for deep sleep night after night contrasted highly with my insomnia and made me wonder how a person with so much to be sorry for could be able to sleep so peacefully, so unrepentantly. Did he even have a conscience? If he did, I am not sure he would even know.

After hours of staring at gravity carrying away the pouring rain into the sewer, I was (probably for the better) taken out of my momentary trance down into the endless pit of dangerous thoughts by my parent's car entering our street—just the kind of Deus ex machina I was in desperate need of. We shared a long, warm and much-needed hug, and went inside the house. You see, parents are like unobstructed nostrils or toilet paper: their presence is rarely appreciated and usually taken for granted, but it's their absence that is truly felt and should be feared by all. It was only when I found myself in the same room as them since I had left for a better life in Switzerland, that I realised how much I had really missed these perfectly flawed yet boundlessly kind human beings. We spoke for a while in the hall before deciding to order some Chinese takeout for a late lunch/early dinner. It had been eight hours since I had arrived at the station, twelve since I left Geneva, so I was naturally starving to the point of questioning my vegetarian belief system in the presence of a succulent roast beef in the fridge that seemed to be enticingly whispering my name.

"And why were you waiting out there, all on your own? Don't you have your keys with you?" my mother asked as we awaited the food delivery.

"I left them at the flat, I forgot to carry them with me, I guess" I replied, being fully aware that such a statement would be followed by Mom's characteristic "Oh, my dear, always losing things! One of these days you're gonna lose your head." And it was. It just rolled off her tongue.

"What a shame that you had to wait outside in the rain. If

only you had arrived a bit earlier, your brother could have let you in," she said, paying absolutely no attention to the damage she was about to cause. This kind of behaviour meant the legacies of the person my brother had built me to become in their eyes, were still very much present. Once again, it makes one think how a single comment can trigger the most horrid of acts; how an innocent remark could make the unthinkable become the inevitable for a person with as fragile a disposition as mine. And my constrained reaction of not taking the bait and entering the purposeless conversation I had had a thousand times too many revolving around my brother Diego, was the best that I could do to keep this family away from a permanent fracture. Given such a conversation was one bound to arrive at no clear destination whatsoever, as had happened time and time again in the past, I resigned myself to following the same cycle that had been in place in my family: I swallowed the pain to keep my mother from experiencing it herself. It is heart-breaking when the one doing the harm labels the one doing the damage control as the culprit, but some are put on Earth to do the working and some to do the collecting. However, this time something was different, not on hers but on my father's face. He looked at me, truly looked at me, and nodded, as if he understood, as if he knew exactly what had just happened, as if I had finally found some witnesses to corroborate my reality, my own floating wooden panel across the mad ocean I was forced to swim in every time I stepped foot on that house.

Omitting this incident, the three of us actually had a great time, as we usually did when left on our own. They filled me in on the juiciest local gossip, I gave them some brief updates on the latest trips made with the girls in Geneva and the lack of exciting (or otherwise) developments at work, and we remained happy in our ignorance of the painful episodes that had happened in each other's absence which we chose to keep from one another to try to enjoy our presence as much as we could. My father and I had a similar sense of humour, and always made a never-disclosed competition to see who could make my mother laugh first, a woman who laughed frightfully little for the amount of joy she brought into the world. She was a sufferer first and an enjoyer second, meaning that she would be the one helping people out of a burning building, and the last one to leave, the one breaking her back on her job as a schoolteacher in spite of her advanced age in order to provide for her family, and, above all, the one willing to suffer in silence the pain of having two children who (in her mind) inexplicably hated one another in order to continue having a family to speak of.

As we carried on with our conversation, enjoying each other's company and planning our forthcoming trip (they were going to come visit me in Switzerland two weeks from then), I sat back to take the entire moment in, and saw the way they looked at each other. Two people who had never dated anyone else except each other, who had been through all the phases a couple could go through, and still managed to retain nothing but an abundance of love for one another. When one looks at the world, at the rising divorces and the decreasing rates of marriage, at the toxic nature of most relationships—all with a characteristic expiration date—it would be easy, and statistically reasonable, to assume true love is a hoax. But they keep proving to me and to the world at large that 1) genuinely everlasting love does exist for some people, if you are willing to work hard enough to find it and be resilient enough to fight to keep it; 2) you should only marry people that you love, but more importantly, people that you *like*; 3) a marriage is not sustained on emotion, or spark, or on surprising your partner, or on spicing things up—a marriage is a full-time job, which is why steps one and two are so important in the first place.

This brief internal deliberation was interrupted when, out of the corner of my eye, I managed to see the small shadow of a dark figure standing outside, peeking through our window. At first, I assumed it to be the person delivering the food we had just ordered, but I eventually dismissed that theory and opted to believe it was someone who might have stepped onto the wrong house, and so we continued planning our exciting trip across Swiss landscapes. My mother was only a few months away until she finally reached her retirement age and finally left her energy-draining, physically taxing, often thankless teaching job, providing the perfect opportunity to travel around the world with my father, which made her eyes glimmer with a palpable excitement which manifested itself each time she spoke about it, a kind of excitement which I suspected we had deprived her of showing with as much frequency as someone as graceful and tender-hearted as her, truly deserved.

Right after my father let out one of his remorselessly poisonous farts, our gathering was abruptly interrupted by the sound of my mother's phone ringtone.

"Hello, darling. (…) WHAT? But…but are you okay? (…) Oh, dear, are you sure? (…) We're on our way, honey, don't you worry, we're coming to pick you up," she said, before hanging up the phone. "I'm sorry, dear: we have to leave, your brother's car has broken down in the middle of the highway," she said. "Iván, let's go," she said to my father. They picked up their coats and prepared to immediately leave. "I'm sorry, honey, we will celebrate your birthday tomorrow, I promise. But right now, your brother needs us," she said before closing the door behind her.

"And so do I, Mom. And so do I," I thought. So, there I was, alone in my own house, on my birthday, where once again my brother Diego had managed to monopolize all eyes on him. This utterly talentless man still possessed an exceptional ability to ruin my days in the most discrete and unnoticeable of ways. With Geneva now completely outside of my mind, I found myself metaphorically holding a lit match right next to the pile of flammable agony he had carefully assembled just for me during all those years. And the fire had never looked so real, and the need to put it out had never felt so unnecessary.

XI

LIGHT AND SHADOWS

My arrival at my own birthday party was marked by a lack of enthusiasm on my part, which I made every effort humanly possible to hide in the face of my friends' notable dedication to organize a special occasion just for me, and by the impending feeling that I was not deserving of being there in the first place, as I arrived at Sara's house with the emotional backlash of the recent events still freshly imprinted upon my already fragile soul. With my characteristically limited consciousness and attention span, I wandered from empty conversation to empty conversation, pretending my mind was not completely elsewhere and doing my best to acknowledge all the effort my friends were putting into making this night stand out—for the right reasons this time. Sara's radiating smile and natural aptitude to provoke in me therapeutic laughter continued to incessantly challenge the views of those who claimed that deep down, we are nothing but our traumas, because, at the end of the day, most of what we are is not determined by our unshut wounds, but by the people that we surround ourselves with...or such is the truth I aspire to believe in. Luna calmed me down, as she always did, after I finished venting out my hypochondriac theories about the imperishable tachycardia which had ferociously re-emerged that very night after weeks of total disappearance—the described symptoms were apparently within normal parameters, considering my energy-engulfing depressed propensity, which entailed natural death was unluckily not on the cards for me, or so kept everyone saying.

And even though I had made a mental note not to cry before dessert, I was ultimately unable to mask my feelings any longer after Mónica asked me how the reunion went with my parents. The hesitation it took me to finally reach something that resembled an answer, paired with the nonsensical mess that came out of my mouth, confirmed what they already suspected. Because while I was never able to get the support from my family on such complex matter, all guilty of being immersed in their different degrees of complicity, my friends had become my de facto therapists, the only ones who remained immune to the "Peter and the Wolf" myth being effectively spread amongst my family, and the ones with whom I could be completely candid about the reality that had been imposed upon me without the fear of incredulity or retaliation for speaking out. Having entered into the entire ordeal by leaving all preconceptions at the door, they had become more than acquainted over the years with the real person behind it all, behind the mind games and the fractures on my family's emotional well-being.

With this problem having been left undealt with for so long, it had become prominent enough over the years to the point of having rearranged my priorities and rescheduled my entire day-to-day life, forever altering the way I behaved both at home and outside of it, no longer feeling safe, at ease or comfortable in my own house, my own family, or my own skin. The problem of living with the constant fear and tension that I experienced materialised in the eventual survivability skills that I developed by doing the worst thing one can do in that situation: getting used to it. Being always exposed to the likely outcome of crossing paths with him made me feel like each time I dared leave my room I was permanently being forced to drive one of the trucks in *The Wages of Fear* (1953), in which every step I took down the stairs had the possibility of becoming an opportunity for him to step up and come up with a way to ruin my day in the way only he knew how to.

Forever active and physically incapable of stopping for a single second this twisted web he had managed to wrap all around me, instead of taking some quality time for a much-needed process of self-reflection, the worst part of his actions became the holiday period, where it almost seemed like all was forgotten once Christmas arrived and he laid on my parents' feet a myriad of gifts whose legal status left a lot to be desired, to say the least. A dick-measuring contest in which my intern salary prevented me from actually competing, the results of which were later on preached to the rest of the family so they could all know exactly how much each of us cared about our parents. Part of me wants to think it was his way of demonstrating his love for them: with material elements, in the presence of his inability to do so at an emotional, intangible level. Gifted clothes will likely be worn off with time, colognes will be used and cease to exist, and books will be read and forgotten, so I found comfort in thinking that my parents were intelligent enough to see beyond the shockingly obvious attempts to win their love in the short run by a person who would clearly be the first one to abandon them at the very first sight of a need for emotional support, the first one to flee once funerals and bureaucratic processes would begin, the first one to offer gifts when it mattered least yet the last one to appear when you needed him most.

This constant state of anxiety he effectively enforced upon me did not remain within the compounds of our home, however, as he developed a penchant for obsessively following me whenever I left the house precisely in the hopes of escaping the way he made me feel and the nauseating environment he had single-handedly created. Following the third movie screening where I casually saw him sitting in the front rows, pretending to (be able to) read the credits rolling on the silver screen, I stopped going to the movies altogether, unless I was certain he was out of the country, mostly during holidays. Then came the four different gyms I enrolled myself in after seeing him night after night, exercising in the machines right next to mine—him being perfectly aware of that I considered that place a refuge I *had* to go to so as to let off steam and forget about him for a while. It did not take him long before he emerged successful in his attempts to make me quit going to the gym altogether. I even stopped going out with my friends to nightclubs, as he always inexplicably found a way to be at the same places I went to, however random they may have been. And even if he wasn't there, he ruined the night nonetheless, as I knew fully well that as soon as I stepped through the door whenever I returned home and tried to get some decent sleep, he would immediately get out of bed to slam his fists on my door and wake this light sleeper again and again by purposefully engaging in ultimately trivial yet considerably noisy behaviour for the remainder of the day.

After a while, I no longer had the strength to continue having the same incessant thought in my mind, so I stopped going out altogether because I never knew if I was going to be forced to see him or not, but the prospect that I did was a sufficient incentive for me to stay at home. Going outside on my own was no longer possible, as I was always accompanied by the asphyxiating presence of the incessant thought looming over me at every corner I turned, every subway station I entered and every café I stopped by. Thus, I became a domestic animal, meekly repurposed to fit his needs, ultimately unable to enjoy even life's most simple pleasures. Perennially weary of making any noise at home that would reveal my presence or activities within my room, always listening to his moves and looking for a moment where he was no longer around to get out of my cave, my existence became entirely determined by someone else's choices. My life, no longer my own.

The problem was that my friends did what they could—and a little more than anybody typically would—to help me survive under such conditions. In fact, on more than one occasion where we encountered him at the club we went to, they, in an attack of bravery arising from their collective realization that my inability to stand up to him stemmed not from cowardice but from years of experiencing nothing but harsher retaliation every time I tried to confront him, made an attempt to let him know he was not welcome there. Yet, they were ultimately treated with the same frustratingly condescending replies my parents experienced every time he got caught performing one of his tricks in broad daylight, without following the precautions he typically did. A frustrating and seemingly unresolvable situation of such magnitude, big enough to taint all aspects of my life in some form or another, revealed both my friends and myself were all comprehensively unequipped—and admitted as much to me—to help me deal with it all, with answers such as "why don't they kick him out" or "have you tried talking to him?", constantly filling up our conversations every time I brought up the topic, as if those had never crossed my mind, and as if they would have been remotely effective. How could my parents kick him out of their house for something they didn't believe in the first place he was guilty of? How could they delude themselves into thinking that driving a car against a wall was not going to end in a violent crash, as it had every single time in the past? For instance, you would not kick your alcoholic son out into the street, for he is a sick person in need of help. Instead, you would book him a trip to therapy, support him along the way and hope he gets better, right? But to do all those steps, you need to have parents that recognize their son has an illness that needs to be dealt with for the sake of all the people whose lives he affects, and you also need the person in question to admit he is in serious need of help, so he can actively participate in the process of seeking it and recovering from whatever it is that lies at the root of his behaviour. And the truth was, none of those things were present, and by the looks of it, it seemed like they never would.

So there we were once again; he had won yet another battle by monopolising my attention and shattering any outlook of happiness I might had foolishly sought for on my birthday, since we found ourselves talking about him when his name should not be said out loud by anybody except the priest at the feet of his unmarked tombstone saying a final prayer in his name to little success—because, Father, you can pray all you want, but if there is a Heaven and there is something resembling afterlife justice, he will be headed elsewhere. As I looked around my friends' faces, I could see that they were just as tired about this topic for which it had become apparent there was no viable solution in sight, as I was, perhaps even more, because it was a situation which they had to *stand*, to *hear about*, but not *suffer* in their own flesh and bone.

As of lately, part of me, the irrational brain hemisphere, the one where He exercised the biggest influence ever since I could remember, began to beguile myself into thinking that in my friends' mind, the problem I was presenting to them in actuality was not as tangible and painful as I claimed it was, given my penchant for exaggerating and colouring reality, and that a large part of what my brother did and had done was either a figment of my imagination, or at least somewhat justifiable. Because if that were to be true, it would indeed be a manageable problem with a foreseeable solution and not the immeasurable one I claimed to have to deal with. And that thought I thought they were all thinking, I wondered, perhaps made them feel comfortable at night after our endless conversations always unavoidably ended up revolving around the same exasperating topic. Being a writer at heart—or so I claim—it should come as no shock to anyone that I am indeed guilty of occasionally peppering up stories with a few minor additions of my own to the real events that actually transpired. It is not only for the sake of entertainment, but also due to knowing that accuracy could potentially cloud the truth of the events when telling any story, so I tend to ensure the latter is always prioritised over the former, I admit that much. In my defence, describing the occurrence of a particular event is often inevitably paired with an innocuous need to alter reality—to a greater or lesser extent—in order to optimally present certain events, after considering it necessary to sacrifice verisimilitude and an exact portrait of reality at all times, in favour of the depth that can emanate from a slightly altered yet optimally told story. However, those slight modifications I certainly was responsible for were not only meaningless: they were <u>never</u> related to incidents involving my brother, because reality always remained way ahead of fiction in that particular aspect of my life. How foolish it would be to fake the pain that I wear inside, the sleepless nights, the anxiety attacks, the inability to hold any social interaction after a few years of prolonged suffering. And for what would I exactly feel the need to pretend? For attention?

That wasn't the Carla they knew, because the Carla they knew did not skip a day without wishing she wasn't desperate for the kind of attention, help and advice that I badly needed. But in their hypothetical defence regarding my friends' apparent opinion on this matter which as far as I knew existed uniquely in my mind, it was easy to understand their position in this scenario were they to indeed think in this manner. After all, what I told them stood in direct contradiction with reality and with the image of my brother which he portrayed to others—if he was such a wicked and perturbed individual, then how could I explain his extreme popularity among his numerous friends and his wonderful girlfriend? Or how our parents loved him unconditionally and our grandparents adored him, while I had never had a partner, had a rocky relationship with my mother, and the number of friends I had could barely be counted with the fingers of both hands, and you'd end up falling short?

    The nature of the relationship with my mother is for sure a path filled with bumps along the way, which is the only natural result of two powerful forces going at a rapid speed and coming into contact with one another on a daily basis. Underneath the occasional screaming one comes to expect from any mother-daughter relationship, lied a selfless love for another, which we developed from an early age. She set the standards as high as she followed them with her actions, which can be quite a tough act to follow. And I admit the pressure made me lose my temper on more than one occasion, but I was careful never to do so in front of her, always in the comfort of my own room, with nobody but my Alfred Hitchcock 4K DVD collection as witness. At the end of the day, she was a masterful poker player who knew better than placing all her bets on the same horse. Being more than aware—as only mothers can—of the person her son was poised to become, yet making no attempt to show her dissatisfaction with the direction his life had taken in the hopes of not adding fuel to the fire that his complex of inferiority had already created, I deduced long ago she knew that I was the one on whom to place the majority of her expectations for a better life. And the result paid off, because all interactions between her and my brother were one of four things: a short conversation where he essentially asked for—more like *demanded*—money, a heated argument about the most trivial of things (usually related to his inability to pass a single college course), a one-sided talk where he plainly ignored her presence while refusing to take off his headphones or, more often than not, all of the above, sometimes in that order, too. I knew what while it caused her great pain to live like this, evidenced by the progressive increase of bottles of wine on our garbage can, she found great comfort in knowing our relationship was always built on trust and communication—even if that meant telling one another that we hated each other every now and again—which, by the way, I believe is one of the signs of a healthy relationship: taking out of your system all those feelings with high toxicity levels, which when we fail to externalize with words, have the potential of fracturing relationships, tainting our entire view of reality and the way we perceive and are perceived by others. After one of such encounters between the two of us, we would cry, order some McDonald's and watch Leo McCarey's *Love Affair* (1939) until we transformed into two sobbing messes tightly hugging one another. Our love often came in the shape of silences when all we needed was for someone to listen, of close embraces when we felt like the world was closing down on us, of looks when, at family dinners, it seemed like we remained the only two sane people sitting at the table. Love was knowing exactly when she needed my help, and whenever I needed hers.

Simply to be, as we were, there for one another. So years after I had finished the money-grabbing scam that were those hypnotherapist sessions and I began to internalise the pain I suffered to make as little waves as possible, I came to the conclusion I needed to go see a therapist—a proper one this time—which I disguised in the eyes of my parents under the façade of studies-related stress levels, with the excuse of my upcoming final year exams coming up. As she always did, she supported me and asked no questions, only for the check. And when she underwent critical surgery to reconstruct her intestines as the result of a bacterial infection, and had no other choice but to leave work for an entire year to recover at home, I took care of her every day of the week, night and day, as I should, and as I gladly did.

While you already remember my dear Grandma Lupe from my tales about nearly killing a pair of baby twins, my Grandpa Agustín was an equally remarkable man whom I adored and who was the living personification of a moral compass: a man who served as a constant reminder of what a person should stand for. The loving father of seven, plus three angels along the way—as he used to say—he never kept for himself the wealth he worked tooth and nail to amass so as to rise above the poverty which had been endemically installed in his family for generations. Even when he began leading a luxurious life after reaching the destination of success at the age of forty, he never enjoyed it in solitude but with his family, always making his best to ensure we all had the life we wished we had. His health had steadily declined after he reached eighty years of age, a condition unquestionably worsened by his furtive numbers of escapism to the bar around the block, and his passion for Cuban cigars and tall pints of Guinness. It would take two additional years for the

Alzheimer's to start making him imagine furniture flying around the room and late-night visits from his long-deceased sister, and three years for him to leave an immense void in our hearts after his illness got the worst of him. Always an avid moviegoer, we shared a strong cinematic connection and, by the time he lost his ability to even speak, I used to learn as much trivia as I could from his favourite films— relegated mostly to John Wayne and similar embodiments of toxic masculinity—and then rewatch those movies together, filling hours and hours on end with all the fun facts I had learned exclusively for that occasion. That smile that was painted on his face surely redeemed all the sleepless nights I used to spend with him at the hospital, when his heavy medication made him believe it was my brother Diego who was taking care of him. But while I was never kind to him because I wanted some form of recognition, as in my mind, that is exactly what defeats the purpose—to me, Love is selflessly devoting yourself to someone else, with no expectation of getting anything in return—it instantly made my blood boil every time I thought that all the good deeds I had done were now undone and wrongfully attributed to my brother, a person who didn't even bother to give my grandfather as much as a courtesy call for his birthdays, not in the least because it made me torture myself thinking of all the other potential situations that had and would be wrongly attributed to him. It was a lesson in humility, though, as it taught me that when you love someone so deeply, someone who deserves to be loved only in that way, your love must come unconditionally, even if the one taking the credit is someone else, and even if that someone else does not have the capacity to love anyone unconditionally—least of all, himself.

  As to why I have never had a serious partner other than Irene and the occasional one-night stands, well, not to get too analytical, but the events of my life led me to have a short-lived childhood and to plunge myself right into adult life from an early age, whether it was by quickly getting a job, by burying my head deep in my studies or by voluntarily secluding myself into the world of movies, two to three hours at a time, occasionally in movie theatres only in those scarce moments when sufficient distance came between my brother and I. It might seem as if I am pinning all my troubles and shortcomings on Him and the damaging dent he has forever made in my life, perhaps unduly using him as a scapegoat through which I can aspire to trade off some peace of mind. But either originated from source A or B, it is an unmovable fact that social anxiety severely undermined my chances of meeting new people, unless it was by sheer *force majeure*, like the incredible friends I had miraculously managed to make in Switzerland, because I would be lying if I said that it did not help that I was not comfortable walking around in my own skin. You see, when you tell someone that they're not good enough, as true or false as it may be, the danger is not the possibility of causing harm, but the certainty that the other person will end up believing such things about themselves. In order to consider the possibility that others may find you likeable and attractive and someone whom they enjoy spending time with, you must consider yourself somebody worth everyone else's time in the first place. And if self-love is not the starting point, but the finish line, then, like me, you are bound to eternally wander around on your own.

So, while there might not be any truth to any of these sombre thoughts which I was somewhat confident my friends were surely having, once your brain gets to that space of *conspiracy mode* where regardless of actual probability anything has the potential to become a tangible reality, there is no turning back. As

Christopher Nolan cleverly exemplified in *Inception* (2010), there are few more pervasive and effective things in this world than an idea. Because money and power move mountains, but the pursuit of an idea is what fuels the collective imaginary: the pursuit of love, of money, of power. And when an idea takes roots in your mind, it has the potential to imprint upon your psyche an indelible, ineliminable memory, as if Leonardo DiCaprio himself had figured out the combination to your mind safe. And it will stay there for good, for even if you manage to eliminate it, the aftertaste will remain with you forever.

***

After the party was over, I walked through the foggy streets of my hometown with my headphones on full blast paying half of the *Camp Rock* (2008) soundtrack, until I arrived home roughly thirty minutes later. Walking up to our doorstep, I noticed our kitchen light was on. I was then prevented from knocking on the door by my family's roaring laughter—the three of them, in unison. Lowering my gaze and staring into our street, I saw my brother's car poorly parked into two separate spots, leaving no room for anybody else to leave their car outside. The tips of my fingers began to tingle, my legs to uncontrollably shake, a sudden heat wrapped itself around my face and an incoming wind of anxiety grabbed my throat so tightly I could barely breathe anymore. Just then, I was invaded by the overpowering impulse to make the kind of decision that you are sure to end up regretting. With only forty Swiss francs in my wallet, I took the car keys out of my pocket and headed towards my derelict-looking car parked on the road opposite to my house. Right there, in the middle of the night, I miraculously managed to start the *experienced* engine, which sounded less like an engine and more like Gilbert Gottfried coughing up his left lung, and headed to a place I was unaware of. From the mirror, I could see my parents peeking their heads out the window, watching me drive away, possibly thinking (perhaps not for the first time) that I had positively gone mad, completely unaware that our home had now become a place where there was simply no room for me. At that moment, I knew myself enough to know that all I needed was to be somewhere where I could get some perspective, where I could get my thoughts and my life in order, if possible. After a couple of hours behind the wheel I inexplicably ended up, of all places, at the natural park of *Los Calares del Mundo y de la Sima*, where my father used to take us on hiking trips when we were kids. There was not a soul anywhere to be found, only the sound of crickets served as a companion on that cold night. For a person who had lost faith in life and her fear for death, that was exactly the place to be.

Aided by a flashlight I found on the glove compartment (one of Dad's Christmas presents), I aimlessly wandered around the woods for at least a few hours, analysing in excruciating detail the events that had transpired that night; trying not to give in to my most primal instinct along the way by preventing myself from pushing the Nuclear button; striving to understand if I deserved this life or if I purposefully designed it this way; making every effort to see if this problem was a creation of my own, if it was a story I told myself to evade responsibilities in life, and if so, if I was ever going to find a way out of this corrosive obsession. Oh, how easy it is when you have someone to pin all your troubles on, when you can define the "other", the villain, the "Knock" character from F. W. Murnau's exquisite theft of Bram Stoker's iconic novel, *Nosferatu* (1922). Having left Geneva, all the progress made up until then was now long behind, and everyone there whom I had met were nothing but a distant memory. My mind was readier than ever, and it would not be long before my body would follow suit. The improvised hiking trip came to a sudden end once I unexpectedly (or perhaps, not necessarily) found myself at the highest point I could possibly reach in the mountainous park: the perfect spot to look down at the entire landscape and get an uninterrupted view of the progressively clearer horizon, slowly conforming itself into an expressionist painting that hid the potential to irreparably alter a lifetime full of memories. I could see the water placed roughly a couple hundred meters below my feet, calmly calling for me, yearning for the arrival of the sudden impact of a body which became a walking corpse long ago. But what the Hell was I doing up there? Was I rushing into this? If I somehow managed to make it out alive, would it always be this way each time his and my path inevitably crossed? Was I just looking for the smallest excuse to prove he was right about me all along?

The first, more primal impulse came in the shape of a thought: a (somehow) considerate idea to give others peace or at least illuminate their forthcoming darkness by leaving a note—at least that was what I had seen in movies. So, I mechanically took out my phone and started drafting my final text. And I knew just exactly who I was going to send it to. As soon as I started writing, a sudden inspiration rose and took control of me, becoming unable to stop myself from typing. Anxiety led the way for adrenaline to burst into scene. The total loss of inhibitions, the freedom that inundated me as soon as I understood all future consequences for my actions were about to fly out the window, the realization that I was about to go somewhere where He could not get to me anymore, made me hold no bars when it came to expressing how I felt, how he made me feel, and how I never wanted to feel ever again. The sensationalist—albeit true—nature of the flammable contents of such a message, and the pain with which it was written, made me sense the full weight of my family's future stability hanging in the balance. The three scenarios that I contemplated were the ones we all do when moving across life and daydreaming at any chance we get: the one you wish for, the one you could get, and the one you will get. In my mind, perhaps an ultimate dip into the pond of wishful thinking, the cosmic energy that reigned over us all would make my last wish come true by ensuring that the text I was writing—and the act that would ensue—would finally make my brother understand the scope of his actions, and the fact that although he was not the one about to push me down that cliff, he surely was guilty of the impending death about to take place. An equally devastating (although much more likely) outcome was that Diego would opt for deleting the text and writing my story as he pleased. This nihilistic scenario would only be possible if the content of the message pierced through his thick skull and actually had somewhat of an effect on him. So, even if the text was not shared with all, it would reach its intended target and hopefully encourage him to make of his life something other than a full-time job of enforcing misery upon others. Yet, deep down, I knew he would not hesitate for even a second to use the message as a brush with which he would refine his previous painting of my long-abandoned role as the family's villain, as the ultimate proof that I was a deeply disturbed human being who tried to pin all my deserved misfortunes on my saintly brother, in a last-ditch attempt to break up the family. Once again, I would be giving him the ink with which he could rewrite history, with nobody in his way anymore to counter his manipulation of reality. And as much as it distressed me to admit it, I knew this latter was the scenario with the highest chances of materialising.

Either in the shape of a blessing in disguise or a curse in plain sight, the little residual agency that I still possessed over my body was severely curtailed by the presence of a variable which I had failed to consider when internally computing the mathematical probability that my suicidal tendencies could end up materialising on that night: the appearance of an overwhelming, superior force that fell well out of my jurisdiction. Thus, before I could (perhaps for the last time) wrap my head around the possibility of effectively falling prey to my darkest nature—a process whose ramifications, emotional or otherwise, I was verifiably unable to fully comprehend—the first gleams of sun started to illuminate the incoming vans and cars of early hikers down below, successfully preventing me from succumbing to the sinister ideas which by now had acquired permanent residence status in my mind. It seemed like a cop-out, but it was genuinely true that I would never do something so personal, so traumatic, so irreparable, in front of others, not in the least because with an audience came the possibility of non-consummation of the act, as it is only instinctive to ultimately appeal to our human kindness and empathy. Such an anticlimactic interruption made me wonder if I really wanted my darkest tendencies to actually become fruitful, for I had expressed the same readiness to face both the end of my life as well as its momentary salvation. I decided the answer was inconclusive given the intervention of another variable on the equation. Indeed, the presence of others had effectively taken me out of the path I was about to walk along, almost making me feel ashamed for frequenting it as much as I had.

The walk back to my initial starting point on that park was

slow, almost methodical, certainly medicinal. When I arrived at my old, thoroughly chipped and unapologetically scratched monstrosity of a car—Grandpa Agustín's old Ford Focus, which I inexplicably continued to drive around despite it being a full two years older than I was—I was surprised to see a car parked right next to mine. It was a black Kia with a trunk so large it often got mistaken for a hearse: Dad's car. As I approached him, I realised I was not going to give my brother the satisfaction of seeing my lifeless body in a coffin. For once, I acted with the rational side of my brain to sacrifice short-term satisfaction with the endgame in mind, when I permanently deleted the long, and highly destructive text, and I tightly wrapped my arms around my father, who was waiting outside of his car, characteristically smoking a cigarette with a Coca-Cola Zero in his left hand.

What could I say about a man so larger-than-life that any combination of words, as flattering and descriptive as they may be, was surely bound to fail to capture his true essence? Of short stature yet immeasurable heart, he used discreteness and agreeableness as his weapon, a fanatic of quietly standing on the side-lines to remain out of trouble whilst always managing to get a good view no matter what. He too had been cursed with a somewhat similar sibling relationship, only he had his younger sister to console him, and my grandparents always made their reluctance of affection and disappointment of having had children unapologetically clear—Grandma Gabriela used to say in virtually every single Christmas dinner how miserable her life had been, and how happy a life she would have lived had she married Juan Alberto Álamo, a steel worker who asked for her hand in matrimony and who died when he was thirty after an incident at the factory. But I always knew my father acted not as a passive spectator, but as an active listener. He talked a lot, too much sometimes, yet too little when required by the situation, but always remained the first to stick to his own advice as, when he did open his mouth, you knew there was a good reason for it. And we all remained quiet as soon as he did.

What did a man who had seen all the filmography of the Nouvelle Vague pioneers, of the Kurosawas and the Fellinis, the Kubricks and the Altmans, the Langs and the Wong Kar-wais, the Hawks and the Welles, the Wilders and the Wylers, what did that man watch when he turned on the TV? A man who had experienced the many beauties immortalised on silver nitrate across time and space? A man who had (mostly) seen all that humanity had to offer as immortalised on the Seventh Art? Well...he watched MTV's *Ridiculousness* (2011—). The explanation for this lied in his assumption that all that was worth saying, worth filming, worth showing on a movie...had already been said, filmed and shown, many times before. And though many aspired to come close to that *je-ne-sais-quoi* which others had masterfully achieved before, they were only doomed to fail from the beginning, as that which came before could never be matched. Thus, my father routinely chose to watch something reliable, something that ensured a stable, flat encephalogram, which is the best way in which I can describe how this man was (and so far, is), someone with clear priorities, a distinct vision of life, and a robust work ethic, all three of which enforce a total dominance over his life choices. Always deeply devoted to his wife, and discretely (yet consistently) available and present for whenever we needed him, my father was, simply put, a deeply flawed individual whom I admired with every single bone in my body, unhealthy as they may be due to poor life choices and genetics (thanks, Grandma; you could have given me a little bit more of your musical talents instead of what soon will manifest on my body as premature osteoporosis). For that reason, I was surprised when my father decided to take off his paternal mask, which had instantly placed him many times before in a de facto position of deifying his children, and for the first time in years, had an honest talk with him about the biggest taboo topic of conversation in my family: my family.

We sat down on the hood of his car, with the stars that previously had illuminated my night now being eclipsed by the sunrise slowly painting the horizon as the background curtain for a father-daughter moment, the kind which we hadn't had in a very long time. After Dad remained characteristically silent for a while, always careful when it came to choosing the words that came out of his mouth, he took in a mouthful of air, and braced for the impact that conversation was about to have on both of us.

"You see, little one, parents are born with a special gift: the gift of sight. And trust me, your mother and I, we see it all: every good grade at school, all the points scored during basketball games, each laugh and every smile...but also every ounce of pain, each fall and every tear, the tantrums, the lies...your scars and your bruises, the desperation tattooed on the bags underneath your eyes and the loneliness within yourself in the decreasing frequency with which you get out of your room. We see you not touching your plate at family dinners for the past ten years. We see your isolation in the presence of an inability to deal with a reality imposed upon you. We see all your hugs being refused by him on every birthday and special family occasion, carefully dodged away from everyone's sight. We see the lifesaving need you had to leave our house and go work in jobs you had never had any interest in before, in countries you had never heard of before going to live there one summer at a time. We see how you no longer enjoy that which you used to love, and how you have progressively pushed your mother, myself, and your friends aside when we have proven ourselves to be the persons you need most, but who are unable to help you carry a burden too large for anyone to bear—especially on their own. We see the hate you feel for yourself and your body and the person you have become, growing every day a little deeper. We see the marks on your door after it has been kicked at every morning to wake you up, and the prescribed anxiolytics on your left drawer. We see the scars on your wrists and on your thighs, and the injuries on your knuckles and the holes on your walls. We see your past and your present, and know, as your parents, a truth deep down of ourselves…even if we will not dare to admit it. We know that as things currently stand, your future will likely not be to outlive us."

Although I had begun crying from the very moment he started his first sentence, this last lapidary statement took a while to process. At first registered in my brain as relief that someone finally understood exactly what I had been going through—his blatant honesty standing in sharp opposition to my mother's characteristic "your brother is just misunderstood…and we're all to blame" delusional approach—it immediately gave way to a brewing frustration, a genuinely felt disappointment at him for not having intervened and failing to rise to the occasion when he should have in the face of my unsuccessful attempts, and finally turned into a more powerful, legitimate feeling: pure rage.

"You knew? All this <u>fucking</u> time you knew? And you didn't do anything? What kind of a father does that?"

"I—uh, well, we're here so I might as well be honest with you. I—I must admit that at first your mother and I thought you were just being kids. That was the way we were raised. Hell, the way most children are raised. They constantly fight, they annoy one another and then, after that rivalry phase is done, they are finally mature enough to leave all differences aside and become siblings once and for all. But the truth is that, by the time I realised the scope of the problem and the deep roots it had taken, the damage was already irreversible. In any case, darling, our job was done with nothing but the best of intentions, as flawed as it might have eventually turned out to be."

"But if you were aware of the kind of person he was—which, by the way, Mom continues to refuse to see—why now? Why did you choose today to find the courage to come clean about this, instead of when I needed you most?"

"Because, darling, look at where we are right now. It is not a coincidence that both of us are standing in the middle of a forest at 6.42 a.m. in the middle of a Saturday. You're my daughter and I've known you all my life, far too well. So, when tonight I looked into your eyes, I could see that possibility that has always lingered in your mind become more real than ever: the willingness to finally concede on the verge of materialising; the sheer tiredness pushing you to yield and give up this unwinnable fight. You will do whatever you want to do with your life, I am nobody to stand in your way. And trust me, I have seen far less resilient people who have surrendered to their impulses for considerably less painful suffering than yours. But before you do, you must remember that your mother and I—"

"I'm sorry, Dad. But these words come far too late, and frankly, they mean nothing to me. I needed your help years ago. 'Needed' as in *past* tense, not now, when all you have is compassion and understanding in the place that should have been filled by the real solutions which I needed from both of you ten years ago."

"The truth is, as much as it may hurt you to hear this, Carla, that we acted that way because your brother needs us, and you don't. Or at least not so badly. He is a deeply troubled man, little one. For a long time now, I have learnt to treat him as what he is: a sick person in desperate need of help."

"Then get him some help: take him to a fucking psychiatrist so that the rest of us don't have to go, instead!"

"God knows we have tried, and each time he has become more and more violent. Last attempt I made he came close to sucker punching me, right there and then. I now fear that if I even come close to once again offering him the possibility of going to a therapist, I would be the one ending up in the hospital, instead. Your mother and I are giving him all the love that we can, in the hopes that it eventually leads him to reach that conclusion by himself."

"And what are you going to do with him, then? Are you going to stand the way he treats you, the way he treats Mom, forever? Because he's not gonna leave your house—trust me, I waited for long enough to realise he has no plans of ever getting out of there. And you two offering life on a silver platter for him does not help, either."

"What do you mean?"

"I mean giving a far-too generous allowance to an unemployed twenty-six-year-old whose only task is to routinely raid your pantry. Wake up, Dad, you have been paying his college tuition for the past seven years. I was never great at Math, but all it takes is four years to get a degree—perhaps three in the case of that private university he goes to, I hear bribes are never off the table…"

"Listen, I am going to be frank with you, perhaps more than I have been to your mother and certainly more than I have ever been to myself. There are two options: either your brother is a deeply troubled man, who so far has been completely incapable of letting go of his childhood traumas and move past his resentment…or…shit, your mother and I have been living with a maniac for the past twenty-six years."

Before I went ahead with the inflammatory words inside my brain which yearned to come out, I took an instant of deliberation where I hesitated on whether to water down my thoughts with the intention of making the blow a bit easier to digest. Ultimately, I began to understand that I was no longer a child, as I understood right then and there that regardless of the circumstances, the truth must always prevail, as painful as it might end up being.

"For a very long time, I thought none of you understood what he had done to me; that you were oblivious to how much it fucking hurt me to wake up day after day after day to live whatever remained of the life he now has effectively ruined. But it turns out you knew—you just didn't care. All you could do was to sit comfortably on the bench, as you always have, and tell me all about your 'powers of sight'. Well, Dad, we all have eyes. But you prove to me that not everyone has courage. At least I did everything but take my life to try to put an end to it, while all you could do was to just stand still whenever you saw that he was obviously behind—"

At that point, I found myself running out of air, completely incapable of finishing the sentence. As refreshing as it had been to finally get some light on a topic that had become distinctively opaque over time, the torrent of information that had just come my way became far too overwhelming—I needed some space to think, so I jumped out of the car hood and started pacing in front of my father, trying to remember my breathing exercises in an attempt to pull myself together. With the sleeve of my hoodie, I dried out the tears running down my cheeks and the snot pouring out of my nose, and purposely lost my gaze on the nearby woods until I had gained enough clarity of mind and felt capable enough to look at him in the eyes. My father came closer to me, extending his arms, trying to get a hug from me. It was the first time in my entire life that I had seen him cry. His honest tears slowly made their way across his blushed cheeks. It pained me to see him in this manner, but I refused his friendly advance and took a step back, nonetheless, remembering both my priorities and where we both stood at an emotional level at that point in time.

"Just tell me…if—if you knew all of this, then how could you two be foolish enough to send the wrong kid to therapy all these years?"

"You were a very emotional kid, and you still are. You couldn't go through life losing your temper in the ways that you used to, and you needed some serious assistance to help you handle your emotions and become the one who rose above the petty power dynamics of your brother. Deep down, you know that it wasn't ludicrous for us to get you some help. For Christ's sake, you have had insomnia and anxiety attacks since you were eight. How many eight-year-olds do you know suffer from that, huh?"

"I don't know, how many people do you know have a brother like mine? None of those things happened out of nowhere, Dad. So don't you even dare to try to blame any of this shit on me, because there was a clear reason why I stopped sleeping well at night."

We sat in silence for some time, only surrounded by the sound of robins merrily flying to their nests, until my father took out a package of cigarettes which I knew my mother would go absolutely ballistic if she were to see, lit two cigarettes and offered me one, somehow having learned I had started smoking back in Geneva. Must have been that gift of sight he claimed to always have had, I guess. After a few minutes, I finally managed to speak up, feeling the need to put all the cards on the table once and for all and understanding that chances of opening up to my father were hard to come by on those days.

"Well, I am not going to lie to you: explaining all of this will not make me forgive you. All these years, you have known what he has done to me, and I assume Mom, in her own way, also has. I mean, have you forgotten about the conversation we had two years ago on New Years' Eve? You told me you had the same problem with Uncle José María when you were kids, and you could not find a single shred of empathy in you to prevent your own daughter from suffering the same experiences you suffered? Isn't that what parenting is all about? Making sure your children don't make the same mistakes as you did?"

"After it became apparent that it was too late for us to do anything to stop it, as we knew the damage by then was irreversible, and by my own experience—like you just mentioned—knew that only time would put everything and everyone in its place, what kept us on the side-lines was not entirely cowardice, *little one*, but also the belief that despite the pain you were and still are suffering, that something good could come out of it. I know that either passively or actively, we all took your childhood away from you, but not intervening in the matter has also given you all the tools necessary to go out into the world. Your brother Diego represents every single thing that you will have to face in this life: tyrannical bosses, unreasonable landlords, neglectful doctors, and twisted divorce lawyers. Your mother, you know her, she loves him too much to even dare to look reality in the face, so I had to make the best out of what I had. Him going away was never an option we considered, otherwise your mother would have finally had the breakdown she had feared since the size of this problem started to become apparent; and you could not be the one who had to go away, because it was not your burden to carry. I tried calling your aunts and uncles, but your mother would refuse to break up the family and insisted on living her deluded fantasy of keeping the family together, instead. We are all to blame, Carla, me being the first one. And I wanted to say that not a day goes by in which I don't wake up thinking of all the pain you have had to carry on your shoulders for so many years, all on your own. So please, I hope you find the love in your heart to forgive me, or to at least understand why I did what I did. I can bear one of my children hating me, but not both of them."

A hurricane of feelings wrapped a tight knot in my stomach, making me feel utterly unable to comprehend the entire ramifications of the conversation that had just taken place. After staring at my father for long enough to grasp that both his guilt and emotions were real, and that this was not a well-intentioned ruse being played on me to make me come back to the land of the living, the feeling that eventually came out on top, however, was the one with which I returned home alive: for the first time in my life, someone from my family had fully acknowledged me and my experience, and had put words to the complex web of entangled feelings hatching inside of me. Finally, I was no longer alone, in the shadows. My dear father had just opened a small crack on the walls of the inner cell where I had spent the majority of my time, and through it came a shy ray of light, of opportunity, of hope that someday I could perhaps aspire just like everyone else to the chance of having a happy, meaningful existence.

XII

MANY HAPPY RETURNS

With the comfort of no longer bearing the brunt of being the crazy outcast in the family, and with a renewed faith in my family's vision of ourselves and of the reality we all inhabited, I arrived in Geneva with a new outlook on the suffocating problem I left behind; my brother no longer playing the role of a torturer in the play that this life of ours was, but of a tortured soul desperately in need of our help and support. It did not instantly expunge him of all wrongs committed up until that moment, as even the sickest individuals who carry out abundant atrocities under any kind of influence still have some agency in them, and his offences were too exact, too tailor-made and far too twisted to be dismissed, or worse, excused as an uncontrollable impulse of his. Still, it was a much healthier perspective, nourishing the desire of perhaps one day eventually making it bearable to live with a problem that by now had become a fundamental part of my identity, for so long having cast a long shadow over the chance of a mildly optimistic existence, under which lied the desire to make his condition and, by cause and effect, *my condition*, no longer irreparable.

Coming back to the flat in *Carouge* was an almost religious experience, making me feel like a shell-shocked war combatant returning to the tender embraces of his beloved family, having lived in an almost mechanically engineered spot of constant torture, and now invigorated with having been presented with the possibility of taking back my life, which stood at a sharp contrast with the reality I had left behind merely hours before. In the absence of Richard and Agnes, the place was now inhabited by a senile Swedish old gentleman named Ingmar, who every time he stepped out his room believed he was in the battle of Algiers all over again, and an attractive young doctor, from Switzerland nonetheless, who went by the name of Jean Luc. As if perfectly orchestrated by my mentally-unstable landlady, whom I was constantly knocking on wood for having been spared of talking to since that whole Greek yogurt incident, she had placed me in a premature madhouse, with a lunatic who later on would repeatedly start his mornings by taking his little pickled herring and urinating on our downstairs neighbours' garden, and his remedy in the form of Dr Jean Luc who, as it would turn out, actually administered old Ingmar with a sedative three times a day. Little did I know that when Jean Luc went away for work, as he often did, the responsibility for the old man's health fell onto me. The first time I succumbed to my inner human decency inherited from my parents after I agreed to administer Ingmar his morning injections, I instantly regretted my decision, as it turned out the location where the needle had to penetrate his body was located immorally below his hip and unfortunately above his knee, forcing me to constantly circumvent his pendulous *Köttbullars* as if I were in the midst of a dodgeball game, praying with all my heart to keep my balance steady.

  The return was also marked with high anticipation for the one perk my job truly had, and the one thing that had actually kept me motivated throughout the endless eight hours a day over those months which I spent pretending not to dedicate my entire workday navigating IMDB, Letterbox and Netflix: the possibility to deliver a statement on behalf of the organization that I worked for at the United Nations' *Palais des Nations*, located at the very heart of Geneva. While we're being honest, neither the actual content of the message nor the people on whose behalf it would be delivered mattered in the least to me. But the opportunity of being in that room, reading a message that would be simultaneously broadcast in virtually all countries around the world, right at the core of the most prominent international organization that ever existed, was certainly as thrilling an experience as one could get in my line of work as an intern. It was also a way to ensure that for the next three years I would not have to starve anymore to get a thankless, probably unpaid, desk job which I would without a doubt be completely unqualified for, as my CV could just as well be relegated to a link of the statement's internet retransmission and the emoji with the halo hovering on top.

During, before and after the period of the Human Rights Council's sessions at the United Nations, the building where our office was located—right across the Broken Chair statue—radically transformed from a quiet, insipid atmosphere analogous to watching paint dry or sitting through a Vincent Gallo movie, into a hectic succession of people running in and out of rooms, frantically sprinting in heels to carry documents from one side to the other as if in the middle of the most inconsequential triathlon in history, given essentially all its tenants worked for human rights NGOs being thoroughly involved in the bureaucratic processes related to the United Nations. It was not unusual to find empty bottles of alcohol in the bathrooms, probably laid there by workers at higher or lower floors in an attempt to prevent their bags from making a whistleblowing sound on their way out the door with the clinking of the bottles contained therein. By this time, those of us at the office who had been doubly vaccinated against the pandemic virus were all progressively returning to work and began temporarily forging a mild spirit of camaraderie and teamwork. Such spirit was of the "marriage of convenience" type, which can only arise in moments of crisis when you have nothing and nobody else to hang onto for help, all stemming from the frenzied preparations of the statements and the handling of the post-United Nations "Council" aftermath.

Despite the momentary glimpse of something resembling a kind of faint emotional attachment other than the "purely business" approach we'd been shunned with up until then, it had become more than apparent to everyone in our organization that the problem of cohesion amongst colleagues resided on their side, evidenced by Vero and I's close relationship both amongst ourselves and with the staff of the NGO standing opposite our corridor—where Anna, Michaela and Montserrat worked, and whose bosses we ended up having vodka Martinis with after work every now and again. This must not have gone unnoticed by our otherwise purposefully absent-minded team, as suddenly both Cassandra and Lucille were quick to express the interest they had failed to manifest before in planning out of post-work drinks every Thursday, plans for which Vero and I subsequently became unable to attend given the high frequency of dead silences and shared feeling of wanting to be elsewhere with literally anybody else, which tended to preside over those gatherings. In a devilish attempt to get them out of their comfort zones which they seemed to rarely get out of, and under the pretence of my late birthday celebration, we decided to quietly yet unwaveringly get them drunk and make them loosen up a little by taking them to karaoke night at a bar we knew far too well.

And sure enough, after the first couple of beers came the

surreptitious tequila shots, and then the cocktails which Vero expressly went behind the bar to haggle with the bartender to include an indecent amount of alcohol in. Before they knew it (even if we perfectly did), we were drunkenly zigzagging our way out the bar in the pursuit of singing a Britney Spears-filled song repertoire. Located just a few streets from *Gare Cornavin* and right opposite *Les Brasseurs* bar (where, on a drunken night, Vero and I ended up fondling the unfathomable breasts of the lively owner Emmanuele, much to her—and our—delight), the karaoke joint was run by an Armenian gentleman named Simon, who was a mix between *Dune*'s Baron Harkonnen (2021 and, regrettably, 1984), *Austin Powers*' Fat Bastard (1999) and Santiago Segura's *Torrente* (1998)—rapist vibes, hirsute forearms and much-too-tight yet confidently stained Hawaiian shirt through which you could (unfortunately) get a glimpse of his massive Famous Amos-sized nipples.

All it took was for Spice Girls' *Wannabe* to loudly resound over the empty bar for Lucille to throw her monotone voice out the window and replace it for a maniacally-possessed-in-desperate-need-of-contacting-the-Vatican-for-an-immediate-exorcism-heavy-metal-singer one. Still, Cassandra seemed unconvinced, even when I purposefully started playing the tunes of ABBA's infallible discography in an attempt to finally reach out onto that carefully concealed heart of hers.

"What could it be? What could make her tick?" I wondered. Simon served us all another tequila shot, courtesy of the cocaine hustle he probably had on the side to keep up the lights on that place only Vero and I ever frequented, and the idea instantly hit me. As quick as lightning, I energetically grabbed the mic from Lucille's claws—unbeknownst to me effectively propelling her onto a table and then onto the floor due to my vigorous mic-grabbing thrusting move—and gave it to Cassandra. We locked eyes, as the first piano notes of the ever-iconic song began to play. A song they should teach in schools across the world. A song I wish one day becomes the hymn of the United Nations. A song objectively regarded as being universally and unequivocally note-by-note-beat-by-beat impeccable: *High School Musical*'s "Breaking Free". Immediately, her eyes began to spark, unable to contain the emotion of receiving a gift she was unaware of needing that badly, her face finally painting a genuine smile for what looked to have been the first time in quite a while. In that magical moment which we shared, I could see the person who for over four months had been tasked with the challenge of being my supervisor, a person more uncomfortable with being herself than even I was to be myself, who was now forsaking the corseted role she had been playing and giving her all on the dance floor, for once unbothered about the opinions of everyone else around her. It was entrancing to see her peeling away her inwardly imposed self-consciousness barriers, and made me feel like following along, not just in that disgusting joint that looked like a Catholic Church-sponsored façade for an international web of choir boys trafficking, but in every aspect of my life. If even the most uptight person I knew could let go of her troubles every now and again, then it was absolutely conceivable that I, too, could tone down the self-awareness rotting my desire for any social interaction, and eventually achieve a somewhat moderate level of carefree energy which my life was so desperate for.

The following morning, the day when I was scheduled to finally make the statement at the United Nations, we progressively began to collectively regret all of Simon's cheap tequila shots, with an honourable mention to the deeply shameful trip we ended up taking to the falafel place after the karaoke, where we ingested unethical amounts of hummus and chicken shawarma, despite all of us following a vegetarian diet. Even though I was dressed in an impeccable double breasted grey suit that made my ass instantly dethrone the *Jet d'Eau* as Geneva's main tourist attraction, the break dance moves that yesterday's late dinner were performing on my stomach made me curse the moment I decided to wear a grey suit on the day where it statistically looked like I was poised to endure flatulent incontinence, perhaps dipping my toe on deeper waters—we would see, the day was still young. The commotion of the moment prevented me from absorbing the entire experience, as I was quickly rushed through a thorough security control and then guided through underground passages until reaching the locally famous yet globally irrelevant Room Twenty of the *Palais des Nations*. Only a few NGOs had been allowed to make an in-person intervention, which only served to make the experience even more daunting, as the words of the panellists slotted to speak before me loudly bounced off the ample walls of such an opulent construction. Had I not been experiencing profound stomach aches that made me seriously question whether I was about to give birth, I would have noticed the naff multi-coloured ceiling looming over us like one of Scorsese's or Brian De Palma's zenithal shots; the excitement of being surrounded by the eminent characters whose work and roles I had thoroughly studied in college; the importance of the statement I was about to deliver on behalf of the people of Nigeria; and, above all, the appreciation for the moments before my intervention was to be indicted (in the shape of the world's tiniest footnote) into the history book of the United Nations trajectory.

My legs were trembling, at this point remaining unable to determine whether it was because of the hangover, the demonic presence nesting in my stomach, or the IMAX camera with which they were apparently going to record my statement. I sat down, making my best not to breathe too deeply or else the physical integrity of the buttons on my shirt would risk being mortally compromised, legs crossed to prevent any leakages—aerial or otherwise. Sitting a few seats to my left, I saw the Nigerian Ambassador attentively listening to the speakers. Always a powerful presence, the nearly seven-foot man slowly turned his head in my direction, until our eyes finally met in an exchange that, given his characteristic stoicism and the heavy sweat pouring down my forehead possibly being interpreted as a severe cocaine addiction, brought about inconclusive results other than the mutual awareness of one another's presence. A tall man wearing a wrinkled, purple velvet suit quickly came by to let me know I was next in line to speak. After taking a sip of water to clear my throat, and draining all visible sweat from my body (a futile attempt when wearing a clear grey suit, as I later learned), I quickly read the statement for the last time and adopted a power-pose I had discovered in the film *Broadcast News* (1987), which consisted of sitting on the tail of your suit to make your chest stand out while getting rid of all wrinkles, or so they said. Because in the movie, the people who tried it were Albert Brooks and William Hurt, both of which are men and none of which have the monumentally large bosoms me and my chiropractor have to worry about, the trick did not have its intended effect on me, instead resulting in the tearing of my left shoulder pad, the opening of four of my shirt's buttons and the somewhat naughty look of an out of place left breast, trying to get a peek outside. There was no time to rearrange nor dry out the extensive sweat stains slowly advancing around my armpits, as I only had ten remaining seconds before going live on air and out into the world.

My family, my friends, my colleagues, and thousands of interns taking notes of the event in the face of their superiors not being able to be bothered to listen, were attentively watching, waiting for the moment for me to appear. It was precisely at that instant, my possibly life-defining big moment at the United Nations, that my brain decided to lose all control of my sphincter and launch two flatulent winds that sounded like someone hitting on a pair of nineteenth century knockers, which instantly began hovering around the room as soon as the camera operator told me they had started recording and I was live on air.

Being aware that the live nature of the intervention made it impossible to start over, I began reading the statement out loud, propelled not by common sense but by sheer inertia and survival skills. As I continued reading the statement, managing to mispronounce the names of the child soldier victims I was supposed to honour—a result of having skipped rehearsals on that cursed Friday morning—the tension in my body was so that three additional, sinfully loud bangs coming out of my posterior effectively ensued. The person in charge of editing my intervention apparently had a blast over at the recording booth, as he did not miss a chance to close in on the astonished Nigerian Ambassador, whose initial reaction was coughing once he got a taste of the lethal gas I had let out in the world, the kind after which a climate conference would have to be scheduled to deal with its environmental impact on the ozone layer. He then looked at me, somewhat scared, but with a hint of admiration in his eyes. After all, I could've easily torn a pair of holes on the metal chair I was sitting on with my flatulent prowess. The reactions of everyone else present in the room did not take too long to arrive, instantly eclipsing the content of the statement, which had already been overshadowed by my colicky creations and by the noticeable waterfalls of sweat staining my suit and pouring onto the table. With only one paragraph left to go, I sprinted my way across those final lines, not realising I had failed to say, "We urge the Government of Nigeria to pass a more comprehensive amended child rights bill that addresses all inconsistent and discriminatory clauses," and instead openly stated, at the United Nations, in front of the world, of the Nigerian Ambassador I had nearly murdered, of the President of the Human Rights Council and of God Almighty if she were to exist, the words, "We urge the Government of Nigeria to *ban* a more comprehensive amended child rights bill that addresses all inconsistent and discriminatory clauses." As I uttered the words "I thank you" to close my indeed life-defining speech, the left shoulder pad I had carefully put in its place before the intervention, fell out of place, leaving me both literally and figuratively in deep need of repairing.

The red light on the camera went off and the same man that had ushered me in, escorted me out of the room, this time visibly reluctant to come near me, standing at a distance as large as medically necessary. The Ambassador and I shared one last look, containing a mix of disappointment and perplexity, and I exited the room, heading straight to the toilet. All things considered, my experience at the United Nations had proven itself to be nothing short of unforgettable, especially when it came to its bathrooms, which I totally demolished by punishing that porcelain toilet with the fiery falafel remains which finally saw the light of day after eternally yearning for freedom. Once such a sacrilegious act was consummated, I entered the waiting room, where I found Cassandra pacing from one side of the room to the other, awaiting my arrival. Other than us two, there was only a man hectically texting on his Blackberry phone, sitting on a chair next to the large windows at the far end of the room. I could tell she was not happy, even if her British default mode was back in place.

"How did I do?" I asked.

After some hesitation, she replied, "Well, nobody gets it right the first time. And at least you said most of the lines correctly!" certainly in an attempt to put a positive spin on the fiasco that I had single-handedly orchestrated.

"That is a very low bar, Cassandra," I replied.

At that instant, the man with the cell phone stood up, now carrying a manila envelope in his hands, looked straight into my eyes and said, "Oh, honey, that's the one you just set," before leaving the room.

"Tough love," I thought, "always hurts less and helps more when delivered by people who mean nothing to us."

XIII

ANOTHER DAY OF SUN

11th February, 2018

I have never seen myself as the kind of person who would even entertain the possibility of keeping a diary.

"Too much of a cliché and far too time-consuming for me," I often thought. But in an attempt to try not to be my worst enemy during these past months and avoid succumbing to the rut and depressive cycles that come with a little bit of an unsatisfactory routine life, I decided to finally listen to Dr Nguyen. She claims it is important for me, and she is about the one person I trust in this hospital. I guess it all has to do with healing through a more accurate knowledge about oneself, or something along those lines. So I can use these pages to express that which I feared saying out loud, to externalize the thoughts that would make the people in here move me to a more secluded section, one with plastic cutlery and padded walls, a space that I can use to reflect on my own convictions and ponder questions like: "is it weird that I keep fantasising about my own end?" or "is it healthy to finally stand up to Death and try to go out on my own terms?"

It has always baffled me how, from a very early age, we are systematically taught the perpetual lie that Life, a time that can only be accurately described as a constant succession of struggles, can be lived without stopping every once in a while to ask ourselves about the meaning and potential shifts in spiritual perspectives that stem from its finite nature, that Death is nothing but an obstacle in our way of life, one which brings far too many head scratchers for us to acknowledge it—that is, until it becomes far too late. We can neglect it alright, but it always comes knocking on our door. Having a close, frequent and strong relationship with Death merely entails that I am more than ready to go out at any time. In fact, I feel like I have been looking for the right moment to die for a couple of years now. "I could die right now" is what I think whenever I have one of those scarce moments of happiness: an attitude of perennial readiness to leave this planet with which to face the anxiety of the sand running out of our own internal clock, nothing more than a wholesome lens through which to stare at the inextricable problem that is the loss of Life. Since we keep thinking the moment in which we are currently living is no time to die, I guess our death is almost inevitably destined to come either too soon or too late, depending on which side of the boot-throat dynamic you've always been at. If you're doing the choking, life has been good to you, even if you haven't in return.

Yesterday, my emotional frailty began to show when I almost slipped and told the first person ever—other than the doctors—what exactly it is that for so long I had seriously considered going through: my grandmother Gabriela, who had come to visit me for the first time since I arrived at this place and the person I least expected to share this information with, who right then seemed like a good shoulder to cry on and in which to confide my most obscure secret. A couple of beers (courtesy of my friend Roberto down at the cantina) made the hermetically deluded lady mysteriously open up when she confessed—inverted commas here—that the past three years of her life had been the worst time of her existence on this planet so far. Statistically speaking, that should not come as a shock to anyone, as my grandfather passed away exactly three years ago. Yet, this lady for whose needs my father was perpetually looking after on his own (in the absence of his sibling's capacity for empathy, remembrance or decency), had apparently forgotten (or purposefully erased from her mind) the hopeless devotion my father had for her when she blatantly confessed to me that my Dad, Patron Saint of Lost Causes and Infinite Patience, was her least favourite son. Just like that. Didn't matter in the least that he'd dedicated his life to doing everything in his hand to make his sick mother's life a little more bearable, because it turned out my father was nevertheless poised to end up forgotten, dismissed and vilified by the rest of the family, whether he liked it or not.

Being subjected to someone else's distortion of our collective reality is something I have grown accustomed to, and that I could clearly see not only in my brother's actions, but in my grandmother's as well, as the story she went around telling the few family members who still replied to her painfully long e-mails every once in a while, differs substantially from the actual events that transpired. According to her, nobody ever talks to her, she's all alone; my father has never taken care of her, or so she claims, so now she is dead set on going away to live with my aunt Sandra in Paris. Like that parable of Slavoj Žižek about the married man who dreams with leaving his wife for a life with his lover, how foolish are we to sacrifice a life we had for the prospect of one we will never reach, for a hypothetical reality that will never materialize because it only existed in our mind in the first place, a fantasy perfected over the years with no base in reality and fuelled entirely by a chronic inability to give answers to all our problems, soothe our anxiety and prevent us from facing our failed aspirations and broken dreams. Because the devastating reality is, when she finally moves to my aunt's home—an even bigger, emptier house—she will have to face the reality of the person she has become on her own, which is exactly the same person she was before arriving there. Because loneliness is inescapable; it follows you around, doesn't matter if you're surrounded by hundreds or all alone in your bed. During this conversation of ours, as furious as it initially made me feel, discussing this topic served as a pseudo-therapeutic remedy for me, making me come to the unequivocal conclusion that my brother was not the problem in the reality that I faced, because now that I find myself in this place, where people are trying to take good care of me and I feel like I am getting slightly better (albeit at a much slower pace than I wished), it is more than apparent that I will not be happy even if he is not in the picture, for the reality is deeper and much more complex and harmful than that. The damage created is now irreparable. All I can do is, from now on, measure happiness in contrast to the distance between him and I. But that distance will never be far enough, and it will often be close to zero.

My guess is that, having had few honest conversations in her life, my grandmother felt the need to reveal to me her hardest kept secrets, perhaps in the hopes of reaching some form of forgiveness, or merely after realising there simply was nobody else interested in listening to them, when she proceeded to tell me all about her multiple extramarital affairs and her intimate life in general—never a great thing to hear from an elderly person, least of all if it's a member of your family. At one point, in reply to her light question—one of those she loved to ask—on the reasons why I didn't believe in God—a human made creation responsible for arguably the worst events in human history, ideated for the sole purpose of quenching our anxious panic attacks after finally understanding that this purposeless void is all there is—I replied to her quite optimistically, following that trend of mine where I had positioned myself as a self-assured counsellor who, paradoxically, was utterly illiterate when it came to applying the theories I had developed into my own life.

"It doesn't matter who you believe in: Buddha, Jesus Christ, Joseph Smith or Nicholas Cage—nobody cares. The most important thing is that, since the only guarantee is the life we currently have (that is, provided we have taken the right pill from Morpheus), we must try to, in essence, avoid being a complete piece of shit to ourselves and to others, too. Who cares if you eat meat on a Friday, or if you pick up the phone on a Saturday, or if you skip church on a Sunday? I honestly can't imagine Malala arriving on Heaven's gate and being received by Meryl Streep—yes, if there is a God, I'm betting my money it's her—and sent down to Hell just because she did not believe during her lifetime in the 'right' God. If you manage to walk the tightrope of not being too naïve while avoiding (in as much as possible) behaving too much like an asshole to others, you'll be alright, I guess. Or at least I like to think that you will be," I replied.

My eighty-seven-year-old Grandma stood in silence, and then replied with one of the saddest things anybody has ever told me, given the realization of the irredeemable pain it implied. She said, "You see, I don't think I've done a whole lot of good things in my life." The worst part is that she was completely right.

Since we were both at that sweet spot of self-hatred and, most importantly, self-awareness of the kind of person we were, at that moment of shared vulnerability I felt tempted to ask her for a cigarette and calmly tell her about the dark plans that for so long had been stored in my mind, and on whether that melancholically doomed destination was something I wanted to achieve at all, or if on the other hand there was an escape for me and for people like me. This sort of *Harold & Maude* (1971) situation where the youngest individual's readiness for Death in the midst of an inability to appreciate Life sharply contrasts with the oldest person's deep appreciation for Life (in her case, one filled with regrettable choices) despite her impending Death, only works if the other person has no stake in the game. If I was another late octogenarian, then the story would be quite different. But being as young as I am, as well as being her one and only granddaughter, she wouldn't approve of my plan and refuse to have *the* conversation, the one I have yet to find someone to have it with other than the doctors here. In fact, more likely than not, she'd end up shaming me into growing old, morally broken and perennially regretful of chances not taken in a life seldom lived and scarcely enjoyed—not much different from where I currently stand.

Suffice to say, I did not tell her anything in the face of what I perceived was a predisposition to fail to understand my readiness to capitulate, which made me wonder, "Who did I have in my life with whom I could possibly talk about this?" I guess that's the side of the coin that we are not comfortable discussing, because my friends would most certainly be scared to death, probably forever traumatised, and would positively never look at me the same way ever again. In my place, they would see a fragile porcelain doll, constantly fearing that even the slightest wind would plunge me into the void and smash me into a thousand pieces. Quite understandably, this subject being of a considerable magnitude, they would be overwhelmed by it all, and recommend I go see a therapist. My parents, as parents always do, would eventually find out; Dad would understand…but Mom…this has the potential to send her six feet under even before I reach that destination myself, and I simply cannot do that to her. She would torture herself to sleep every night thinking she could have done more. Because suicide never kills just one person. Your parents. Your friends. Your family and acquaintances. Your colleagues and teachers and old pals whose lives you used to be involved in. They are all, in radically different ways, forever changed, marked by your loss and by the gruesome way in which your life story has come to an end. It is always cathartic, unavoidably so, and a part of them dies with you.

Because the truth is that the first thing that immediately came to my mind on the prior occasions where I almost consummated the act, both as something to avoid magnifying as much as possible in any way that I could, as well as something to prevent me from carrying it out in the first place, was the emotional toll it would take on those around me. It is devastating to know that I have people around me that love me, and yet I don't see them. That I have friends that want to help me, yet I feel they wouldn't be capable of doing so. But also, how could they? I provide them with little to no information about my real emotional state, I am more often than not in a moody, melancholic and reclusive disposition, and give them absolutely no guidance as to whether I need help either from them or from others and, if so, what shape it would need to take to successfully complete its desired objective. But what am I supposed to say? "Save me from myself?" And more importantly, do I even want to? It's like the chicken and the egg: I stay silent because I know the truth would scare them, and we all collectively agree this is a situation best dealt with by professionals. And I scare them because I refuse to share with them the uninhibited truth. And so, the all-encompassing pain keeps growing, never stopping, neither for me nor for those unlucky enough to find themselves around me. Nobody gets help and we all inevitably lose.

In a beautifully eloquent scene of the movie *Malcolm X* (1992), the reverend Mohammed tells Malcolm about the need to teach others the faith in Islam not as a glass of water mixed with ink, but as a glass of clean and clear water that allows others to finally see reality (in this case, their religion) for what it truly is. An unobstructed look at life, with all its colours, with all its troubles and tribulations. When others ask themselves why suicidal people often fail to ask for help or only do so after it has become far too late, part of the explanation stems from the fact that people who suffer from the same affliction as I do continually experience life through the inked glass of water. That is what it feels like to have depression: a horde of people around you, willing (and eager) to help you make your burden a little lighter, lies at the other end of the glass; but the dark, invasive and pervasive presence of depression prevents us from seeing that support, from properly valuing it, and from asking for help and emotional support when we need it most. It is that frustration attributable to being mentally deluded into thinking our problems are only our own, and have no solution, and nobody around us is capable of even grasping the ailments that break down our spirit, that eventually forms the perfect breeding ground for a suicidal wish to emerge, regardless of whether it makes the jump from wishful ideation to actual realization, or not.

And it is easy to see why others succumb to the social stigma playing an important part in the Rubik's cube that this epidemic has become, by thinking of it as a cowardly act; how they think of it as a safe passage to successfully evade responsibilities, bills, toxic relationships or unsurmountable problems. Cowardice, at the end of the day, for failing to deal with reality, and for putting an immovable burden atop the shoulders of those who dared be close to you. Yet, what many fail to realise is that it takes bravery to commit suicide, more than many are capable of even imagining, because, going down this path entails that you are renouncing the most precious thing you'll ever have: your own life. And the person snatching that away from you, is yourself. Judge, jury, condemned and executioner. What a horrible place a person must be in, what pain and suffering one must endure, what inextinguishable anguish one must feel, to even remotely consider the possibility of taking their own life. Those that opt for this option are not cowards. And they are also not a product of a vacuum. They are you, and the person next to you. And your mother and your girlfriend. And the man bagging your groceries. And the CEO kissing his seemingly perfect family in the forehead before leaving for work. And the preacher with a gambling addiction. And the successful tennis player with a Rock Star life. And the old widow living in the suburbs all by herself. And the homeless man addicted to heroin that sleeps underneath the stairs leading to the local bank. And the postman who delivers your letters with a smile on his face. We are all one bad day away from taking that irreversible decision, whether we like to accept it or not.

Mental health erosion is on the rise, that's one of the things that I found here. And with suicide becoming a common cause of death, it worries me that we—particularly us young people—are completely incapable of finding safe spots to open up about these taboo issues which, incidentally, are the ones that trouble us most. We feel judged, stigmatised by a society who has only been partially exposed to this depressingly tangible reality. The hypocrisy around it makes me sick. We collectively put on the fake masks of progress which we never achieved yet constantly find in the mouths of others when we underscore the vital importance of mental health and the collective need to be a little more broad-minded to be able to openly discuss matters related to it. Yet, the only suicides that we ever hear about are the most sensationalised cases surrounding this problem, the tragic ones, the celebrities, the mass shooters, the young people... Rarely do we get into why that happens, because sweeping the important questions under the rug is a much more comfortable alternative which allows us to sleep better at night. Imagine if the only cases of alcohol addiction that we ever saw on the news or heard from professionals on talk shows or on the radio, were those extreme cases of people seeking to be wasted during every moment of the day, unable to walk, talk, think or blink, twenty-four hours a day. That is not alcoholism. Alcoholism is bringing to work a coffee flask filled with whiskey and quietly taking a sip every once in a while. Alcoholism is going out for dinner and struggling not to order one beer after another. Alcoholism is drinking countless bottles of wine all alone in your room every night you arrive from work. It can take so many subtle forms, that reducing it to the most evident and noticeable cases, only adds fuel to a fire that is consuming the lives of millions of people around the world, myself included.

At least in the way through which I see the problem, it is not an opaque and isolated phenomenon relegated to a few people, locations or times in history. Bad things happen to all of us, events that are rarely under our control, and we always manage to get back up and do it all over again until something that may or may not be the direct result of our actions hits us right in the face, and turns our lives and every conviction we had ever had upside down. But suicide is an entirely different thing. It is a product of our own creation directly emerging from the choices that we make. When someone voluntarily opts for this road, it can be the result of putting some thought into it and concluding there is simply nowhere else to go and nobody that could steer them away. But, by and large, and even if you have clearly delimited the steps to follow and have mentally put yourself through it all, suicide tends to be the outcome of an impulsive, rather than premeditated, decision. Such impulses keep knocking on my door a couple of times a day and have come very close on more than one occasion, but they dissipate as soon as rational thinking and *pros and cons* lists enter into the scene to calm down my panic-stricken episodes. That is partly why I started to write this diary, in the hopes of finding myself along the way, of finding solid ground above which my feet can stand when my neck is being tightened by an imaginary, yet potentially real, rope. But I keep thinking, am I just an attention whore, hungry for others to notice my existence and take care of me? Or is this a cautionary tale, an exercise to bring a little more clarity into such an obscure topic? Perhaps all of the above. Perhaps none of them. Be that as it may, so far, the only ground I have found is the one where my grave stands, and each day that passes by, the hole grows a few inches deeper. When not even your comfort zones can help, when you've become accustomed to the remedy—or worse, indifferent—then you know there is little else to do. Perhaps I am just being short-sighted; I can feel my mind betraying me, like when you endure a breakup—or so I am told—and it uses its pernicious selective memory to only play its top-ten selection of the greatest moments you shared with your partner.

 Attempting to find some comfort after pouring all my frustrations on the world out on these pieces of paper, I now play out loud the sharp notes from Phillip Glass' heart-breaking work on *The Hours* (2002), while I think about the eternal fight. The one nobody has won yet. The race we are all forced to compete in, and the one where we always inevitably end up losing. The perpetual struggle to defeat our own mortality. Like an internship, just when you start to grasp the way it all works, to get really good at it, to develop some skill and wisdom, to learn the rules of the game, that is exactly the moment when you have to leave the table and free up some space for new players. Players who will soon forget you, who will use you as a cautionary tale, as the dear friend or the friend of a friend or the girl they occasionally saw at the supermarket, as the need not to give in to one's passions. But now, all that moral superiority, inner monologues and furtive whispers are no longer deafening; all the pain I will leave behind does not trouble me anymore; all the opportunities not taken, and the destinations not visited seem trivial to me; all the unheard songs and unseen movies and kisses not given, did not play a part in my story anymore. Once your mind is set, there is nowhere else to go. But before I can even start to think about my funeral, I have to start thinking about the methods that eventually propel the celebration of such a solemn ceremony.

"Pick your poison," life seems to ask me in the face of minor challenges or personal tragedy. Hanging seems to be the preferred way out, and self-mutilation like Hannah Baker or the Roman elites could eventually seem appealing, were it not for the mutilation part. No, I am not able to do that to myself. If I am to inflict pain upon myself, it has to be an invisible one—just the kind I have grown accustomed to by now. Thus, in my mind nothing beats a fatal sleeping cocktail. I can already imagine it...

"After writing down the very last page of what would eventually become this very book, I went down into the kitchen, opened up my mother's drawer and took out her sleeping pills and muscle-relaxing sedatives. Perhaps my grandfather's genes led me to pick vodka out of all the bottles of alcohol on the kitchen shelf, and to pour a tall glass of the silently deadly liquor. On my way up the stairs, my lovely Mia approached me, head down as she always did when she could sense I was about to go on an eternal sleep, wiggling her tail and looking to be petted to try to keep me idle and make me momentarily forget about the dangers ahead, as if every second I stood away from myself and closer to her was already a victory. She knew, in her own primal way, that something was about to take place. I kissed her one last time and closed my bedroom door. Outside, I could hear her crying on the stairs, clawing at the door, already anticipating the period of grief that would soon follow. Inside my room, I headed towards the table and put all the envelopes in a neat order: Mom, Dad, Grandpa Agustín and Grandma Lupe, my ladies from Geneva, the friends back at home, and Diego. Making my best to fight back the tears, I ran my fingers through the manila envelopes and nodded to myself, finally coming to terms with the biggest and ultimately final decision of my life. On the CD player, I introduced my favourite film (the gift that kept on giving that was Damien Chazelle's third feature film), and comfortably sat down, staring at my reflection on the black mirror that was the screen of my TV. I turned the phone off, fearing the possibility of someone abruptly intervening and making the battle uphill much harder from then on, then proceeded to erase the search history on my computer—not because of the porn, but because I knew it would kill my mother to see 'suicide methods' rank amongst my most popular searches—after which I finally allowed myself to enjoy the movie as it began to play. I could already hear the various car horns of hundreds of vehicles stuck in an LA highway on a sunny winter morning. With the opening song's humming as the backdrop of my demise, I did not fail to notice that the bottle with the sleeping pills now seemed bigger than ever. Ah, if only those pills from *Silent Night* (2021) actually existed in reality, I would at least get a somewhat dignified death, away from the vomiting reaction increasing my survivability chances. But this wasn't about giving up; it was all about knowing when to stop. It was not a matter of losing a fight, it was, in fact, about winning one. I subsequently emptied the contents of the bottle into my mouth, added muscle relaxers to the party and, aided by the vodka, chugged it all down in one firm sitting. The first notes of 'Another Day of Sun' began to play. And then…silence. Finally, silence…"

What I am purposefully omitting from this imagined future, is the image of my mother coming back home after a long day at work, her patience drowned out by the impending verbal battles that were likely to ensue as soon as my brother returned from the gym—over money, most likely. He would keep on shouting, her health steadily diminishing, until she'd eventually give up the fight and find her way to the kitchen where, after pouring herself a tall glass of white wine, she would open the top left cabinet next to the microwave, and insert her hand inside a cardboard box of laxatives, inside of which she had hidden a bottle of highly-potent muscle relaxers, to put an end, if not to the shouting, to the deadly pain on her back, and then head to the bed to get some rest before starting it all over again. To this day, imagining her face of realization after noticing the emptied cardboard box, the image of her inconsolable crying on my father's shoulders at my funeral, the haunting visualization of her broken life from that moment on, is what is stopping me from accomplishing what I am most certainly going to do. For that reason, and in spite of my inability to ask for help, the thought of planning the entire ordeal as an accident did have a frequent spot at my personal table of self-destructive thoughts.

"What if I make it look as if I had mistakenly taken a few too many sleeping pills?" I kept thinking. Or perhaps I would steer a bit too hard on the highway and have a perfectly innocent, yet ultimately fatal, car crash. Despite the initial frustration those around me would surely feel as soon as they heard the news, the incident would also bring them some peace and closure, as they would not have to wake up every day trying to figure out why someone that brought them so much joy could take away her own life for no apparent reason. In my case, I am not that great of a poker player, and the truth loomed heavily over my shoulders: it would surely hurt and cut deep, but would not surprise anybody, because it was there in broad daylight all along. Since even if I were to arrange it as an accident, the unmistakable reality would be patently manifest to those around me, I might as well carry it out in the most painless way available to me and let others worry about the mess left behind. After all, I have done enough suffering for a couple of lifetimes. As a non-believer who likes to keep an open mind when it comes to potentially choosing from the ever-growing religious buffet, the endemic feeling of abandonment and existential crisis which perennially fills my days now has emerged not necessarily from being disappointed by the expectations placed on a God-like entity, but from being left all by myself by a world who never cared about me in the first place. Sooner or later, we are bound to arrive at a point of ultimate introspection where the endless pile of insufferable pain born out of a successive cumulation of broken dreams, of the intolerable ruthlessness lurking at every corner, of understanding our own narrow existence is ultimately purposeless, all becomes self-evident. And the only result of properly grasping the actual extent of the anguish inflicted by the life I've lived and by the equally disheartening future that awaited for me, was a chronic loss of faith in the possibility of salvation, neither by internal renaissance nor by external intervention.

    After this outcome had set in my mind as a perfectly palpable scenario, what soon followed was a period of imagining/fantasising about my funeral, which I now find myself revisiting on a daily basis. Less so since I have been here, but every single day, nonetheless. Who would give a speech? Who would even come? I feel that a part of all the people present in that church would know, to some degree or another, that I was unwell. Ignoring for a moment the total disregard for the desire of the deceased (because, contrary to the fact I am a well-reported agnostic who only visited churches on weddings and funerals, and to my repeatedly expressed wish not to have a Christian funeral, my mother just wouldn't be able to stop herself from arranging the service was held at my hometown's famous Cathedral of *San Juan de Albacete*; after all, she could not hold the funeral at a Satanic church, which now that I think about it, I kind of deserve and I desperately want), the first pretence for a funeral to take place is the permission being granted from the Catholic Church. Now, as if it was not painful enough to endure what my parents would—and will—endure, the Church would more than likely refuse to hold my funeral, given my chosen method of death, despite the fact the Bible does not condemn at any point the act of taking one's life (in fact, the reported people who took their own lives in their—perceived as "holy"—book are hailed as heroes: I'm looking at you Saul, Samson, Ahithophel or even, to some extent, Jesus himself. But they must retain their very much earned position of moral highness, I guess, and continue to avoid addressing (whilst actively enforcing) child molestation, misogyny, and homophobia amongst its ranks. But a funeral for a suicidal woman? Well, that's simply beneath them.

So, let's avoid relegating the Church to a tax-free cult of child fuckers for just a second and imagine the funeral does indeed take place. Leaving aside all the friends and family who I assume would likely be filling the various rows of wooden benches, I chuckle at the very likely possibility of people whom I had nothing but contempt for, actually attending the funeral in an attempt to perform something resembling a publicity stunt. Because words of my suicide would travel fast, as scabrous and morbid details always do, and it would become the talk of the town. If I concentrate, I can almost hear it: the whispers, the gossip, the "she was always a weird kid," and the "her poor mother" murmurs bouncing off the walls of the cathedral, filling the mouths and ears of those too limited to understand that effectively blaming the suicidal person and passing down moral judgement onto the person's reputation and her family only contributes to further ostracising those whose lives were already heavily inflicted with a depressed outlook for their remaining existence. The name of my family would forever be tarnished, my parents would be recognised on the street as the "Mother and Father of That Girl Who Killed Herself," and the shadow of my demise would forever lurk heavily in every family gathering, every celebration and every interaction, as idle and apparently irrelevant as they may be. Indeed, this way of dying is one of the vestiges of a time where most people experienced that being alive was a crime and taking your life was just as much: a privilege for some and a punishment for the rest left behind, a stigmatised practice treated by our society in the manner of a shouted whisper, a cautionary tale we think is relegated to the mentally insane yet lurks surreptitiously all across and between us.

But more than the social stigma, and leaving the rest of unpacking on that subject for each one's own moral homework, I fantasised about the blame everyone around me would place on my brother. Not in a sadistic way, as if enjoying someone innocent being crushed with all the weight of an unlawful and prejudiced punishment. More like witnessing the engineer of the gas chambers being sentenced to the electric chair. Not necessarily poetic justice, not even moral justice, really—as evidenced by the presence of a dead body in the equation—but popular justice, something that usually brings others an easier way to travel along the rocky path of grief: a culprit. Because suicide, at the end of the day, is nothing short of an accusation. Pointing our finger right back at those that have inflicted us pain, that have made of our lives a sustained sequence of uninterrupted agony, at a society that has neglected us, maniacally inflicted a perpetual silence that only serves to further marginalise those who are unlucky enough to experience the kind of behaviour labelled as "problematic". Looks would be thrown at him, and everyone in that cathedral would know that, even though the body lying on the casket in front of them died from her own hand, a murderer lurked around the church, and was sitting in the front row—right next to the victim's parents. Although it would cost her an exorbitant amount of self-hate, even my mother would come to the inevitable conclusion that her eldest child wreaked upon her younger kid a degree of suffering profound enough to want to die by her own hand before she even reached the age of twenty-five. Being an avid follower of Hitchcock myself, what remains from the creative side of my brain pushed me to develop one more variant in this scenario: the unlikely outcome that Diego would suddenly grow a spine and develop a moral compass with its heart in the right place, right enough to seek punishment for his crime, and follow in my footsteps. This must be contemplated, because even if I have lost faith in my life, I must never lose it in humanity. Still, if we were to stick by logic and rational behaviour, the history books will not be unkind to him, something heavily aided by my mother's refusal to portray him as anything short of a cancer to my family and to myself. So, let's not ever forget he's no Raskolnikov; he was always more of a Judah Rosenthal.

The last piece of this fantasy of mine was a rather optimistic one, where my friends would gather around for the first time ever, mixing groups and people from all the different spheres of my life. It comforts me to think they would eventually become friends amongst themselves: letting life and friendships bloom out of death, growing out of the pain imposed upon them, and becoming better along the way by using my example as the extremes one must not reach before one reaches a point of no return. If my death served to illustrate a point, and to prevent others from doing the same; if it served as an excuse to never let down our guard when it came to our mental health; as a way of nipping in the bud all toxic relations before they consumed us; of grabbing onto whatever and whomever makes us feel alive for as long and as tight as we can, then it would have been worth it. Mistake me not, I am not contemplating doing this as a kind of messianic sacrifice; but, if it can bring an additional value other than finally putting to sleep the deep anguish that runs through every vein, bone, and organ of my body, then I am glad I could be of assistance. If not, I was not doing it *for* you, anyway; I was doing it *because* of you. *J'accuse*, indeed. I lift not my responsibilities from my own shoulders, as those weigh heavily over my soul and forever will. I am merely attributing additional blame to all others who stood quiet when they should have intervened, those who actively drilled a hole in my soul, and those that made life become the death of me. So no, even if they may be actively contributing or passively assisting in the perpetration of a self-inflicted death, the responsibility or, for lack of a better word, *blame* for the commission of a suicide lies on its perpetrator. The duty to help someone carry their troubles in a bearable manner, is something different entirely.

So, from the bottom of my deeply feeble and barely functional heart, I just hope that nobody goes through the pain of going to bed praying to a god you don't believe in that you never wake up, only to awake the following morning to beg the same god that you still don't believe in that you don't make it to bedtime. To tell you to stay safe, look for help, and talk to your loved ones to avoid ending up like me, would not only be hypocritical, but it would also be contradictory to everything that I have written here so far. It is hard to stay safe when you're the one who poses a threat to yourself; it is tough to look for help, particularly when health services are not widely available nor helpful; it is heart-breaking to talk to your loved ones, particularly if you think they will not understand, will be scared off, overreact and will not see you again in the same way. I feel you and I see you, and I hope whatever it is that is keeping you alive, continues to do so until you get on a path towards recovery and self-improvement. Although far from my finest moment, what these few lines contain is that, despite my plans and fantasies which I am dead-set on turning into realities, I still have plenty more I could do before actually reaching rock bottom, something which I am sure will come later, much later... There is plenty more to do before reaching that destination, or so I keep telling myself, and I hope the same is true for you, too, dear Reader, whoever you are...and *if* you exist.

XIV

EMOTIONAL RACKETEERS

And just like that, as if not a single day had gone past, all the chaotic energy that characterised *Abordaje* came back to us as soon as we all found ourselves in Geneva once again. We immediately headed to *Bains des Pâquis* to catch up with our respective summer trips over a delightfully decadent fondue, and then took one too many Aperol Spritz that encouraged us to end up—as we always did twice a week—at the nightclub *Village du Soir*. It had been at least twenty minutes since I had obsessively played the song *Pepas* by *Farruko*, so naturally the first thing that I did once we arrived at the club (knowing fully well that the previous DJ I had previously done this to had recently announced on social media he was taking a break from work mere hours after we—"we" in the broadest sense, fundamentally meaning "me"—incessantly chased him around the club in the aggressive pursuit of listening to *Pepas* one more time), was to head over to the DJ booth and ask him to play the song.

"We've played it three times by now," he screamed.

"Well, let's go for the fourth one, then!" I replied, drunkenly winking an eye at him. Although his stone-cold stare was clearly an attempt to make me realize he was not in the mood of playing it again, he failed to learn that, unfortunately for him, that was not for him to decide. To make the plan work, I naturally asked every one of the girls—calmly, individually, discretely, without the others noticing—to go to the booth and ask the DJ to play the song. One by one they went over there and progressively tested the patience of the skinny guy whose only sin was being hired to play on the same night these emotional racketeers were regrettably in the mood of giving their all on the dance floor. After the strategy did not bear its intended fruit, I expanded my pyramid scheme overseas, in turn targeting every girl dancing next to us with the task of effectively making the poor man regret the moment he gave up his mechanical engineering studies to pursue a career in music. Sooner than expected, the DJ had been forced to hear nearly two dozen requests for *Pepas* to play on that night, which ultimately made his morale crumble when he finally succumbed to my sheer stubbornness. In my defence, as soon as the first words from Farruko's lyrical masterpiece became audible, the room went ballistic with excitement as everyone instantly clicked in a beautifully improvised communal experience and started harming their lungs and vocal cords (and, quite likely, their high school Spanish teacher's job satisfaction) by passionately mispronouncing the lyrics with the conviction of a pro-life Karen shouting anti-vax slogans at the Q-Anon gathering of JFK Jr's resurrection.

Aside from effectively bestowing upon the club a renewed energy that kept the party going for more hours than it previously had any right to, that night became as good a time as any to practice inside the club a tradition we had been carrying out for quite some time. On one of those drunken nights when inspiration knocked on our door with frighteningly ingenious yet illegal ideas, we came to develop a competition we baptised "Trophy Night", which we insisted on enforcing each time we went out. The dynamics were simple: all we had to do was to find the most invaluably valuable object to take home each night. Had we dedicated a single second to thinking about the consequences our latest plundering project could have on the lives and jobs of others, we would have probably never done it in the first place, but since we hadn't, we didn't. The rules of Trophy Night were clear:

1) Find the most inexpensive yet irreplaceable item. Examples include flowerpots, street signals, teapots, virtually anything from the public domain, flags, cutlery, chairs, streetlights, fences, cobblestones, oak trees, cranes, lorries, phone booths and gazebos.

2) Except those cited in rule n°1, no expensive items (nothing beyond the hypothetical price tag of ten Swiss francs). Thus, money, wallets, bicycles, jewels, watches, phones or any kind of object that will make its owner's life much more difficult, are excluded. After all, we are not thieves, but mere collectors.

3) Children and other wild animals are off limits.

After the song was over, Anna and I succumbed to our recently developed kleptomania and took one of the rubber mats they put on bar counters, as well as a bottle of tequila when the bartender was momentarily distracted by the incoming wave of thirty-year old bachelors still living in their parent's basement and dying to sexually assault her. It was all fun and games until Claudia noticed a slobbery, disgusting macho man, wearing velvet moccasins and enough cologne to sedate Elizabeth Taylor, dancing with a girl half his age—a young lady with a kind face and round glasses, who wore her slightly ash-coloured, gorgeous blond hair in a tall ponytail. They seemed to know one another from before, but she was far too drunk to notice his frequent red flags every time he passionately choked her—the rage in his eyes becoming apparent underneath the pretence of the "passion of the moment"—and slapped her ass, clearly enjoying himself far too much, with the pain of each slap registering in her eyes, if only for just a second, the heavily anaesthetised reality creeping inside of her and attempting to get out.

Captained by Claudia, with just one look and zero words spoken, we instantly organised and split into two teams: one to separate the two of them and have a conversation with the repulsive man, and one to talk to the woman and make sure she felt safe and comfortable. At one point, Arantxa had to hold Claudia—a whole metre shorter than the guy—to prevent her from knocking the man's golden tooth out of his entitled, Dorito-shaped, sweat-filled, rugged little face. The commotion made the security guards intervene and eventually kick the guy out after he kept screaming at us in the middle of the club, where by now everyone knew who we were—especially the DJ. It was soul-crushing when, at first, the girl, who later told us her name was Cristine, refused to see reality for what it was, and dismissed the entire episode as just the way her boyfriend tended to be whenever they went out at a club. Being fluent only in whining and random movie trivia nobody cares about, I opted not to embarrass myself by talking to her in French, but instead opted to let Cristine know (in English) that we were there for her, and that we would not be leaving the club until she felt safe enough to walk through her home's door with her head held high.

That moment transported me back to the conversation I had with my friends at my farewell party right before I arrived in Switzerland, where an argument broke out after Pablo, a friend from school who had grown up to be someone nobody at the party could even remotely tolerate, told us about an incident he had experienced that day. He was on his way to his morning walk in *Parque de la Pulgosa,* close to the city's virtually abandoned airport, when he noticed a man who had clearly had a dozen too many, unshaven, wearing a stained old suit, his smell of rotten trout being noticeable from a mile away. The man had apparently not found a better thing to do on a Friday morning than to harass a young lady carrying her groceries back home, following her around, gratuitously telling her in the middle of the street about all the sexual fantasies he would've liked her to fulfil, even though it is more than likely he would have been unable to perform any of them past the thirty-five-second mark. The way Pablo described the look on her face reflected a familiar, collectively shared reality, which made me think of the polyhedral excellence with which such phenomena had been portrayed under a heavy cloud of cynicism and dark humour in the generation-capturing movie debut of Emerald Fennell, *Promising Young Woman* (2020). My argument was, and still is, that there is a conspiracy on this planet in which we are all a part of, because even if we don't like to admit it, we all naturally belong, are assigned to or choose to perform any one of three roles: victims, perpetrators or enablers. People like Pablo and the frightening majority of my male friends, even if they don't want to admit it, and even if they fail to realise the effect their actions could have on women—a topic of conversation in and of itself worthy of a collection of books—have all harassed women at some point in their lives, with the most likely scenario being while partying, where inhibitions tend to be dialled down and we have collectively accepted that responsibilities and moral duties fade away…only for some. The fact that by and large, most men look for—more like *hunt*—for drunk women at the club, in the hopes one will provide them with the personal gratification and approval they desperately crave, has become so ingrained in our collective imaginary that it is no longer registered as an act of depraved individuals: it has become the norm.

Watching men getting into fights either in or outside nightclubs has become not only a common trope, but something that is bound to happen at some point during the night; an event permanently fixed in the agenda, all stemming from an unfulfilled sexual desire women have been charged with failing to satisfy. And all that testosterone discharge is something accepted and ignorantly justified with the mortally charged expression, "Boys will be boys". Well, that is just a poor translation of "inability to handle emotions" and "fragile masculinity". No wonder we're progressively running out of safe spaces; generation after generation of men are being taught (encouraged, even) to have ape-like behaviour and react to sexual frustration with violence, often directed against women themselves for having the common sense of not wanting anything to do with people who give Max Cady vibes. And while the hashtag #NotAllMen is often thrown around by those who want to be on the right side of history (perhaps undeservingly so), the truth is that men by and large have been, are and will be either enablers of abuse or active enforcers of it. Who has not seen a man at a club or a party taking advantage of a drunk woman, and not done anything, huh? Well, many reading this right now, just like Pablo did back in the day, will claim they do not fit into either category, but I'm afraid his girlfriends would disagree, and I am positive that a lot of girlfriends, ex-girlfriends, wives and ex-wives around the world would, too. Now, while it would be unrealistic to claim that all men act in the same manner as Pablo—a self-appointed *womanizer* who tried a bit too hard to overcompensate for his severe erectile dysfunction and for the fact the only woman he had ever managed to make scream in bed was his mother during childbirth—it cannot possibly be denied that a lot of them share more than a couple of traits with him, whether we like to admit that level of self-awareness as a species, or whether we keep pretending that such a behaviour can only be found in a few "bad apples."

The point here is that that morning at *Parque de la Pulgosa*, Pablo had a choice to make, and he chose the coward's side. Because while a lot of men pride themselves into thinking that they have never abused any women nor coerced them into having sex with them—as if that was something to be applauded, God we have set such a low bar—most men who come to that thought are also thinking like what they are: men. And chances are that even if they didn't notice—which is part of the problem as well—they more than likely have overstepped their boundaries (to put it mildly) on more than one occasion. But Pablo described the anguish resulting from his decision that day, when he chose to lean not on the active abuser but on the passive enabler. Turning a blind eye, arguing it's just not his—*our*—problem, and that there is nothing that he could have done to change it because they were both grown-ups and make their own decisions—you know, the kind of lies one tells oneself just to be able to sleep at night. That's what motivated his decision, or so he claims. Which is why when he saw the fish-smelling man and the woman carrying the groceries looking for help, bearing the brunt of an imposed obligation she had no duty to bear, and she locked eyes with Pablo, he turned around and opted to go somewhere else. What could he do? Change her life? That's for people who are in command of their bodies and their lives, and for people looking for trouble. But I wonder, just between you and I, while nobody else is looking…if you were faced with that situation, what would you really do?

Anyway, after we managed to calm Cristine down, we all went outside to get some air, where we were offered nearly a dozen cigarettes from men deliriously expecting to get into our panties, like that scene from *Malèna* (2000). It took a few additional reassuring moments for Cristine to come back into her senses, not because she was not a bright person. Far from it. But the mixture of alcohol with the high toxicity component of the relationship she had found herself into had prevented her from, first, seeing the problem—at least its full scale—and second, asking for help, because how can you ask for help for a problem you don't even know you have? How can you even begin to search for real answers to what is gnawing your emotional stability and self-worth from the inside out if you have no choice but to face an imposed-upon inability to discern gaslighting tactics from the right questions that should actually be posed?

Once she started talking, it all came crashing down: the lies, the abuses, the cheating, the obsessions, the control, the nauseating feeling that filled her nights, the manipulation. A story told time and time again at such a terrifyingly frequent rate that by now had become a cliché. By the end, Cristine was a mess, and so were we.

"Come, let's go get breakfast. This is no place to cry, and he is no man worth crying for," I said, pretending to be someone with the confidence of Marlene Dietricht. Being the flora and the fauna of the night as depressing as it was, we took an Uber and headed downtown to *Chocolaterie Martel*, in the hopes of finding a redeeming ending for that night.

As the crackhead of our driver blazed past the streets of *Carouge* with the same regard for public safety as the cast from *Fast and Furious* for acting lessons, I gazed at Cristine's wide eyes, who, having sobered up and with her face now looking considerably more relieved after having found in our shoulders a safe space to cry in, now appeared to be in a much better place, in all possible senses, and we could not be happier to have met her on that eventful night. The same way that it takes a village to raise a child or make a movie, as it is often said, it takes the entire half of this world's population to ensure its own survival through an instinctive need to keep an eye on one another, as sad as it might be, to mutually support and protect us amongst ourselves in the face of there being no certainty that anybody else would be willing to.

With the morning rain slowly dripping down the car windows, I looked at Cristine's imposed-upon fragility, at the abuse she had endured, whose real depth and scope we would never get to truly know about, as the deepest pain can never be accurately described, only felt, and in her I saw myself, my own reflection, like two drops of water who had crossed paths in the middle of the race this life puts all through. And in her eyes, I realised that, though our pain had been engineered by a different author, we both had found ourselves trapped in a relationship from which there just did not seem to be any viable way to get out of, either by sheer impossibility, the delicacy of the subject and those around us which were affected by it, or our self-imposed blindness in an attempt to continue omitting the darkest parts of a relationship which was not in the least worth saving, yet we find ourselves in desperate need to preserve—her, as she told us, to not let go of the high school sweetheart with whom she had fallen in love five years prior; me, in the hopes of avoiding being perceived as the culprit for having irreparably fractured my family. But most importantly, in the relief that now flooded her reddish cheeks, in the way her eyes lit up with the comfort she clearly had yearned for and had now found in our soothing voices, I had an epiphany where I realised exactly the thing that needed to be done, the one which often seems too daunting of a task, the one that requires the most courage, the one we deny ourselves of being in need of, and yet the essential condition for getting out of the hole we find ourselves in: asking for help.

Whether it is to friends or siblings, to parents or therapists, or even to strangers like we were to Cristine, human beings feel the need to make a connection with one another and to momentarily let others make our suffering more bearable by opening up, by becoming vulnerable and letting out all the traumas and the suffering which, just like secrets, are hard to keep for oneself and have the potential to end up destroying you from the inside out. By allowing ourselves to get rid of our pain through honest conversations in sufficiently safe spaces—be it a therapist's office or your best friend's kitchen, your college dorm room or your trusted bar in front of the town square—taking that step to be willing to have that conversation, as hard as it may be, is the key to unlocking the path towards a potential recovery. Whether the problem has just started and you fail to pay it the attention it deserves or whether you're at the point of thinking it is unsolvable; whether you have trouble trusting others or instead have received no help in those instances when you asked for it; whether you have already exploded and are broken down into a thousand little pieces, or you are about to; whether you think you can carry this on your own; whether you think you are beyond redemption and unworthy of help; whether you're thinking of doing something from where there's simply no turning back or have already tried to head there… We act as a magnifying glass every time the pain is secluded within the compounds of ourselves, and when that becomes your sole reality and you choose to have nobody to confide it to, then, just like Plato's cave, all we will see will be that pain, progressively becoming our entire reality, severely incrementing over time, and eventually taking control of our own fate.

Like the liberating feeling I saw in Cristine's eyes, I yearned for a release I thought had never been at the tip of my fingers, until I comprehended that not only was I suicidal, I was also blind. Very much in the line of the clichéd "You never know what you've got until it's gone", I began to see all the times my friends back home had attempted to reach out, to penetrate into my thickly insulated skull, and their resulting frustration from being unable to help the person they knew needed it most because she did not want to be helped in the first place, even though in reality, it was because she initially did not know she *needed* to be helped, and when she did, she foolishly and arrogantly thought those others would be unfit, unable and unwilling to do so. As long as we remain incapable of trusting and confiding in others so as to aspire to get better, our troubles will do nothing but worsen over time, our despair nothing but multiply and our darkest thoughts nothing but materialise. Now I realise the hole is deeper than ever before, when I could have used the support of those I had single-handedly managed to push aside, even after they had many times lent me both their hands to get out of my bottomless and sadly often undetected pit of depression. Perhaps they had not done so directly, but in their own way, maybe in the shape of going to a movie they did not want to watch but knew I'd definitely enjoy, or by cheering me up with their jokes when they knew I needed it most, no doubt by constantly texting to check up on me even when I gave them no motivation to do so with my cold or inexistent replies, or possibly by simply remaining a bright lighthouse that would eventually lead me back to shore whenever I was as lost as I had found myself over those months. Like the love of relatives, we often take for granted the pillars of friendship around us and rarely utter how thankful we should be for them, both to ourselves and externally for them to hear. Without speaking a single word, Cristine had in that moment, in that car, on that rainy morning, made me finally come to terms with that specific side of the reality around me I had failed to acknowledge and appreciate; not only the friendships I had been lucky to have made there in Geneva, but especially the ones with those kind souls that had inadvertently put up with me since we were innocent kids. Now that I saw their true impact, the *supporting* role they played in the wild tragedy that my life was, instead of their role as extras in the background which I had erroneously assigned to them, made me realise that, perhaps, my situation was bearable enough if I had them all by my side.

We arrived at the store and had an absolute feast with our newly found friend, coming as near as I have ever been to a chocolate-induced coma. Even though Cristine's journey towards recovery was far from over (quite the contrary: it had just begun), we collectively felt, as only tight friendships can feel, something we never uttered amongst ourselves: a feeling that we had altered her life course, and she had become aware—awakening me in the process—of who she truly was, allowing her to begin to make a distinction, for the first time in a long while, between the life she was living and the life she deserved to live. We exchanged phone numbers and Instagram accounts with that girl whom we would regretfully never see again, and parted ways to head home to an awaiting and more than earned hangover.

Alone at the station in front of *Parc des Bastions,* waiting for the tram that would take us home, Michaela and I, the only ones who lived in the northern part of the city, decided to crown that Trophy Night—at that point, "Trophy Morning", all the more power to us, as robbery in broad daylight always brought in extra points when it came to computing the calculations to determine the real winner of the competition—by infiltrating the life-sized game of chess at the entrance of the park, and stealing a bishop, two queens and a knight, before sprinting over to the incoming tram. Before we could finish catching our breath, the ticket inspector arrived—always in time when it comes to the possible outlook of collecting other people's money—and quietly stood in front of us both. On that cold morning, Michaela and I were the only passengers of the tram: two women who were incidentally holding onto large chess pieces that unmistakably seemed like they had been illegally acquired, looking like two wet raccoons after our eyeliner had been ruined by Swiss weather.

My attention being absorbed by the realisation we had failed to buy the tickets for our trip back home, and trying to put into practice all those years of Kegel exercises upon noticing the fiendish incident being concocted inside of me and which was about to ensue as a result of the mixture of chocolate and booze (very much bringing back memories from the analogous incident one a week prior over at the United Nations), I was unable to reply to the inspector when he inquisitively asked in French, "Where did you get those chess pieces?" in a perceived tone of moral high ground which did not go unnoticed nor was appreciated in the least by us, particularly given that public property theft fell well out of his purview.

To her credit, Michaela played an award-worthy performance by never letting him know of the true extent of her drunkenness, as she managed to convincingly utter, "My grandmother gave them to me."

"At seven o'clock in a Friday morning?" he quickly followed up.

"Yes, you see, *Mister Inspector*, it was…it was before she

died," she answered, as a tear began running down her cheek. A moment of silence ensued where none of us moved a muscle...until one of the most powerful flatulencies I have ever produced escaped from the claws of my rectum and tore apart the moment of quiet that reigned in that tram car, surprising even myself and effectively ruining Michaela's performance. Such unexpected turn of events had—unbeknownst to me—prompted me to let go of the bottle of tequila I had been holding on my right hand. The bottle started to roll, propelled by the back and forth of the tram's movements, and landed right on the Inspector's feet.

We all stood there at an impasse where it seemed all movements had been outlawed for what amounted to a lifetime, but in reality turned out to be merely ten or fifteen seconds, after which he slowly bent his knees to pick up the bottle, unscrewed the cap, took a sip that was equivalent to a quarter of the bottle, and then menacingly declared, "Consider yourselves warned," in a French accent, missing a moustache to twirl to become an animated movie villain. Michaela and I did not dare to react to that statement, feeling as if we were back in eighth grade trying to unsuccessfully gain control of our laughter in front of the headmaster, fearing otherwise the exemption from a two hundred-Swiss-francs fine we had just been granted would turn out to be nothing but a fantasy. He then exited the tram at the *Bel-Air* stop, and started wandering aimlessly, clumsily tripping over construction work and nearly falling straight into the river, very much personifying the floating plastic bag from *American Beauty* (1999). Michaela tenderly laid her head on my shoulders, and we sat there in silence as we watched the city awakening from its deep sleep with the arrival of a few timid rays of Swiss sun. A new day awaited our arrival.

XV

LA PETITE MORT

Cinema and Death are unexpectedly linked together by the thread of Life, forming an intrinsic relationship often rooted in co-dependency: Life only exists in the absence of Death, and Cinema only exists in the presence of Life (with the former often managing to successfully bring the latter into our days). Yet, the same way that someone can reach a climax when having proper sex—a scarce commodity these days—one can actually experience a momentary orgasmic state of postcoital pseudo-death analogous to a phenomenon which some have coined as "*La Petite Mort*": a fleeting instance whereby our consciousness is weakened to the point of momentary abandonment. When extrapolated to the cinematic experience, such moment takes place when you and the work you are bearing witness to suddenly merge and become indistinguishable, and everything around you slowly fades away: your mind completely hijacked by a story that quite rightfully demands your attention; your limbs and organs no longer responsive to rational behaviour; your pulse accelerated; your lips forming a grin that results in an infectious smile; your pores invaded by sudden goosebumps covering every inch of your being. As if assaulted by an uncontrollable, immersive joy that inundates your body in a way that makes you feel unable to contain it all, cinema slowly wraps its tentacles around you until your entrancement leads your body to fall for a second, a shot, a dialogue, a scene, a movie, a filmography, under somebody else's control. This sustained crescendo speaks to the most irrational part of our being, an ungovernable feeling that makes us suddenly lose control of ourselves, and hand in the keys of our consciousness to a director who is perfectly in command of the concatenation of poetic images being presented to us in a profoundly poignant way, inspiring in us the emancipation of our best side residing all along within ourselves.

There are few better feelings than having the certainty that someone has invaded your brain, toyed around with your mind, and left you a different person by the time the credits start rolling. That is the deeper reason behind our persistent attendance to movie theatres over time: the hope that the person that enters and the one that emerges are no longer the same. Perhaps the change we experience is not necessarily produced in the way we perceive life. Perhaps it is less transcendental, like being exposed to situations we never had seen before. Perhaps it comes in the shape of an unheard song or a movie reference or the discovery of a promising up-and-coming actress. Because cinemas are places not unlike churches, places of worship, where we are told—on some occasions more enthusiastically than in others—a certain set of ideas that we can either reject or adhere to. Although, come to think of it, more than a place of worship, they fit best the description of places of knowledge, where you learn with failed incursions into reaching cinema glory, and are encouraged by successful ones to continue expanding your hunger for the art of moving pictures. Places of lovemaking, too, albeit not necessarily in a sexual way—although, I have certainly been made love to countless times during Andrzej Żuławski's movies—but as a means towards experiencing a love letter of a filmmaker to the unknown we desperately crave to know in the shape of *2001: A Space Odyssey* (1968); or to real-life figures that have made an indelible mark—for better or worse—in world history like *The Social Network* (2010) or *Judas and the Black Messiah* (2021); to the cities and towns deeply unappreciated by some and borderline-obsessed over by others as portrayed in *Wings of Desire* (1987) or *Manhattan* (1979); to the intense summer romances of *Before Sunrise* (1995) we dream with some day experiencing; to unexpected friendships formed in unexpected places like *Les Amants du Pont-Neuf* (1991); to periods we never lived through yet fill nostalgia for, like the 1960s lived through the kaleidoscopic *Last Night In Soho* (2021); to cultural snapshots that immortalise the previously inconceivable as relevant urban day-to-day life of ordinary people, as in *Berlin: Symphony of a Great City* (1927) or *Man with a Movie Camera* (1929); to reflecting the most troubling realities plaguing our societies, with some authors' dearly-troubled neighbourhood serving as the setting stage, be that a small block in New York, as in *Do the Right Thing* (1989) and *In the Heights* (2021), or the streets of Compton in *Boyz in the Hood* (1991); to the perceived loss of faith in humanity harrowingly portrayed in *Bicycle Thieves* (1948), and the restoration of our hopes in its future from the ever optimistic Frank Capra in *It's A Wonderful Life* (1946); to cinema, for its controversial implantation of the seed of voyeurism in all of us through *Rear Window* (1954) and *Peeping Tom* (1960), for the passion with which it inspires us to keep daydreaming and telling stories in the face of catastrophic existential crises as in *8 ½* (1963), for its ability to make us pull through life in the face of adversity in as beautiful a film as *Le Scaphandre et le Papillon* (2007), and for the inspiration it brings even in the most remote of locations, astoundingly showcased (if sometimes dipping its toe into oversentimental waters) to the tune of the master Ennio Morricone's score in *Cinema Paradiso* (1988).

It is often overlooked how crucial it is not only to nourish ourselves with as many stimuli as available around us, but also to, once exposed, carry out an introspective analysis of ourselves in order to identify that which brings us, personally, idiosyncratically, unapologetically, pure pleasure, and what doesn't, and to be able to determine so in a way that is decided by nobody other than ourselves. And when you find that thing that makes your troubles disappear, you want to start to schedule your life around it as soon as possible, because this discovery has allowed you to find a small piece of this Earth where you know you can go to whenever life comes crashing through your door, and be momentarily happy in the midst of all the chaos presiding over our daily lives. A refuge for the storm, an island for when you find yourself adrift, a painkiller for when the anguish reaches maximum levels and refuses to accept your truce offer. That certainty is there and will remain there as long as you need it to be.

How essential it can be to, after having developed an enthusiastic obsession with cinema, avoid crowning ourselves with a perceived moral superiority stemming from enjoying unconventional movies or titles that are perhaps relatively unknown for audiences at large, to never lose track of the persons we once were. This can be said of virtually any type of artistic creation which, whilst carrying a certain objective value, allows for pretentiousness to creep in through the cracks of its vast subjective nature, populating blogs and local Q&As with troubled individuals who delude themselves into believing to be better than everybody else just because of their penchant for trashing beloved films—many of them in search of validation from others when, ironically, the validation they should have been looking for all along was their own, and now find themselves unable to obtain either one. What a world.

Likewise, the endlessly incommensurable nature of cinematic production makes it impossible to ever read every single line written about the art form, or to watch the entire catalogue of movies shot, or to listen to every film study carefully analysing in excruciating specificity even the last detail of a particular director's filmography. Yet, bearing in mind that Cinema mirrors Life and vice versa, part of their appeal lies in the fact that, like any David Lynch movie, we will never get all the answers to our questions, only more questions. Because the truth is we will never get enough time to enjoy all of cinema. There is so much to learn and to watch and to read and to write, and yet so little time to do so, so we can only hope to do it one movie at a time. That is why we should spend our preciously scarce moments wisely, in the hopes of achieving all the answers to Life and to Cinema and to the Cinema of Life and to the Life of Cinema, though remaining aware throughout the way of the impossibility of our task and the nobility that lies in trying, nonetheless. Given the ticking sound that accompanies us everywhere we go, some conceive the limited time we have on Earth in relation to cinema not as a way to, each time they eventually sit down and commit to watching a film, make sure they pay as much attention as possible to truly take in the experience, but, instead, as a kind of list that they force themselves to constantly cross off names from, as if in the midst of grocery shopping, a futile task analogous to preparing for a race against the competitor nobody ever defeats, the one who will always remain faster than us, the one nobody can outrun, the one who has never lost a race: our own finite existence. So, since it is a race you know you can't win, then why not enjoy it? Why not make it last? In the end, we will all end up dead one way or another, so if all you can do is remember how fast you have been going instead of how much you have appreciated the view along the way (be it watching four or four thousand films), then you are as blind as the executives who refuse to finance Martin Scorsese's movies.

The entrancing spell filmmakers struggle to cast around a quick-to-learn audience that knows most of the tricks they may or may not have up their sleeve, provides a magnetic escape, a façade, a way to teleport, to travel in time to a destination and period which changes with each viewing, even on repeated screenings. Forever relevant, forever changing, forever influencing our lives and, in some cases, saving them. It has stood the test of time like no other medium, surviving in the era of streaming and blockbusters, inspiring artists to break away with screenplays that came out of a lab, maintaining the pertinence of period pieces and genre films through sheer innovation and willingness to speak a truth never heard before by audiences, and standing up to the dominating capitalist empire that drowns the artists' voices and promotes automatons who enjoy being moved by the strings of executive committees. When you enjoy something as much as you enjoy sex, then you know you have to keep it in your life the same way doctors prescribe their patients to incorporate physical exercise into their lives: at least once a day and for ninety minutes or more.

Referring to his magnum opuses *Persona* (1966) and *Cries and Whispers* (1972), Ingmar Bergman famously admitted in his book *Images* that by carrying out his work on these two films in an environment of relentless, unobstructed freedom, he had been able to reach the limits of his potential, of the very best that he could do as a movie director, all of which endowed him with the ability to uncover truths only reachable, only perceptible, only transmittable, through the Seventh Art. Which got me thinking: isn't that what we should strive for, then? For reaching those hidden secrets only unveiled in a movie theatre? For bearing witness to the best version of what a moviemaker can offer? For being inspired by seeing others reaching the summit of excellence? Without anything resembling an inch of envy or inferiority complex at sight, merely sheer admiration wrapped in solidarity, an aspiration to one day become the very best we could possibly offer; for putting our lives into what we do in the hopes that, when the time comes, we are able to call it a day and pick up our chips from the poker table. For living, at the end of the day, like you could die at any moment without any remorse.

A couple of weeks ago, my friend Vero and I decided to embark on one of those plans that seemed like a horrible idea in theory, standing in stark contradiction with the person I had been up until then, when we entered a screening of *Once Upon a Time in America* (1984) carrying four cold beers, two bottles of wine and more than a few snacks—which turned out to be a blessing in poor disguise, as the projectionist forgot to pause the movie at its intermission, eventually making it feel longer than sitting through one of Frank Coraci's movies. A fierce opposer of making noise, eating, and making noise while eating in as sacred a place as a movie theatre, I found myself becoming exactly the kind of person which I previously loathed. Like Harvey Dent's villainous turn, I had turned into the kind of person which I swore I would never become. The worst part was that it was not the first time such an occurrence had taken place, with the memory of a children-filled screening of *Mary Poppins* (1964) being noisily interrupted by the sound of our wine bottles being uncorked, effectively tearing up the impetus of the movie's narrative pacing and instantly quieting the talkative children, whilst simultaneously making their mothers salivate with envy at our Pinot Noir wine tasting event. Of course, after the wine came the Twinkies, and then the lemon pie, and the cashews and the sandwiches and the hummus and the bread—we had a five-course meal in reverse order, as we always did. During moments like those, I kept thinking about how I had never thought of happiness as a destination, as a permanent achievable state of mind, as a feeling that could potentially be elongated through time. Happiness, to me, was moments, glimpses, brief instances of joy whose existence we often become aware of only after they are long gone, moments such as those movie escapades, perhaps in the shape of an impressive camera technique in a film, or a long take, or a coordinated fight scene or a stunning dance sequence, or an overwhelmingly witty dialogue exchange between charismatic characters or, simply put, an objectively admirable, goddamn great movie. Those moments in between two to four hours, were where happiness mostly lay for me: seconds, minutes, hours when I was able to defy all laws of physics and float out of my body and merge with the silver screen to become one and the same.

Right now, things may seem dire for our depressed adults, disappointed due to our lost youth—a broken generation who have inherited the shattered dreams of their ancestors; climate catastrophes and potential war outlooks always in the cards; hunger and starvation constantly lurking at every corner. The chances are we will not last for long, and if we do, it is more than likely we will not want to live in the future we are currently constructing (or destroying), one oil refinery at a time. So, as a result of a desire to put into practice my most nihilistic tendencies, and very much sounding like virtually any wealthy twenty-year-old entrepreneur who preaches others to "follow your dreams like I did" (minus the astronomical loans of their billionaire parents), just enjoy the ride, my mind says, because who cares at the end of the day? Who cares whether you like Fritz Lang or Pasolini or both or neither? Who cares if you hated *12 Angry Men* (1957)?[1] Who actually pays attention to whether you gave *Un Chien Andalou* (1929) three and a half stars instead of four stars in your attention-whore Letterboxd review? Who in their right mind is going to prevent you from enjoying *Godzilla vs. Kong* (2021)? Do not call them guilty pleasures anymore: call them pleasures, period.

We must respect the cinematic experience and steer away from pretentiousness and incorporate and respect a varied intake of diverse art into our bodies and souls, creating a space where we can humbly enjoy any piece of work that speaks to us on any level—be that a Dwayne Johnson franchise or a Julia Ducournau movie. Or at the very least, we must try.

So next time you enter a movie theatre, just sit down, turn off your phone, let the characters do the talking, and enjoy the film. You might learn a thing or two. And, if you're lucky, you will experience a *petite mort* along the way or, in the best cases, from start to finish.

Posted on August 2, 2021 by **Carla J. Galván.**

This article appeared in the August edition of ***The Silver Nitrate Magazine****, our free online newsletter featuring original movie reviews, interpretations and analyses.*

---

[1] Actually, *I* care, but you do you.

XVI

ONE VIRGIN, THREE SINNERS

With my parents having contracted COVID from my brother and thus no longer being able to come to visit me in Switzerland—you know, because when you're only twenty-six years of age there is no way of understanding that when you become infected with the virus, the first and only thing in your mind should be to lock yourself into a room and do the mandatory quarantine, instead of casually continuing your far-too-comfortable life alongside the high-risk people (both of them having entered by then into sixty-year old territory) who had been doomed with the burdensome task of being your parents—I decided to go on a trip with the girls to take a small break from the accumulated stress of doing absolutely nothing at work. Michaela, Claudia, and Lara were unable to join us, and so was Vero, who had already spent all her days off at work. So it was just Anna, Arantxa and myself. Having the bank accounts of the twenty-something-year-old interns that we currently had, as we currently were, luxury was never a part of our plan, unless provided by someone else—like all those endless nights of free drinks, courtesy of repressed male sexual desire over at *Village du Soir*. Instead, we opted for a plan whose appeal partly lay in its simplicity, as most enjoyable things in life do, which chiefly consisted of renting *proper* bikes for Anna and myself—that is, electrical bikes instead of the machine of anal torture that my bicycle had become by then, a turn of events which the sportive Arantxa did not realise until it was too late to come back to the store, just as we had planned—and cycling around Lake *Léman* during the weekend, making a pitstop at *Vevey* to rest for the night.

Neither our minds nor our bodies were ready for riding those bikes for nearly two hundred miles a day, which only made me think I had absolutely no idea how my eighty-year-old rusty heart and Anna's tobacco-loving lungs could have possibly made it past Geneva had it not been for the motor propelling our bikes and doing most of the heavy lifting while Arantxa, more in shape than a WWE-steroid induced wrestler, cycled the many roads uphill without a worry in her mind. We looked like the Beatles, had the Beatles ever felt the need to carry their bodies to near exhaustion, forming a straight line along the road: Arantxa leading us as the natural captain she was, me in the middle constantly reminding myself to close my mouth with each bug that I continued to obliviously swallow, and Anna standing last as the last piece of the pack of lonely wolves we were, fearing we would laugh at her cycling abilities. Her fears were ill-placed, as I turned out to be the first one to fall from my bike in one of the treacherous curves which the inner roads nearing *Versoix* hid, my mind being occupied with that time the highly overrated and incessantly pretentious Jared Leto opened the door for all of us to stare at his completely delusional perception of reality when he described his laughably misguided and entirely make-up-sustained performance in *House of Gucci* (2021) as a declaration of love to the country of Italy.

"Must have been Mussolini's Italy," I wondered right before smashing my bicycle onto a streetlamp and being subsequently propelled head on right into a perfectly placed, three-foot wide, tender Swiss cow excrement.

The girls' bike tires came to a screeching halt, and I could hear Arantxa asking in the distance, "Are you okay?" to which I replied, "Yeah, last night I had Claudia's enchiladas so...not my first time eating shit." After that sudden burst of cosmic justice served me a much-needed portion of humble pie, I literally shook the shit off my body with the help of a nearby fountain, laughed it off and carried on with the show.

Very much in-character, Anna characteristically took a long drag out of a cigarette while we had our pagan midday beer by the local town church in *Nyon*, with a sun brighter than we had ever seen before in the country hitting hard on our faces. That small stop brought us back to life, after effortlessly climbing the steep road leading up the hill—this time, Arantxa nearly coughing up her right lung when facing the nearing ninety-degree inclination of the path leading up to it. The trip continued with a few pitstops along the way, followed by more beer to the point of making us a public safety hazard by the early hours of the sunny afternoon. It was only around the time we found ourselves in the midst of devouring our hummus and cheese sandwiches at the city of *Lausanne* that we realised we had no place to sleep on that night. We still had three hours to pull through until our arrival (two of actual cycling, and one of most certainly getting lost along the way), so I took a puff of our heavily loaded joint, and a sip of the cold Belgian beer I had bought at the supermarket, to conjure up the little French residing somewhere in the vastly unexplored territory that was my brain. After Googling and subsequently phoning a number of hostels with no available (nor affordable) rooms for us, given the immediacy of our request, I no longer knew the telephone I was dialling anymore, but I went through the same process once again, expecting to get rejected quicklier than a naive, mid-western Broadway-singer wannabe with big dreams coming to New York City for her first time. This last-ditch attempt was carried out without an ounce of hope in emerging victorious, as we were all by then mentally preparing to sleep on the cold, hostile streets that night.

"Well, we've been through worse," I said. Arantxa nodded, but Anna relegated to taking a drag of her cigarette. To their surprise, and very much to *mine*, I unexpectedly managed to book a reservation for that night. I thanked the clerk who had picked up the phone and had managed not to laugh at my disregard for French grammar, and we continued our adventure.

By now, the road was illuminated by the bright colours of the sun setting. So exceptional was that sight enveloping everything around us that we had no choice but to stop midway, despite being already late to our reservation at the hostel, and admire the most remarkable sunset I had ever seen in my entire life. Almost a religious experience—the sun slowly taking refuge into the vastness of Lake Geneva, the infinite shades of gold covering every inch of the mountains surrounding such a colossal piece of genuine beauty, the local people walking by as if having gotten used to such a stunning image, the immaculate reflection of the sun into the windows of the passing cars—the three of us sat in total silence on a perfectly placed bench near the road. Being well aware that no words could possibly come close to describing such an irreplaceable view, none were spoken, as when in the presence of something as extraordinary as what was in front of our eyes, the only thing one can do is try to capture every second of it as best as one can and store it in the box of unforgettable memories one will spend the rest of her life remembering. That moment was, to me, like that scene in *The Barbarian Invasions* (2003) when Natalie describes Rémy the wave forever chased by all junkies who are permanently on a manhunt to replicate the experience they had the first time heroin entered their bloodstream. That would be the wave to pursue, the one to try and reproduce yet possibly never reach again; for that moment, and every other in our lives, it could never be repeated, as hard as we tried, and as much as it ached us. It is common sense, then, to approach every second of our existence as what Lara once described as "taking pictures with your eyes", for we only have today, right now, this moment. And nothing else is certain. And nothing else matters.

We reached *Vevey* two hours after the agreed-upon time, and the mildly tipsy band of irresponsible peril dynamos that we were soon realised we had indeed booked up a place to stay for the night, yet had no idea of what place that was, nor its name, nor how to get there. With my phone battery long dead, and all hostels looking like exact replicas of one another on the Internet, I had the humbling experience of channelling an alcoholic, forty-year-old cougar who arrives late at her adoptive son's school play of "The Wizard of Oz", when I had no choice but to call each hostel one by one, in French, at ten p.m., audibly intoxicated, blubberingly asking the astonished night clerks whether they had a reservation to my name, and if so, what was the name of their hostel…until one of them replied affirmatively. This little manoeuvre set us back an additional half an hour, but we managed to finally arrive to the place: a derelict-looking small apartment located above a Thai restaurant which seemed to be a cosy hideout at the heart of the town's criminal underground, and inside looked like someone else's place had been quickly (and ineffectively) cleaned in a rush. I say this because the person in question had left his family pictures hanging on the walls, as well as his toothbrush in the bathroom and colossal purple dildo under the bed. As far as welcoming presents go, it was quite thoughtful of him, if I might say so.

Once we had left our bags inside the tiny apartment, and, fearing the owner of the place would come in with a chainsaw and make us leave the room in weekly fascicles, we headed downtown to satiate our starving stomachs with a typically Swiss dinner of pizza and beer at a locally traditional Italian-themed restaurant—a much fancier place than we were used to frequenting, yet the only one which remained open at that late hour of the night.

"Never have I felt more underdressed in my life," said Anna upon noticing the other customers were all in a suit and tie, and delicate summer dresses, very much standing at a sharp contrast with our leggings and sweaty running tops. The two one-litre beers that each of us impressively chugged down in a matter of minutes helped our bodies rest after an entire day of cycling in the sun. Whilst Arantxa and I spoke about the job she would be starting soon in Jordan, Anna, having long left her inhibitions elsewhere, began raising her left leg in the middle of the restaurant, unknowingly to her but very much knowingly to everyone else, and stretching out like a chimpanzee struggling to lick his testicles. Her recently emancipated leg kept rising without her noticing, and Arantxa and I made a silent pact with a complicit one-second look not to say anything until she did. Soon after, a waiter of minuscule size and long acrylic nails came to let her know that not only were we severely underdressed, but also Anna was not allowed to be doing whatever it was she was doing in her restaurant, to which Arantxa and I replied by surreptitiously raising our right leg in solidarity. It would not take long for the security staff to escort us out, but it did not matter to us in the least. On the contrary: we had just gotten away with free drinks.

We continued stretching a little more on the stones placed in front of the Charles Chaplin statue (commemorating this world's tolerance for cruelty after it inexplicably secluded an exiled Chaplin into that town until he took his final breath), right in front of that hideous, purposeless fork inexplicably inserted onto the lake like a metaphor for the established recognition gained in Hollywood by the objectively talentless Affleck Brothers. Once we had finished up all the weed we had for that trip, Arantxa began improvising the meaning of the star constellations hovering around our heads and painting up the dark Swiss skies, to a perfectly gullible Anna and I. After a while, it became colder than humanly bearable, so we decided to call it a night and get some rest. On our way to the cholera-infected mousetrap we were about to sleep in, I had the great idea of popping into the most unappealing bar in town, perhaps in the country: a barely lit, ominous-looking, hole-on-the-wall frequented by even less people than Simon's Armenian karaoke.

"Okay, but just one beer," Arantxa sentenced.

By the time we got out, it was plain daylight. The sun relentlessly imprinted its presence onto our hungover retinas and the streets and grey-coloured walls of the identical-looking buildings covering the main avenue. Just then, Anna had the impending and all-encompassing need to, as she put it herself, "See the Virgin Mary", as if we had found ourselves in the middle of the scene from *La Dolce Vita* (1960) where a whole village impetuously gathers at the very first irrational hint of divine apparition. She started sprinting down the street, until—sure enough—she found a somewhat ramshackle building on top of which an oscillating rusty plaque read "...Church". The top part of the plaque was unreadable, a consequence of time, filth, meteorological phenomena, or, perhaps, of intentional misdirection.

"Anna, wait up!" we shouted at her.

"No! I just need to see Mary!" she replied, slamming the door open so energetically it smashed onto the wall and broke the tainted glass into a few uneven pieces.

The deafening sound effectively woke the entire village of Vevey, yet Anna felt the need to ask us, in a childlike voice, not entirely in command of herself, "Do you think they have heard us?"

"I don't know, Anna, depends on whether they are as deaf as you're drunk," Arantxa replied. We walked up the spiral staircase of that church until we arrived at the top floor, the three of us heavily panting after a night of having too much of everything.

Looking like Inspector Clouseau, Hrundi V. Bakshi and Lieutenant Frank Drebin, respectively, we entered a vast room filled with austere metal benches and presided over a colossal wooden cross where an altar lay, covered in a pale tablecloth. Arantxa and I discreetly sat down on the rows nearest to the door, while Anna, apparently ecstatic by the presence of Christ and the Virgin Mary, went on her knees and started praying like the fierce devotee that her acts whilst in Geneva had heavily come to contradict. A tall, white-haired man with noticeably long sideburns yet no neckline anywhere in sight, made a dramatic entrance into the room.

"Excuse me, can I help you?" he asked.

"Oh, no, we just came in to say a little prayer," I said, and after noticing his cassock added, "...Father." He remained silent and looked at us: three sweaty ladies with greasy hair, wearing dirty (and, by his church's standards, much too short and way too tight) clothes, and sporting baggy eyes long enough for us to qualify as Parisian brothel Madammes.

"I see...have you had breakfast yet?" he kindly asked. Anna's face instantly lit up, even interrupting the prayers she had previously been so deeply invested in, and looked at us like a playful puppy with a *Shrek 2* (2004)-Puss-in-Boots-look, begging us to follow up on the Father's apparent invitation.

"No...?" I managed to say, being as convinced with my reply as I was of the real value which my bachelor's degree in International Politics actually had in the labour market.

"Well, then, come with me, 'my children', we have plenty of croissants and coffee for you," he said, before disappearing into a nearby room. Alcohol, hunger and sheer carelessness led us to accept his invitation, which could have easily resulted in a newspaper headline, yet turned out to be nothing but a selfless gesture from a genuinely kind individual, regardless of his or our religious (or otherwise) beliefs.

After we had devoured all his croissants and were well on our third cup of hot chocolate, it became apparent that, as luck would have it, and out of all places in town, we found ourselves at that moment at a Christian Evangelical Church, which widely differed from Anna's Catholic Church, and with Arantxa's Judaism, and with my agnostic faith.

"So...you *don't* have a Virgin Mary?" a disappointed Anna wondered, as if her world had just irreparably crumbled apart.

"Yes, that's pretty much what makes us different from your Church, my dear," he calmly replied. Arantxa's head started uncontrollably falling up and down, a result of our accumulated tiredness, while my mind somehow found enough strength to regurgitate a TikTok I had seen a few months prior in which I seemingly learned that raising one of your legs prevented you from falling asleep. To his credit, the friendly priest took compassion in us, as he painstakingly explained the core pillars of his faith to a drunken Anna, remained calm at Arantxa's struggles to fall asleep, and made no effort to acknowledge me when I started, without any previous explanation, calmly raising my leg above the ground, just like Anna had done on the night prior at the Italian restaurant.

Soon, the need to sleep was trumped by my still insatiable hunger, so, while avoiding eye contact with the priest yet being positively noticed by him, I reached out to the table right next to us, and with my left eye twitching and my right leg being lift up high, I clumsily grabbed the first item of food I could get my hands on, unknowingly pushing a silver platter into the ground and effectively letting everyone in the building know of the theft I was in the midst of carrying out. I smiled, as they carried on with their conversation and Arantxa remained a lifeless corpse, had her head not been endlessly wandering around in a futile attempt to stay awake. Eventually, I gained enough courage to take a bite of the bread I had just stolen—bread which the priest would later kindly let me know, was the sacred bread of the mass he was about to give—its rough texture and dry content making me instantly cough and instinctively grab the first thing containing liquid that I could get hold of: a silver chalice that— yes, indeed—contained the sacred wine for the forthcoming mass.

The priest now turned his attention to me and asked, "So, tell me, my child, other than saying your prayers, why did you come to this Church in particular, out of all places?" I guess in an attempt to determine whether he should call the police or the psychiatric ward. After gagging on my sacred booze, and very much in the midst of a panic attack (never been one to excel under pressure), all I managed to say was "...because...we're getting...married...?" which turned out to be, of course, one of the few wrong ways to answer that otherwise perfectly simple and easily navigable question. Without any prior warning, Arantxa's head suddenly smashed onto the table, having finally succumbed to gravity, and effectively made her fall into a sleep deep enough not to notice the heavy blow her face had just taken.

"Oh…" the befuddled priest said. "In that case, wait here, my child." He left the room—to get his murder weapon of choice, I assumed—and returned with a Bible that had a bookmark on Genesis 2:24, which he handed to me as he walked us out. Having made enough sins in that sacred place to burn in our respectively believed or denied Hells for all eternity, we managed to get a confused Anna, now bubbling with probably worthless knowledge about this new faith we had stumbled upon, and the still inanimate object by now Arantxa had become, out of that Evangelical Church with filled bellies courtesy of Jesus Christ, and headed over to the hostel we miraculously managed to find without encountering any major difficulty along the way, for a change.

The two of them went straight into bed, not even undressing nor realising the picture of a married couple placed right next to their head, atop the bedside table. Sat down on my bed, right above the purple dildo, I looked at those crazy ladies I had been blessed with knowing, and questioned myself whether it was worth it to get out of a world where they were a part of and into another where they weren't; whether my catastrophic intentions could ever be drained out; whether my death was, as I had intended myself on believing, inevitable or whether there was still joy to be had, with them, with my friends back in Spain, with my parents, or even all by myself; whether another chance was possible, and whether I indeed deserved it. How radically different life can be when looked at from the right lens and in the right company.

"Thank you, ladies, for making me experience something other than misery for a change," I thought before whispering it to the two sleeping beauties. "Thank you for not letting me forget even for a second what happiness really feels like."

XVII

FOR SHE HAD EYES AND CHOSE...US

Two hazel-coloured lamps faintly light up the living room, with the switched-on TV loudly playing Laurence Olivier's (now infamous blackface) rendition of Othello (1965). Metres away, on the adjacent open-doored kitchen, Carla and her mother finish eating dinner, while casually taking initially shy (yet progressively more sizeable) sips of their wine glasses. On their plates we see an uncomplicated tomato salad next to some "croquetas" and "recently-prepared "carrilleras". In the background, at a slightly fainter tone than the TV, we can hear Carla's father loudly snoring, the vibrations of his clamorous breathing felt on the walls and the titillating lights hovering atop the living room.

MOM: ...which reminds me of that one time I pissed my pants in church—oh, what a day! Anyway, I need to call *Centanni* to make a reservation. Does Sunday work for you for a little brunch, just the two of us? It's been a while since we last—

CARLA (*over*)**:** Hang on, hang on. You WHAT?

MOM: ...need to call *Centanni*?

CARLA: No, no. The other thing.

MOM: Pissed my pants in church. Haven't we all at some point?

CARLA: Mom, the only grown-ups who still piss their pants are Members of Parliament, heroin addicts and probably Maluma. That's it.

MOM: Oh, darling, you've clearly never been pregnant, so don't play the puritan card on me. There are to be no prudish attitudes in this house as long as you live under this roof.

CARLA: I'm not being puritanical.

MOM: Oh, I know—your newly acquired, ten-pound sex toy can vouch for that.

CARLA: Would you please stop LOOKING AT MY AMAZON PURCHASE HISTORY?

MOM: It's my account, too!

CARLA: And, by the way, it's not a ten-pound sex toy… (*Beat*). It's a six-pound one.

MOM: Oh, honey, there's no need to explain—we've all been twenty-three at some point in our lives. Anyway, about pissing myself—

CARLA: Ugh. When was it, by the way? The church thing, I mean.

MOM: When was it? Hmm, let's see. Oh, right: yesterday morning, during the eleven a.m. mass. It's so funny, HA, everyone could hear the drips throughout the service, and blamed it all on a leaking pipe. It was a leaking pipe alright!

CARLA: Jesus Christ...

MOM: Exactly! After it was all over, I noticed the pool of pee around us. So, I did what anybody would have done in my case...

CARLA: Please tell me you didn't blame Mrs Santamaría.

MOM: I blamed Mrs Santamaría.

CARLA: Mom! She's an invalid!

MOM: Precisely!

CARLA: And hearing-impaired!

MOM: Even better. Who's gonna ask any questions, huh? I rest my case.

CARLA: You're one crazy lady, I'll give you that.

MOM: The one thing I got from your grandma. (*Lets out a deep sigh*). Ah...my darling. What am I going to do without you?

CARLA: Don't be dramatic—it's only six months, Mom...

MOM: Six months too many! Before you know it, you've opened a Swiss bank account and have started working for the Swiss government, married to a Swiss cheese maker and visiting a sperm bank to have blonde children who will grow up to be watchmakers.

CARLA: Did you leave out any clichés out of that fantasy?

MOM: No, I think I managed to stick them all inside.

BOTH (*after a brief pause of defiance*)**:** That's what she said!

MOM (*they laugh for some time, then*)**:** Ah…never gets old. What is it about misogynist jokes that always stand the test of time?

CARLA: That the patriarchy is still in place, living in even the best of us.

MOM: Amen to that.

CARLA (*quickly finishing up her dinner*)**:** I'm going to sleep now: tomorrow some of us have a busy workday ahead of us filled with pretending that we do something useful at our job.

MOM: What exactly do you do at this place, anyway? I know, I know. Hang on, let me do it before you do (*Putting on a funny face and getting cross-eyed*). "I've told you before, MOOOOOOOOOM." I know you have but, what can I say—I'm drunk, and I probably was all the other times when you told me, too.

CARLA: You're really starting to sound like the fifth member of the *Desperate Housewives* club.

MOM: Hey, as long as it's not that bitch Samantha.

CARLA: Wrong show.

MOM: Not all role-models have to refuse a glass of wine every now and again.

CARLA: Mom, you pissed yourself—

MOM: Oh, like you have never answered the call of nature unprepared for the occasion.

CARLA: NOT AT CHURCH!

MOM: Wasn't my first time, either.

CARLA: Oh, for fuck's sake, what has gotten into you!

MOM: Chardonnay, baby. Tonight is momma's night of rest after ten days of working non-stop, correcting the final exams of those ungrateful little unsuccessful abortions over at school.

CARLA: Mom, they're twelve.

MOM: That's the worst age. Your brother started breaking shit at that age.

CARLA (*under her breath*): ...and hasn't stopped ever since.

MOM: What was that?

CARLA: Nothing, nothing...

MOM (*after a long, meditative pause, looking straight into her daughter's eyes, in a more serious tone now*): You know, I am aware of what you think about him.

CARLA: About whom?

MOM: We are not blind, your father and I. And we hear it all and we see it all, and we suffer, just like you do—if not more.

CARLA: Please, let us have one dinner in peace, one in which he is not the topic of conversation, for once.

MOM (*taking one step forward, all hints of joking long gone*): You think you're the only one in this house with years-long anxiety? The only depressed person under this roof who wakes up every morning feeling like she has a deep hole on her chest?

CARLA: Please, Mom, let's not.

MOM: No, no—let's. Because you seem to be under the wrong impression that you are not to blame for this mess.

CARLA: Excuse me?

MOM: When a person hates himself as much as brother does, any additional rejection from others only magnifies whatever it is that he carries inside.

CARLA: He is the one who has earned that spot on his own, Mom. (*Looking at Frank Finlay's Iago entering into scene on TV*). Just like he did.

MOM: Oh, please don't tell me we're about to get inside of that like we're in some Woody Allen movie.

CARLA: Wouldst yond beest so lacking valour? What art thee afeard of?

MOM: Enow.

CARLA: Look, I know your love for him blinds you, and believing that he is a different person is more comforting than realising exactly the kind of person that he has grown up to be, but...

MOM: Your brother is not a bad person, Carla. (*Her daughter replies by instinctively scoffing, exhaling with disdain*). He simply lacks...emotional intelligence, and the sensitivity to know he needs to act on his problem, because it has gotten out of hand.

CARLA (*after a brief pause*)**:** Wow...that is the first time I have heard you admitting he is the one with the problem here, instead of me.

MOM: I said no such thing. We all have a part in your brother's story, and as far as I remember, you have had more than a few instances where you've lost your temper and said some deeply hurtful things to him. I am sure those did not help.

CARLA: You never saw what came before that, did you? What actually led to those moments. You only saw the result, the spectacle, the show he loves to put on just for you and Dad to see. That is why you will never be able to see the entire scope of the problem, or the kind of person that he really is. I mean, how could you? You only see him as the person he claims to be in your eyes, and you only see me as the person he has convinced you all I am. I'm sorry, Mom, but you have never been able to look at this from an objective point of view. And I don't think you ever will.

MOM: The human mind is very, very complex. And I am not a psychiatrist, but it is very clear that your brother is a troubled person—nobody is saying otherwise. But honey, if anybody needs therapy, that's the two of you, not just him. I think saying that is fairly uncontroversial, right?

CARLA: It's very different to be the one who needs therapy because of her own actions than to need it because of someone else's.

MOM: And what am I supposed to do, huh? Stop loving him? He is my child as much as you are.

CARLA: No, Mom—I am not asking you to stop loving anybody, but I am *begging* you to start loving yourself. Life is slipping through your fingers, and you keep defending someone for actions that cannot be defended; blindly praying for someone who does not deserve your prayers; irrationally trusting that one day, a person who has never shown any remorse nor willingness to change miraculously understands the scope, the depth and the long-lasting consequences from the pain he has caused.

MOM: I am not abandoning my child, Carla, even if nobody believes he can get better. <u>Especially then</u>. We never stop loving our children—that is not what mothers do. Mothers stand by, rain or shine, against all odds, against whatever comes our way, against any problem our children may face. And we remain in our place, and suffer in silence, even when you think I don't care about this problem or refuse to deal with it. I deal with it the best way that I can. Your brother needs love; how could I possibly refuse to give that to him? Could you even imagine where a person like him would end up without his mother's undying love and support? I play the role I can play, and I try to do my best. (*Tears start rolling down her cheeks, yet she remains in full control of herself*). You two, and your father, you're the most important thing that has ever happened to me. And when I see your relationship...my heart shatters, and I don't think it can ever be repaired. But that has never stopped me from believing that one day it will. And there is nobody that can take away that hope from me, including you, because in the absence of your brother's ability to express his love for us, that is all I have left. (*Wiping away the tears with the cuff of her wool sweater*). So, I will remain right where I am, giving your brother all the love he needs and more, even if he doesn't deserve it, and hopefully some of it will get through and one day we can all finally aspire to have something—anything, really—resembling a proper family. But do not ever mistake my lack of progress with your brother with a lack of trying.

CARLA: Well, do not mistake my lack of trying with my lack of wanting to. Because I have tried, Mom, and failed many times before. Four times in which I humiliated myself for you when I came knocking on his door, literally, and apologised to him and asked forgiveness that I did not need, taking blame for actions I was never responsible for, all in the hopes we were all collectively in a better position to sleep at night. Well, four times he either refused to talk, listen or even see me. Four times that my heart, too, was broken. Four times that made me give up and realise that some causes are not worth fighting for. I'm sorry, Mom, but you have no right to lay all the blame, or even part of it, on me.

MOM: Just do me a favour, Carla. I know you don't believe in God, at least the same way your father and I do, but you need to learn to forgive, even if you don't think he deserves it. You must take this weight off your shoulders, off your chest, if you want to properly breathe, if you want to have a life beyond your brother. The best thing you can do for yourself, and for him, is to forgive and cast hate out of your life.

CARLA: How can you stand there and seriously ask that to me, instead of him? He is the one who had hated me since I was born, for some <u>fucking</u> reason I am sure he doesn't know himself well enough to even understand.

MOM: It's not hate…it's misunderstood love and affection that he has no way of knowing how to give. But he doesn't hate you, Carla, even if he doesn't realize that himself.

CARLA: Well, while we're being honest here—I think *I* hate him.

MOM: Don't say that; you know it is not true. Underneath all of the anger that you feel right now, whether misplaced or not, lies love waiting to be freed. You will see, in time, that your brother is not deserving of your hate, nor your pity. He is only deserving of your understanding.

CARLA (*a brief silence ensues; only the TV and Carla's father's snoring can be heard now*)**:** Sounds like he won't be coming to dinner after all.

MOM: Oh, you know…he's too tired these days, the night shifts are taking the life out of him. He's our big, round angel, so all is forgiven for him, even his ungodly snoring. (*After a brief pause*). …so, now that we've got that out of the way…tell me about this mysterious new job of yours.

CARLA (*clearing her throat*)**:** Well, it's not very exciting, really. It's another internship at an NGO. In Geneva, this time.

MOM: Oh, another one of those. Does this one pay you, at least?

CARLA: Well, yes…most of it will go straight into my future landlord's pockets, though. Switzerland remains relentlessly undefeated when it comes to setting unethical rent prices.

MOM: I see… Well, at least this one isn't unpaid like the last four…

CARLA: No, it isn't, but the next one probably will be. Most of them are, anyway. It's a tough sector.

MOM: But aren't non-profit organisations supposed to be based on, well, non-profit? Seems a little on the nose that they, out of all organisations out there, are the ones who deny your human rights by either paying wages below the minimum salary or offering no salary whatsoever. Oh, sorry, what do they always say? Ah, right: "They pay you with experience." That's funny. Next time I go grocery shopping I'm going to pay the cashier with experience—let's see how fast I end up at the police station…again.

CARLA: There is no time to unpack all of that, and I am honestly too afraid to ask about that last story. All I can say is that this NGO looks to be a little different from the rest. It mobilizes and coordinates action to defend vulnerable children around the world. It is more of a noble profession than the others, you have to give them that.

MOM: Noble aspirations should not be a priority for an international politics graduate, in my humble opinion. But I'm proud you have found a job that encourages you to channel the best part of yourself. (*Raising her glass*): Let's drink to that!

CARLA (*smiling, taking a sip of her Chardonnay*)**:** I don't have a clue about what exactly my day-to-day tasks will be, to be honest. My latest professional experience over the past months has been mostly relegated to just clicking on shared Excel documents all day long and putting ticks on tasks I have not completed before I go ahead and watch a couple of films a day on my computer. And so far, nobody has asked any questions and I have refused to give any answers.

MOM: I see. Let's hope they don't demand any references from past managers, or dig in too deeply on your CV, then.

CARLA: The world is such an unfair place because there are people like me in it, right?

MOM: Agreed. I bet if *you* worked for *yourself*, you'd immediately get fired.

CARLA: Quite likely.

MOM: So, tell me, while we're dealing with intense topics tonight…what exactly do you intend to get out of life?

CARLA: Oh, so we're having this conversation now, are we?

MOM: What better time to tell your mother about the future that you're planning? I just want to see the direction you think your life is taking, and whether everything you're doing is all part of a (*air quotes*) "bigger plan" or, if like most of us, you're just making it up as you go. And if it is the latter, see if there's anything I can do to help.

CARLA: Well, you know this NGO-anti-meritocratic-reserved-only-for-the-most-privileged-thankless-job kind of situation was never *really* my true passion…

MOM: Uh-huh.

CARLA: But if you play your cards right, I guess it could potentially be a *profitable* job…

MOM: I feel we're speaking different languages now: you're talking profits, I'm talking passion.

CARLA: Sorry, Mom, but that kind of "pursue your dreams" idealistic bullshit has no effect on me, anymore. I mean, no offense but, look at you: did you want to become a middle school English teacher, really?

MOM: Yes, I did, you elitist little bitch. (*They both let a vociferous laugh fill the room*). I love changing those kids' lives by forcing their eyeballs to read Mary Shelley and Jane Austen and Virginia Wolf, even if they are as ungrateful as they come. Sure, your grandfather made us all enrol in college, but there is no doubt in my mind that he would have supported me if I had wanted to be a lion tamer, or a stripper, or a nun, or all three at once. And you know I will be just as supportive with you as he was with me. So, what do you *really* want your life to look like?

CARLA: (*long pause*): I guess I've never really thought about it as a real option, because it just seems so far away, but for some years now, I keep daydreaming about being a writer. Yes, I would love to write for a living.

MOM: There you go.

CARLA: And if possible, to somehow combine that with movies.

MOM: Like a film critic?

CARLA: Sure, but not necessarily, because this world will never run out of critics, anyway. It would be more focused on analysing films, debating their meaning…in the shape of a book, or a screenplay, or something in between, perhaps. Or maybe a reflection like one of those essays that I published, remember?

MOM: Oh, yes. They were really helpful to cure my insomnia.

CARLA: Mom!

MOM: Kidding…though not really. (*Carla looks at her, irritated*). Don't look at me like that, sweety; there's nothing wrong with being an acquired taste. You don't need my approval to know your worth, both as a person, as an artist and as a writer…but you have it, nonetheless. You know that, right?

CARLA: Uh-huh.

MOM: (*opening her arms*): Come here, you grumpy little Pauline Kael. (*She tenderly hugs her daughter*). If there is a time to be lost in life, it is precisely right now, when you still have time to gain the perspective that you need so you don't make the mistakes most of us ended up making. If you want to keep the life that you have, then go for it. There is nothing wrong with doing a job that you half-like and find half-interesting. Besides, you can still combine that with your writings, right? *(Carla nods)*. Good. So, while you continue to search for yourself, you can sort of feed both beasts simultaneously, and after some time, see which one grows faster and demands your attention with more urgency. Hopefully, personal and artistic fulfilment will result if you choose the path that nourishes your soul the most.

CARLA: How can you be this insightful when you're *this* drunk?

MOM: Oh, darling, practice—a lot of practice. And it's been finals week, so you can't blame me. Besides, what are four nights in a row getting drunk but the warm-up to a fifth one?

CARLA: An assured death, that's what.

MOM: We've been through worse.

CARLA: ...and through much better, too.

MOM (*brief pause*)**:** I love you, Carla. I know I say it far too often but, it never hurts to say it more than it should be said, only to say it less than it should. I may not always *like* you, but—

CARLA: ...and you ruined it.

MOM (*sharp laugh and tight hug*)**:** Oh, I'm gonna miss this.

CARLA (*gently into her mother's ear*)**:** Are you going to be okay without me?

MOM: (*she takes a moment to reply*): I will manage, but I will not be okay. When a mother's children refuse to talk to one another, she can never be okay. All she can hope for is to be better. So no, I will not be okay, Carla, but hopefully I will be a little better. (*Beat*). Now, off to bed with you—I'll clean this up tomorrow. (*She kisses her daughter goodnight, and warmly stares at Carla as she starts to go up the stairs*). ...Darling?

CARLA: Yep?

MOM: You will be whatever you want to be. And the world will have no choice but to get ready for whatever it is that you come up with. (*A tender smile was painted on her daughter's face hiding a much larger smile yearning to come out; no more words were uttered, yet none were needed*).

XVIII

ALL'S WELL THAT ENDS WELL

With the terrifying reality of our stay in Geneva having an expiration date slowly dawning upon us all, we all decided to save up three days of our respective schedules to make a trip, the entire group together one last time before Arantxa left for her new job in Amman. I still had some money left, courtesy of my birthday present from Grandma Lupe, which she insisted on delivering in the manner legally agreed upon by the Grandmother Syndicate: surreptitiously, whispering as if uncovering State secrets and looking both ways before forbidding me from telling my mother. So that night, after going to the bouldering club down in *Annemasse*, we had all agreed to gather at Anna and Lara's place to plan the trip, even if we were very much aware that such an objective would prove too exhausting a task, and we'd more than likely end up postponing the planning phase one day at a time.

    Inside the bouldering spot, it did not take long for my forearms to be sorer than my ass cheeks after twenty minutes of riding my bike, so Lara and I, being the proud title holders of biggest asses, albeit most inexperienced ones of the lot, decided to call it even for the day, and waited for the rest of the girls at the bar over a tall pint of beer. By then, my body had developed an immunity of sorts to alcohol, where I was able to drink amounts that used to get me drunk merely a year prior in the span of fifteen to thirty minutes, which was simultaneously an asset in terms of stamina, and a shortcoming in terms of my financial stability or, more accurately, its lack thereof.

"So, what are you gonna do after you finish your internship? Any plans?" Lara said, as she took a long sip of her beer.

"I'm trying not to think too hard about it; that *reality dose* will have to come much later on."

"You have nothing planned out? Not even something like babysitting or bartending, or—"

"Not really. Thing is, I came to Geneva without thinking at all about what I'd be doing here other than the internship at the organization. That was the first time in my life I did not obsessively overthink the decision I was about to make. And somehow, it worked out. My life seems to run smoothly whenever I don't put a lot of thought into what I do, so I plan to follow that strategy for the time being. Besides, at least now I am out of my house, so that's all that matters to me."

"Because of your brother, right?"

"Uh-huh."

"Well, I'm twenty-five, you're twenty-four…if there is an age to be lost in life, I would confidently say this is it. But listen, I don't want to sound like a broken record, and you know all I want for you is to be happy, but you cannot keep ignoring the problem you have back at home. Because, from what you tell me, he's not going anywhere. So, pretending like he will not be there as soon as you arrive there next month is only going to make that "reality dose" hit much harder, like it did last month when you came back for your birthday. Or at least much harder than it should."

"I know, I know. But what do you suggest I do? I have gone through all possible scenarios in my mind, and I can find none where this problem can be solved. So, I have to force myself to choose to be stoic about it, like Lucas always says, because if I worry now, then I would only be renouncing to being happy here in Geneva, where he can no longer get to me. And I cannot let him take that away from me. Not again."

"So, if you're happy here, then why don't you stay?"

"My contract is up next month, and my bank account has been in red numbers pretty much since I arrived in the city, so I can't really afford to stay in my place. Or anywhere near Geneva, really. There are no jobs for non-students—at least paid ones—and you can't live here on a waiter's salary."

"Then go somewhere else! The EU has really great jobs at the European Parliament."

"But I'm not sure I want to keep on working as a—"

"I know, I know, but you don't have to: there's plenty other jobs to keep you going while you figure out what you want to do with your writing, uh, *inclinations*—I'll send you some links tomorrow morning. In the meantime, start thinking about the conversation you're gonna need to have with your brother. Because ignoring he's ever existed or flying to another country is not going to make the problem or the pain he causes go away. Start small, like writing a letter, an email, whatever you want."

"You know I can't do that. I can't really tell him all that I feel, as much as I may need to do so. Even if for some reason he decided to listen to me, the effect it would have... My mother would just—"

"Forget about your mother when it comes to this, honey. This is a separate topic. It may be a bit hard to say this out loud, but she is collateral damage here: you're the one who has to live with this problem, day in and day out, without a break, on your own. And if she cannot get to terms with the son she has, then that should not be an additional burden for you to carry. If you keep letting the hypothetical effect that your actions will have on others get in the way of your happiness, then you will never get past your life's starting point and always let others decide your life for you."

"But even then, even if I do what you say, he's not gonna want to hear whatever it is that I write to him."

Lara tenderly grabbed my face with her strong hands.

"Haven't you been listening? Who cares what he thinks? You say what you have to say, get a clear conscience, get it out of your system and let him carry the full weight of your words. Let him know exactly what and who you are and why and where you stand. And if you want to keep living in that house and manage to find a way to make it bearable, then fine, go ahead; but if you don't or you can't, then you shouldn't. Either way, you no longer have the sickening regret of having failed to tell him what a fucking asshole he is, and how much damage he has made."

A quiet moment ensued, during which I carefully processed her words.

"What?" Lara asked while nervously chuckling.

"Nothing…"

"What? Tell me!" Lara said, getting progressively nervous as she always did once she knew we were keeping something important from her.

"It's just that I don't want to sound corny or anything, but I…I am just so happy that I was lucky enough to cross paths with you. I don't know, it's probably the beer talking but I…I honestly don't know how I would have survived here if it hadn't been for you all."

"You know we love you too, bitch, and without you this place would have been a much darker one, that's for sure," she said, jokingly pushing me aside and caressing my cheeks. "Now, let's finish this up and climb up that red wall over there: I saw the cute guy I told you about and I'm wearing my lucky panties."

"Fingers crossed," I replied, before going ahead and finishing up my drink in one sitting.

In terms of planning the trip, we did none, essentially relegating ourselves to figuring it out along the way. The one thing that we knew was the destination—Interlaken, a mountainous region in between Lake Thun and Lake Brienz, located at the very centre of the country—and the dates, which we had to decide in advance to ask for a day off. That is, most of us had, because Lara pretended to be working from home that day during the train ride, which might have caused some confusion over at her office when in a staff meeting they could hear *"Prochaine étape: Interlaken Ouest"* courtesy of the Swiss public transport and Lara's unmuted microphone.

The hostel we had found, this time ensuring we did write down its name and telephone number ahead of our arrival, was in *Lauterbrunnen*, close enough to the main landmark locations to visit in the area, barely a couple of minutes away from the train station, and with incredible views facing Mount *Jungfrau*. We were all living a vivid dream, it seemed, as the iconic destination appeared to be straight out of a postcard: lush emerald pasture fields, snow-covered mountain tops and colourful flowers all around. That day, making the most out of the surrealistically sunny day we were having, we took the train over the mountains and into *Schynige Platte*, a summit where one could see the entire region as if it were a map laid out just for us to observe. Once again, I got the perspective one could get only from the top of one of those nature-made colossal skyscrapers, making me see my life troubles for what they really were: their size no longer inscrutable, their solution no longer unforeseeable.

On our way down by foot and, needless to mention, having made a quick stop at the bar on the top of the mountain, we stumbled down the hills singing *Pepas* at the top of our lungs, making a three-hour intensive cardio workout feel like five minutes at mild speed on the treadmill. The unlucky soul that had built a freely accessible, small wooden shelf within which one could find a number of locally produced cheeses and a tiny wicker basket with money inside, as well as some carefully written yet thoroughly ignored instructions in a nailed piece of paper, had certainly done so as a result of a deep belief in human kindness and moral rectitude, and an equally profound oversight that people like us existed in the world, because we took the three smelliest cheeses contained therein and left the little (and far too unethical amount of) cash we had: Clara's two hundred Chilean pesos, Arantxa's two Swiss Francs and Lara's twenty cents. Were we horrible people? Indeed, we were.

By the time we arrived at the hostel, a multicultural spot had been formed at the kitchen and adjacent dining hall, now filled with dozens of people from all ages, countries and creeds filling up the long tables there placed. The hostel's owner, an attractive lady in her late thirties with perky breasts and her artificially atomic blonde hair tied up in a top knot, entered the kitchen and introduced herself as "Mrs Charlotte". She let us know, not before taking a look at me top to bottom, that the place had a no-noise policy past ten o'clock.

I nodded and she laid her hand on my shoulder before saying, "Good night, honey," successfully fogging up the lenses from my round glasses. The ladies started whistling as soon as she left, but I made an effort to make nothing of it—high expectations are bound to end up in equally profound disappointment. The one item of food at our disposal was the four kilograms of pasta which Michaela had stolen that morning as part of an early rendition of Trophy Night, so we used the pots at the kitchen and mixed the obscene amount of spaghetti with the recently acquired cheese, and the result was far too much delicious pasta we had no choice but to share with the group of American frat boys in the midst of their gap-year-after-college-identity-crisis who asked us for food, given all stores had closed down three hours prior. They were pushing it a little too hard with their flirting, which we initially dismissed as thankfulness for the food we had given them, but seemed nice enough for us to have a perfectly fine dinner with them. In fact, if one were to temporarily omit their off-putting Republican Party energy and love for uttering the words "dude", "sick", and "bro", one could even see the appeal in their muscular bodies and chiselled jawlines and scruffy hair and deeply perforating clear eyes and bright smiles and provocative lips, all urgently demanding our attention. Suffice to say, some of us did not end up sleeping alone that night, as it became clear after a few minutes of talking to them that, while standing at polar opposite sides on most things that mattered, sometimes in life one must be guided purely by one's own instincts. And so did Claudia when, approximately thirty minutes after dinner, she and Pedro—a tiny guy who stood as the shyest of the bunch—quietly left the scene. We would not hear anything from them until Vero and I headed to the bathroom and heard a sharp sound echoing across the hostel, similar to a wild boar being executed, but it was just Claudia's Latin passion and Pedro realising what being properly fucked actually felt like. So much for the no-noise policy.

    The next morning, we took the trip all across the valley until reaching the *Jungfrau* Mountain and linked two hiking routes together to be able to walk past the *Eiger*'s North Face, eventually walking for twelve miles until reaching the vibrant streets of the town of *Grindelwald*. Although the trip was more of an inner journey of sorts, as each one of us walked by ourselves for the majority of the trip, it only meant in my mind that we were comfortable enough with ourselves and with each other to know when we needed some alone time and when we didn't. You know those artsy films that the most radical(lly misguided) mobs at Letterboxd would cream their jeans on by laying out the deep meaning heavily imprinted upon a remote copy of a film only two people have ever seen and only four have ever heard about? I am referring to the kind of movie that would feature a forty-five minute still shot of a pine tree being slightly tossed around by incoming winds to symbolize the rise of repressed artistic expressions in a small village in 1892's Austro-Hungarian Empire. That's a leap of faith those people take every time they start drafting a review nobody but themselves will ever read, the kind of jump into the void that, before arriving at this country, I thought I could never take. But the leap I took when I decided to come here, and the subsequent ones that followed each time I met one of the ladies, randomly ended up becoming some of the best decisions I had ever made, even if they began as accidents, sheer luck, or mere instances of *force majeure*. What we had right there, was like capturing a lightning in a bottle. It is a hard thing to realise, but being silent among other people without it being awkward but organic only means you are lucky enough to be surrounded by those with which you can truly be yourself, no bars held, in all aspects of your life: when partying, when talking, when crying, when laughing, when singing and when remaining in silence. Thus, for the most part of the hiking route, we each walked straight ahead, deep in our own thoughts, enveloped by the natural beauty of Swiss landscapes, trying to permanently record those sights for posterity by "taking pictures with our eyes".

From *Grindelwald*, and with the sun slowly setting by now, the train led us straight into the barbecue spot located at a natural riverbed near our hostel, where the Americans were already waiting for us, like salivating stray dogs. And while Claudia and Pedro went on a trip of their own, we saw the sun setting over the mountains right next to *Lauterbrunnen*'s iconic waterfalls. It was truly a sight to behold, with the grazing animals all around us, the fire progressively becoming the sole source of light illuminating the area, the all-encompassing sound of the waterfalls calmly ironing out our inner troubles. When we finally arrived at the hostel, it would only take a few drinking games before the stage was set for us to have an eventful night: Lara and Anna went to the remaining Americans' rooms for some *English lessons*, Vero and Michaela stayed outside making friends, as they always did everywhere they went, and Arantxa and I went to bed. While Arantxa's reasons for an early retreat were reduced to a painful headache, mine arose from the combination of running out of social battery and physical exhaustion from our hiking trip—my body could take a dozen beers, kilos and kilos of pasta, and twelve-hour movie marathons, but anything beyond three hours of physical exercise and my muscles would start to walk the line towards non-responsiveness.

After I grabbed my toothbrush and headed to the bathroom, I was almost tackled to the ground by a five-year old running around the corridor.

Chasing after her was Mrs Charlotte, who apologised for her daughter, and after an awkward pause—me, toothbrush in hand and pink slippers on my feet, her, holding a toddler of her own making in her arms—asked in a morally wrong yet sexually enticing, seductive voice, "Got any plans for tonight?"

For some reason to this day I am unable to know, I had the nerve to innocently pull down my glasses and reply, "Perhaps," before winking an eye and heading downstairs to the bathroom. Two, three, four deep breaths it took me to come back to my senses. Fucking American beer. I tried to pretend like that incident had not happened, and quickly brushed my teeth to get to bed as soon as possible so that I could forget the embarrassing moment I had just orchestrated all by myself.

"For Christ's sake, I have just flirted with a woman that might as well be my mother, right in front of her infant daughter...is there no decency anymore?" was all that flooded my mind, although my actions and fashion choices had already answered that question, I reckoned. When I entered my room, I found Arantxa completely knocked out after taking her nightly sleeping pills concoction, and before I could take off my slippers, I heard a knock on the door. Standing out there was Mrs Charlotte, with a neckline low enough for me to see half of her right nipple peeking through.

"Am I interrupting?" she said, confirming she had seen far too much porn in her teen years.

"No, not at all," I said before exiting my room and, before realising it, promptly entering *hers*—a place where I would go on to have the most fulfilling sexual experience of my entire lifetime. What can I say, forbidden or inappropriate loves are the ones that taste the best.

That morning, every single one of my muscles ached—partly due to the recent days spent hiking outdoors, partly due to the hiking I did in Mrs Charlotte's room—and as I was in the midst of my *walk of shame* back to the room, I saw Anna and

Lara in the middle of theirs, as well as Vero and Michaela exiting the laundry room holding hands. Just then, Claudia came upstairs from the bathroom, and we found ourselves, six bitches who had just been destroyed in a way only matched by bank account receipts after a night of heavy partying, doing a Mexican stand-off in that corridor, before bursting into laughter and erupting into our room to have a group hug with Arantxa, who was still mid-trance, courtesy of Big Pharma. When we arrived at the dining hall to quench the hunger from our yearning bellies, having spent the previous twenty-four hours burning calories in various different ways, we pleasantly discovered Mrs Charlotte had prepared us breakfast, and as soon as I stepped through the door, her daughter came running over and gave me a tender hug. We chugged down our meals, me in resignation at their fruitless attempts to try and repress their laughter stemming from the fact I had apparently become a mother overnight. In their defence, they were right to laugh, I guess. After all, had Mrs Charlotte and I's nightly adventure been discovered three hundred years ago—perhaps even less—we'd have been stoned and burnt on a pyre, and I kind of liked that thought. Made me feel that sleeping with that voraciously insatiable lady was dangerous, and certainly not regrettable, for all the right and wrong reasons.

After quickly finishing up our meals and, with little more than three collective hours of sleep, we headed to our last trip that weekend all the way to a natural pool in the midst of an ancient glacier tongue. Up there, at nearly three-thousand metres above the ground, lay a glamorous SPA where we saw a group of elderly individuals taking their clothes off and diving into the outdoor jacuzzi. Wanting nothing to do with vaginal candidiasis, we instantly cancelled all plans to take a bath over there, instead opting for playing a game of pool at the indoor resort with a margarita on one hand and a penchant for poor life choices on the other, while Lara and Arantxa briefly popped into the small museum inside the resort and did the customary touristic route on behalf of all of us. When we finally entered the train to take us back to Geneva, my memory started to get a little fuzzy, as all I could remember was our arrival at Interlaken, not our departure, very much in direct opposition to our vital memories. Noting that time flies by when you're a piece of shit, and we were indeed seven big, fat pieces of shit, by the time we arrived at the *Cornavin* central train station, the entire trip had flown by in what appeared to have been a mere couple of minutes. The morning after I returned to the flat, I woke up unable to remember when I had had such a deep, repairing sleep before. Perhaps in the womb, but nothing else seemed to come closer.

Having achieved a point in my life in which pain had become an option and no longer the general rule, I realised that during those three brief, intense and highly unpredictable days we spent together, I barely wrote a word in my personal diary, attributing the diminishing number of dark thoughts and the taming of the need to write down my feelings as a way to cope with my emotional handicaps, to being surrounded by the right kind of people. No longer worried about fitting in or going out on my own or being surrounded by couples all around, I had begun, just like Cristine did back in the day, the journey towards self-improvement, for I had understood the role that I played in my own life, and planned to take control of it eventually…or so I thought…and so I hoped.

XIX

TRADING PLACES

A sea of faces filled up the seats of the surprisingly (and faith-restoringly) packed *East of Eden* (1955) screening over at the *Grütli* cinemas as part of their 1950s cycle; a true gem of the shooting star that was James Dean, and a testament to the dangers of letting nature sort itself out without intervening before it is too late in those kinds of relationships we see a crystal-clear potential for blooming into worrisome rivalry down the line in a future not too far away. Or at least not far enough.

Even if I've already bought the tickets in advance, I've always loved arriving shockingly early to movie screenings. There is a sort of additional spectacle that comes with the price of admission, one which often goes unnoticed and in which we all are—unbeknownst to us—part of. Like an orchestra conductor softly shaking her baton before starting a concerto, I ritualistically took in a mouthful of air before entering the popcorn-smelling room and sat on my carefully chosen seat located right in the middle of the theatre at a symmetrical distance from both the back of the room and the screen in front of me, as I always did. I then dedicated a few instances to carefully examining the strangers' faces with whom I was about to collectively share a cinematic experience over which we had absolutely no atmospheric authority whatsoever: a journey whose final destination nobody but the projectionist knew about, where laughter would be magnified and comfort during terrifying moments would be found in the reassuring feeling of being a part of something being communally felt. While each pair of eyes was about to see a movie through a different lens, knowing that such feeling—on the tip of our fingers, on our sweaty palms, on our panicked moves of instinctively grabbing onto the armrests, on the tingling sensation on our toes, on the beating of our pounding hearts, on the goosebumps covering every inch of skin on our bodies, on the tears rolling down our cheekbones—had the possibility of being replicated on every single person around me, made me feel part of a collective, a group of strangers I may again cross paths with in the future without realising: a sisterhood of sorts, all weaved together through the sheer power of cinema.

As the commercials began to play, I could feel a symphony was about to begin. First came the popcorn wave—the sound of loud chewing and scrambling for the snacks at the bottom of their boxes flooding the room and combining in unison to form a calm, steady sound, like raindrops falling on otherwise-overcrowded streets. Then, the momentary disco ball rave of bright lights coming from the smartphone screens of those souls kind enough to mute their ringtones. Finally, just before the movie started, and accompanied by the sharp sounds of caffeine-addicted spectators anxiously slurping on their Coca-Cola's through turtle-killing plastic straws, four kinds of audience members walked into scene—as they always did—right before the production logos appeared on the silver screen: the myopic and deeply absent-minded man wearing a grey beret and a wool scarf, carelessly meandering around, effectively rendering the rest of the viewers blind by illuminating the quest for his seat with his phone in flashlight mode; the family of five that walks in holding their kids' hands while impossibly carrying a wide array of Paw

Patrol-themed toys into a positively non child-friendly movie, unaware of the lengthy bills they will have to pay in psychologist fees over the ten years to come as soon as the film credits started rolling; the lady in heavy makeup texting on her phone who trips on her way up the stairs and drops anywhere from fifty to seventy-eight percent of her popcorn onto the ground—in the best cases onto someone else—before letting out a redundant comment that confirms exactly our first impression of her; and finally, the Adam-Driver looking, left-femur-higher-than-my-student-debt tall middle-aged man, who (obviously) sits right in front of you and unavoidably deprives you from approximately a quarter of vision from the screen, thus relegating your ability of understanding subtitled foreign movies to your vast imaginative skills to fill in the gaps. Phones will nonetheless ring, babies—if inexplicably present in the room—are likely to start crying, sneezes, coughs, whispers, screams, snores…all forming a perfect musical composition, an unrepeatable soundtrack that always accompanies movie screenings, yet morphs, like jazz music, with each session, with each performer, with each viewer.

During the film, I had one of those realisations that only happen when a well-written character falls into the hands of an experienced director and is portrayed on screen by a movie legend that redefined some of the unwritten laws of performing for the camera and the audience at the other end of its projected image: I saw myself in them. As different as we were, I could see bits and pieces of my story—our story—being told with the eyes and faces of James Dean and Richard Davalos. Though falling into the specifics could potentially render any comparison worthless, my brother and I were, at the end of the day, two siblings in a troubled relationship, where fatherly favour for one or the other had in some form ended up creating a chasm big enough to forever doom the family: a shared inability to forgive over mutually perceived damages in a quest for a truth no longer present in the face of distorted realities taking power for themselves and growing into a life of their own, eventually leading to a tragic end which stood in the way for any resolution to come to light. The pain we endure and the pain we choose to endure more often than not go hand in hand. But like every toxic relationship, it is hard to see where the blame of others ends and where your own responsibility for the state of affairs actually begins. I could not keep postponing it; I was not getting any younger and my seemingly irresolvable traumas had so far showcased no inclination whatsoever to disappear any time soon. Yes, it was about time that I confronted Him head on, putting fear and regret, and the emotional resolution which my life depended on, each on one side of the scale, hoping the latter would outweigh the former, yet bracing for impact and a bloody outcome.

As soon as the movie came to an iconic end, I decided to finally put into practice the advice I had been given by one of the most understanding yet fiercer voices in my life, this time in the shape of Lara. Immediately after I walked through my apartment's door—successfully ignoring Ingmar's *au naturel* nightly yoga stretching—I locked myself in my room and began the process of emotional regurgitation in the shape of writing a letter I knew I had to write, but which I had refused to do so up until then in the face of the potential pain it would most certainly bring. It takes courage to bleakly confront oneself, to be willing to dig deep into the nest of wasps that our mind can turn out to be, in the hopes of reaching a candid awareness about your own self: what we like, who we love, who we are, what makes us complete and what makes us want to instantly reach for a gun and blow our brains out. After all, you can never expect others to accept you if you don't even know who you truly are.

Although the prospect of reaching something resembling an enlightenment of sorts was certainly better than drowning in pills and subsequent morning coffees to be able to survive coping with that animal I had no choice but to call my brother, just the thought of this hypothetical confrontation made me nauseous, gagging at having to stand in his fictitious presence, a sort of Pavlovian reaction of getting my dopamine to worryingly decreasing levels with just the thought of picturing his face. Even though I had avoided making eye contact with him for the past ten years, I could remember very distinctly every idiosyncratic mannerism he made, like the shiver-inducing sound of a metal spoon hitting his teeth that preceded his irritating chewing habits each night he monopolised the kitchen to have a protein-exclusive dinner; or the way he closed doors with enough fury to make the hinges crumble—probably as a subconscious way of feeling the need to remind everyone else of his existence; or the way he would alternate inaudible footsteps for times where he wanted his presence to go unnoticed by me, with the cardiac arrest-inducing sprinting down the stairs early in the morning whenever I had a big day ahead of me; or the repulsive guttural noises he made to expel phlegm out of his system before going to bed; or his total disregard for flushing the toilet after his repeated trips to the bathroom and always unapologetically drying his hands on my face towel; or that penchant for infesting our home with a latrine-like rancid smell after applying that reeking muscle-growing lotion that was unable to hide his flat-chested heritage; or the way he used to take out the dishwasher by forcibly putting all plates and cutlery anywhere but in their proper place with so much repressed anger each time he chipped a different item; or the poor

DJ skills he showcased by being able to only play the exact same plagiarised song he bragged to his circle of friends with having created over and over again at full volume during long hours of the night, times which the rest of us spent battling to fall asleep; or the oxymoron that he embodied by alternating his verbose disposition when talking with his anonymous online friends while playing Call of Duty, with his inability to make conversation during family dinners; or the incessant sound of his cracking knuckles each time he found himself in the same room as I did, as a way of menacingly announcing his presence; or his vicious daily rants directed against my mother, always with his left arm on his hip and the right one waving in the air frightfully close to her face.

    The years may pass, the ink may dry, but my memory will never falter. That face, those hands, that unnatural gaze behind which lay the architect that had orchestrated some of my darkest thoughts... As soon as I sat down, put a pen to a paper, and decided to confront him through me, everything came back all at once. My wrist began to move swiftly, propelled by the grief over the person I had been prevented from being and from the incandescent rage carefully stored over countless years in an unnamed box on the deepest compartment I managed to find within my psyche. The pen struggled to keep up with the hurricane of ideas that flooded my mind, excitedly moving up and down, sacrificing spelling accuracy for the realistic portrayal of a hypothetical event. As if Tilda Swinton herself had sent me to the Astral Plane, in the middle of my writing frenzy a part of me abandoned my own body, flying into the ether, calmly floating towards the large, full-bodied mirror located on the far right corner of my room, where this excision of mine stood in silence, staring at its own reflection, while paying close attention to my physical self over at the desk, writing like there was no tomorrow because, potentially speaking, they may never be. From out there, my reflection began to scrutinize every inch of the part of myself sitting just a few meters away, deeply immersed in the telling of the only story I felt worthy enough of writing. It was right then, from the cautious distance, that my projected self began to remember what for so long I had forgotten, that which had been drowned out by the new language of anxiolytics, self-deprecation and depression that I now spoke in, the true essence that had been lost in translation: self-love, the most important kind, and the stepping stone that opens the door for others to join in. Unveiling the truth that had been there all along, I began to notice how I used to frown like a heroin-addicted accountant each time I became deeply immersed in my writing duties; how I constantly blew up a lock of my hair which got in the path of my eye; how I nervously tapped my foot against the floor when I wanted to get a sentence out of my body and into the page, and how I smiled when I knew I had done it successfully; how my eyes lit up whenever I thought about the movie I was just about to reference; how I kept looking at the Polaroid pictures over my head, of Grandma Lupe and my parents, looking for inspiration in their bright smiles, for warmth in the hugs distance prevented us from giving; how I loved to take my bra off to be able to properly breathe and walk around in a grey XXL T-shirt with an imprint of Agnès Varda's face; how I clicked my tongue and rubbed my hands across my face whenever inspiration went out the door; and how I failed to allow myself to let my tears roll down my cheeks every time the pain from the story I was writing got too real, too present, too tangible for me to bare. With the last remnants of sunset light slowly creeping through my window, I looked so peaceful in moments like those, when my mind was occupied and I felt I had a purpose, and my life had, if only for just a second, something resembling a deeper meaning. If only I could see myself the way that my reflection saw me then; if only I could find it in me to remind myself each day of the inherent value that I, and my life, had; if only I could make that scared little girl that had grown up to be a scared little woman comfortable in her own skin, feel capable enough to navigate her life, and strong enough to face her troubles head front; if only she knew the value I knew she had always had.

At the other end, staring at my own reflection in the mirror, I noticed how a whisk of incoming wind shook my dark hair, with each to and fro making it progressively shorter until it acquired a length of a crew cut, considerably thinning at the top area. My dark skin was progressively whitened; my breasts replaced with tight, hairy pectoral muscles; my thick thighs now had the shape of two skinny—yet equally hirsute—legs; my eyes had lost almost all their blue tones; my nose had grown considerably larger; the shoulders began to widen and the veins in my arms and forehead came to light for the first time in my life; my lips nowhere to be seen, my ears very much present: an impostor stood in the reflection of the mirror where I had just seen the replicated image of my body. I was no longer staring into my own eyes nor bearing witness to a one-sided inner conversation—he had finally arrived.

We stood there in silence, properly observing one another's faces for the first time since any of us could remember—all the early wrinkles found at the outer corners of his eyes and the scars on my cheeks left by the uninvited presence of acne during my teen years, finally becoming apparent for the other. All we had been through and all we had become had taken us both to that exact moment in time when we finally locked eyes and shared a sustained, honest look: one charged with regret, reproaches, anger and disgust. He tilted his head to his right in response to me doing exactly the same a second prior, then continued in this vein as he proceeded to mimic my moves most certainly in an attempt to once again try and make me delude myself into considering a Doctor Caligari/Shutter Island-*esque* twist (2010) in which the prisoner and the cop had been one and the same all along.

Underneath all the layers of hatred through which I had tended to see him over the years, I was shocked to realise how much we looked alike once we got rid of the stigma I had imposed over his presence, most certainly in the hopes of separating as much as possible the person I was from the person he chose to become. Yet, our shared DNA ultimately remained victorious and came to light in a most unexpected manner; like the way we would pensively look into the distance whilst in the middle of a conversation, looking for inspiration in the faraway horizon; or the sudden tics in the shape of deep blinks that plagued our facial expressions whenever we attentively listened to someone else speak; or how much of our father could be seen in our bone structure; or the clearly shared inheritance of my mother's kind eyes, apparent only when looked at from the right perspective; or our obsession to take as much time as needed to thoroughly clean the specks from our glasses; or how much we enjoyed a similar taste in TV shows, as exemplified by our virtually identical Netflix viewing history. It was a revolting realisation to come to, to learn that such a large part of him could be found within myself. To see that two people who had dedicated varying degrees of effort to distance themselves from one another had ended up having so much in common, as if nature was playing a twisted trick on us by giving us only the illusion of choice. As if destiny could not be escaped from, no matter how hard we tried.

DIEGO: You wanted to see me. (*Opening his arms*). ...here I am.

CARLA (*after remaining momentarily unresponsive, her mind collapsing with every single little detail she had wanted to say for so long, all battling, unsuccessfully, to come out at once, yet failing to find the precise words to utter*)**:** I wanted to...uh, you, you have to—

DIEGO: Wow—I was really hoping you were no longer dumb enough to struggle with putting two words together. Good to see nothing's changed. (*He takes a long look at Carla's projected self standing in front of the mirror, at the body of Carla sitting down at the table a few meters away, and at the room around her*). This is your place, I assume. I can see you're still single. At least you look the same way you've always looked—only a bit, uh, *meatier*—so I'm guessing you still haven't found someone to stand that much, ahem, *weight* on their shoulders, have you?

CARLA: Always good to see you, too.

DIEGO: I don't have time to play any of your little games so, please, stop wasting my time—what do you want?

CARLA: Look, I don't want to talk to you any more than you want to talk to me, trust me. But if you ever want us to never see each other again—

DIEGO (*putting both hands together, as if about to pray*): Please.

CARLA: ...then all you have to do is to be honest with me. Just this once.

DIEGO: And then?

CARLA: Then you'll never hear from me ever again.

DIEGO (*he remains quiet for a second, nodding to himself, smiling*): Sounds like a good deal to me. What do you want to know, *little one*?

CARLA (*in a soft, whisper-like voice*): I guess I want to start from the beginning: I want to know why...why you did it.

DIEGO: What? Speak up!

CARLA (*as a tear runs down her face, trying to gather enough courage to speak louder*): Why did you do it?

DIEGO: What are you talking about? Do I have to call the hospital...again?

CARLA (*ignoring his remarks*): What did I do? All I ever wanted was to live a normal life, just like everybody else. But for some reason, you decided to take that away from me. (*He lets out a deep sigh*). So, I think I deserve to know why you have treated me, treated us, this way for all these years. (*Running out of* breath, failing in her battle to hold back tears; her emotional breakdown is met with silence from him). I just want to be able to sleep at night, that's all. If you told me, whatever it was that I did—something I assume to be horrible enough to make you behave the way you have been behaving all these years—then I could do something to try and fix it. And who knows, maybe we can repair this relationship before it is too late. But for that to happen, I need to know, I *must* know why you... (*After more silence*). What have I done for you to hate me as much as you do?

DIEGO (*cackling laughter*): You're such a drama queen.

CARLA: This is important to me, it's not funny, Diego.

DIEGO: ...to you it certainly would not be. And do me a favour: don't say my name, it disgusts me to hear it coming out of your mouth. (*Looking around, noticing her crying*). Ah, you were always such an emotional little girl. And what good did it do to you? (*Beat*). I'm sorry, but I can't help you; you're asking for something I don't think I can give you.

CARLA: I am only asking for the truth.

DIEGO: No, you're not. What you are asking for, if you look deep enough within yourself, is forgiveness. And the person that asks for forgiveness does so because they know they have done something wrong. You seem to be under the impression you should be apologised to, when in reality, you're the one who should be on her knees, begging me for clemency for all the things you have done.

CARLA: There are two people in this room, and the person standing in front of me is qualified for very few things in life—*very, very few*—amongst which forgiving others can most certainly not be found. Besides, we're way past the point of forgiving, and all the damage is already done, so you have nothing to lose by telling me the truth.

DIEGO: But what truth is there to tell?

CARLA: You know very well.

DIEGO: Okay, then. But I warn you, it's a simple story, the one everyone knows, and the one you are no longer able to rewrite as you please: once upon a time there was a bratty little girl who envied her older brother and made use of her far too wide imagination to fabricate facts into the reality that fit her whimsical world best, a world that constantly orbited around her, where everyone but her—always pure, immaculate, free from any sin—was to blame for all the misfortunes in her life. Anything but take responsibility for her actions. When things, as they inevitably do, failed to go according to her plan, she kept losing her temper in incidents that turned progressively more violent, until she found herself swallowing pills as a frequent resident of the local psychiatric facility. After she was released years later, members of her family—people guilty only of having tried to help her carry the burdensome self-hatred she directed towards them—were met with total rejection from her side: rejection of their help, rejection of word, rejection of acknowledgement of their presence, rejection even of the food and drink we kindly prepared for her. That is, until she let everybody know we were beneath her when she finally fled out of our house like a dog in the night, and into a foreign country, in the hopes of starting it all over again with a new set of characters who would temporarily remain unaware of the kind of danger she posed to them and, most importantly, to herself. (*Beat*). Am I getting any closer to the truth you desperately seek, *little one*?

CARLA: Wow. (*Heavy laughter*). And *I'm* the one with a far too wide imagination? Jesus Christ…are you seriously expecting anybody to believe that load of crap?

DIEGO: There is no need to expect anything—that is the word going around back home, which has become common knowledge at this point. It only remains an imaginary story as long as everybody refuses to believe in it, and right now, nobody does, because it is a very seductive narrative, and you have made it far too easy to consider accepting it as the truth. And all that creativity of yours you have used in filling the minds of the three friends you still have—those poor souls—and in poisoning their minds with tales that never happened anywhere but in that rotten brain of yours, all those stories about the things that I do to you, and to Mom, and to Dad, and about how everyone in our house despises the sight of me and feels threatened by my presence, and how your sickness, your disgusting disease, your weakness of character, is all the result of my actions…all of that is forever gone, just like you should be.

CARLA: You must be delusional to think that what you just described is not the reality that you have forced us all to live in.

DIEGO: Let me ask you something, then: out of the two of us, who is the one that has been *intensively* going to therapy since they were a kid, huh?

CARLA: And whose fault is that?

DIEGO (*calm yet menacing*)**:** Answer me. (*Silence*). That's right, *little one*. I'll do you one better: out of the two of us, who has been widely known by our family to throw tantrums and accusations and scream in public for no apparent reason?

CARLA: You know there was a reason. There always was—you made sure of that.

DIEGO: It is about time that you understand that it does not matter what you claim I have done, only what others think they have seen you doing. Right now, if those stories that you go around telling your friends—

CARLA: THEY ARE NOT STORIES!

DIEGO: And here we go with the shouting once more. You know, other than successfully making Dad go broke, all those years of therapy have accomplished absolutely nothing, it seems; you're still completely incapable of controlling your impulses.

CARLA: I'm not a kid anymore, you know? You cannot make me believe things so easily now. Mom and Dad and Grandma and my friends and everyone with an ounce of common sense is able to separate fiction from reality in that absurd, self-indulgent, little story of yours which you take so much disgusting pride in going around telling others. *Fiction* is the comfort you must get out of projecting myself as the author of the harm you have created;

reality is torturing your little sister day in and day out, for no apparent reason and for as long as she can remember, to the point of making her want to reach for a knife and slide her wrists open at every chance she gets. It's about time you learnt the fucking difference.

DIEGO: Oh, and what else? What else am I to be blamed for? (*Pointing at her from head to toe*). Am I supposed to also take responsibility for this? What about Ebola? COVID, perhaps? Your dyslexia, too? You know, at one point it becomes time to take responsibility for your own actions and for the person you, through nobody else's but your own actions, have chosen to become. It is far too easy to blame all of your problems on somebody else, to make others take the blame for the poor choices you have made. But guess what, *little one*, if I were to disappear right now—like in one of those vivid fantasies that you keep flying off to, to the point they are coming frighteningly close to becoming your reality—, you would still be the same fucked up, twisted little child that has nothing better to do with her time than going around ruining everybody else's lives.

CARLA: What are you talking about?

DIEGO: Mom's, for starters. And Dad's, although he is too proud to admit it.

CARLA: What about them?

DIEGO: You are too blind to see this, or at least pretend to be, but each night they cry themselves to sleep—in separate beds now. And *I* am the one that has to be there each morning, because of the agony you make them go through as soon as they wake up, and for as long as they go back into bed at night. It's because of you that Mom has been taking refuge in booze and pills—

CARLA: IT'S BECAUSE OF *YOU,* YOU FUCKING IDIOT!

DIEGO (*paying no attention to her remarks*)**:** ...and it's because of you and your stupid, pointless little therapy sessions and hospital bills that Dad can no longer afford to pay the electricity bills—

CARLA: Are you even listening to the things that you're saying?

DIEGO: ...and it's because of you that they are now considering getting a divorce.

CARLA (*the pain of this last statement lingers for a little while*)**:** You fucking liar.

DIEGO: Okay, if this is the level of conversation that you want us to have—me telling you the truth you've desperately asked for, and you refusing to believe it once I clearly spell it out in front of you (just like you always have)—then so be it. It's just that I thought you had called me to have a proper talk about the way in which you have destroyed our family forever. That's all.

CARLA: Nobody can generate more damage than you already have, that's the one thing you've ever been truly good at. *I* am the one who is there each night to pick up the pieces of whatever is left of Mom after you're done venting out your frustrations at her, or worse: *I* am the one who takes care of our grandparents and helps them run their errands and drives them to their appointments and spends endless nights at the hospital right by their side, since their only other grandchild was only capable of miserably locking himself in his room and playing his Xbox with his equally mentally challenged online friends; *I* am the one helping Dad in building and running his business' website and social media accounts, and *I* am the one he trusts enough to say to me how much of a fucking maniac you are. That is why, when you say that I have ruined this family forever, I wonder, what have you done to keep it together, other than successfully managing to unite us all in the common hatred we deeply share towards you?

DIEGO: Now you're the one projecting, *little one*. Listen, there is no trick here. No reality you are not seeing, no code, no conspiracy, no underlying reason for us to have the relationship we have, other than the fact that, deep down, all this mess you've put us all into stems from the fact that twenty-something years ago, when you were but a little child, you consciously chose the path of envy: a road of futile attempts to win our parents' favour, to define yourself by using me as a reference of the person you would like to become—either as something to aspire to or as something to steer away from. Of *you*, at the end of the day, being defined as the absence of *me*. Because, let's face it, without me there would not be any Carla to speak of. All you have ever achieved, as little as it may be, has been because of me.

CARLA: You know what? I feel pity for you. You're just a delusional, self-conscious little tumour that somehow made it out of the operating room and is now committed to making others as miserable with ourselves as you feel about having to wake up every day in that body of yours. No steroids and no amount of surgery will ever be able to fix the kind of person that you truly are. And I hope one day somebody makes you see—because God knows you are too dumb to realise on your own—that you have broken all of our hearts. I mean, don't you even have any regrets? Are you capable of having those, even? There are no cameras here. No audience. No witnesses. Nobody to trick into despising me; no friends of mine who you can turn against me. (*Beat*). If you knew yourself as much as I know you—which is way too much and far more than I wished—you would be able to see our family's continued yet hopeless willingness to reach out into that thick skull of yours to offer our help. If only you had asked instead of making us want to ask for a kind of help we did not need prior to your actions; if only you had developed anything resembling redeeming qualities; if only you had shown love and respect and support for someone other than yourself; if only you had not chosen to gaslight me and make me want to become somebody else, then you would not be drowning in the worthless life that you're currently living. You would obtain no satisfaction from making those around you endlessly suffer. You would not find comfort in the tears of your mother, in the bankruptcy of your father, and in the early grave of your own making of your sister. I would tell you that you will get what you deserve, but life only has rewards, never punishments, for people like you. But one thing is clear—your unkindness may defeat my life, but never taint my love. So, I hope you will one day have children that grow up to be just like their father, so you can finally experience first-hand what it is to have in your life someone you're desperately willing to love who nonetheless makes you hopelessly desire to take your own life.

DIEGO: Don't be so dramatic. What do you want me to say? (*In a mocking tone*). That you're my little sister and that I love you deeply and that I want to be forgiven for whatever crimes you claim I am guilty of?

CARLA: That train is long gone and was never meant to be for us.

DIEGO: Then?

CARLA: You can start by apologising. Would that be so hard?

DIEGO: No, it would not, but it would be dishonest of me. And what purpose does an apology serve if it is not an honest one?

CARLA: I don't know, depends on the price that you're putting on saving this family.

DIEGO: I am sorry, but in what version of this story are you supposed to not be the villain? I thought we were doing this so you could finally get some closure and arrive at the conclusion the rest of us already reached a long time ago.

CARLA: What do you mean?

DIEGO: Understanding your disease, and why you have to leave us. That is why I am here, so you are better prepared for your final destination, to pay the price for what you have done. Don't you feel better now, knowing exactly the problem that you have?

CARLA: What problem?

DIEGO (*leaning in*): Come closer. (*She does so*). Closer. (*Carla bends forward*). A little more. (*She is now leaning with her head against the mirror*) You are still alive. (*He suddenly grabs Carla, and vigorously shoves her inside the mirror, swiftly managing to switch places; he now lies outside while Carla remains trapped inside the tall glass*). You claim I have made you no longer want to live. That I made you desperately want to take your life. (*He begins to slowly move in the direction of the nightstand by Carla's bed, takes out a bottle of sleeping pills—the strongest ones of the lot—and slowly walks towards the desk where her physical self is still deeply immersed in her writing*). Then, by all means, follow up on your promise. (*Carla remains immobilised inside the mirror*). I am not getting in the way of your destiny. You know you want to do this—think of me as a humble facilitator of your deepest desire. (*He takes the pills out of the bottle, taps her physical self on the shoulder, and puts the pills in the palm of her hand; from inside the mirror, Carla is forced to witness, unable to move a muscle, how her real self gives Diego a confused look; he looks back at her, reassuringly, and with his index finger pushes the glass of water on the table forward in her direction*).

CARLA (*from the mirror, pounding at the glass*): But I want to live!

DIEGO: Do you *really*?

CARLA (*from the mirror*): Yes, just... Just not the way I am living now...

DIEGO: It's too late for that now, I am afraid. (*To Carla's physical self on the desk as she stares at the pills placed in her hand*). Yes, that's it. Go ahead. Take them. Take them and let it all go away. (*He takes the glass of water and puts it on her other hand*). Make me disappear forever. Allow your ears to never hear my voice again. Free Mom from her suffering. Make Dad finally gain a chance at being happy once again. Do the right thing, for us, for them...for you. Bring the villain forth and make her pay for her crimes.

CARLA (*from the desk*): I...I can't—

DIEGO: Of course you can. Isn't this what you have been dreaming of all these years? All that *La La Land* bullshit? Here. (*He takes her phone, enters Spotify, and starts playing "Another Day of Sun"*). There you go.

CARLA: (*from the desk*): I said <u>I CAN'T DO IT</u>.

DIEGO: Why not?

CARLA (*from the desk*): Because...because that would mean that you've won.

DIEGO: If you're even considering going through with it, then I already have. (*Beat*). Sooner or later, you are going to end up right at this moment. It's better that you spare yourself from more suffering. Think of it as going into a deep rest. No more pain, no more tears, no more sleepless nights. Everything will finally be over, just like you wanted.

CARLA (*from the desk*): I don't want to do this. I...I shouldn't have to do this.

DIEGO: There is only room for one of us, and you know I am not going anywhere. It is up to you to go to the one place you will have the certainty of not seeing me ever again. (*Putting the glass next to her lips*). It's alright, *little one*. It will all be over soon.

CARLA (*from the desk*): I... (*She hesitates and, for the first time, stares at her reflection trapped in the mirror; she stands up, still holding onto the glass, and heads to her bed, where she lies down and takes the glass to her lips; Carla looks at her reflection once more, both of them now drowning in tears, and instantly signs a silent pact with her to finally carry out this final plan of hers; no future in mind, no prospects of happiness on the horizon, she takes a moment to examine the pills in her hand; after some hesitation, she nods in approval, having long come to terms with a decision beyond repair, and just as she is about to shove in her mouth all the pills in her hand...her phone rings; she ignores the ringtone, still decided to take the pills when...she receives yet another text; Carla begins to fight an inner battle with herself, feeling the pressure of the imagined presence of her brother looming heavily over her shoulder...until the rational part of her brain ultimately prevails and prompts her to head towards the table to check her phone; she notices a couple of text messages from Anna, one of which reads "Ready for tonight?"*).

DIEGO (*expectant*): Well?

CARLA (*she stares at her computer wallpaper, an image of Bette Davis and Anne Baxter sharing a tense look from 'All About Eve' (1950); Carla becomes more aware than ever of the choice she must make, one for which her life hung in the balance; both on her computer and on her right hand simultaneously lie the two possible cures to the illness she faced—one for the short-term* *and one for the long haul; she stumbles and runs as many scenarios in her mind as the adrenaline allows her to, her mind inclining itself for the quicker solution, the one that would require less effort, less battling, less resistance; Carla then sinks her gaze on the pills in her hand, thinking about the consequences, at all she would be giving up, at all the kisses never to give or be given ever again, at the pain in her mother's eyes, at her flatmates picking up her dead body, at the sorrow in the lives of those around her, at the inability to open the door to falling in love with life once again...and just as she was about to enter her own epilogue, Bette Davis stares at Carla, with that wickedly mysterious look only she possessed, making Carla feel as if she was the only person left in this world of ours, and suddenly clearing all doubts momentarily taking root in her brain)*: Not tonight. (*Carla vigorously opens the door, passing by the illusory projection of her brother and the mirror where her reflection continues to be trapped in, and heads to the bathroom where, with unequivocal clarity, Carla flushes the pills down the toilet*).

DIEGO (*his voice echoing through the tiles of the bathroom, his presence very much felt yet his face nowhere to be seen*)**:** Demand me nothing. What you know, you know. From this time forth I never will speak word.

When I came back to my room, there was nobody there anymore other than myself and the palpable feeling that a crisis had been averted, although for how long it had been postponed remained a question mark heavily looming in the darkness that now covered the four walls inside of which I found myself in. An appointment for a deeply inner examination remained pending, one where I would need to come to terms with the fact it had taken me alarmingly little to carry out something I had long thought discarded; a danger I did not consider threatening anymore; an apparently banished idea, now more tangible than ever, which had quickly come back to haunt me with a speed and a certainty that made me question everything that I stood for. The ultimate truth persevered, unchallenged: all it takes is one bad day. And no matter how much progress one makes, we are never in the clear. We must never let our guard down, for those are the preferred moments for the darkest thoughts to manifest themselves. Be that as it may, and regardless of whether I deserved it or not, I had managed to emerge victorious. I had, against all odds, managed to live to see another day of sun.

XX

CARLA SAYS GOODBYE

It took a long, warm shower and an indelicate amount of concealer to get me in the mood of going out that night, although the chance had proven to be a lifesaving escape of sorts as well as a convenient excuse to get the aftertaste of that traumatising albeit non-existent encounter I had just had out of my mouth. Sporting some stilettos that threatened to render my ankles purposeless, and rocking a silver one-shoulder crop top with the tight leather pants that I had finally managed to fit in after my sustained choice of cycling over the past months as a de-facto mode of transportation, I joined the girls at the Ethiopian restaurant near Mr Pickwick's for a dinner that was only bound to end up regurgitated on the sidewalk hours later. Although I would not realise it until some hours later, when it became much needed in the face of the arising circumstances, I was carrying inside my jacket the notepad on which the week prior, after attending a much-needed session of Jean Renoir's *La Grande Illusion* (1937) down at the Cinerama Empire, I hosted a one-person evening of self-therapy in the shape of writing down as many of the feelings and fond memories collected since I arrived at this unexpectedly lovable city, in the hopes they would not be corroded with the vast repertoire of toxic memories I had so painfully experienced throughout my lifetime, and before my mind (aided by the global pharmaceutical industry) tricked me yet again into erasing the little remnants of the civilization now in decadence that was my own personal happiness, perhaps as part of an exercise of trying to simultaneously remember and forget.

With the food coma we induced ourselves in starting to slowly diminish the willingness to go out on the night in which I needed it most in order to keep myself away from myself, Vero had the brilliant idea to inaugurate that night with a remedy to cure our creeping somnolence: taking ecstasy. Now, I am a nervous person by default, having a mental crisis every time I have to talk to a stranger and more often than not quietly refusing to correct waiters whenever they bring the wrong order of food, failing to honk the car horn at reckless drivers putting everyone's life in peril, remaining silent in the presence of disrespectful moviegoers who loudly talk over the film's dialogue, and leaving the airplanes last so as to avoid interacting with anybody as much as medically necessary. So, taking that blue pill directly from the palm of a slim Senegalese gentleman's hand—a guy inexplicably wearing a white fedora and Apostle-like leather sandals in the middle of a cold October night, who went by the name of "Cornichon Endormi", standing at the door of the club *L'Usine*, right on the shore of the river *Rhône*—was perhaps not the smartest decision I had ever made.

At the very door of the building that technically held something resembling a club inside of it, though it looked exactly like the meeting place of the high spheres of Geneva for satanic rituals, *Eyes Wide Shut*-esque orgies (1999) and deeply unsettling sadistic ceremonies that would make the events portrayed in *Salò, or the 120 Days of Sodom* (1975) look like content apt for children. Without bearing in mind that the powder-keg we had just ingested was slowly brewing a far-too consequential personal crisis on the horizon, we confidently walked inside the graffiti-filled place, struggling to take any step forward without our fancy shoes sticking to the floor, and dodging pools of vomit, blood and beer as far as the eye could see. On our way up the sixteenth century staircase that held numerous (apparently) deceased bodies on its stairs, I stumbled onto a leather jacketed, septum-pierced, heavily tattooed emotional reject who screamed something to me in French and gave me his beer cup before he instantly passed out and loudly fell down the stairs. Nobody rushed to help him, and thus, like another piece of heavily mistreated furniture of the building, he became part of the flora and fauna that conformed the club. Being not of sound mind, I decisively held the glass he had given me in my hand and did not think twice before drinking the contents it contained. After all, this was a night whose sole purpose was to help me escape from earthly troubles, and there was no better way of starting that process than drinking from that cup, I concluded.

It took a few long looks around to get used to such a strikingly grotesque environment, a place that felt like the club where most people would not have ended up in had they been neglected a little less by their emotionally withholding parents. It was indeed a sinister construction filled to the brim with individuals that looked like the personification of that useless fold of skin that hangs out on the nape of the morbidly obese. Nonetheless, Anna, Vero and Michaela seemed to be perfectly in their element surrounded by that crowd—to all intents and purposes a likely group of ex-convicts playing extras in a *Sid and Nancy* (1986) sequel—which made me experience with a clarity analogous to noticing what the first stomachal sounds after eating a kebab at two a.m. will certainly bring, that I, with my belly hanging out of my cute top and my tight leather pants and stilettos, did not even remotely belong in there, and everybody—from the DJ whose face I could not even see, to the courageous bartender fiercely holding her position in the perennial presence of male aggressiveness remaining in its full splendour courtesy of abundant drugs and alcohol flying around—could most certainly tell.

We pulled through and walked into the dancing floor, where we were greeted with a scrum of men violently shoving each other from one side of the room to the other to the tune of the music—monotonous, deafening variations of the same song, which I am sure they use in "enhanced interrogation tactics" over at Guantanamo Bay. Thankfully, our last working neurons managed to dodge the vomit viciously propelled by a couple of fifty-year-olds in Mohawks for whom that scene looked like just another Wednesday, making me effectively forget about the *mine vaganti* inside of me that was about to go off and take everything in sight with it.

Despite clearly perceiving from the very beginning my state of non-belongingness in that place, courtesy of my dreaded sensitive nature, I was nonetheless subjected to the inquiries of a bald man in his forties inexplicably wearing a parka indoors and smoking a joint big enough to pass as a battering ram, who felt the impending need to condescendingly ask me whether I was lost or if I indeed enjoyed the kind of ape-brutality-inducing music that was being played—more like *inflicted upon*—at that club.

"I'm just asking because…you know, with your shoes and all…" he eloquently mansplained.

Sick and tired of not being able to enjoy my own social anxiety in peace, I nonchalantly shouted in his ear, "We are who we are," and started dancing with Vero, Anna and Michaela, fist held high in the air, turning my back on the guy who that night would most likely return empty-handed at his permanent residence for the past four decades: his parents' downstairs cellar.

Certainly playing a role in my perception of the club was the fact that the image which I had of these sort of places was relegated almost exclusively to expecting a pseudo-Margot-Robbie-in-*Once-Upon-A-Time-In-Hollywood* (2019) vibe of dreamlike spirituality all around, where good vibrations and lack of inhibitions in the presence of hard drugs, made everyone friendlier than usual, with the impending sense of collective enjoyment of a state of superb elation wrapping everyone's minds, souls and bodies all around. But such a reality soon came crashing down mere seconds after standing in the midst of a place that was the living personification of the bathroom *and* toilet from *Trainspotting* (1995): thirty square metres filled with a total disregard for your eardrum's well-being, sudden outbursts of repressed masculinity-fuelled violence from which nobody was to be spared, and frequent loss of consciousness all-around of those who lost the battle against their bodies' integrity and effectively joined the puke, blood and shattered glass on the floor. From across the ocean of substance-induced sweaty bodies, my gaze suddenly halted at the girls: their figures being colourfully illuminated by the fluorescent lights, their self-awareness nowhere to be seen in a way that made me feel envious of their unobstructed freedom, their bodies carelessly engaged in a symphony of seductive, spontaneous dancing.

Vero, with a wide smile brightly painted on her delicate face, looked at me, eyes half opened and said, before taking a drag of her cigarette, *"Estamos de puta madre,"* and then kept on dancing as if the world wasn't watching, the key to going unnoticed even in the hole we then found ourselves in.

Mere instants before my social battery had completely ran out and I entered the well-known space of self-deprecation for not allowing myself to enjoy having anything resembling a mildly amusing moment, the catastrophe in my stomach started to go off—not quietly, not progressively, <u>but all at once</u>—and took hold of my body like the butterflies one feels when in love—I guess—or the most primal moments of entering into contact with grief, or the sudden gravity-defying drop one experiences when sitting at a rollercoaster as it rapidly descends into the void. With such a powerful chemical reaction bubbling inside of me, my body was squatted by a foreign feeling of overwhelming and uncontainable energy that yearned to get out in whichever way was readily available at my disposal. The four of us were taken over by this all-encompassing bliss that made us suddenly feel the urge to tell how much we dearly loved one another, that is, all but Michaela, who exited stage left and started puking all over the ironically redundant VIP area. Looking at Anna and Vero tenderly hugging one another, on their own and to their own rhythm, I once again found myself having so much love and euphoria inside of me…yet having nobody to give it to.

Ecstasy, as all drugs do, does not turn you into a completely different individual, despite the lies that religious organizations and self-declared intellectuals with as much relevance as the script supervisor in a Terrence Malick film, like to tell us; it merely accentuates the kind of person you already are. There are no bad trips, only people who do not know themselves enough to realise the person they are when they are high is the person they have hidden deep enough inside themselves, under layers of masks they put on each morning, and a reality that disgusts them to look straight in the face, at least enough to never allow themselves to confront the lurking shadow projected by their real personality, which will forever follow them around. And so, the pill inside of me brought out the most pervasive, paranoid, anxiety suffocating side of myself which, up until that night, I had otherwise thought I had managed to tame into a small corner where it could not hurt me like it used to. I was thoroughly unprepared to confront the ferocious beast that came out which, after starving for so long, had been subconsciously provoked mere hours before in the comfort of my own room.

Looking around, I saw my friends as unreachable: them, far deep into processing their mutual love, as only ecstasy can make you do; me, as unworthy of their love, slowly stepping away until I found myself standing in a corner like I used to do at each party I ever went to. With my mind anxiously awaiting to be possessed by the darkness it had fallen prey to becoming far too comfortable with, I failed to notice the incoming presence of a face in the crowd of someone I unluckily knew well enough for the sight of him to induce me into a sudden state of shock. My brother Diego walked decisively, opening his way across the dance floor into the far-right corner where I was standing, shoving with his muscled arms everyone in his way, until he came face to face with me.

He took a long, disgusted look at me, scanning me from top to bottom, as he always did, after which he proceeded to put a hand on my shoulder whilst leaning forward with a smile on his face, and calmly whispered in my ear, "Why don't you do us all a favour and kill yourself once and for all?"

Our eyes met for a brief instant, and I felt the need to look down, struggling to breathe, uncontrollably gasping for air almost to the point of nearly choking to death right then and there. A loud voice kept bouncing back and forth in my brain, and when I finally managed to look up, I saw the bald man in a parka, instead, worriedly laying his hand on my shoulder, trying to make sure I was alright.

"Everything okay?" he managed to say while holding a tall drink in his right hand. Squinting my eyes in an attempt to find anything and anyone to hold onto, I started to notice how the ceiling became taller and the drug-fuelled people all seemingly looked to be staring at me in unison while Anna and Vero kept being entranced with one another. Just as I could feel my heartbeats earsplittingly pounding on my chest, another scrum broke out near the DJ booth, this time followed by bottles being tossed around, flying through the room and resulting in broken glasses, teeth and bones. The nauseating environment gave me the feeling that if I did not get out of there, I would not get out of there at all. Fuelled by the impetus that now artificially flowed through my veins, I took a few steps back, away from the girls, from the noise and from the bald man in a parka who had come to check up on me in the face of my self-concocted distortion of reality. And almost without realising it, I started methodically walking towards the door, with the intention of reaching the bathroom to wash up my face being impulsively discarded for a more permanent destination.

As I walked down the stairs and left the deafening music behind, my ears struggled to adjust to the sudden change of environment. For a few instances, they registered what sounded like insulting words in French by the comatose people which lay at the stairs and saw me walking out in a clearly mismatched outfit which posed a stark contrast with the location around us. With the powerful dissonance in reality perception that one experiences after being inside an airplane as it takes off or putting on noise-cancelling headphones, I walked out into the cold of night, with a new melody entering into my ears: a requiem of sorts formed by drunken people on the street, the garbage trucks beginning to do their early rounds, the desolate cats standing at the border of the lake launching defiant looks at the fiery swans, the non-stop sound of the Rhône River energetically flowing through the heart of Geneva, the flickering street lights on the river pathways under the bridge, the old engines of fleeting cars wandering through the cold darkness of the night... A combination of a recently expropriated body with my characteristic lack of peace of mind, gave me enough fuel to keep on actively walking across the polar twilight, purposeless and without looking up even once, for what amounted to well over an hour. By the time I took my phone out, having now reached a solitary forest by the shore of the river, I saw fifteen missed calls from the girls.

"Where are you?" (...) "Honey, please talk to us." (...) "Carla, where the fuck are you, I have called Leo: we're taking his car to go look for you." (...) "Carla, please answer, we are out here looking for you." (...) "We're worried, please pick up the phone." (...) "Please let us know, Carla. You know no matter what, we're here for you." (...) "Carla, my dear, you cannot be on your own." (...) "Where are you?" (...) "Whatever it is, we're your friends. Please, Carla, please, we want to help. Let us help you." (...) "You should not be alone right now, let us take care of you, please." (...) "We love you, Carla. Please pick up the phone."

I looked up for the first time during my walk, the inner part of my lips having been viciously devoured by an uncontrollable masochistic impulse to bite it until it bled, and set my eyes on the nearby forest. The trees were being carefully caressed by the freezing wind of a day minutes away from beginning, the river vigorously carrying an unstoppable stream, the area completely uninhabited by another breathing soul. I closed my eyes and took a deep breath—the kind we rarely ever take— trying to come to terms with what I was about to do, and emerged victorious, now being able to clearly see something that I had lacked for so long: purpose. Sheer, uninterrupted, crystal clear, unequivocal purpose. Without thinking for an instant longer, I turned the phone off, and jumped over the small fence that led to the nearby forest. My stilettos landed on some metal stairs that took me down to the ground level, where the water was flowing, with the depth and darkness of the woods and the inhospitable time of the day hiding my actions, and with nothing but a humble bridge hovering atop the river, eminently placed to get first row tickets to the entire show, standing as witness. My footsteps could be calmly heard approaching the shore, and I quietly sat down on a nearby rock to reflect on my final moments. I just stood there, a couple of meters away from the flowing water, waiting for the kind of last-minute salvation that spared Fyodor Dostoevsky from an imminent execution, patiently hoping for the improbable eleventh-hour arrival of inspiration to burst into scene and seduce me to come back to life once again. But that moment did not arrive, because when you set your mind on convincing yourself there is no other choice, then no matter how many options are presented to you, such a final outcome is going to be inevitably executed in the face of a chronic loss of faith in yourself.

    Thus, not impulsively but serenely and totally in control, with the drugs flowing through my system merely performing the role of accelerating an already ongoing process, I took out the notepad stored in my jacket. Without hesitation, and very much inspired by that character from Dostoevsky's *The Idiot*, I started drafting my final words with the sound of Geneva's nightly atmosphere playing the final tunes of my vital finale, making sure to also reserve—like the character from the novel—a few final instances to reflect upon my own course of life and take one last look around before abruptly ceasing to exist. Words seemed to appear on my mind so naturally, so fluently, that I wondered for how long I had been thinking about them; no writing mistakes, no babbling or meandering thoughts: entire sentences materialised, conveying in an orderly fashion and with relieving precision what exactly it was that was going through my mind both at that moment and on the long years leading up to it. An externally perceived yet internally felt force swiftly guided me towards accurately expressing all the existential angst that I wanted to get rid of once and for all, allowing me a last courtesy of at least getting out of this world knowing that those around me would find comfort in their pain by learning the reasons that led me to that exact moment in time. With no rules other than actively avoiding falling into pointless accusatory remarks that were beneath me and may give others the chance to spread the wrong perception of the roles played in my life and the opportunity to dismiss my claims as utterly unfounded and nonsensical, I began to write, with the intent that the questions raised were outnumbered by the answers provided.

"But how do you say goodbye to those you love most, or those who you need to send one last message to? How do you even begin to express such indescribable, years-long, intricately complex ailments?" I wondered. Well, I guess you must start from the beginning.

To my friends back home,

Ever since I can remember, my fondest memories have been spent by your side. Although I rarely opened up to say this, the moment that I met every single one of you marked a <u>before</u> and an <u>after</u> in my life. And throughout all these years that I have been lucky enough to have had you all right next to me—an invaluable time which we have certainly made the most out of, and forever will seem like it wasn't enough, like we didn't see one other enough, like we didn't party enough, like our hugs could have always been tighter and our "I love yous" more frequent—this scared little girl that spent her entire days and nights in agony found herself mostly free from pain when in your company. As you probably know, maybe because I keep bringing it up again and again, I have never conceived happiness neither as a tangible state nor as something that can be achieved and sustained for a prolonged period of time. Instead, I see happiness as moments. But, if I have ever come close to extending a concatenation of happy moments for longer than expected, it has been during the time that I spent with every single one of you. Because there are very few better feelings than laughing until tears come to your eyes, and even fewer people that can say they do it every time they see their friends. For what has amounted to a lifetime, every second I have spent with you has made me feel like I was part of a true family, one that gave me plenty of reasons to hold onto the possibility of more promising outlooks: **<u>Miriam</u>**, with your constant smile and contagiously positive mindset, always the first one ready to help as needed and the one on whose shoulders I have found solace time after time; **<u>Mónica</u>**, a selfless, caring soul who loved me unconditionally and asked no questions and provided answers whenever I needed it most; **<u>Antonio</u>**; one of the few people on this planet who could make me laugh like no amount of movies ever could, and the source of stoic energy that gave me sufficient fuel to escape from countless problems, one night at a time; **Luna**, my first true love who always refused to let me forget my real, inherent value, and a reason that kept me on my feet during my constant struggles to become a better person; and **Sara**, my eternal companion and confidant, with whom I learned to live life a little better and with a lot more passion.

But even the best of us can sometimes be blind enough to push those that love us most aside, preventing them from providing us with much-needed emotional stability to support the crooked house that we all eventually become. I simply cannot envision a life without you, and I wish I had expressed more often how much your love meant to me. But I hope you understand that you did all that you could, and what you did was more than enough. Now that I begin to see everything a little darker, you and I both must not forget that for there to be a great shadow there must be an even greater light behind. Looking back and being unable to look forward, it doesn't seem real that soon, you will all be gone. But before I leave, I just wanted to let every single one of you know from the bottom of my heart, that I love you with as much intensity and honesty as one possibly can, and that I will forever be grateful to all of you for having made of a life that initially did not promise me anything, acquire value in your presence; and years that seemed transitory, a life to never forget.

To my grandparents,

It is an act against nature that grandparents see one of their grandchildren pass away before they themselves do, but appealing to your infinite wisdom and capacity for empathy, I hope you understand that there simply was no other way for me to go. All you ever wanted was for me to be happy, and since I cannot get that in this life, maybe I can get a shot in the next one—if there ever is such a thing. You have always remained a constant source of inspiration for me, an example of perseverance in the face of difficulties, and, simply put, the kind of people everyone should look up to. And in the remarkable life that you have led, you have created a family in which all of us have felt truly loved, and have stood day by day as a perpetual presence for all of us to lean on, igniting in us a constant desire to continue to improve our lives in the hopes of someday reaching the best version of ourselves, just like you two have. The sorrowful times that will soon follow will certainly bring with them a great deal of pain that I wish I could prevent you from experiencing. But precisely in these times, it is important to see life with some perspective, and recover the complete vision of what one has and has had. In the same way as the character of James Stewart in <u>It's a Wonderful Life</u>, this world would have been a worse place had there been no room for your stories and anecdotes, for your doses of wisdom that taught us how to shine a little brighter and made me appreciate at all times the people I had around me who, very much like you two did every day, made me feel this life of mine was a little more bearable.

This world, this family, and this granddaughter in particular, owe you far more than words can contain. In these final moments, I would like to remind you both of how important you have been in my life, what an incredible influence you have been in showing me through your actions everything that is good and pure, and what a privilege it has been to grow up surrounded by your kind, loving souls. I hope that you find it in your heart to forgive me for the damage I will bring upon your lives, and from now remember me not in this way, but as the granddaughter who has always been by your side; as the little girl who has always admired you, and who will never stop loving you.

To my ladies from Geneva,

To say that I feel fortunate to have met you would be an understatement, because it's not that you have made the time I have spent here better, it's simply that without you all this would not have been worth it. You gave me light when I needed it most, you gave me life when I thought I no longer had it in me, and you gave me a sore stomach every morning after endless nights of constant laughter and slutty dancing—of course, always to the tune of "Pepas". Because Geneva without you girls is not Geneva. It is just another city. Everything that makes it special has been sitting right next to me on all those nights filled with regretful choices, smelly cheeses and cheap wine. And when you are surrounded by idiots, any plan becomes a memory of the kind that one never wants to forget.

They say that friendship is a soul shared in two bodies, in this case, a couple more: **Claudia**, our bottomless well of positive energy and intense "perreo"; **Arantxa**, my most random Tinder match but the one I'm most glad I had; **Michaela**, my favourite partner in crime on our night robberies and movie sessions; **Anna**, the author of my stomach aches after nights and nights of crying with laughter, never failing to fill our days with contagious optimism; **Lara**, with whom I return to adolescence with just one look, as when our neurons come together they inevitably register null cerebral activity; and **Vero**, simply put, the older sister I never had and the boss everyone wished they had, and my island in the middle of an initially inhospitable ocean. But time, like the decibels of Michaela's snoring, is relative. And the fact is that the higher you climb, the harder the fall will be. And that's why this farewell will be so hard for us all, because we have set an incredibly high bar, effectively proving that quality always beats quantity, and people you know from just a few months can prove to you infinitely more than someone you may know for forever. It is important that you focus not on what could have been but on what has been; not in that we wish we had met before, but in how lucky we actually are for having actually met. If during these short months I have become a better and happier person, and if I have found moments of pure joy that made me want to carry on and not give in to my inner impulses, it will have been because of you. Thank you for making my last days impossible to forget, wherever it is that I go next. Don't you ever forget the light that you all radiate. I love you, *marujillas*.

To Mom,

Mother-daughter relationships have always been known as a minefield, as tumultuous waters filled with conflict and tough love. But you have made it so easy to be your daughter, so effortless to love you, so comforting to be in your presence, so hard to now let you go. You, dedicating your days to solving our problems before they dare to appear, wrapping your arms around me even from the distance, letting me know I was never alone in those moments where there was only room for feeling otherwise, have made a full-time job to bring joy into our days, even when it meant renouncing to your own. Even in death, I will remain forever grateful to you for gifting my days with your tender voice and encouraging words, for believing in this lost cause, for refusing to give up even when I deserved so, for remaining an incorruptible bastion of the kind of person we should all aspire to be, and of everything good this world has to offer. In these final moments, no other feeling fills my mind other than suffocating remorse, an agonising but ultimately idealistic wish of a life where I could spare you of the pain of the years to come. It is my deepest regret to know that I cannot shield you from the inevitable collateral debris that is going to come your way. If it is any consolation, it has been one of the main reasons why I have kept on living up until this moment, for I could not bear to cause you any harm in any way, nor be the reason for your tears to appear. You do not deserve that; you do not deserve to be treated that way. You do not deserve to stare at my lifeless body during the funeral I know you enough to be sure will most certainly be held within a church I never wanted to belong to. You do not deserve to be looked at in the way you will be looked at by the neighbours, friends and strangers on the street, when word spreads about my demise, and particularly by the way such demise took place. But you also do not deserve to blame yourself for what I am going to do, because even though in these cases the natural thing to do would be to torture yourself by thinking you could have always done something to prevent it, this ticking time bomb would have eventually found its exact replication a few years down the line.

So just know that this destination was always the final stop, but you made the trip here a lot more bearable by filling it with the kind of love that made me want to remain on my two feet for a little longer. You deserve a daughter that brings you happiness instead of the pain I am about to fill your life with. For all of that I apologise, dear Mom. I hope someday you can understand that if I did what I am going to do, the oppressive suffering must have been excruciating enough to make me want to renounce everything and everyone, and carry on despite being fully aware of the devastating impact it would have on you. So, I beg you to navigate the sea of grief coming your way, and see that my eternal love for you will never die, even if I will. This world will never live to see a mother that comes even remotely close to being half of the mother you have been to me, so find solace in knowing that if there is one certainty in this uncertain moment, it is that this life has been worth living for having spent even a single second by your side. Just the thought of you will keep me warm on my final moments. It is you, Mom, it has always been you. I love you.

To Dad,

Keeping in line with your characteristic brevity of word, I will keep it straight to the point. Since I was a kid, and I became able to notice how other parents behaved and to see the (often non-existent) relationships others had with their fathers, I knew how lucky I was to have in my life the father everyone wished they had. Because the same way that knowing a spoiler before you watch a film makes you appreciate everything else in the ensuing movie a little more, the truth is that being aware of the inherent value residing in having a father that is the living and breathing evidence that true, selfless, discrete kindness still exists, makes you truly appreciate how utterly lucky you are for having always had your biggest fan, your constant supporter, right by your side. The wisdom in your eyes and the love in your acts made me feel loved and supported, and made me want to carry on even when all odds were against me, and the deep connection that we shared for the love of cinema—an art form I would have likely been indifferent to had you not properly introduced me to it—gave my life some meaningful albeit temporary purpose, which palliated the harshest parts of my days with their inspiring beauty and endless possibilities.

I will not lie and say that I will not miss our trips across 'Plaza de Callao' on those lonely Saturday evenings we spent around Madrid when I was but a child and it seemed everyone was having fun at parties I was not invited to, which we spent looking for bootlegged versions of the latest films we were unable to afford watching in movie theatres, only to illegally watch them at home, just the two of us. I will miss knocking on your office door with a problem and having the certainty I would come out of it with peace of mind and a handful of solutions. I will miss going to movie theatres with you and hearing your loud comments overshadow the dialogues in the film. I will miss the smell left by the smoke of your cigarettes which surrounded every inch of our house, and the way you always managed to turn any dead moment into an opportunity for laughter. I will miss having you around, making my life a little better, one smile at a time. Because nobody is as lucky as I am, for I could not have asked for a better role model to grow side by side with. I only wish I was the daughter you deserved, Dad. I hope that you understand what I am about to do, and that you forgive me for refusing to go on like this. Because you have carried similar burdens to the ones I have lived with, even though you had more dedication to push through it all, when I now find myself unable to live for even one second longer. No words can come close to describing my love and admiration for you, and I really hope you live the rest of your long life knowing you have been the very best father one could ask for, and that if I have an ounce of decency in me, it was surely learned from the example that you set every day. Find reassurance in knowing that you did the impossible, Dad, that you did your best and even more, and that you have proven that heroes are not confined to fiction anymore, for day by day you make those around you want to be better persons. Simply put, the world is an instantly better place for having you in it. Goodbye, Dad, I loved you as well and as intensely as I could, and I always will.

To Diego,

The pain I leave behind is far larger than I ever wished, but not more painful than the thought that we could have been more than enemies if only you would have taken my hand; that before we were darkness, there remained some potential for a meaningful relationship between us both; that I wish I could have been the support you clearly needed and you the brother that I never felt I had; that I yearn for a life in which you do not exist anymore, one in which I no longer hate the person that I am, one in which your deficiencies do not come crashing into my world, demolishing through a domino effect every single thing that I once held dear to my heart. But now, the problems created either by your hand or mine or a combination of both have become far greater than the joy I get out of living. Because when the foundations of a building are jeopardised, the entire structure is only poised to crumble, and the small lies and apparently innocent forms of mistreatment that grew into fully-fledged emotional torture and abuse have turned you into a monster that only finds satisfaction in the face of other people's lack of it. Now that there is no way back for me, and I am unable to cope with you anymore, I would like to steer away from sensationalist comments like "I hope you know you are the main reason why I am doing this", in part because there is no reason to do so, as deep down, once you dare to take a good look at yourself, you will see you are already aware of the part you have played in this, but also because I would like my final words to you to be helpful rather than just hurtful.

From the bottom of my heart, I sincerely hope you get the help that you truly need, so that it helps you carry the traumas and emotional shortcomings you have displayed and felt the need to project onto us. Right now, I am unable to see what kind of phenomenon is powerful enough to make you finally see the full extent of the excruciating damage you have single-handedly inflicted upon me, upon Mom and Dad, and upon yourself. For me, there is no longer any hope: the fate has been sealed and the decision is final. But you have the potential to change course, and finally find yourself along the way by realising the mistakes you have made. You can't change what you have done so far, and your time will surely come to face those acts, but you can perhaps mend what you will do to others. It is up to you to put an end to the behaviour I can no longer suffer, and it is up to you to remedy all the harm generated by making sure you never make anybody else go through what you have inexplicably made me experience. To help you in your journey of self-discovery and awareness of the environments you have engineered, I encourage you to go through my laptop and take a look at the document I have named "Swiss Death of Mine," where your presence and subsequent effect throughout all these long months, as well as the even longer years that came before, have been carefully put into words. With nothing but your best interest in mind, I wish you all the best, and sincerely hope with every last breath I have left in me that you forgive yourself and manage to become the son our parents have needed for all these years, and cease to—whether consciously or unconsciously—be the villain in your own story. Good luck, and always remember the person you have been all these years, to never let yourself forget where you come from and to make sure you never return to being that person ever again. Not only for your sake, but for everyone else's.

With surprising skill and delicacy, I carefully used my pair of shaky hands to fold the notebook and store it inside my jacket, right before taking my clothes off and stripping down bottom naked, intently, and for the last time.

"Here comes the kind of person with nothing to lose which James Baldwin warned us about on the verge of doing something permanent," I thought. Before allowing as much as a minute of hesitation to potentially open the way for a Deus ex machina to appear, I calmly introduced my left foot first into the freezing cold waters, with the rest of my body promptly following suit. As I began to weightlessly float, my mind fixed on being carried away by the river to an uncertain destination, a tear came out of the corner of my eye, camouflaged by the gentle waves of the river, and took it away the same way it was going to take my last breath. The last beams of moonlight before the impending arrival of the morning sun struggled to illuminate such a disheartening scene. This sweet form of death began to subtly make its way through my body: the cold waters meticulously perforating my lungs, pacing their way towards a fatal pneumonia; the muscles starting to let the door wide open for total paralysis to arrive at any time; my breasts no longer firm; my legs no longer movable; my broken heart about to emit its final beat; my body no longer mine; my mind, at last in peace. And thus, I closed my eyes, the real ones, and in that darkness, I took a proper look at myself, at the person I had been and the person I was now going to become. Of little importance was all that would remain after I was gone; all that mattered was the destination that I was headed to, finally reaching somewhere I truly belonged. That always sounded like a good life—a proper life—filled with exactly what I needed and ached for: silence.

The noise on the streets was drowned out by the voracious sound of the river flowing, and I braced for impact by exhaling my final breaths before giving in, not in resignation but in gentle acceptance of defeat. Defeat of a battle I had long lost before I even stepped foot on this country. Defeat that had proven to be inevitable, even after having encountered face-front true happiness around my newly found friends, and having learnt to appreciate the love of my parents and friends, who tightly surrounded me from the distance with their gentle arms. Defeat that was always irreparably destined to be.

And in those final moments before my body succumbed to the less-than-ideal circumstances I had managed to put myself through at that moment, I was invaded by instances of true, honest self-reflection in the face of an impending exit; a simultaneous feeling of clarity that headed in opposite directions with equal strength, making both sides of my brain fiercely battle to the death in pursuit of reaching either the light or the light at the end of the tunnel...

RIGHT SIDE: Okay, so...I guess this is it. Our body temperature will soon reach worrying levels; our limbs will promptly stop shaking; our lungs will cease to produce any more oxygen; our faulty heart will come to the halt it desperately aches for... (*Beat*). Our pain will finally stop being present.

LEFT SIDE (*after a long pause*): ...you know it doesn't have to be this way, right?

RIGHT SIDE: What do you mean?

LEFT SIDE: We've been through this before—you know very well there is more to life than just a few miserable moments, as close together as they may be, and even if they are prolonged over a long period of time.

RIGHT SIDE: Don't start with that shit again, you're not convincing me this time. <u>This is it</u>.

LEFT SIDE (*in a mocking tone*)**:** *This is it.* Look at you being dramatic, where was this when Mrs Fernández was casting for the school's Romeo and Juliet in eighth grade?

RIGHT SIDE: Just shut up, please. Don't ruin this for me. Save your time; no amount of words is going to change that we have failed: we're a fucking failure. There are just no more reasons left to live, how many people can actually say that? And I am just sick. Sick of being sick of myself all the time. Sick of not being comfortable in my own body. Sick of finding no meaningful ways of coping with myself and with him. Sick of not being understood. Of knowing that what awaits me if I keep on going is more of the same. Sick of the certainty that whatever I manage to do with my life, it is inevitable that I will end up alone. This is just not for me anymore.

LEFT SIDE: Okay—there's a lot to unpack there. First things first: my darling, are you really so ignorant so as to avoid confronting the fact of all that you would be leaving behind?

RIGHT SIDE: Like what, exactly?

LEFT SIDE: Well, for starters, what about all those movie nights that made you feel like the world was not such a bad place after all?

RIGHT SIDE: I cannot spend my days locked in a movie theatre, escaping from reality one film at a time. That is no way to live—constantly in hiding from others, from myself, from the life that is waiting for me as soon as the credits start rolling and I step out the door. Make no mistake, the only things that I leave behind are those which I don't want to see ever again.

LEFT SIDE: There is nobody here but us, so there is no point in lying, my friend, but okay. Then, what about the people you will never see anymore, those you are abandoning? What about your friends in this city and back in Spain? What about the heartbreak you will force them to suffer for the rest of their lives?

RIGHT SIDE (*inner dismissive hand gesture*)**:** Ah...they will be fine. Deep down, a part of them already knew, anyway. You and I have both been on borrowed time for the past couple of years. Besides, my life choices cannot be solely based on the impact they will have on others. At one point, my own personal interest must come into play, right? The eternal grief that I suffer for myself on a daily basis is far greater than what anybody else might experience, regardless of how much they may love me. The biggest victim in this death is myself; everyone else around me is collateral damage.

LEFT SIDE: Collateral damage? What about Dad? What about the pain it would bring Mom to see your inert, lifeless body on a casket? Are they also collateral damage? They have given everything they had, every fibre of their being, to giving you the best life you could possibly get. You always say happiness is not an attainable state, that it's only ephemeral instants, but you forget that happiness can also be a place, a film...or even a person. And you are theirs: everything they wished they were, a life filled with everything they wished they had. You're not only their main source of emotional support, their embodied happiness: you're their life project. And you want to throw it all away? A parent without their child becomes an orphan, inconsolable, forever incomplete, forever grieving, forever lamenting they could have done more to save you. You are condemning them to the same type of depression, if not more severe, that you're currently experiencing. You will therefore become the perpetrator and no longer the survivor, just like your brother. In fact, you will become exactly the kind of person you have worked all your life to avoid becoming. I mean, do you have any idea of the suffering they will—

RIGHT SIDE: Do you have any idea of mine?

LEFT SIDE: Yes, I do.

RIGHT SIDE: Good, then start talking like you do. No need for the petty emotional manipulations: I am well aware of the impact this will have on them. They have been nothing but kind and supportive to me, effectively preventing me from going down a permanent spiral of self-hate, even if they occasionally contributed to it by turning a convenient blind eye every now and again... And yet, whatever they did wasn't enough, which does not reflect on them as parents, but on the magnitude of the problem at hand. Suicide never kills only one person, you know that as well as I do, but if they love me as much as we know they do, Mom and Dad will have to realise, as painful as it may be, that this is what is best for me.

LEFT SIDE (*loudly exhales*)**:** I feel you; I've been with you every step of the way. And I'm not going to lie to you: if you only looked at the evidence you are presenting—and omitted all the details I keep bringing up only for you to leave them out of the picture—right now one could say you had a pretty solid case. But it's just...it's just that I don't want us to go like this.

RIGHT SIDE: Like what?

LEFT SIDE: Like we gave up before trying all other possible avenues.

RIGHT SIDE: Oh, please...you're better than this. Spare me the optimistic outlook that will never be a part of our reality, as much as you try to fool us into thinking otherwise.

LEFT SIDE: You have to get worse before you can get better.

RIGHT SIDE: True, but the thing is I have been getting worse for the past ten years, if not more, and there is no future in sight where I get better. I am sorry, but this is my decision, and my decision is final. This is not rock bottom; I reached that a long time ago. You just don't see it yet, because you refuse to understand that—

LEFT SIDE: I understand just fine, better than anybody else could. All I am trying to do here is to make you see there is more to life than suffering.

RIGHT SIDE: Life *is* suffering. I have tried and failed to find meaning to my days, and even when that proved to be an impossible task, I settled down for trying to reach a state of mild numbing of the pain, but that too turned out to be unsustainable. There is honour in the noble task of having tried, as most humans do. I mean, the truth is that the true beauty of life is something often chased, and rarely appreciated at its right time, for when we think we have reached it, we have long lost it. And it has escaped through my fingers, as even when I was certain of having finally attained it—the solution to living my days in peace, the purpose found in those twenty-four frames per second—I no longer thought it enough to keep me alive.

LEFT SIDE (*cackling laughter*): What the hell do you know about living? You are twenty-four years old, and your entire experience has been reduced to an almost complete seclusion in movie theatres to evade yourself from facing a reality tinkered by a megalomaniac sibling with autocratic aspirations—to all intents and purposes, a very partial, fragmentary, and reductive view of a life that has considerably more to offer. You don't know life; you have barely even begun living it! Just because you have tripped at the beginning of the race doesn't mean that the race is over.

RIGHT SIDE: Oh, my God. You just don't get it, do you? I WANT TO DIE! What is so hard to understand about that? Please...please, just give me this. Just let me die... Why is it so hard for you to get it?

LEFT SIDE: Because you are about to make the most important decision of your entire lifetime without being fully aware of the consequences of your actions, nor of the alternative choices that are at your disposal. You just have to find the right way of—

RIGHT SIDE: That ship has long sailed. Perhaps for someone else, someone with options, someone who truly belonged, those "alternative choices" are genuinely at their disposal. But for people like me, like us, that was never on the table. The circle is growing tighter and tighter and everyone else finds a spot in the universe except me. Except us.

LEFT SIDE: Well, if you are unable to find your spot in this world that does not make you unworthy of love or unfit for living—that only makes you human. Look around! You are not the only one who cannot find her place. The roles that have been imposed upon us leave plenty of misunderstood people standing along the sidelines. Of individuals who, like us, have been wronged in one way or another. And that is not the end of the world. Because, unlike those that are a part of the heavily greased machinery that is our society, the fact that you have been dismissed by many and struggled to find somewhere you truly belong has given you something they will struggle to ever possess: perspective, empathy and the willingness to avoid repeating the mistakes others have made by consistently hurting—in some form or another—people like yourself. You have a role to fulfil, a contribution to make, so that you can assist in the cause of making sure nobody has to go through what we have.

RIGHT SIDE: But I am just one woman.

LEFT SIDE: And one woman is more than enough. Of course, on your own you simply cannot make sure that people like your brother keep existing, but any effort in that direction is necessary, and every action counts—and that includes the simple act of stepping out of this river right now.

RIGHT SIDE: The thing is, I remember back in college, whenever I tried to solve those ridiculously intricate math problems as part of that econometrics class we took with, uh, what was her name? Alicia...Escudero? I lost my virginity with her in the faculty bathroom, but I can't even remember her face now... Anyway, what was I saying? It had something to do with numbers... Oh, right, econometrics. Well, in one of those exams I would always double-check the result with, at the very least, three different methods (including checking on the neighbour's exam): if it came out the same, then there simply was no other solution. Well, I've run down the numbers—a few times over a few years—and the result has been the same. The idea has already appeared in my mind, and there is simply no turning back now. We can stay here, floating in this river, as long as you want, but at the end of it all the truth would remain that there is only one way out. You know there is.

LEFT SIDE: But there isn't. Listen, few are as lucky as you are to have all the people you have by your side, ready to support you the moment you let them know about your troubles, about this reality that they have no idea exists.

RIGHT SIDE: No amount of friendships and selfless love and support will ever prevent me from feeling, deep down, with as much certainty as I have ever had, that there is no reason why I should keep on living, because I simply don't want to live anymore.

LEFT SIDE: And I can tell you with as much certainty as I have ever had that that is <u>exactly</u> what is going to prevent you from feeling the way you are feeling now.

RIGHT SIDE: Come on, we've already been through this. And frankly, it's starting to get on my nerves that you keep talking like you are unaware of how exhausting it is to pretend like I am fine day after day, conversation after conversation, party after party, dinner after dinner. And if you think that I am stupid for leaving it all behind when I have so many people that love me and support me, then just think of it the other way round: how deeply damaged I am to want to die in spite of having them all in my life.

LEFT SIDE: If this is about Diego, which I know is only partly true, surely you must be aware that you don't have to live with him! You don't have to share a life with him. Hell, you don't even have to share a surname with him if you don't want to!

RIGHT SIDE: It's not that easy...

LEFT SIDE: Of course it is not. What is easy is to refuse to fight for your life. What is easy is to let him continue doing this to others. What is easy is to leave before having tried and failed every possible way of defending your value in the face of those who blindly insist on its non-existence.

RIGHT SIDE: Don't you dare insinuate I am a coward.

LEFT SIDE: I am not. All I am saying is that you are actively refusing to take charge of our own life, declining to actually do something about our state, about how we can approach him, about how we can help him and try to fix our—

RIGHT SIDE (*over*): Help *him*? You must have a pretty short memory to have already forgotten about how all the times we've tried to confront him have backfired and we've been the ones who have ended up at an even worse place than we initially began in, as hard as that might have been to believe. How all of the sudden I was turned into the violent one out of the two of us. How in the eyes of all I was the one breaking apart the family. How I became the reason why my mother's bloodstream was almost entirely polluted with a mix of alcohol and anxiolytics. And it has, is, and will keep on growing and growing, forever, like it always has, because it no longer belongs to me anymore: it belongs to them. And once they find in me the butt of the joke, the perpetual culprit, there is nothing else to do. Doesn't matter if I kill myself or not, I am always going to be the one who bares the blame. There is no fixing him, no fixing the mess he has made, no fixing my role in this family, and I want no part in it, even if there was room for a hypothetical solution to our relationship. He doesn't deserve it.

LEFT SIDE: If not for him, or for your family, do it for yourself. Just think about all we'd be losing.

RIGHT SIDE: I cannot keep on living like this; it would all be so much easier to just give up…to give him the satisfaction of winning. I have no control over what he does or what will happen after I no longer do, but I know history is written by the victors, and when the one with the pen in his hand sets out to write his own story, he will not disappoint my expectations, I'm sure, after he labels himself as the hero in his own story. Right now, all I can see is the pain from thinking I will be forced to see him every day, even when he is not present, following me around, forcing me to once again schedule my life around him.

LEFT SIDE: Then look further, look at those on the sidelines, tending their hands to you, so close you can feel their fingertips... Nobody wants to live like we have been, and nobody should. But you are luckier than most because you still have other choices, plenty of them, in fact. You have a life worth living waiting for you as soon as you step out of this river and put on some clothes. An infinite supply of movies to be seen. An abundance of moments yet to be shared with your friends. Hugs not given to your parents. Relationships in your life which are awaiting to appear, to be repaired or to be permanently ended.

RIGHT SIDE: I think you have an idealised version of what our daily lives look and feel like.

LEFT SIDE: Even if in the twenty-four hours of the day you are only able to get out a single second of happiness, isn't it still worth trying?

RIGHT SIDE: Not anymore. That part of my life is over now.

LEFT SIDE: But there is a way out. At this moment, you are not able to see it, how could you? The solution is right there but there is a thick fog around it that prevents you from visualising the entire picture. You cannot live through your days on a scale of black or white, because it is in the greys that one must navigate this life we have been given. Do you have any idea of the privilege we currently have? Think about your parents emigrating across the Atlantic Ocean, working fourteen hours a day when you and Diego were kids. Think about the life they spared you from having. Think about how lucky you are to be able to walk on the streets freely with the remaining battery on your headphones being the one worry plaguing your mind. To be able to temporarily move to a different country, Switzerland of all places, and work at an NGO that actually changes the lives of some of the people who need it most. To find friends that have made you feel at home even when you are thousands of miles away from it, and to know that when you *do* arrive home, your childhood friends will be right where you left them and welcome you with open arms. Think about the life you have lived, even in the circumstances we have, which many would kill to live just for one day.

RIGHT SIDE: Just because other people have it worse than we do doesn't mean that my claim here is invalid.

LEFT SIDE: Yes, but at least it gives you enough perspective to make you see that even the worst moment of your life would be the best moment of someone else's existence if they were given the chance to live it. I am not saying that what you want to do has no merit or that it is unfounded or that you don't have the inalienable right to do it—your life is your own, and even though a part of it lives on those you love most, it belongs to you and to you only. But you have to try all other options before doing something from which there is no way back. And you need to work on it as soon as you leave this place.

RIGHT SIDE: Like what?

LEFT SIDE: Like learning to ask for help. Nobody can reach out to you if they don't know you need their help; nobody can come to your rescue if you keep pretending and letting everyone know that you are all right when you are everything but. There is nothing wrong with admitting our own shortcomings, about displaying our own vulnerabilities, about opening up and letting others know about our most embarrassing and darkest thoughts, as long as we do not act upon them. Because guess what we become when we let others see the damaged people we really are? Just another human being. Nothing more, and nothing less.

RIGHT SIDE (*finally breaking down, bursting into tears*)**:** But I just don't get why this is…it is just so fucking hard. Any time I want to speak up, I know nobody will be able to understand this emotional state, this permanent damage that I carry with me. They will stare at me in shock, instantly traumatised, (understandably) unable to know how to react or how to help me. Who knows if they want to keep being friends with me after they learn of the kind of thoughts that constantly come back to haunt me—

LEFT SIDE: Whatever their reaction may be, this is a reality you must never keep to yourself. The longer you do, the bigger the impulse to want to do it. It is only in isolation that our worst ideas become irreversibly doable. We need to take it out of our system and share it with our most trusted and loved ones, to keep ourselves from the worst side of ourselves.

RIGHT SIDE: But they will never understand.

LEFT SIDE: They won't if you refuse to give them a chance. At first? Sure, they will freak out—who wouldn't? With the dominating lack of exposure to this issue that is currently going around, and the only reported cases being relegated to the most gruesome sources of gossip, it is only natural that they will initially be shell-shocked and react with certain precaution. But you need to let them know, so they can help you get out of this dark hole. What do you want me to say, that nothing will change, and they will see you the same way they see you now? Why would I lie to you in such an obvious way? And more importantly, would that be so bad, that they change the way that they behave around you? Would it really be the worst outcome in the world if your friends learned of the true extent of your problems so they could actively intervene whenever necessary to make sure you never find yourself where we currently are now?

RIGHT SIDE: I just…I don't want to do this. But I cannot keep waking up every day feeling like this. Feeling like I am not enough and knowing that I never will.

LEFT SIDE: Listen to me: everything will be okay.

RIGHT SIDE (*more tears ensuing*): How do you know?

LEFT SIDE: Because that is what I do: it's your job to set out the alarm and it's mine to put out the fire. So listen to me once again: everything will be okay, Carla. The road ahead is going to be long, and I cannot promise that we will not encounter problems so severe that would make us want to end up right here once again, because there always will be. The reasons for us to want to commit suicide will not diminish, and never will—all we can hope for is that those are outnumbered by the reasons to keep us alive. Because the problems this life puts us through are so severe and so universal that nobody is spared from experiencing them; it is how we deal with them that ultimately defines us. That is why I refuse to tell you that it is not a possibility that the day comes when we find ourselves pouring a bottle of pills all over again on the palm of our hands, with "Another Day of Sun" in the background and the certainty that there is no other way to go on, because we now know that such a scenario could very well materialize. In those moments, whose occurrence is not remotely improbable, all I am asking you to do is to take a long, hard look at what you are about to do, at the consequences, at all you would be giving up…and at the inability to open the door to falling in love with life once again. And really ponder about the full extent of your decision, and on whether the pain is inevitable, or if there really are ways of either numbing it, palliating it, or putting a temporary or definitive end to it. And if your decision is final, don't rush into the endless night. Wait. Wait for a day. And the following morning, and the one after that, ask yourself the same question. You will be amazed at how quickly a couple of days suddenly turn into a week, and a week into a month, and a month into a year, until you run out of sufficiently substantial reasons to carry out an early demise orchestrated by your own hand. Our time ahead, if you make the decision to step out of this river right now, is going to be a perpetual battle. Even if we make it through today and survive this struggle, the following morning we will have to get up and fight some more, because winners today are fighters tomorrow. It will never go away, and this inescapable feeling will never let us go and will forever remain a part of us, whether it is to a larger or (hopefully) lesser degree. And if we do get out of here, we can no longer afford to keep our people away from the truth: they must know, and we must live with knowing they will always know. And yes, it will be uncomfortable. But think that underneath that inner (and probably unfairly perceived as excessive) preoccupation lies an abundant, if not infinite, amount of love. We have a lot of work to do, you and I, and the hardest task that we will ever have to undertake is to learn to love and live with ourselves, *and* to learn to let others love us, too. As long as we are in good company, including just us two, everything will work out for the best. It is a matter of being blind and being helped by others into finally seeing. Horizons widen and perspectives open up whenever we are surrounded by those who make their lives to lift us up whenever all we do is bring ourselves down. And what can I say, we are pretty lucky, because those people are already right next to us, just where they always have.

RIGHT SIDE (*long pause*): Thank you…just…thank you.

LEFT SIDE: Nothing to thank me for: thank yourself and those that have made you who you are. Have I made myself clear? (*After I nod to myself*). Good. Now get your ass out of this river: there's a life ready to be lived waiting for you out there.

Baptised by the wisdom found all along within myself, my brain sent the order to the rest of my body to immediately abort all plans of entering an eternal sleep, and I began to steer away from my floating position by slowly straightening up. With my lungs firmly refusing to follow wherever my mind had intended to go mere minutes before, the blood flows being progressively restored to their proper place, I ran my fingers through the delicate factions of a face that had been given a second chance. The cold suddenly made its presence felt all at once, and as I gasped for air, every sound piercing the morning air sounded at first so apparently distant, so remote. My vision still remained out of focus, only managing to discern shapeless figures gesturing at me in the distance, across the thick steam coming out of a body nearing hypothermia. Using every last bit of energy stored in that body of mine, I began walking to the shore, now completely in command of myself. The strenuous process which I had forced my body to endure had taken a toll on my physical stability, which had effectively prevented me from previously hearing the screams of local pedestrians halting their morning trip to work in a selfless act of looking for help in the face of my non-responsiveness whilst floating across the river. On my way to reaching solid ground, I found a friendly face navigating her way across the forest to come and get me: Vero, dear Vero. Without hesitation, she jumped into the river to gently wrap her arms around me, and carefully guided me to the shore, where Anna was waiting for us. With the tears in her eyes having made furrows across the make-up carefully applied on her otherwise elegant face, Anna put her leather jacket over my naked, shivering body and warmed up my heart with a tight embrace. A whole row of curious passers-by had gathered at the bridge, but much to my surprise and in an act of anonymous solidarity, no phones were taken out, no pictures were taken nor posted online. Right next to the bridge, and with the sounds around me beginning to acquire a gradual sharpness, I saw Michaela and Leo, waiting by the newly arrived ambulance and pointing to the paramedics in my direction.

As I was carried inside the vehicle, I took a lengthy look at my beloved friends, now gathered around the open doors; a tender glance into their eyes, into the warmth with which they were ready to receive me, into how their willingness to save this soul invigorated my existence with newly found meaningfulness.

"We are here for you now, darling. Hang on tight, we're right behind you," Michaela managed to say, before the doors were closed on them and the ambulance promptly begun its trip to the nearest ER. While the girls got inside Leo's car to swiftly chaperone the ambulance, a discombobulated Anna, still deep into a state of shock, trembled on her way to sit down on the very same rock I had stood before jumping into the river. Her quivering hands managed to reach for a cigarette, which she lit with an anxious impetus as the tears began to profusely roll down her cheeks. Her gaze stumbled upon the clothes I had left near the shore, and when she grabbed them and tenderly held them in her hands, Anna accidentally dropped the notepad containing the final words plucked without anaesthesia from the entrails of my heart. That moment served as definitive evidence in her mind that the events that had just transpired were no accident at all: no drug-fuelled hallucinations, no foul play—just the inescapable truth. Anna took a drag of her cigarette and gathered enough courage to use her shaking hand to grab the notebook and read its contents. Just the first sentence made her heart instantly shatter into a thousand small pieces, a rupture she knew she would never be able to fully recover from. Unable to contain her frustration to herself anymore, she finally burst out into tears, noisily sobbing all alone by herself under that bridge where a tragedy had just been avoided. For just a second, she looked at the suicide notes, hesitating on whether to throw them into the river and let the water carry away the pain. But before she could carry out such a regrettable act, the Genevan sunrise came out in its full splendour: the amber sky looking as promising as it had ever been, the starry night finally coming to a much-needed close, the daylight now in full display projecting itself onto Anna's face.

"Get some rest, my friend. You have earned it," Anna murmured to herself, before introducing the notes into her pocket, and carrying the clothes over to those inside the waiting car. The river stream kept its course, witness to all that had unfolded, yet unchanged by its ultimate resolution; the water had somehow used its erosive abilities to take away the sorrow no longer hosted by a tortured soul.

That night, a part of me died, forever lost, and a part of me was saved, forever found. Whether that was to be permanent or not was another matter entirely, as I emerged as someone who no longer thought of the option of Death as the only destination where I could potentially, hopefully, finally find happiness at. And even though I had managed to step out of that river on my own two feet, the question remained, however, whether the rational part of my brain would prevail in the days and months and years to come, or whether I would eventually fall prey to my frequent impulses.

"Just like most things in this life," I thought, "you are the one who must make the first move, for sure with as much help from others as you can get, but indeed the initial step must come from you and you alone."

On that eventful morning, I had a vivid dream as I was being carried to the hospital. A colourful vision in which all the suffocating weight had been finally lifted from my shoulders; where I had surprised myself by leaving behind all hints of reticence to open up to others about the suffering I carried inside; where I no longer had to hide or pretend or overthink or project traumas onto others; where the sour and unwelcoming faces diluted in the presence of a materialised possibility of more promising outlooks. A dream where the Carla who started thinking about how to survive eventually learned how to properly live and, above all, where the better life promised by the left side of my brain seemed finally attainable.

Outside one of the small, round windows of the ambulance, I could vaguely make out the incoming beams of sun beginning to colour up the city of Geneva. It was the light of a life that was no longer whispering but shouting, calling to me, shaking me out of the deep sleep that had kept me entranced for so long: a life that was waiting for the real Carla to finally step out into the other side of tomorrow. And, for the first time, I felt ready to answer the call.

EPILOGUE

WINNER TODAY, FIGHTER TOMORROW

News of my sister's death understandably sent shock waves down the spines of every person who had played a role in her eventful life, myself included. Though her reckless actions on that cold morning when she jumped into the Rhône River led her to a severe pneumonia, she was nonetheless taken good care of at Geneva's HUG University Hospital. After three weeks went by, and making sure she was well recovered, my parents decided during their prolonged emergency visit to the country that it was best she returned back home, to begin a new stage in her life—one in which they could contribute, finally, to slowly craft a previously non-existent willingness to live. As if helping a suicidal person into falling back in love with life wasn't already an arduous if not nearly impossible task, I take no pride in admitting such was a process in which not only did I not contribute positively to, but actually found my way to seriously endangering on more than a few occasions.

However, despite Carla keeping a moderately healthy lifestyle, a month later we were meeting the doctor who had performed her autopsy on that cold December evening. After a handful of demographic statistics were quickly laid out at our proverbial feet to soften the blow of what was to come, the doctor concluded that my sister's fatal cardiac arrest was nothing short of inevitable, as she had "the heart of an elderly woman", with the tissues surrounding her heart muscles having been severely deteriorated through the years. Then again, what is a cardiac failure in an otherwise healthy twenty-four-year-old but the result of a heart that has long been broken. The only comfort my parents found during that time, and the one I recently became acquainted with after intensive periods of therapeutical interventions and the unconditional support of a finally united family, was to learn how happy she was during her last days, surrounded by people who truly cherished her presence even when she refused to do so herself. She made the most out of her final moments on Earth, where at last she came to genuinely appreciate the unwavering support of her childhood friends who never, not even for one second, stopped loving her, even in the moments where she behaved in a way that made her undeserving of such love, and coming back to a devotion deeper than ever for our supportive parents, eternal bearers of secluded suffering, who never skipped a chance to let her know how lucky they were for having had her. A few final blissful months where, at long last, she came to terms with what she had done, and where the person that she was and the person she wanted to be for the first time became one and the same.

And what a way to go. I only wish when my time comes, I am able to do so in such a perfect way, a send-off note for all the ages—just the way she envisioned it, albeit under a different set of circumstances. Her body laid on the empty movie theatre of the *Capitol Cinema* located a few hundred metres away from the city's emblematic cathedral, a wide smile painted on her face as the credits of *La La Land* (2016) continued to roll, as if they had been consciously designed with the sole purpose of playing her life's epilogue. How reassuring it is to know that even though she could not handle her life in the manner she would have liked to, at least she managed to get out of it on her own terms. Far from the only future she accurately predicted, all those scenarios that she imagined after she was long gone, did indeed take place. At her funeral, acquaintances were made, friendships bloomed amongst her different groups of friends and scolding looks were rightfully knifed at my then-irredeemable heart. At home, the blame was laid on me after one of the friends Carla made in Switzerland gave my father Carla's suicide letters, which inevitably led him to her diary, too, and the flammable content that laid therein. As predicted, my mother fell down a deeply pervasive inner well of depression, alcoholism and sleeping pills to numb the pain of a loss she always knew she'd witness, but always prayed for its inexplicably reversion. And, sure enough, I came close to following Carla's attempts, in the midst of all the fingers pointing at the one common denominator in this equation, the one immovable truth, the one cause that stood out amongst all others, and the reason that would explain such a medical anomaly. It was only thanks to my inner raging impulses that, in the midst of an attempt to burn down everything that had ever belonged to her in the hopes that it would erase the image of "Saint Carla" everyone seemed to have after her death, that I, for some reason I still remain unaware of, started reading the words she had carefully vomited onto those hundreds of pages that made up her diary and ended up becoming her final words.

 In this diary of hers which she had for so long (and rightfully so) kept private from any pair of eyes other than her own, a lengthy book eventually retitled "Swiss Death of Mine" whose contents you have just borne witness to, she described with relentless clarity of mind and of passion her last moments in the city that had provided her with the few moments of happiness I now wish I could have filled her life with. As if a part of her already knew she would soon be gone, Carla managed to put words to the feelings and images everyone else tends to ignore on their day-to-day routines, instantly awakening inside ourselves a desire to truly take a look at the world around us and appreciate the beauty hidden in plain sight, only enjoyable for the eyes which are able to truly see beyond themselves and past the troubles haunting their lives. Like the way the streetlights illuminated the falling snowflakes delicately covering the tiles of *Place du Marché* in her neighbourhood of *Carouge*; or the three pairs of footprints on the snow—two large ones on each side followed by a much smaller set on the middle—left on the *Pont de la Machine* bordering the *Rhône* River by a newly-formed family on their way to the supermarket; the vision-impaired gentleman who warmly sang cheerful songs on the packed tram nearing the streets of *Rive*; the sound of songs by the Bee Gees on an old radio in one of the food stands at the Christmas market surrounding the park near *Jardin Anglais*; a couple in their early eighties, sporting psychedelic hats, holding hands and intertwining smiles whilst walking across the rainy streets circling the *Place des Grottes*; the shrieking sound the tram of line fifteen made when it violently turned left near the UNHCR office as it was nearing its final destination of the Broken Chair Square; the smell of dust in the old books written by pretentious authors trying to exploit their nostalgia for a time they believe cinema really meant something, over at *Librairie du Cinéma* store near *Terrassière*; the way the sky lit up in a thousand shades of gold during the early hours of the day, merging its irreplaceable landscape with the yellow scaffolding perennially installed over the *Veyrier* area—a perfect fusion of old and new…

 This therapeutic experiment of hers symbolised a massive,

unyielding block of concrete in the middle of the road, one against which I may have as well crashed, but eventually managed to pull the brakes just in time after the pain she experienced and carefully described started to flow through my own veins, in the first instance of empathetic connection I had ever shared with her. Pain that I inflicted upon her, upon those around her, upon myself; pain that I refused to let anybody else feel ever again; pain I no longer wanted to see in my parent's eyes or in my own reflection every morning staring at me, inculpatory, recriminatory, passing down judgement, in the mirror.

In the end, it wasn't pills that took or saved her life. It wasn't therapy, either. The former can momentarily help at a time of profound despair, like a tequila shot before a family dinner. The latter can help you build a path *out* of the emotional vacuum you have locked yourself into and *towards* the person you wish you had been all along. But none of those, either on their own or combined, can mend a deeply broken heart, especially one which does not believe it needs to be repaired in the first place. Relegating each of our self-improvement paths to any one of those elements would be overly simplifying a phenomenon that is deeply complex on its own, and has the potential to generate as much damage as doing nothing at all. After studying every word she wrote, every picture she took, every friendship she made and going through every movie list she carefully prepared for her friends, I began to slowly yet methodically get to know the person that for so long I had refused to allow a way into my life. Someone that would have made me a better person, and who I now see was only guilty of wanting desperately to love this twisted heart of mine. It is devastating to go through a dead person's computer and personal files, but for those of us that are left behind, it opens up a window of opportunity to finally see into the truest side of another person, a part only a few have access to, and a way into understanding not only their place on the world, but also our own, both in relation to them and their death, and on the role that you play in your own life and in the way in which you want to be remembered by others.

In her diaries, I wept when I learnt how much comfort she could have brought into my life, how our struggles mirrored one another with a complexity that I could have never dreamed of, how my traumas accentuated hers and vice versa, perversely feeding into a cycle of self-hatred directed towards one another. Morning after morning, I wake up after the effect of my elephantine Eszopiclone doses wither away, thinking it's been five years since Carla left us on that rainy evening on the day of my twenty-seventh birthday. Yet not a moment goes by where I don't think about how easy it would have been for me to prevent her early exit from this world, had I known that the scorching hate that I felt for her was, in fact, hate that I felt for myself. But of no use it is to dwell on "have nots" and hypothetically optimal scenarios, of past lives in which we gathered enough courage to do the right thing and do good even in the moments where it resulted in a detrimental outcome for ourselves. Since time cannot be reversed to mend all that's been broken, all that matters is how we choose to face the days to come. Simply put, and very much embodying the famous line by Ernest Hemingway, on each of our idiosyncratic paths towards the development and constant improvement of our individual growth, we should not aspire to be better than the rest, only to be better than our past selves—a little more than we were yesterday, and a little less than we will be tomorrow.

Living with our condition requires more than the customary understanding of the existence of our problem, as well as the subsequent materialization of a willingness to act upon it. It also needs its host to be able to develop a pragmatic disposition so as to avoid falling into complacency, resignation, sheer acceptance of life's *tos and fros*, and, ultimately, the final destination we are perversely seduced into visiting earlier than we probably should. Once you have accepted the person that you are, and established yourself as a fighter who wants to break out of the chains around your body and the subliminal noose tightly wrapped around your neck, the true journey will begin for you. A journey that will (hopefully) be over when nature itself seizes command from your own hands in regard to the determination of when to put an end to your own mortality. In order to appreciate the entire voyage, you must avoid driving in darkness and necessarily include on the pitstops along the way sufficient time to learn about what it is that is brewing inside of you, where that fire could be stemming from, never falling shy of acknowledging both shortcomings and offences, sins we are responsible for and sins committed against ourselves, and to always maintain the willingness to act upon those so as to change the course of our future in the face of an immutable past. And if you find it in your heart to carry out such a journey in good company, welcoming with open arms those who wish to help—be it relatives, friends, strangers, past or present offenders or health professionals—then, by the time you reach your final destination, the one memory that will remain would be that of a long, thoroughly enjoyed, properly experienced, deeply moving journey.

    The prospect that we will all be dead in a matter of years should bring everything into perspective. What if I were to die ten seconds from now? What would I do? What would I regret? As much as your inner impulses, much like my sister's and not unlike my own for many years, might make you wonder "does an entire life count?" as the answer to that question, that should only be interpreted as a self-imposed-against-our-will blindness which, once awakened and aware of our external surroundings and inner confinements, can be remedied (at least partly) through every means at one's disposal. In one of her entries, Carla wrote "...because, how foolish was I to consider dying before watching my dearly beloved Stanley Kubrick's filmography for the twenty-ninth time in a row. Or without travelling around the world to places as remote and untravelled to as New Zealand or Iceland or Wisconsin. Or without hugging Grandma Lupe once more or telling Mom that I adore her for the last time. Or without going to the movies with Dad and having him loudly talking throughout the entire picture. Or without laughing once more with the girls at *Village du Soir*. Or without spending an entire evening of endless beer, bad decisions and gossip with my friends back at home..."

And yet, with all those wonderful things either out there or up for grabs if one works hard enough to get them, one does not include such variables in the equation when computing our death calculations. Once the variable "X" is clear, there is only one path. Everything else around it is white noise. Thus, the first thing to remedy is to wake up and understand that, as redundant and Instagrammer-wishful-thinking as these pieces of advice may sound, to some degree or another, this is what saved my life, and I wish with all my heart that it had saved hers, too. So, I hope within these pages you can find something—a sentence, a chapter, a character, an experience—to help you save yours, like Carla intended. Just one life is reason enough for these lines written on these pages to exist. So regardless of gender, sexual orientation, physical appearance, creed, culture, political beliefs, socioeconomic status or any other element that might falsely lead us towards a perception that we are not all made from the same fabric; this story is for you, for people that may feel like you, or for people you know could feel like this. Embrace your differences, your perceived weaknesses, your hidden talents and lifelong passions. It is easy to look at others' fabricated happiness and be envious of all the vacations with friends and the dreamlike weddings and the everlasting loves and the successful job positions. But if a house has shaky foundations, it is only bound to eventually collapse by its own weight. People will get fired, faithful couples will cheat on their spouses, children will be born and irreparably link two people together for the remainder of each other's lives... So next time you look around, do it as close as you can, for you will realise your journey is not comparable to anyone else's, as your journey is only your own.

And for those who consider themselves immune to the pressures of this condition, it is not irrelevant to restate that we all have a responsibility to be awake, present, mindful, and alert. To watch out for that lonely kid who is misunderstood and left behind. To always be active lookouts, not passive enablers of this problem that is all around us and, statistically speaking, is either in your group of friends, or in your family or in both or in yourself. To let our loved ones know how much devotion we have for them. To try and be the very best version of ourselves. Because kindness takes effort, and is almost never profitable. It is much easier to look the other way. But, the same way that all it takes to give up is a bad day, all it takes to carry on is a good one. Oh, how selfish it is to think of others when considering whether to take your own life, but how right we are to do so, for it is others that can keep us alive in those moments when there is nothing else between you and a handful of deadly pills.

So, whether you are a passive enabler, an active sufferer, or a direct enforcer of pain, I hope you can all find yourselves along the way, to learn to forgive and to be able to realise the mistakes you have made—if that is your role in someone else's story—and understand that, while you can't mend what you have done to others, you can certainly mend what you *will do* to others from now on. Putting an end to other's suffering inflicted by your own hand is something that, while its arrival may be preferred at an earlier rather than later stage, is always more than welcomed, in any shape or form it eventually arrives in, as it has taken me five long, regret-filled years to finally learn. When you find yourself in deep waters such as these, it takes a blunt "reality dose" (as Carla used to say) for us to begin to comprehend our afflictions. In that line, and being very much aware that she was one of the few people on this planet who had, in some degree or another, found the true meaning and purpose of human existence, Carla wisely wrote in the final entry of her diary, "I would like to say to the authors of my traumas, amongst which I include myself and my ability to dramatize and magnify every and any problem that comes my way, that I am thankful. I am thankful for making my life a mess, for making me hate life in order to be able to love life once again. For waking me up from the collective lie that happiness is something achievable, and for making me understand that it is only momentary and when it comes our way one must seize it with all one can."

Forever in my mind is and will be that Richard Burton interview my sister mentioned in one of her writings, a video where the actor described alcoholism as a constant daily battle involving yourself and a bottle of liquor: you may win the round, but you will have to face the opponent tomorrow. And he will be even tougher than he or she was today. And regardless of all the people you have in your corner or cheering for you on the seats around the ring, regardless of all the training you have done until then, regardless of all the times you have rejected a glass of wine or a casual afterwork beer, when you enter the ring, you are on your own, and only you can defeat the vicious opponent. That is exactly what being suicidal is, with the other fighter in the ring being a constant search for reasons that make you want to cease and desist your attempts to keep on living. Though what prevented her previous attempts from being successful ranged from sheer luck to mere incidents of *force majeure*, her latest one was frustrated by her own hand, having come near to being knocked off her feet, yet ultimately standing up before the referee could count to ten. And even though the ways to come out victorious seem easily achievable and blatantly obvious to many, the vision of the one doing the fighting in the ring is deeply clouded to the point of total distortion of reality, unable to see those around, extending their hands, eager to help, the willingness to fight no longer as clear as it once was, the life that awaits after the fight no longer desired. As much as we may try for others to step out of their dark-tainted glasses to appreciate the world in all its multi-coloured splendour, some fighters are bound to end up knocked out, and that is also an acceptable outcome in which we must separate our pain from that of the fallen boxer, and understand the former's must have cut so profoundly into every inch of his or her existence for that person to want to inflict such excruciating pain on those whose only sin was to try and help mend a broken soul in whichever way they could. For Carla, it was the world of celluloid and being surrounded by the right kind of people, both of which—to varying extents and in widely different ways—made her come back to a reality she had long thought to be lost, and successfully managed to keep her alive until her body was found on that fateful evening. But there are only so many movies one can watch, and so many hours of the day that your loved ones can spend with you, so there will always come a time when not even your remedy is effective. Or at least not effective enough. Tomorrow morning, the ring will be right where you left it the moment you close your eyes tonight, and the day after that, and every single day of the rest of your life. The possibility forever lingering in your mind, the scenario always on the table, the pain always seductively pushing you into opting for that outcome. And that is a reality those like my sister and I will have to live with and forever remain alert and willing to keep on boxing, until there is no life left in our bodies to keep up the fight. Even if there are few things on this Earth that make you move, that make you live, that keep you grounded, with both feet firmly onto the ground instead of suspended a few inches above the earth or a couple of meters down below, it is only fair to try and do everything in your hand to spend as much of your precious time doing them at every chance you get. Whatever it is, I hope it works for you. And if it doesn't, don't be ashamed. Life is not for everyone.

So here's to the one million "Carlas" of the world who every single year find their lives to be the death of them; may our active gazes and progressively broken social stigmas allow for nobody else to follow suit. It is our turn now to take a good look at ourselves and take the first step towards fulfilling our inner and collective responsibilities. After all, the cameras are already rolling…and the whole world's watching.

AUDIOVISUAL INDEX

- 8 ½ (1963)
- 12 Angry Men (1957)
- 13 Reasons Why (2017-2020)
- 2001: A Space Odyssey (1968)
- After Hours (1955)
- All About Eve (1950)
- American Beauty (1999)
- Atonement (2007)
- Austin Powers: The Spy Who Shagged Me (1999)
- Before Sunrise (1995)
- Berlin: Symphony of a Great City (1927)
- Boyz in the Hood (1991)
- Broadcast News (1987)
- Bicycle Thieves (1948)
- Camp Rock (2008)
- Cape Fear (1962)
- Casablanca (1942)
- Cinema Paradiso (1988)
- Cries and Whispers (1972)
- Crimes and Misdemeanours (1989)
- Desperate Housewives (2004-2012)
- Doctor Strange (2016)
- Don't Breathe (2016)
- Do the Right Thing (1989)
- Dune (1984)

- Dune (2021)
- East of Eden (1955)
- E.T. The Extra-Terrestrial (1982)
- Eyes Wide Shut (1999)
- Fast and Furious (2001-forever, apparently)
- Gaslight (1944)
- Godzilla vs. Kong (2021)
- Harold and Maude (1971)
- Harry Potter franchise (2001-2011)
- High School Musical (2006)
- His Girl Friday (1940)
- House of Gucci (2021)
- Inception (2010)
- Interstellar (2014)
- It's a Wonderful Life (1946)
- Judas and the Black Messiah (2021)
- Killing Eve (2018-2022)
- La Dolce Vita (1960)
- La Grande Illusion (1937)
- Last Night in Soho (2021)
- Lawrence of Arabia (1963)
- Les Amants du Pont-Neuf (1991)
- Le Scaphandre et le Papillon (2007)
- Les Diaboliques (1955)
- L'Événement (2021)
- Love Affair (1939)
- Un Chien Andalou (1929)
- Madres Paralelas (2021)
- Malcolm X (1992)
- Malèna (2000)
- Manhattan (1979)

- Man with a Movie Camera (1929)
- Mary Poppins (1964)
- North by Northwest (1959)
- Nosferatu (1922)
- Once Upon a Time in America (1984)
- Once Upon a Time in Hollywood (2019)
- Othello (1965)
- Paris, Texas (1984)
- Peeping Tom (1960),
- Persona (1966)
- Promising Young Woman (2020)
- Monsters Inc. (2001)
- Ratatouille (2007)
- Rear Window (1954)
- Ridiculousness (2011—)
- Salò, or the 120 Days of Sodom (1975)
- Sátántangó (1994)
- Sex and the City (1998-2004)
- Shrek 2 (2004)
- Shutter Island (2010)
- Sid and Nancy (1986)
- Silent Night (2021)
- Talladega Nights (2006)
- The Accidental Tourist (1988)
- The Babadook (2014)
- The Barbarian Invasions (2003)
- The Cabinet of Doctor Caligari (1920)
- The Dark Knight (2008)
- The Father (2020)
- The Godfather (1972)
- The Great Director (1940)

- The Hitman's Wife's Bodyguard (2021)
- The Hours (2002)
- The Hunt (2012)
- The Machinist (2004)
- The Matrix (1999)
- The Naked Gun: From the Files of Police Squad! (1988)
- The Party (1968)
- The Pink Panther (1963)
- The Power of the Dog (2021)
- The Purple Rose of Cairo (1985)
- There Will Be Blood (2007)
- The Sacrifice (1986)
- The Shawshank Redemption (1994)
- The Tinder Swindler (2022)
- The Wages of Fear (1953)
- The VVitch (2015)
- The Worst Person in the World (2021)
- Toni Erdmann (2016)
- Torrente: El brazo tonto de la ley (1998)
- Touch of Evil (1958)
- Trainspotting (1996)
- Trading Places (1983)
- Treasure Planet (2002)
- Veep (2012-2019), Season 1, Episode 5 "Nicknames".
- Wings of Desire (1987)
- Zodiac (2007)

LITERARY INDEX

- Bergman, I. (1998) *Images: My Life in Film*. London, England: Faber & Faber.

- Clarke, Gerald. "Books: Sunny Boy". *Time Magazine*. February 20, 1978.

- Dostoevsky, F. M. (1992) *The Idiot*. Translated by A. Myers. Oxford, England: Oxford Paperbacks.

- Dostoyevsky, F. (2001) *Crime and Punishment*. New York, NY: Signet Classics.

- Shakespeare, W. (2005a) *Hamlet*. London, England: Oberon Books.

- Shakespeare, W. (2005b) *Othello*. Edited by K. Muir. London, England: Penguin Classics.

- Tarkovsky, A. (1989) *Sculpting in time: Reflections on the cinema*. Translated by K. H-. Blair. London, England: Faber & Faber.

- William, J. (2021) *The Longest Suicide in Hollywood: The Death of Montgomery Clift*. Edited by D. Constan. Aplomb Publishing.